U0136434

全民英文單字力檢定

Vocabulary Quotient Credential: B~C Rank 7000 words

VQC 7000字級

附VQC線上英文單字能力檢測系統

劉振華 編著

VQC
線上英文單字能力檢測系統
（價值550元）

收錄Rank B~Rank C

D 勁園・台科大
SINCE1997　www.tiked.com.tw

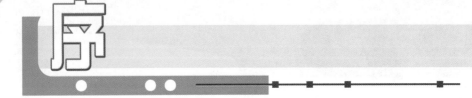

序

　　一個人究竟認識多少英文單字？大多數人面對這個問題時，都回答：「不知道」。由於過去沒有客觀普及的方法與工具，老師、學生、家長都無法好好探究此重要能力。本書將恩師何宏發教授的理論與方法實踐出來，期望對教學者與學習者有幫助。本書期望能有下列效用：

◎提供背單字計畫，幫您輕易執行，習得大量單字，英文能力大幅提高。

◎幫助學校制訂單字習得計畫，並順利執行、考核檢討，提高全校升學考試英文平均成績。

◎幫助老師、家長、學生隨時瞭解自己的單字實力、單字商數 VQ。

◎幫助你取得英文單字檢定國際證書，擁有更多英文國際證照。

◎特別針對高職學生設計從最基礎的單字開始，以統測為目標。

作者　謹識

1 文獻摘要

1-1 單字是英語文的根基

楊懿麗教授，政治大學語言學研究所退休教授（楊懿麗，2006）指出：

「詞彙是語言的根本，是語句形成的素材，就像是蓋房子的鋼筋、砂石、磚塊、與水泥，沒有詞彙，語言的藍圖畫得再漂亮，都無法變成真正的言語行動或語句篇章。一個人所擁有的詞彙量的多寡，與他的閱讀理解能力，乃至於整個語言能力，有密切的關係：詞彙越多，能力越強」（Willis, 1990；Meara, 1996；Coady & Huckin, 1997；Lewis, 1997, 2000；林麗慧等，2003；蔣佩珊，2004）

1-2 曝光次數越多越熟悉

Bertram, Baayen & Schreuder（2000）指出學習者接觸單字的頻率越高，針對這些高頻單字的口說與語言理解處理越快速且精確，反之亦反。

單字習得與單字曝光次數有關。學習者在閱讀時、溝通時、考試時，遇見從來沒見過的關鍵單字，必定產生困難。遺忘也與曝光次數有關。對於英語是外語的我們來說，大量閱讀是個重要的好方法，可惜多數學習者認為大量閱讀的時間花費太大、太困難、可行性低。因此，集中式背單字的學習策略應運而生，至少確保單字的曝光次數達到基本認識。

單字曝光的種類有多種，不是只有拼寫。單字曝光的方式包含：看到單字、瞭解字義、聽到單字發音、唸出單字發音、拼寫出單字、習得單字知識、用法等。尤其以前科技還不夠進步時，單字的發音需靠音標，聽力不容易好，現今電腦與電子科技進步，學習者可以輕易聽到外國老師的發音，對聽力提高很有幫助。學習單字時，接觸、曝光各種單字呈現方式有利於學習與記憶。

學習時若能聽單字發音、唸出單字發音，對於口說與聽力方面會有很大的助益，畢竟這是人類學語言的自然方法。多數學習者還停留在只用眼睛與頭腦學習單字，很可惜。單字聽力的測驗也很重要，本書的工具能幫你測出你單字聽力能力。

1-3 「單字量」測試很重要

Meara 與 Buxton 提出的 Eurocentres Vocabulary Size Test（Meara and Buxton, 1987）被當為分班測驗（placement tests）的工具呈現很好的效果。因為 Meara 與 Buxton 的單字測驗測試了單字的知識，且一個測驗測試了大量的單字，因此得到可靠的決策依據，所以 Meara 與 Buxton 的單字測驗是有用的診斷與分班測驗。

你的單字量是多少？因為沒工具，你可能不清楚，多數人不知道。本書提供你一個很好的工具，可以測驗出你的單字量。

1-4 VQ, EVQ 與 VQC 簡介

何宏發（Ho & Lin, 2010）提出單字商數（Vocabulary Quotient, 縮寫 VQ）、估計單字量（Estimating Vocabulary Quotient, 縮寫EVQ）、與單字商數檢定（VQ Certificate）概念，對英語學習與教學有幫助。VQ 是以現代測驗理論的「項目反應理論」Item Response Theory（Baker & Frank, 1992; Hambleton & Swaminathan, 1985）為基礎的一種詞彙能力測驗，提出低成本、有效率、可行性高、信度與效度良好、鑑別度高的測驗與電腦軟體工具。

對學生而言，VQ 測驗可準確估計學生的單字量 EVQ，提醒學生距離目標還有多遠。升學考試通常有目標單字量的要求，例如：高中生至少需具備 7000 字才能有機會在考大學時，獲得良好的成績。如果高三學生認識的單字數只有 3000 字，就應該加強習得更多單字，還有大約 4000 字需要學習。很可惜，大多數學生自己不知道自己具有的單字量，以及距離目標還有多遠。VQ 可以具體量化。

對老師而言，VQ 測驗可幫助老師瞭解學生的單字量，依據學生的單字量，選擇教材、安排教學計畫。假設學生只會 1000 字，老師選一萬字的教材，一定不適合。也可以當為分班測驗（placement tests）的工具。

客觀的VQC檢定可幫助學校、老師、學生驗證英語文單字能力。過去主觀又缺乏量化的方法，使得學校與老師因為不瞭解而幫不了學

生。利用VQC不但給學生目標、客觀量化數據、與信心，更可以增進學生對英語文的更濃的興趣。

參考文獻

1. 楊懿麗（2006 年 9 月）。〈國內各級英語教學的詞彙量問題〉。國立編譯館館刊，34：3，35-44。

2. Baker, F. B. (1992), *Item Response Theory: Parameter Estimation Techniques*, New York: Marcel Dekker.

3. Bertram, R., Baayen, R. H. & Schreuder, R. (2000), Effects of Family Size for Complex Words, *Journal of Memory and Language* 42, 390-405.

4. Hambleton, R. K. & Swaminathan, H. (1985), *Item Response Theory: Principles and Applications*. Kluwer-Nijhoff Publisher.

5. Hong-Fa Ho and Ping-Zong Lin, (2010), May, Chinese Word Learning System on Mobile Device with Dynamic Timing of Review, *Proc. of the Sixth Canada-China TCSL Conference*, Canada.

6. Hong-Fa Ho and Ping-Zong Lin, (2010), July, Chinese character Learning Review System with Item Response Theory Analysis, *Proc. of Research in Reading Chinese (RRC) Conference 2010*, Canada.

7. Meara, P. and Buxton, B. (1987), An alternative to multiple choice vocabulary tests. *Language Testing* 4, 142-51.s

2 同學習得必要單字的「難點」與方法

2-1 想成功？很簡單：天天背單字

想在英語文上取得成功，很簡單，從天天背單字開始。學習外國語言的困難點之一就是：做不到天天學習。無法做到天天學習，熟悉度就不會高，廣度與深度方面也就不會更廣更深。英語文的內容既深又廣，每個人都希望「面面俱到」地學習好、學習到，可是真正做到的人很少。與其將目標設定在「面面俱到」的學習好、學習到，不如將目標區分為基礎目標、考試目標、與長期目標。先達成基礎目標，然後才去追求更高目標，成功的機會可以大大增加。基礎目標可以先包含：自然發音與單字。單字的數量很多，單就認識單字的意義一點，就需要花費比較長的時間，需要毅力，這往往是你失敗的關鍵。大多數人學習的「難點」在於「無法做到天天學習」，想成功，可以先從天天背單字（習得單字）開始，先把基礎紮好，學習英語文才能輕鬆。天天學習時，還要注意後面的方法。

重要的方法：聽、唸、認識、例句

　　　每天背單字，也要有好方法。大家容易忽略的是：沒有聽外國老師唸單字的發音、沒有跟著外國老師唸單字的發音、沒有仔細認識字的意義與相關知識、用法等。多數人都側重單字的拼寫與字的意義，這樣不夠。運用本書時，你可以善用本書所附檢測系統聽外國老師唸單字的發音、跟著唸。拼寫的能力建議放在熟悉所有目標單字後，才開始學習拼寫。這是個很有效的方法，如果你有興趣瞭解，可以上網聽何宏發教授的「線上演講」（網址：http://taipei888.com/speech/）。

2-3 自我單字量測試

　　　定期自我檢測，瞭解自己的單字量，有助於達成目標。假設你的近期目標是考大學，至少需要熟悉 7000 字。你現在究竟熟悉多少單字呢？如果你自己都不清楚，誰會清楚呢？你又如何安排何時學會哪些單字呢？這樣的情況突顯出你對單字量的不科學態度。利用本書提供的「線上英文單字檢測系統」，只要大約一個小時，你可以科學地、客觀地量測出你大約熟悉的單字量，根據測出的單字量，你可以安排更好的學習策略。

　　　例如，你是高一新生，打算採用最佳策略「高二之前背完 7000字」，高一開學時，測出只熟悉 2000 字，還有 5000 字要學習，可安排高一上學期學習 2500 字、高一下學期學習 2500 字。到了高一下學期開學前，自我檢測看看，單字量是否已經達成 4500 字，高二開學前，自我檢測看看，單字量是否已經達成 7000 字。最佳策略讓你高二、高三時，不需花大量時間背單字，當其他同學還在背單字時，你早就熟悉 7000 字了。

3 本書用法

3-1 級別說明

　　　本書內容含有教育部公布的第一個千字表、第二個千字表，與高職考統測至少需要熟悉合計 3893 字。並再細分為四或三個部分，可以區分為各年級適用的內容。各級別的區分與「全民英文單字檢定VQC」完全吻合，適用於國小、國中、高職各級別。本書的內容也已經內含全民英文檢定的單字。

3-2 你的必要單字量是多少？有哪些單字？

　　知道自己的目標，有利於安排自己的步伐。國中考高中至少需要熟悉教育部公布的第一個千字表與第二個千字表、高職學生考統測至少需要熟悉 3893 字。所有單字都已經收錄於本書。

　　為了避免學習時，好像在背字典，特意將單字安排成不像字典的順序。

4 學校如何幫學生習得必要單字？

4-1 單字習得計畫

　　在國際學術論文中曾經有人指出：英語文教學活動中，學習者的單字量是最難管理的一部份。學校的校長、主任、召集人、老師們如何掌握學生的英文單字學習呢？建議學校制訂「英文單字能力管理辦法」給師生依循，書末附錄所附文件是我國在這方面領先的兩所學校制訂的辦法，一所學校是國立的，一所學校是私立的。管理辦法的目的是：讓學生的單字學習是可以管理的，進而幫助學生提高英語文成就、升學考試成績全面大幅提高。

　　學校制訂計畫、公告實施，老師帶領全校學生學習，並利用「線上英文單字檢測系統」評量。電腦測驗，免出題、免閱卷、隨時測驗。可以輕鬆讓全校學生的單字能力管理好，老師教學更有成就。如果學校沒有管理辦法，學生多數採自我學習，往往造成許多學生連單字都不足，如何會有良好的英語文成就？

　　何宏發教授常說：希望各級學校都能有「英文單字能力管理辦法」，並認真執行、考核，國人的普遍英語文能力一定可以大幅提高。

4-2 單字學習護照

　　老師可以利用「單字學習護照」幫助學生背單字。護照內詳細紀錄學生每天學習本書單字的紀錄，讓學生家長簽字，老師（導師或英文老師）檢查。最好配合「線上英文單字能力檢測系統」定期評量，一方面可檢視單字學習的成效，也可以找出需要特別輔導的學生。

4-3 每學期舉辦校內或區域單字比賽，順便檢定

　　建議學校每學期舉辦一次「全校的」或聯合多個學校「區域的」單字比賽，可提高英語學習興趣、營造英語學習氛圍、提高全校升學的英文成績、同時檢定。務必讓「全校學生都參加」，活動的效果遠比「只有極少數英文高手」參加的演講、作文、話劇比賽要好。學校每年辦學術活動的目的究竟是只為少數同學？還是為了全校學生？

　　以前，因為舉辦全校參與的活動很累，人數太多，不可行。現在，有了「線上英文單字檢測系統」，利用電腦教室，可以一天內全校學生都參加了。免出題、免閱卷。下面簡介美國的 SpellingBee 與我國的「全國英文單字大賽」，學校可以輕易地複製「全國英文單字大賽」的方式，每學期舉辦單字比賽。並派出校隊選手參加「全國英文單字大賽」。

　　學校舉辦單字比賽，可向 Certiport（國際檢定單位）申請「比賽同時檢定」，讓參賽同學可以同時在校內參賽又參加檢定，成績達發證書標準者，可以申請國際全民英文單字檢定證書，增加學生的英語文國際證照，對推甄有不小的加分效果。

1. 美國的 SpellingBee

　　美國的 SpellingBee（http://www.spellingbee.com/history）從 1925 年開始，至今已經超過 80 年，目前在美國全國，美國領地薩摩亞群島，關島，波多黎各，美國維爾京群島，歐洲國防部學校，巴哈馬，加拿大，加納，牙買加，利比里亞，紐西蘭，和韓國都有舉辦 SpellingBee。

　　美國的國語是英語美語，為何還要舉辦SpellingBee?因為單字是根基。單字不會就無法聽說讀寫。美國人希望寫字時，能正確拼寫，以免貽笑大方。

　　美國的中小學每年都舉辦校內 SpellingBee，各校的校內冠軍，參加 County 舉辦的 SpellingBee，各 County 的冠軍，參加 State 舉辦的 SpellingBee，各 State 的冠軍，共 50 人，參加每年都固定在美國華盛頓 DC 舉辦的 National SpellingBee，各大媒體都會大幅度報導。

2. 我國的「全國英文單字大賽」

　　我國的「全國英文單字大賽」在教育部指導並出錢，由台灣師大何宏發教授於 2005 年主辦創辦第一屆，參賽對象含小學、國中、高中、高職共四級。第二屆時，還是由教育部指導，台灣師大主辦，參賽者繳費。第三屆至第六屆（2010），還是由教育部指導，財團法人溫世仁文教基金會主辦，台灣師大承辦，溫世仁文教基金會承擔所有經費，讓比賽成為公益活動，全國分為十個區域先舉辦區賽，一場全國決賽。每年參賽者均為各校派出的校隊，每年參賽者總人數大約 3500 人至 4500 人。官方網站：http://vq.ie.ntnu.edu.tw。

5 老師如何幫學生習得必要單字？

　　從「學習動機」的觀點分析，人分四類：全自動、半自動、被動、與不動。學生多數是被動的，需要老師的幫助，既使是全自動的學生，也需要老師的引導。老師可以善用本書與工具，執行下列事項，必定可以幫助很多學生進步。

1. 講解單字習得計畫的重要性與影響。

2. 要求每天學習單字。

3. 要求每個月做一次單字量測試。

6 軟體工具簡介

　　善用電腦幫助學習者，不但可適應個別差異，語言學習有發音，老師與學生都輕鬆，學習成效提高，學習速度增快。利用工具之外，科學化與量化的單字量也可應用於「學前評量」與「學後評量」，或「前測」與「後測」。下面這兩個工具是「全國英文單字大賽」比賽的工具，也是「全民英文單字檢定」的正式工具。軟體可從隨書光碟中取得，或可從網站取得 http://taipei888.com。

1. 電腦軟體單機版-英文單字 X 光機。

2. 線上英文單字能力檢測系統。

Contents

VQC 單字力 C Rank

VQC 單字力 B Rank

VQC 單字力　附　錄

讀者申請免費授權流程

1 註冊再啟用

Step 1 讀者從書中隨書光碟取得序號（刮開刮刮膜）。

Step 2 連結 http://vqc.tiked.com.tw 網站進入「註冊」畫面。

Step 3 填寫以下基本資料，並將序號鍵入後按「註冊」鈕送出。

Step 4 伺服器將直接發送「啟動 email」給讀者，讀者請至註冊之 email 信箱收信，按下啟動鍵即可使用。

Step 5 逾時 10 分鐘收不到「啟動 email」，請電洽 0800-500-699 勁園認證中心，由專員代為啟動（請於營業時間致電）。

2 光碟使用說明

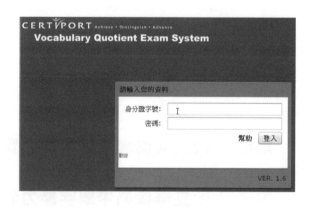

Step 1 帳號啟動後，按光碟操作步驟進行安裝。

Step 2 安裝完成，確認網路連線正常，直接點選桌面「線上」圖示，或以「開始/程式集/3RRR/VQ Online Testing」連結。

Step 3 依畫面輸入身分證字號及密碼，即可進入系統進行練習。

◎完成註冊手續即可免費使用授權半年。
◎帳號售價：300 元/1 季/1 帳號
　　　　　　550 元/半年/1 帳號
　　　　　1000 元/1 年/1 帳號
欲購專線請洽 0800-500-699 勁園認證中心

VQC

單字力 C Rank

S2 高中二年級
V2 高職二年級 編號 3894～4103

3894

cooperative [ko͵ɑpə'retɪv] [-'ɑprətɪv]

adj. 合作的,協力的

The students in this club are very cooperative.

這個社團的學生非常合作。

3895

cooperate [ko'ɑpə͵ret]

vi. 合作,協作

He cooperates with others in the company.

他在公司內與他人合作。

3896

outstanding ['aut'stændɪŋ]

adj. 傑出的,突出的,未解決的

This singer had an outstanding performance.

這位歌手有場傑出的演出。

3897

yogurt ['jo-gərt]

n. 優格

She eats yogurt everyday.

她每天吃優格。

3898

realistic [͵rɪə'lɪstɪk]

adj. 現實的,注重實際的,實際可行的

The method is realistic.

這個方法是可行的。

3899

scarcely ['skɛrslɪ]

adv. 幾乎不,簡直沒有,剛…就…,僅僅,剛剛,決不

I can scarcely breathe.

我幾乎不能呼吸。

3900

seagull ['si͵gʌl]

n. 鷗,海鷗

I saw seagulls near the sea.

我在海邊看到海鷗。

3901

shaver ['ʃevə]

n. 刮鬍刀

I use an electric shaver.

我使用電動刮鬍刀。

3902

sightseeing ['saɪt͵siɪŋ]

n. 觀光,遊覽 adj. 觀光的,遊覽的

This is a famous sightseeing spot.

這是個著名的觀光景點。

3903

settler ['sɛtlə]

n. 移民者,居留者,定居者

They are early settlers in Australia.

他們是早期定居澳洲的人。

3904

researcher [ri's3tʃə]

n. 研究員,調查者

He is a researcher.

他是研究者。

3905

regarding [rɪˈgɑrdɪŋ] prep. 關於,注重,注意,考慮,關心,尊敬,尊重,器重,注視,凝視

Do you have any problems regarding your work?

你有任何關於工作上的問題嗎？

3906

registration [ˌrɛdʒɪˈstreʃən]

n. 登記,註冊,掛號

They charge a small registration fee.

他們收一點註冊費用。

3907

capitalist [ˈkæpətḷɪst]

n. 資本家,資本主義者 adj. 資本主義的

I am a capitalist.

我是資本主義者。

3908

lawful [ˈlɔfəl]

adj. 法律許可的,守法的,合法的

It's not lawful to smoke here.

在這裡抽菸是不合法的。

3909

lecturer [ˈlɛktʃərə]

n. 講演者,講師

He is a lecturer.

他是演講者。

3910

lotion [ˈloʃən]

n. 乳液,潤膚液

He puts lotion on his body.

他在身上擦乳液。

3911

lousy [ˈlaʊzɪ]

adj. 汙穢的,糟糕的,差勁的

He is a lousy manager.

他是一個差勁的經理。

3912

marathon [ˈmærəˌθɑn] [ˈmærəθən]

n. 馬拉松,耐力的考驗

He decides to run a marathon.

他決定參加馬拉松比賽。

3913

homeland [ˈhomˌlænd]

n. 祖國,家鄉,家園

Taiwan is my homeland.

台灣是我的故鄉。

3914

hostel [ˈhɑstḷ]

n. 便宜的旅舍,旅館

There are many youth hostels in London.

倫敦有許多青年旅館。

3915

appointment [əˈpɔɪntmənt]

n. 約會,指定,預約,職務

I'd like to make an appointment with Doctor Lee.

我想約個時間見李醫生。

3916

cunning [ˈkʌnɪŋ]

adj. 狡猾的,巧妙的,取巧的,可愛的 n. 詭計

He is as cunning as a fox.

他像狐狸般地狡猾。

3917

accompany [əˈkʌmpənɪ]

vt. 陪伴,伴奏

Kids must be accompanied by adults.

小孩必須由大人陪同。

3918

obedient [əˈbidɪənt]

adj. 服從的,孝順的

Mary has an obedient child.

瑪莉有一個聽話的小孩。

3919

association [ə͵sosɪˈeʃən]

n. 協會,聯合,結交,聯想

He is a member of the golf association.

他是高爾夫協會的會員。

3920

acquaintance [əˈkwentəns]

n. 相識,熟人

He heard about the news through a mutual acquaintance.

他透過共同熟人聽到這個消息。

3921

ferry [ˈfɛrɪ]

n. 擺渡,渡船,渡口 vi. 擺渡,(船)來往行駛

I took a ferry to England.

我搭渡輪去英國。

3922

jealousy [ˈdʒɛləsɪ]

n. 嫉妒

I'm tired of her jealousy.

我很厭煩她的妒忌。

3923

confusion [kənˈfjuʒən] [-ˈfruʒən]

n. 混亂,混淆,不確定,困惑,困窘,局促不安

I have a confusion as to what to do next.

我對於接著要做什麼感到困惑。

3924

appliance [əˈplaɪəns]

n. 用具,器具

They bought household appliances.

他們買家電用品。

3925

congress [ˈkɑŋgrəs]

n. (代表)大會,[C～](美國等國的)國會,議會

They attended a medical congress on AIDS.

他們出席愛滋病的醫學會議。

3926

mischief [ˈmɪstʃɪf]

n. 傷害,危害,故障,惡作劇,淘氣,調皮的人

Don't get into mischief.

不要調皮搗蛋。

3927

romance [roˈmæns] [rə-] n. 冒險故事,浪漫

史,傳奇文學,風流韻事,虛構 vi. 寫傳奇,渲染,虛構

She writes romances.

她寫浪漫故事。

3928

conscience [ˈkɑnʃəns]

n. 良心,道德心,良知,內疚,愧疚

A good conscience is a soft pillow.

不做虧心事,夜半敲門心不驚。

3929

identification [aɪˌdɛntəfəˈkeʃən]

n. 辨認,鑒定,證明,視為同一

Do you have identification cards?

你有身分證嗎？

3930

glide [glaɪd] v. 滑行,悄悄地走,(時間)消逝,滑翔

n. 滑行,滑翔,滑移,滑音

The American skaters were gliding over the ice.

美國溜冰好手在冰上溜冰。

3931

nonetheless [ˌnʌnðəˈlɛs]

adv. 雖然如此,但是

The book is too long but, nonetheless, it is interesting.

這本書很厚，但是很有趣。

3932

approval [əˈpruvl]

n. 贊成,承認,正式批准

The mother has already given her approval to the plan.

媽媽已贊成這個計畫。

3933

attach [əˈtætʃ]

vt. 繫,貼,連接,附屬

Attach a recent photograph to your resume.

將你最近的照片放在你的履歷裡。

3934

imaginative [ɪˈmædʒəˌnetɪv]

adj. 想像的,虛構的

This is an imaginative story.

這是虛構出的故事。

3935

analyze [ˈænlˌaɪz]

vt. 分析,分解

She still needs to analyze the data.

她還需要分析數據。

3936

atomic [əˈtɑmɪk]

adj. 原子的,原子能的,微粒子的

Many countries have an Atomic Energy Commission.

許多國家都設有原子能委員會。

3937

assure [əˈʃʊr]

vt. 使確信,使放心,使擔保

Her students' future is assured.

她學生們的未來是有保障的。

3938

partial [ˈpɑrʃəl]

adj. 部分的,不完全的,偏向一方的

I'm partial to swimming.

我特別喜歡游泳。

3939

representation [ˌrɛprɪzɛnˈteʃən]

n. 表示法,表現,陳述,請求,扮演,畫像,繼承,代表

The clock in the painting is a symbolic representation of love. 畫裡的鐘是一種愛的象徵。

3940

pebble [ˈpɛbl]

n. 小圓石,小鵝卵石

The beach was covered with white pebbles.

這個海灘被白色的鵝卵石所覆蓋著。

3941

illustration [ɪləs'treʃən] [ɪˌlʌs'treʃən]

n. 說明,例證,例子,圖表,插圖,圖解

The book contains many easy-to-follow illustrations for yoga position.

這本書包含了許多易學的瑜伽體位插圖。

3942

flexible ['flɛksəbḷ]

adj. 易變的,靈活的,彈性的,彎曲的

The straw is flexible.

吸管可以彎曲。

3943

championship ['tʃæmpɪən,ʃɪp]

n. 錦標賽

Our team won the championship last year.

我們的隊伍去年得到冠軍。

3944

despite [dɪ'spaɪt]

prep. 不管,儘管,不論

Despite different class and social status, all human beings have equal value.

儘管出身與地位不同,我們都是生而平等的。

3945

symphony ['sɪmfənɪ]

n. 交響樂,交響曲

I am listening to Beethoven's Fifth Symphony.

我正在聆聽貝多芬第五交響曲。

3946

virgin ['vɜdʒɪn]

n. 童男,處女

adj. 處女的,童貞的,純潔的,原始的,未開發的,原始狀態的

The forest is a virgin land.

這片原始森林是天然的。

3947

terrify ['tɛrə,faɪ]

vt. 使恐怖,恐嚇,使感到恐怖

The baby was terrified by a dog.

這個嬰兒被一隻狗嚇著。

3948

devise [dɪ'vaɪz]

vt. 設計,發明,圖謀,作出(計劃),想出(辦法),遺贈給

n. 遺贈

A new air conditioning system has been devised to regulate your home's temperature.

新的空調系統被設計出可用在調節家中的溫度。

3949

cushion [ˈkuʃ ən] [-ɪn]

n. 墊子,軟墊,襯墊 v. 加襯墊

I bought a velvet cushion.

我買了鵝毛的墊子。

3950

courtesy [ˈkɝtəsɪ]

n. 謙恭,允許,禮貌

Full of courtesy, full of craft.

禮多必詐。

3951

violation [ˌvaɪəˈleʃ ən]

n. 違反,違背,妨礙,侵害,[體]違例

He got a ticket for the violation of traffic rules.

他因為違反交通規則而收到罰單。

3952

commander [kəˈmændə]

n. 司令官,指揮官

He is an American Commander.

他是美國指揮官。

3953

disconnect [ˌdɪskəˈnɛkt]

v. 拆開,分離,斷開

My phone has been disconnected.

我的電話被斷線了。

3954

courageous [kəˈredʒəs]

adj. 勇敢的,有膽量的,無畏的

He made a courageous decision.

他作了很勇敢的決定。

3955

circulation [ˌsɝkjəˈleʃ ən]

n. 迴圈,流通,發行額,循環

She must massage her leg on time due to bad circulation.

她由於血液循環差,必須按時按摩腳。

3956

hurricane [ˈhɝɪˌken]

n. 颶風,狂風

A sudden hurricane scared people.

一個突然來的颶風嚇到人們。

3957

relaxation [ˌrilæksˈeʃ ən]

n. 鬆弛,放寬,緩和,減輕,娛樂,放鬆

I dance for relaxation.

我用跳舞來放鬆自己。

3958

conservative [kənˈsɝvətɪv]

adj. 保守的,守舊的 n. 保守派

He is conservative.

他很保守。

3959

grace [gres]

n. 優美,雅緻,優雅,風度

She accepted his apology with good grace.

她很有風度地接受了他的道歉。

3960

fatal [ˈfetl̩]

adj. 致命的,毀滅性的

H1N1 is a potentially fatal disease.

H1N1 是潛在致命的疾病。

3961

messy ['mɛsɪ]

adj. 骯髒的, 凌亂的, 雜亂

Can you clean the messy room?

你可以清理這個雜亂的房間嗎?

3962

elastic [ɪ'læstɪk] [ə-]

adj. 有彈性的, 有彈力的, 靈活的, 可改變的, 可伸縮的

Rubber is elastic.

橡膠有彈性。

3963

timid ['tɪmɪd]

adj. 膽小的, 膽怯的, 缺乏勇氣的

I was a timid child.

我曾是一個膽小的小孩。

3964

landmark ['lænd,mɑrk]

n. (航海)陸標, 地界標, 里程碑, 劃時代的事

Statue of Liberty is a famous landmark in New York.

自由女神像是紐約市著名的地標。

3965

exhaust [ɪg'zɔst]

vt. 使筋疲力盡, 用盡, 耗盡 n. 排氣裝置, 廢氣

A full day's working exhausts me.

一整天的工作讓我很累。

3966

fort [fort] [fɔrt]

n. 堡壘, 要塞

The soldiers in the fort sallied at dawn.

堡壘裡的士兵在黎明時突擊。

3967

engineering [ˌɛndʒə'nɪrɪŋ]

n. 工程, 工程學

He majors in engineering.

他主修工程學。

3968

damn [dæm]

v. 討厭, 譴責, 咒罵

Damn it!

真糟糕!

3969

errand ['ɛrənd]

n. 差事, 差使, 使命

I was running errands for my mom.

我幫媽媽跑腿。

3970

philosophical [ˌfɪlə'sɑfɪk!]

adj. 哲學的

This is a philosophical problem.

這是哲學性的問題。

3971

fame [fem] n. 名聲, 名望, 傳說, (古)傳聞

vt. (常用被動語態)使聞名, 使有名望, 盛傳

She went to Hollywood in search of fame.

她去好萊塢尋找名聲。

3972

frost [frɔst]

n. 霜 v. 降霜

There was a heavy frost.

霜降得很厚。

3973

emotional [ɪˈmoʃənl] [-ʃnəl]

adj. 情緒的,情感的

She provided emotional support for me.

她給我情感上的支持。

3974

discipline [ˈdɪsəplɪn]

n. 紀律,學科 v. 訓練

Good companies have good discipline.

好的公司有好的紀律。

3975

ambitious [æmˈbɪʃəs]

adj. 有雄心的,野心勃勃的,抱負的,目標的,志向的

He is an ambitious man.

他是一個有志向的男人。

3976

hose [hoz]

n. 軟管,水龍帶,長筒襪 v. 用軟管澆水

He carried a garden hose.

他拿著花園的水管。

3977

socket [ˈsɑkɪt]

n. 插座,托座(燭台的),插孔,管座,孔穴 v. 給…配插座

Please put the plug into a socket.

請把插頭插進插座。

3978

exhibit [ɪgˈzɪbɪt]

vt. 展出,陳列 v. 展示,參展

Her paintings have been exhibited all over the world.

她的畫作已經在全世界參展。

3979

enlargement [ɪnˈlɑrdʒnənt]

n. 放大,擴展,擴建

He is interested in the enlargement of the company's overseas business.

他對於公司擴展海外生意感到有興趣。

3980

leisurely [ˈliʒəlɪ]

adv. 從容不迫,輕鬆的,悠閒的,從容的

I work at a leisurely pace.

我輕鬆的工作。

3981

resignation [ˌrɛzɪgˈneʃən] [ˌrɛs-]

n. 辭職,辭職書,放棄,順從

He sent a letter of resignation.

他遞出辭職信。

3982

diploma [dɪˈplomə]

n. 文憑,畢業證書,證明權力,特權,榮譽等的證書,獎狀

I got my teaching diploma this year.

我今年拿到我的教學文憑。

3983

ginger [ˈdʒɪndʒ⋏]

n. 薑,生薑,有薑味,活潑,元氣,精力,淡赤黃色(的)～

I ate ginger biscuits.

我吃了薑餅。

3984

flush [flʌʃ]

n. 奔流,暈紅,激動,萌芽,活力旺盛,發燒,一手同花的
五張牌,驚鳥

vt. 淹沒,沖洗,使臉紅,使齊平,使驚飛,使激動

She has a flush on her face.

她臉紅。

3985

extent [ɪkˈstɛnt]

n. 廣度,範圍,程度

To some extent, we all remember the good times.

在某個程度上,我們都記得快樂的時光。

3986

horrify [ˈhɔrəˌfaɪ] [ˈhɑrəˌfaɪ] [ˈhɒr-]

v. 使恐怖,使極度厭惡,驚駭

When I saw these figures, I was horrified.

當我看到這些圖片時,我真的被嚇到了。

3987

disgust [dɪsˈgʌst] [dɪz-]

n. 厭惡,嫌惡 vt. 使作嘔

Joan looked at me with disgust.

喬安用厭惡的眼神看著我。

3988

dominant [ˈdɑmənənt]

adj. 有統治權的,佔優勢的,支配的 adj. [生物]顯性的

The country became dominant in the world.

這個國家在世界上佔主導地位。

3989

criticize [ˈkrɪtəsaɪz]

v. 批評,責備,批判,挑剔,指責

They criticize sharply.

他們嚴肅地批評。

3990

glorious [ˈglorɪəs]

adj. 光榮的,顯赫的,值得稱道的,榮耀的,壯麗的,輝煌
的,光輝燦爛的,極其令人愉快的,極為宜人的,陽
光燦爛的,晴朗的

I saw a glorious sunshine in the morning.

我在早上看到明亮的陽光。

3991

elegant [ˈɛləgənt]

adj. 文雅的,端莊的,雅緻的,(口)上品的,第一流的

She is a tall and elegant young woman.

她是一位身材高挑並且優雅的年輕女孩。

3992

equality [ɪˈkwɑlətɪ] [ɪˈkwɒl-]

n. 等同性,同等,平等,相等,等式

The two pairs of pants have the equality of size.

這兩件褲子尺寸相同。

3993

creation [krɪˈeʃən]

n. 創造,創作物

The cake was a delicious creation of cream and fruit.

這個美味的蛋糕是由奶油和水果作成的作品。

3994

estimate [ˈɛstəˌmet]

vt. 估計,估價 n. 評價,估計

The house is estimated to be at least 10 years old.

這間房子估計至少有十年之久。

3995

encounter [ɪnˈkaʊntɚ]

vt. 遭遇,遇到,偶然碰到,意外地遇見,與…邂逅,比賽,
交鋒

They encountered serious problems.

他們遇到嚴重的問題。

3996

functional [ˈfʌŋkʃənl]

adj. 功能的,實用的,機能的

His bedroom is functional.

他的臥室很具機能性。

3997

critic [ˈkrɪtɪk]

n. 批評家,評論家,吹毛求疵者

He is a music critic.

他是一位音樂評論家。

3998

shuttle [ˈʃʌtl]

n. 接駁車,太空梭,梭子,穿梭 v. 穿梭往返

I take a shuttle bus home.

我搭接駁車回家。

3999

tomb [tum]

n. 墳墓 v. 埋葬

The family tomb is in the mountain.

這個家族墳墓在山上。

4000

essay [ˈɛse]

vt. 企圖,嘗試 n. 企圖,散文,小品文,隨筆,短文,評論

He wrote an essay about the country.

他寫了一篇有關於國家的短文。

4001

funeral [ˈfjunərəl]

n. 葬禮,喪禮,出殯,自作自受

The funeral will be held here.

這個葬禮將在這裡舉辦。

4002

revision [rɪˈvɪʒən]

n. 修訂,修改,修正,修訂本

I made some revisions to the novel.

我對於這個小說做了些修訂。

4003

pursuit [pɚˈsut]

n. 追擊,追求

Tom studied abroad in pursuit of a higher degree.

湯姆為了追求更高的學歷,出國讀書。

4004

detective [dɪˈtɛktɪv]

n. 偵探 adj. 偵探的

I like to read detective novels.

我喜歡閱讀偵探小說。

4005

critical ['krɪtɪkl̩]

adj. 決定性的,關鍵的,批評的,批判的

Many parents are strongly critical of the educational system. 很多父母對教育體制有很強烈的批判。

4006

disadvantage [ˌdɪsəd'væntɪdʒ]

n. 不利,不利條件,缺點,劣勢

His bad temper is a disadvantage.
他的壞脾氣是個缺點。

4007

muddy ['mʌdɪ]

adj. 多泥的,泥濘的

The lake is full of muddy water.
這個湖充滿泥濘。

4008

evaluate [ɪ'væljʊˌet]

vt. 評價,估計,求…的值 v. 評價

You should be able to evaluate your progress.
你應該能夠評估你的進度。

4009

graduation [ˌgrædʒʊ'eʃən]

n. 畢業,畢業典禮,刻度,分等級

It was my first job after graduation.
這是我在畢業後的第一份工作。

4010

equip [ɪ'kwɪp]

vt. 裝備,配備,訓練,準備行裝

The course will equip you for being a tour guide.
這堂課程將使你能夠當一個導遊。

4011

sculpture ['skʌlptʃɚ]

n. 雕刻,雕刻品,雕塑,雕塑品,[地理]刻蝕

v. 雕刻,雕塑,刻蝕

He sent me a sculpture of an elephant.

他送我大象的雕像。

4012

proverb ['prɑvɝb]

n. 諺語,格言

'A penny saved is a penny earned' is a proverb.
省一分錢是賺一分錢是一句諺語。

4013

endure [ɪn'djʊr]

vt. 忍受,容忍 vi. 忍受,忍耐,持續

No one could endure such pain.
沒有人可以忍受這樣的痛苦。

4014

frequency ['frikwənsɪ]

n. 頻率,周率,發生次數

Can you tell me the frequency of serious road accidents?
可以告訴我嚴重車禍事故發生的頻率嗎?

4015

dismiss [dɪs'mɪs]

v. 開除,解雇,解散

The class was dismissed earlier today.
這堂課今天提早下課。

4016
efficiency [ə'fɪʃənsɪ] [ɪ-]
n. 效率,功效
I like the efficiency of the train service in Japan.
我喜歡日本火車服務的高效率。

4017
suspicious [sə'spɪʃəs]
adj. 可疑的,懷疑的
They were suspicious about the story.
他們對這個故事心存懷疑。

4018
salesperson ['selz,pɜsn]
n. 售貨員
I go to school to learn how to be a salesperson.
我去學校學習如何當一位銷售員。

4019
furnish ['fɜnɪʃ]
vt. 供應,提供,裝備,布置
The room was furnished with flowers.
這房間用花來裝飾。

4020
tolerant ['tɑlərənt]
adj. 容忍的,寬恕的,忍受的
Luckily, my parents were tolerant of my bad temper.
幸運地,我的父母忍受我的壞脾氣。

4021
faithful [feθfəl]
adj. 守信的,忠實的,詳確的,可靠的,可信賴的 n. 信徒
He is a faithful friend.
他是個可信賴的友人。

4022
dependable [dɪ'pɛndəbl]
adj. 可信賴的,可靠的
I need a dependable source of income.
我需要一個可靠的收入來源。

4023
expand [ɪk'spænd]
v. 擴大,膨脹,擴張,展開
Butterflies expand their wings.
蝴蝶展翅。

4024
imaginable [ɪ'mædʒɪnəbl] [ɪ'mædʒnəbl]
adj. 可想像的,可能的
The travel brochure is full of the most wonderful things imaginable.
這本旅遊手冊充滿了可想像的最美好事物。

4025
publisher ['pʌblɪʃə]
n. 出版者,發行人
Several publishers are competing in the market.
在出版社這個市場出現很多的競爭者。

4026
disorder [dɪs'ɔrdə] [dɪz-]
n. 雜亂,混亂,無秩序狀態 vt. 擾亂,使失調,使紊亂
The room was in a state of disorder.
這間房間一片混亂。

4027

delicate ['dɛləkət] [-kɪt]

adj. 精巧的,精緻的,病弱的,脆弱的,微妙的,棘手的,靈敏的,精密的,精細的

A plastic surgeon performed the delicate operation.

整型外科醫生執行了精細的手術。

4028

demonstrate ['dɛmən,stret]

vt. 說明,示範 vi. 進行示威遊行

The study demonstrates the link between A and B.

這個研究顯示 A 和 B 的關聯。

4029

bracelet ['breslɪt]

n. 手鍊

He sent me a gold bracelet as my birthday gift.

他送我黃金手鍊作為生日禮物。

4030

cape [kep]

n. 海角,岬,披肩,斗篷

A magician wears a cape.

魔術師穿著斗篷。

4031

grief [grif]

n. 悲痛,傷心事,不幸,憂傷

Charles was overwhelmed with grief.

查爾斯萬分的悲痛。

4032

costume [kɑs'tjum] [-'trum] [-'tum]

n. 裝束,服裝,戲服

She changes several costumes during the play.

她在劇中換了好幾套戲服。

4033

generosity [,dʒɛnə'rɑsətɪ]

n. 慷慨,寬宏大量

He treated them with generosity.

他對他們很慷慨。

4034

admirable ['ædmərəbl]

adj. 令人欽佩的,值得讚美的,絕妙的,極好的

He has an admirable achievement.

他有令人稱羨的成就。

4035

divorce [də'vors] [-'vɔrs]

v. 離婚,分離

Why did she divorce with him?

她為何要和他離婚?

4036

professional [prə'fɛʃən!] [-ʃnəl]

n. 專業人員,訓練有素的人,專家

adj. 專業的,職業的

They go on to higher levels of schooling to enhance their professional abilities.

他們持續在高等學校進修以提升他們專業的能力。

4037

needy ['nidɪ]

adj. 貧困的,非常貧窮的,缺乏生活必需品的

I have money to help the needy.

我有錢幫助貧困的人。

4038

convince [kən'vɪns]

vt. 使確信,信服

I convinced myself that this was true.

我說服自己這是對的。

4039

cram [kræm]

v. 填滿,死記硬背

My sister crammed math formulas for the entrance exam.

我姊姊為了聯考(入學考試)硬背數學公式。

4040

establish [ə'stæblɪʃ]

vt. 建立,創辦,設立

Our goal is to establish a new center in North America.

我們的目標是在北美建立新的中心。

4041

emphasis ['ɛmfəsɪs]

n. 強調,重點

The course places emphasis on theories.

這堂課強調理論。

4042

finance [fɪ'næns] ['faɪnæns]

n. 財政,金融,財政學 vi. 籌措資金

Russia's finance minister is on TV now.

俄國的財政部長現在在電視上。

4043

witch [wɪtʃ]

n. 巫婆,女巫,迷人的女子 vt. 施巫術,迷惑

A witch is supposed to have magic power.

一個女巫被認為擁有魔力(法)。

4044

frown [fraʊn]

vi. 皺眉,蹙額,不贊成,反對 v. 皺眉

She frowned as she looked at him.

她皺眉地注視著他。

4045

freeway ['fri,we]

n. 高速公路

There was an accident on the freeway.

高速公路上有車禍。

4046

fantasy ['fæntəsɪ]

n. 夢想,幻想,白日夢,幻想

The student likes to live in fantasy.

這個學生喜歡活在幻想中。

4047

portray [por'tre]

v. 描繪,描寫,以某種印象,表現,扮演某角色

This book portrays the principal as a criminal.

此書將這個校長描寫成一個罪犯。

4048

escalator ['ɛskə,letɚ]

n. (美)電動扶梯,自動扶梯

I took an escalator.

我搭電動扶梯。

4049

copper ['kɑpɚ]

adj. 銅色的

She has copper hair.

她有銅紅色的頭髮。

4050

gallery ['gælərɪ] [-lrɪ] n. 走廊,戲院,教堂等中

最高的樓座,美術陳列室,畫廊,圖庫

Are there art galleries in the city?

這個城市有美術館嗎？

4051

celebration [ˌsɛləˈbreʃən]

n. 慶祝,慶典

The New Year celebration is in the city center.

跨年晚會在市中心舉行。

4052

giggle ['gɪgl̩]

v. 哈哈地笑 n. 傻笑

He can't stop giggling.

他笑到停不下來。

4053

rainfall ['renˌfɔl]

n. 降雨,降雨量

We have a long period of rainfall.

我們有很長的雨季。

4054

differ ['dɪfɚ] vi. 相異,有區別,不同於,

意見相左,持不同看法,不同意,不一致,不同

This dress differs from that one.

這件洋裝和那件不一樣。

4055

sneeze [sniz]

n. 噴嚏 vi. 打噴嚏

She started coughing and sneezing when she got a cold.

當她感冒時她開始咳嗽和打噴嚏。

4056

chore [tʃor] [tʃɔr]

n. 家務雜事

I share the chores with my family.

我和家人分擔家裡雜事。

4057

blink [blɪŋk]

v. 眨眼,閃亮,無視

I blink as I see sunlight.

當注視太陽光時會讓我眨眼。

4058

fulfill [fʊlˈfɪl]

vt. 履行,實現,完成

He has fulfilled the dream of visiting Disneyland.

他完成了參觀迪士尼樂園的夢想。

4059

demonstration [ˌdɛmənˈstreʃən]

n. 示範,實證

He gave a practical teaching demonstration.

他作了一個實際的教學示範。

4060

device [dɪˈvaɪs]

n. 裝置,設備,儀器

He invented a device for separating garbage.

他發明了一個會自動分類垃圾的裝置。

4061

composer [kəm'pozɚ]

n. 作家,作曲家,設計者,著作者

He is a composer.

他是一個作曲家。

The train conductor checked tickets from the passengers.

列車長向乘客查票。

4062

gangster ['gæŋstɚ]

n. (美俗)歹徒,土匪,強盜,流氓

Gangsters got together in the street.

不良分子在街上聚集。

4067

persuasive [pɚ'swesɪv]

n. 說服者,勸誘 adj. 善說服的

He is very persuasive.

他很有說服力。

4063

ballet ['bæle] ['bælɪ] [bæ'le]

n. 芭蕾舞,芭蕾舞劇,芭蕾舞樂曲

We're going to practice ballet tomorrow night.

我們明天晚上要去練芭雷舞。

4068

financial [far'nænʃəl]

adj. 財政的,金融的

They are in financial difficulties.

他們有財務困難。

4064

appreciation [ə,priʃɪ'eʃən]

n. 感謝,感激,正確評價,欣賞,增值

Kevin showed his appreciation by writing a letter.

凱文藉由信表達他的感激之意。

4069

mow [mau]

n. 乾草堆,穀堆 v. 刈,掃除,收割莊稼,掃倒

It's time to mow the weeds again.

該是再次除草的時間了。

4065

idol ['aɪdl]

n. 偶像,崇拜物,幻像,[邏]謬論

She is a pop idol.

她是流行偶像。

4070

fiction ['fɪkʃən]

n. 虛構,編造,小說

He wrote a romantic fiction.

他寫了一本愛情小說。

4066

conductor [kən'dʌktɚ]

n. 指揮,領導者,領隊,經理,指揮管弦樂隊,合唱隊的,

(市內有軌電車或公共汽車)售票員,(美)列車長

4071

deadline ['dɛd,laɪn]

n. 最後期限

The deadline for applications is February 27th.

申請表的截止日期在二月二十七日。

4072

converse [ˈkɑnvɝs]

v. 交談,談話 n. 相反的事物,倒,逆行

adj. 相反的,顛倒的

She enjoys conversing with German.

她喜歡跟德國人聊天。

4073

luxurious [lʌkˈʃʊrɪəs]

adj. 奢侈的,豪華的

There is a luxurious villa on the island.

這個島上有一間豪華別墅。

4074

delightful [dɪˈlaɪtfəl]

adj. 令人愉快的,可喜的

This is delightful news.

這是一個讓人高興的消息。

4075

disguise [dɪsˈgaɪz]

v. 假裝,偽裝,掩飾 n. 偽裝

It is a blessing in disguise.

因禍得福。(塞翁失馬,焉知非福。)

4076

contribute [kənˈtrɪbjʊt]

v. 捐獻,投稿

The volunteers contribute their own time to the activities. 義工們貢獻他們的時間來作活動。

4077

infection [ɪnˈfɛkʃən]

n. [醫]傳染,傳染病,影響,感染

He got an ear infection from a cold virus.

他耳朵被感冒病毒感染。

4078

cord [kɔrd]

n. 繩索,束縛

The shirt was held at the waist by a cord.

襯衫腰際間有帶子。

4079

autobiography [ˌɔtəbaɪˈɑgrəfɪ] [-bɪ-] [-ɒg-]

n. 自傳,自傳的寫作

He published his autobiography last spring.

去年春天他出版了他的自傳。

4080

athletic [æθˈlɛtɪk]

adj. 運動的

He is a strong athletic boy.

他是體格強壯的運動員。

4081

dominate [ˈdɑməˌnet]

v. 支配,佔優勢

My parents dominate my allowance.

父母支配我的零用錢。

4082

eventual [ɪˈvɛntʃʊəl]

adj. (古)可能的,最後的,結局的,萬一的,終於的

We don't know what the eventual outcome will be.

我們不知道最終的結果是什麼。

4083
tiresome ['taɪrsəm]

adj. 無聊的,煩人的

Children's crying is tiresome.

孩子的哭聲令人厭煩。

4084
depression [dɪ'prɛʃən]

n. 沮喪,消沉,低氣壓,低壓,蕭條,不景氣

She was in depression.

她心情沮喪。

4085
convention [kən'vɛnʃən]

n. 大會,協定,習俗,慣例

Shaking hands is a normal convention in many countries when meeting people.

在許多國家中人們見面時互相握手是一種慣例。

4086
surgeon ['sɜdʒən]

n. 外科醫生

He is a surgeon.

他是外科醫生。

4087
depart [dɪ'pɑrt]

vt. 離開,離去,起程,出發,出發,離開人世,去世,亡故

Mary departed for USA last week.

瑪莉上週前往美國。

4088
perfection [pə'fɛkʃən]

n. 盡善盡美,完美,完成

He tries to reach perfection.

他試著到達完美。

4089
prevention [prɪ'vɛnʃən]

n. 預防,防止,防範

Educating drivers is important for the prevention of accidents. 教育駕駛人是很重要的,可預防意外的發生。

4090
motivation [,motə'veʃən]

n. 動機,刺激,推動,積極性,幹勁,行動方式

Jack is a smart child, but he lacks learning motivation.

傑克是聰明的小孩,但是他缺乏學習動機。

4091
strive [straɪv]

v. 努力,奮鬥,力爭,鬥爭

I was still striving to be on time.

我還在努力要變得守時。

4092
envious ['ɛnvɪəs]

adj. 嫉妒的,羨慕的

Everyone was envious of her success.

每個人都羨慕她的成功。

4093
consist [kən'sɪst]

vi. 由…組成,在於,一致

Happiness does not consist in how much money you own. 快樂並不取決於你擁有多少錢。

4094

crack [kræk]

n. 砸開,破開,砸碎,重擊,猛擊,吃不消,崩潰,瓦解,阻止,
　打擊,擊敗,戰勝,打碎,裂縫,劈啪聲

v. (使)破裂,裂紋,(使)爆裂

Don't put boiling soup in the glass or it will crack.

不要將滾燙的湯放入玻璃杯中,不然會破碎。

4095

honeymoon ['hʌnɪˌmun]

n. 蜜月　v. 度蜜月

We went to Hualien on our honeymoon.

我們去花蓮度蜜月。

4096

consistent [kən'sɪstənt]

adj. 一致的,調和的,堅固的,[數,統]相容的

We need to be consistent in our methods.

我們需要在方法上一致。

4097

enforce [ɪn'fɔrs] [-'fors]

vt. 強迫,執行,堅持,加強

The law will be strictly enforced.

法律會被嚴格地執行。

4098

era ['ɪrə] ['irə]

n. 時代,紀元,時期,[地]代

This is a new era of world peace.

這是世界和平的新紀元。

4099

distribution [ˌdɪstrə'bjuʃən] [-'brɪuʃən]

n. 分配,分發,配給物,銷售,法院對無遺囑死亡者財產
　的分配,分布狀態,區分,分類,發送,發行

The distribution center is located in Taipei.

貨品配送中心座落在臺北。

4100

productive [prə'dʌktɪv]

adj. 生產性的,生產的,能產的,多產的

He is a productive writer.

他是位多產的作家。

4101

youthful ['juθfəl]

adj. 年輕的,青年的

She desired to maintain her youthful appearance.

她想要保持年輕外表。

4102

disaster [dɪ'zæstə]

n. 災難,災害

They died from the nuclear disaster.

他們死於核災。

4103

landslide ['lændˌslaɪd] ['læn-]

n. [地]山崩,崩塌的泥石,[選舉]壓倒性勝利

The candidate has a landslide victory.

候選人贏得壓倒性勝利。

S2 高中二年級
V3 高職三年級 編號 4104～4499

4104

species [ˈspiʃɪz] [-ʃiz]

n. 種,類,外形

We must protect endangered species.

我們必須保護瀕臨絕種的動物。

4105

wildlife [ˈwaɪldˌlaɪf]

n. 野生生物

She loves the beauty of wildlife.

她喜愛野生生物之美。

4106

vapor [ˈvepɚ]

n. 水汽,蒸氣 v. 蒸發

Why is water vapor converted directly into ice crystal?

為什麼水蒸氣會直接轉換成冰晶？

4107

spicy [ˈspaɪsɪ]

adj. 香的,多香料的,辛辣的,下流的

I like spicy tomato sauce.

我喜歡辣的番茄醬。

4108

reminder [rɪˈmaɪndɚ]

n. 提醒,通知單

Here is a reminder of what you should buy tomorrow.

這是一張提醒你明天要買什麼的單子。

4109

briefcase [ˈbrifˌkes]

n. 公事包

Mary bought a nice briefcase.

瑪麗買了一個不錯的公事包。

4110

bra [brɑ]

n. 胸罩(brassiere),內衣

Japanese invented bras for men.

日本人發明了男用胸罩。

4111

greeting [ˈgritɪŋ]

n. 問候,致敬

She raised her hand in greeting.

她舉起手歡迎。

4112

gifted [ˈgɪftɪd]

adj. 有天才的,有天賦的

She was an extremely gifted swimmer.

她是極有天賦的游泳者。

4113

goods [gʊdz]

n. 商品,貨物,動產,[英](火車等運載的)貨物,
[英]合意的人(事,物),真貨

I need to buy furniture and other household goods.

我需要買傢俱和其他家用品。

4114

handwriting [ˈhændˌraɪtɪŋ]

n. 筆跡

I can't recognize her handwriting on the envelope.

我無法辨識她在信封袋上的筆跡。

4115

headphone [ˈhɛdˌfon]

n. 頭戴式耳機

I wear headphones when I listen to music.

當我聽音樂時，我戴耳機。

4116

greasy [ˈgrisɪ] [ˈgrizɪ]

adj. 油膩的,滑溜溜的,泥濘的

I need a shampoo for greasy hair.

我需要油性頭皮專用的洗髮乳。

4117

facial [ˈfeʃəl]

n. 美顏術,臉部按摩術 adj. 臉的,臉部用的

Victor's facial expression is interesting.

維多的臉部表情很有趣。

4118

dusty [ˈdʌstɪ]

adj. 灰塵多的,無聊的,含糊的,粉末狀的

The books are really dusty.

書本上的灰塵很多。

4119

distinguished [dɪˈstɪŋgwɪʃt]

adj. 顯著的,卓越的,出色的,傑出的,知名的,著名的,
出類拔萃的

He is a distinguished actor.

他是一個出色的演員。

4120

enclose [ɪnˈkloz]

vt. 圍住,附上,把…圍起來,隨函(或包裹)附上,附入

Please enclose a picture with your order.

請隨著你的訂單附上照片。

4121

examiner [ɪgˈzæmɪnɚ]

n. 檢查人,審查人,主考人

He is the examiner of the test.

他是這場考試的主考人。

4122

flatter [ˈflætɚ]

v. 奉承,阿諛,使高興,感到榮幸

The manager flatters his boss.

那位經理奉承他的上司。

4123

forgetful [fɚˈgɛtfəl]

adj. 健忘的,疏忽的

She has become very forgetful recently.

她最近變得很健忘。

4124

freshman [ˈfrɛʃmən]

n. 新手,新鮮人,大學一年級學生,中學一年級學生

He is a freshman in the university.

他是大學新鮮人。

4125 heavenly ['hɛvənlɪ]

adj. 十分舒適的,很愉快的,美好的,天上的,神聖的,天國似的 adv. 極其

This is a heavenly place. 這是一個十分舒適的地方。

4126 learning ['lɜnɪŋ]

n. 知識,學問,學習,學

I like student-centred learning.
我喜歡以學生為中心的學習。

4127 involve [ɪn'vɑlv]

vt. 使捲入,使參與,牽涉,包含

What will the job involve?
這個工作關於什麼?

4128 isolation [ˌaɪsḷ'eʃən] [ˌɪsḷ'eʃɪ]

n. 隔絕,孤立,隔離,分隔

Because of its geographical isolation, the area is different from others.

因為地理隔絕,這個區域跟其他的不一樣。

4129 itch [ɪtʃ]

n. 癢,渴望,疥癬 v. 發癢,渴望
My feet itch.
我的腳很癢。

4130 housing ['haʊzɪŋ]

n. 房屋,住房 (總稱)
They wanted better housing.
他們要求更好的住房。

4131 democrat ['dɛmə,kræt]

n. 民主政體論者,民主主義者,民主黨員
He is a democrat.
他是一位民主黨員。

4132 informative [ɪn'fɔrmətɪv]

adj. 情報的,使知道消息的,見聞廣博的
This is an informative and entertaining book.
這是本資訊充足且有娛樂性質的書。

4133 wizard ['wɪzɚd]

n. 男巫,術士,鬼才,嚮導 adj. 男巫、巫術的,有魔力的
He is a wizard.
他是巫師。

4134 translator [træns'letɚ]

n. 翻譯家,譯者,翻譯者,翻譯機
Not everyone who knows English can be a translator.
不是會英語的人就能當翻譯。

4135 beak [bik]

n. 鳥喙,鳥嘴,鷹勾鼻
The gull held the fish in its beak.
海鷗用鳥喙刁著魚。

4136
aspirin [ˈæspərɪn] [-prɪn]

n. 阿斯匹靈(一種解熱止痛劑)

I take an aspirin everyday.

我每天吃阿斯匹靈。

4137
syrup [ˈsɪrəp] [ˈsɜəp]

n. 糖漿,果汁

I love ice cream with maple syrup.

我喜歡吃加了楓糖的冰淇淋。

4138
videotape [ˈvɪdɪoˈtep]

n. 錄影帶,磁帶錄影

No one uses videotape now.

現在已經沒有人在用錄影帶了。

4139
gay [ge]

adj. 快樂的,色彩鮮艷的 n. 同性戀

She wears gay clothes to school.

她穿色彩鮮艷的衣服來上課。

4140
administration [ədˌmɪnəˈstreʃən] [æd-]

n. 管理,經營,行政部門

We're looking for someone experienced in
administration. 我們在找有行政經驗的人。

4141
bid [bɪd]

vt. 出價,投標,祝願,命令,吩咐 v. 支付

This person placed the highest bid in the auction.

這個人在拍賣會中出了最高價。

4142
canal [kəˈnæl]

n. 運河,灌溉渠,氣管,食道

Wood is usually sent here by canal.

木頭通常由運河載送到這裡。

4143
rubbish [ˈrʌbɪʃ]

n. 垃圾,廢物,[美式用 garbage]

I have a rubbish bin.

我有一個垃圾桶。

4144
accommodation [əˌkɑməˈdeʃən]

n. 住處,膳宿,(車,船,飛機等的)預定鋪位,(眼睛等的)
　　適應性調節,(社會集團間的)遷就融合

The price for the tour includes accommodation.

旅費包含住宿。

4145
asset [ˈæsɛt]

n. 資產,有用的東西

Our home is our largest investment and our greatest
asset. 家庭是我們最大的投資和資產。

4146
colleague [kəˈlig] [kɑ-]

n. 同事,同僚

She discussed the idea with her colleagues.

她跟她的同事討論這個想法。

4147

tin [tɪn]

n. 錫,[英]罐頭

I appreciate the invention of tins.
我感激罐頭的發明。

4148

accord [ə'kɔrd]

n. 一致,符合,調和,協定 vt. 一致,給與

Her description accords with mine.
她的描述和我一致。

4149

altitude ['æltə,tjud]

n. (尤指海拔)高度,高處(海拔甚高的地方),
    (等級,地位等)高等

We're at an altitude of 1000 feet.
我們在海拔一千英呎以上。

4150

ban [bæn]

n. 禁令 vt. 禁止,取締(書刊等)

Charlie was banned from driving for a year.
查爾斯被禁止駕車一年。

4151

peasant ['pɛznt] n. 農民,尤指貧窮國家的

農民,小農,佃農,老粗,土包子,沒教養的人

Many villagers are peasants.
很多村民是農夫。

4152

compliment ['kɑmplə,mɛnt]

n. 稱讚,恭維,致意,問候,道賀 vt. 稱讚,褒揚,恭維

Please accept these flowers with our compliments.
請接受這些花和我們的祝賀。

4153

boycott ['bɔɪ,kɑt]

n. 抵制,杯葛 vt. 抵制

We boycott all products from Korea.
我們聯合抵制韓國產品。

4154

declare [dɪ'klɛr]

vt. 公布,宣布,表明,宣稱,申報,斷言

I declare you husband and wife.
我宣布你們結為夫妻。

4155

coarse [kors] [kɔrs]

adj. 粗糙的,粗鄙的

I wear a jacket of coarse wool.
我穿一件粗糙的羊毛外套。

4156

abnormal [æb'nɔrml]

adj. 不正常的,變態的

He has an abnormal behavior.
他的行為是不正常的。

4157

barrier ['bærɪɚ]

n. (阻礙通道的)障礙物,柵欄,屏障

The demonstrators broke through the heavy barriers.
示威者衝破了眾多柵欄。

4158 attraction [ə'trækʃən]

n. 吸引,吸引力,吸引人的事物

Taipei 101 is a famous attraction for tourists.

台北 101 是著名的觀光客聖地。

4159 blush [blʌʃ]

v. 臉紅,羞愧,呈現紅色,使成紅色 n. 臉紅,紅色,紅光

She watched him and blushed.

她看著他然後臉紅。

4160 arise [ə'raɪz]

vi. 出現,由…引起

A crisis has arisen in the company.

這個公司有危機。

4161 bankrupt ['bæŋkrʌpt] [-rəpt]

n. 破產者 adj. 破產了的,完全喪失

Many of these companies are now bankrupt.

很多公司現在都破產了。

4162 dictation [dɪk'teʃən]

n. 口授筆錄,聽寫

I am doing French dictations.

我正在法文聽寫。

4163 arch ['ɑrtʃ]

n. 拱形,弓形

This is a bridge with three arches.

這座橋有三個拱門。

4164 amateur ['æmətʃʊr] [-ˌtɚ]

n. 業餘人士

This is an amateur orchestra.

這是個業餘的管弦樂隊。

4165 absolute ['æbsəˌlut]

adj. 完全的,絕對的

I have absolute confidence in the team.

我對團隊完全有信心。

4166 ashamed [ə'ʃemd]

adj. 慚愧的,害臊的

He felt ashamed of going to school late.

他因上學遲到感到羞愧。

4167 circulate ['sɝkjəˌlet]

v. (使)流通,(使)運行,(使)迴圈,(使)傳播

The government circulated currency.

政府使貨幣流通。

4168 coincidence [ko'ɪnsɪdəns] n. 一致,相合,

同時發生或同時存在(尤指偶然)的事,巧合

It was a coincidence that I arrived at the same time as you did. 跟你同時抵達真是很巧。

4169 cigar [sɪ'gɑr]

n. 雪茄

I bought a pack of cigars.

我買一包雪茄。

4170

accomplish [əˈkɑmplɪʃ] [-ˈkɒm-]

vt. 完成,達到,實現

Mission accomplished.
任務結束。

4171

brutal [ˈbrutḷ]

adj. 殘忍的,獸性的

He is a brutal man.
他是粗暴的人。

4172

admiration [ˌædməˈreʃən]

n. 欽佩,讚美,羨慕

Daniel looked at her in admiration.
丹尼爾以欽佩的眼神看著她。

4173

otherwise [ˈʌðəˌwaɪz]

adv. 否則,不然,在其他方面,以其他方式

You'll have to go now; otherwise you'll be late.
你現在必須走了,否則你會遲到。

4174

vast [væst]

adj. 巨大的,廣闊的,廣的,大量的

He has to borrow vast amounts of money.
他必須借大量的錢。

4175

architect [ˈɑrkəˌtɛkt]

n. 建築師

Jones was the architect of the team.
瓊斯是這個團隊的建築師。

4176

blossom [ˈblɑsəm] n. 花(尤指結果實者),

花開的狀態,興旺期　vi. 開花,興旺,發展

The cherry tree is in blossom.
櫻桃樹正在開花。

4177

charity [ˈtʃærətɪ]

n. 慈善,施捨,慈善團體

All the money goes to charity.
全部的錢都會進去慈善機構。

4178

behavior [bɪˈhevjə]

n. 舉止,行為

It is important to reward good behavior.
獎勵好的行為很重要。

4179

satisfaction [ˌsætɪsˈfækʃən]

n. 滿足,滿意

She got great satisfaction from helping people.
她從幫助人們中獲得滿足感。

4180

comedy [ˈkɑmədɪ]

n. 喜劇,喜劇性的事情

A Midsummer Night's Dream is a famous comedy by Shakespeare. 仲夏夜之夢是莎士比亞著名的喜劇。

4181

clarify [ˈklærəˌfaɪ]

v. 使更清晰易懂,闡明,澄清,闡明,純淨,淨化

Could you clarify this question for me?
你可以為我釐清這問題嗎?

4182

fetch [fɛtʃ]

vt. (去)拿來,去取

Shannon fetched some blankets.

夏南拿了一些毯子。

4183

assemble [ə'sɛmbl̩]

vt. 集合,召集,裝配

The crowd assembled in the hall.

人群聚集在大廳。

4184

ascend [ə'sɛnd]

v. 攀登,上升

He began to ascend the mountain.

他開始攀登那座山。

4185

academy [ə'kædəmɪ]

n. (高等)專科院校,研究院,學會,學術團體,學院

He studies in a military academy.

他在軍校學習。

4186

campaign [kæm'pen]

n. [軍]戰役,(政治或商業性)活動,競選運動

vi. 參加活動,從事活動,作戰

He has an advertising campaign today.

他今天有廣告活動。

4187

applicant ['æpləkənt]

n. 申請者,請求者

He was one of the applicants for the position.

他是眾多求職者中的一個。

4188

civilization [ˌsɪvl̩ə'zeʃn̩] [-laɪ'z-]

n. 文明,文化,文明社會,一個著名遊戲的名稱

The book is about the ancient civilizations of Greece and Rome. 這本書是關於希臘跟羅馬的古文明。

4189

equipment [ɪ'kwɪpmənt]

n. 裝備,設備

I am looking for a shop which sells camping equipment.

我正在找販售露營裝備用品的店。

4190

bureau ['bjʊro]

n. 辦公桌,衣櫃,(美)局,辦公署

He is seeking for a job in an employment bureau.

他在就業服務處找工作。

4191

labor ['lebɚ]

n. 勞動,[總稱]勞工

He is a labor.

他是勞工。

4192

aggressive [ə'grɛsɪv]

adj. 好鬥的,敢作敢為的,有闖勁的,侵略性的

Jim's voice became aggressive.

吉姆的聲音變得很有侵略性。

4193

accent ['æksɛnt] [æk'sɛnt]

n. 重音,口音,重音符

He speaks with an American accent.

他說話帶有美國口音。

4194

packet ['pækɪt]

n. 小捆,小包,小盒

I bought a packet of envelopes.

我買一袋信封。

4195

abuse [ə'bjus] [ə'bɪus]

n. 濫用,虐待,辱罵,陋習,弊端 v. 濫用,虐待,辱罵

He is involved in several cases of child abuse.

他涉嫌多起虐童案。

4196

acceptance [ək'sɛptəns]

n. 接受,承諾,容忍,贊同,相信

He wrote a letter of acceptance to the university.

他寫了一封入學接受函。

4197

monitor ['mɑnətɚ]

n. 班長,監聽器,監視器,監控器 v. 監控

Each student's progress is monitored.

每個學生的進度都被檢視。

4198

scold [skold]

v. 責罵,訓斥

He scolded them for arriving late.

他訓斥他們遲到。

4199

alongside [ə'lɔŋ'saɪd]

adv. 在旁 prep. 與…並攏靠著

Charles spent a week working alongside the workers.

查爾斯花了一個星期跟工人一起工作。

4200

mineral ['mɪnərəl] ['mɪnrəl]

n. 礦物,礦石 adj. 礦物(質)的

The area is very rich in minerals.

這地方富含礦物。

4201

anniversary [ˌænə'vɝsərɪ] n. 周年紀念

Jack and Kim celebrated their twentieth wedding anniversary.

傑克跟金慶祝他們二十周年結婚紀念日。

4202

access ['æksɛs]

n. 通路,訪問 vt. 存取,接近

The courtyard has a side access to the rear gardens.

庭院中有一側通道可進入後花園。

4203

pioneer [ˌpaɪə'nɪr]

n. 先驅者,創始人,先鋒 vt. 開拓,開創

He was a pioneer in the field.

他在這個領域是先驅者。

4204

casualty ['kæʒʊəltɪ] n. 傷亡,戰爭或事故

的傷員,亡者,遇難者,受害者,毀壞物,損壞物

Our responsibility is to reduce road casualties.

我們的責任是減少交通意外傷亡。

4205

defense [dɪˈfɛns]

n. (美國)國防部,防衛,防衛物 vt. 謀劃抵禦

They have a firm commitment to the defense of human rights. 他們對保衛人權做出承諾。

4206

league [lig]

n. 同盟,聯盟,協會,聯合會

This is the National Socialist League.
這是國家社會聯盟。

4207

academic [ˌækəˈdɛmɪk]

adj. 學院的,理論的

He possessed academic qualifications.
他擁有學術資格。

4208

damp [dæmp]

adj. 潮濕的 n. 潮濕,濕氣

It is a cold and damp day.
今天又冷又濕。

4209

madam [ˈmædəm]

n. [對婦女的尊稱]女士,夫人

Can I help you, madam?
女士,我可以幫你嗎?

4210

absorb [əbˈsɔrb] [æb-]

vt. 吸收,使併入,吞併,同化理解,掌握耗費,耗去

Plants absorb water from the soil.
植物從土壤吸收水分。

4211

splendid [ˈsplɛndɪd]

adj. 壯麗的,豪華的,極好的

We've all had a splendid time.
我們有一段美好時光。

4212

delight [dɪˈlaɪt]

n. 快樂,高興 vt. 使高興

The kids were screaming with delight.
小孩快樂地尖叫。

4213

communication [kəˌmjunəˈkeʃən] [-ˈmɪun-]

n. 傳達,資訊,交通,通訊

Cellphone is one kind of communication tool.
手機是一種溝通工具。

4214

butcher [ˈbutʃɚ]

n. 屠夫,肉商,肉店老闆

A butcher sells meat.
肉商賣肉。

4215

authority [ɔˈθɔrətɪ]

n. 權威,威信,權威人士,權力,職權,典據,著作權威

Could I speak to someone in authority, please?
請問我能跟某位權威人士說話嗎?

4216

cement [səˈmɛnt]

n. 水泥,接合劑 vt. 接合,用水泥塗,鞏固

I need a bag of cement for my wall.
我需要一袋水泥用來鋪牆壁。

4217
canvas [ˈkænvəs]
v. 徹底討論探究 n. 帆布

I bought a canvas bag.
我買了帆布包。

4218
apology [əˈpɑlədʒɪ]
n. (為某種思想,宗教,哲學等)辯解,道歉

You owe him an apology for what you said.
你應該為你說過的話向他道歉。

4219
agreeable [əˈgriəbəl]
adj. 使人愉快的,愜意的,適合的

We spent the most agreeable couple of hours.
我們渡過了幾小時的愜意時光。

4220
ceremony [ˈsɛrəˌmonɪ]
n. 典禮,儀式,禮節,報幕員

The wedding ceremony will be held tomorrow.
婚禮儀式將在明天舉行。

4221
upward [ˈʌpwəd]
adj. 向上的 adv. [-(s)]向上,往上

They have an upward trend in sales.
他們在銷售上有向上提升的趨勢。

4222
cease [sis]
v. 停止,終止,結束,終了

He ceased being a member of the company.
他終止成為公司的會員。

4223
lecture [ˈlɛktʃə] n. 通常指大學裡的講座,
講課,演講,教訓,訓斥,譴責

He delivers a lecture on medieval art.
他有一場中世紀藝術的演講。

4224
commerce [ˈkɑməs] [-mɝs]
n. 指國際間的貿易,商業,商務

He is a leader of industry and commerce.
他是工商業的領袖。

4225
climax [ˈklaɪmæks]
n. 高潮,頂點

The climax of his political career will finish soon.
他政治職務的高峰即將結束。

4226
refer [rɪˈfɝ]
vi. 提到,涉及,參考(to) vt. 提交,查閱,參考

Her mother never referred to him again.
她的媽媽從不再提到他。

4227
civilize [ˈsɪvḷˌaɪz]
vt. 使開化,使文明,教化

The Romans tried to civilize the Britons.
羅馬人試圖教化英國人。

4228
annual [ˈænjʊəl] n. 一年生植物,年刊,年鑑
adj. 一年一次的,每年的,一年生的

The school trip is an annual activity.
學校旅遊是一個年度活動。

4229

competitor [kəm'pɛtətɚ]

n.競爭者,參賽者,對手

We produce cheaper goods than our competitors.

我們生產比競爭者便宜的產品。

4230

arouse [ə'raʊz]

vt. 激起,引起,喚起,喚醒

Matt's behavior arouses the interest of the public.

麥特的行為引起大家的興趣。

4231

assembly [ə'sɛmblɪ]

n. 集合,裝配,集會,集結,彙編

They were fighting for freedom of assembly.

他們為集會自由而戰。

4232

telegram ['tɛləˌgræm]

n. 電報

My daughter telegrammed me yesterday.

我的女兒昨天發電報給我。

4233

pronunciation

[prəˌnʌnsɪ'eʃən] [pɚˌnʌnsɪ'eʃən]

n. 發音,發音方法

Do you know the correct pronunciation of these names?

你知道這些名字的正確發音嗎？

4234

cashier [kæ'ʃɪr]

n. (商店等的)出納員,(銀行或公司的)司庫

He is a cashier in the supermarket.

他是超市的收銀員。

4235

acid ['æsɪd]

n. [化]酸,(俚)迷幻藥 adj. 酸的,諷刺的,刻薄的

Sulphuric acid will damage your skin.

硫酸會腐蝕你的皮膚。

4236

breed [brid]

vt. 繁殖,飼養

My sister breeds two cats.

我妹妹飼養兩隻貓。

4237

classify ['klæsəˌfaɪ]

vt. 劃分,區分,界定,把…分類

The books in the library are classified according to subjects. 圖書館的書根據主題被分類。

4238

analysis [ə'næləsɪs]

n. 分析,分解

Did you watch the detailed analysis of this week's news?

你有看到這個星期新聞的詳細分析嗎？

4239

companion [kəm'pænjən]

n. 同伴,伴侶

His dog became his closest companion.

他的狗變成是他最親密的朋友。

4240

proportion [prə'porʃən] [prə'porʃən]

n. 比例,均衡,面積,部分　vt. 使成比例,使均衡,分攤

The proportion of graduates has increased in recent years. 近幾年來畢業生的比例已經增加了。

4241

confess [kən'fɛs]

v. 承認,坦白

My brother confessed his mistake.
我的弟弟承認他的過錯。

4242

bond [bɑnd]

n. 結合(物),黏結(劑),聯結,公債,債券,合同　v. 結合

There is a bond between the two companies.
這兩家公司有關聯。

4243

assistance [ə'sɪstəns]

n. 協助,援助,補助,(英)國家補助

We offer financial assistance to people.
我們提供人們經濟上的補助。

4244

grieve [griv]

v. (使)悲痛,(使)傷心,憂傷

She grieved the loss of her only son.
她因為失去獨子而悲痛。

4245

disturbance [dɪ'stɜbəns]

n. 騷動,動亂,打擾,干擾,騷亂,攪動

It can cause a disturbance to local residents when a helicopter lands. 直升機降落時導致當地居民的騷動。

4246

accommodate [ə'kɑmə,det]

vt. 供應,供給,使適應,調節,和解,向…提供,容納,調和
vi. 適應

He bought a huge house to accommodate his collection of sculptures.

他買了一棟可以容納他收藏的雕像的房子。

4247

donate ['donet]

v. 捐贈,贈予

He donated many computers to the poor.
他捐了很多電腦給窮人。

4248

combination [,kɑmbə'neʃən]

n. 結合,聯合,合併,化合,化合物

Water is a combination of two elements.
水是由兩個元素結合而成的化合物。

4249

assurance [ə'ʃurəns]

n. 確信,斷言,保證,擔保

Despite my repeated assurances, Rob still looked very unhappy. 儘管我一再保證,Rob 仍然看起來不愉悅。

4250

appropriate [ə'proprɪ,et]

adj. 適當的,恰當的,合適的,相稱的

Can you wear appropriate clothes for a job interview?
你可以穿適當參加面試的衣服嗎?

4251

awkward [ˈɔkwəd]

adj. 粗笨的,棘手的,使用不便的,難堪的,尷尬的

I hoped he would stop asking awkward questions.
希望他停止詢問尷尬的問題。

4252

murderer [ˈmɝdərə]

n. 謀殺犯

We haven't found the murderer of the case.
我們尚未找到這起案件的殺人犯。

4253

install [ɪnˈstɔl]

vt. 安裝,安置,使就職

They've installed the new computer network.
他們已經安裝好新的電腦網路。

4254

handicap [ˈhændɪˌkæp]

n. 障礙,阻礙,障礙賽跑 v. 妨礙,使不利,阻礙

Jane worked hard to overcome her handicap.
珍認真工作來克服先天的身障。

4255

recipe [ˈrɛsəpɪ] [-ˌpi]

n. 處方,食譜

This is a recipe.
這是一本食譜。

4256

atmosphere [ˈætməsˌfɪr]

n. 大氣,空氣,氣氛

The pollution of the atmosphere is getting worse and worse.
大氣層的汙染越來越糟了。

4257

nutrition [njuˈtrɪʃən]

n. 營養,營養學

Nutrition and exercise are essential to fitness and health. 營養跟運動對體適能和健康是必要的。

4258

sparkle [ˈspɑrkl̩]

v. 發火花,(使)閃耀,(香檳酒等)發泡,用眼神表達,發光閃爍 n. 火花,閃光,光彩,活力,發泡

The sea sparkled under the sun. 海在太陽下閃閃發光。

4259

bridegroom [ˈbraɪdˌgrum] [-ˌgrʊm]

n. 新郎

I enjoyed the bridegroom's speech.
我喜愛新郎的演說。

4260

appoint [əˈpɔɪnt]

vt. 約定,指定(時間,地點),任命,委任

They have appointed a new head teacher.
他們已經任命了新的導師。

4261

occasional [əˈkeʒənl̩]

adj. 偶然的,非經常的,特殊場合的,臨時的

He made occasional visits to Taipei.
他臨時參訪臺北。

4262

enroll [ɪnˈrol]

v. 登記,招收,使入伍(或入會,入學等),參加,成為成員

They are rushing to enroll in aerobics classes.
他們趕著參加有氧課。

4263

compound ['kɑmpaʊnd]

n. 混合物,[化]化合物 adj. 複合的

"Eco-friendly" is a compound word.

"eco-friendly" 是個複合字。

4264

modesty ['mɑdəstɪ]

n. 謙遜,虛心

I hate pretended modesty.

我討厭虛偽的謙虛。

4265

lunar ['lunɚ]

adj. 月的,月亮的

You can see a lunar eclipse tomorrow.

你明天可以見到月蝕。

4266

nasty ['næstɪ] adj. 汙穢的,骯髒的,令人厭惡的,

淫穢的,下流的,凶相的,威脅的

A hot summer is nasty.

酷暑令人難受。

4267

instruct [ɪn'strʌkt]

vt. 教育,指導,命令

His secretary was instructed to cancel all his engagements. 他的祕書被告知要取消他的約會。

4268

electronics [ɪ'lɛktrɑnɪks] [ə-]

n. 電子學

He is a professor in electronics.

他是位電子學的教授。

4269

chemistry ['kɛmɪstrɪ]

n. 化學

He is taking a chemistry test.

他正在考化學考試。

4270

fierce [fɪrs]

adj. 兇猛的,猛烈的,熱烈的,暴躁的,(美)極討厭的,
難受的,(英)精力旺盛的

Tigers are fierce animals.

老虎是兇猛的動物。

4271

inquiry ['ɪnkwərɪ]

n. 質詢,調查

We received inquiries from potential applicants.

我們收到許多應徵者的詢問。

4272

comprehension [ˌkɑmprɪ'hɛnʃən]

n. 理解,包含

The research project will focus on children's reading comprehension.

這研究計畫將著重於兒童的閱讀理解力。

4273

affection [ə'fɛkʃən]

n. 友愛,愛情,影響,疾病,傾向

John had a deep affection for me.

約翰與我有深厚的感情。

4274

community [kə'mjunətɪ] [-'mɪun-]

n. 公社,團體,社會,(政治)共同體,共有,一致,共同體,
　(生物)群落

The local community was shocked by the news.

當地社區被這則新聞驚嚇到。

4275

dynasty ['daɪnəstɪ]

n. 朝代,王朝

He bought a Ming dynasty vase.

他買了明朝的花瓶。

4276

conventional [kən'vɛnʃənl] [-ʃnəl]

adj. 慣例的,常規的,習俗的,傳統的

He is a strong believer in conventional morals.

他是道德觀強烈的人。

4277

hostage ['hɑstɪdʒ]

n. 人質,抵押品

The terrorists took three people with them as hostages.

恐怖分子挾持三個人作為他們的人質。

4278

cucumber ['kjukʌmbɚ]

n. [植]黃瓜

I ate a cucumber for breakfast.

我早餐吃小黃瓜。

4279

carbon ['kɑrbən]

n. [化]碳(元素符號 C),(一張)複寫紙

Carbon is found in all living things.

碳存在於所有生物中。

4280

acquire [ə'kwaɪr]

vt. 獲得,學到

We acquire knowledge by learning.

我們從學習中獲得知識。

4281

cottage ['kɑtɪdʒ]

n. 小屋,村舍

I live in a country cottage.

我住在鄉村小屋中。

4282

acquaint [ə'kwent]

vt. 使熟知,通知

I need to acquaint myself with the new rules.

我需要熟知新的規則。

4283

beneficial [ˌbɛnə'fɪʃəl]

adj. 有益的,受益的,[法律]有使用權的

The drug has a beneficial effect on the immune system.

該藥物對免疫系統有功效 。

4284
kidnap [ˈkɪdnæp]
vt. 誘拐(小孩),綁架,勒贖
Two businessmen were kidnapped by terrorists.
兩個商人被恐怖分子綁架了。

4285
accuse [əˈkjuz]
vt. 指責,指控
I accused her of lying.
我控告她說謊。

4286
concept [ˈkɑnsɛpt]
n. 觀念,概念
Can you explain the concept of infinite space?
你可以解釋宇宙無涯的觀念嗎？

4287
assign [əˈsaɪn]
vt. 分配,指派
The teacher assigned different tasks to the children.
老師指派不同的任務給小孩。

4288
foam [fom]
n. 泡沫,水沫,泡沫材料,泡沫橡皮,泡沫塑料
vt. 使起泡沫
She scraped the foam off her soap.
她將肥皂表面上的泡沫刮掉。

4289
enthusiastic [ɪnˌθjuzɪˈæstɪk] [-ˌθɪuz]
adj. 熱心的,熱情的
All the staff are enthusiastic about the project.
全體員工對此計畫很有熱誠。

4290
devotion [dɪˈvoʃən]
n. 熱愛,投入
His devotion to his church is touching.
他對教會的貢獻很感人。

4291
interpreter [ɪnˈtɜprɪtɚ]
n. 解釋程式,解釋者,口譯人員,翻譯員
Not everyone who knows English can be an interpreter.
不是會英文的人就能當口譯員。

4292
gracious [ˈgreʃəs]
adj. 親切的,和藹可親的,高尚的,優雅的
She is a gracious lady.
她是一位和藹可親的女士。

4293
criticism [ˈkrɪtəˌsɪzəm]
n. 批評,批判
The plan has attracted criticism from many people.
這個計畫遭受到多人的批評。

4294
doze [doz]
vi. 瞌睡,假寐 n. 瞌睡
I dozed off during class today.
我今天在上課中打了瞌睡。

4295

poisonous [ˈpɔɪznəs]

adj. 有毒的

This apple is highly poisonous.

這顆蘋果很毒。

4296

dreadful [ˈdrɛdfəl]

adj. 可怕的,(口)討厭的

What a dreadful thing!

這真糟糕。

4297

instructor [ɪnˈstrʌktɚ]

n. 教師,(美)講師,教練

He is an instructor of English at a university.

他是大學的英文講師。

4298

recite [rɪˈsaɪt]

v. 背誦,朗讀,敘述,[律]書面陳述(事實)

She recited a poem at school.

她在學校朗讀詩。

4299

furious [ˈfjʊrɪəs]

adj. 狂怒的,狂暴的,勃然大怒的,激烈的,熱烈興奮的,
　　極為激烈

Residents are furious at the decision.

居民對於這個決定感到極為生氣。

4300

pedal [ˈpɛdl̩]

n. 踏板 v. 踩…的踏板

I couldn't reach the pedals on my bike.

我無法踏到腳踏車的踏板。

4301

remarkable [rɪˈmɑrkəbl̩]

adj. 不平常的,非凡的,值得注意的,顯著的

She has made remarkable progress.

她有顯著的進步。

4302

architecture [ˈɑrkə,tɛktʃɚ]

n. 建築,建築學體系機構

He majors in architecture.

他主修建築。

4303

accuracy [ˈækjərəsɪ]

n. 精確性,正確度

Don't worry about the accuracy of government
statistics. 不需擔心政府統計數字的準確度。

4304

interact [ˌɪntɚˈækt]

vi. 互相作用,互相影響

Teachers have an amount of time to interact with each
child. 老師有很多時間跟每位學生互動。

4305

commit [kəˈmɪt]

vt. 犯(罪),做(壞事)

He committed a crime in the supermarket.

他在超市中犯罪。

4306

cripple [ˈkrɪpl̩]

adj. 使陷入癱瘓,跛腿的,殘廢的 n. 跛子

The pilot tried to land his crippled plane.

飛行員試圖降落他殘缺的飛機。

4307

astronaut [ˈæstrəˌnɔt]

n. 太空人

He is an astronaut.

他是太空人。

4308

legend [ˈlɛdʒənd]

n. 傳說,偉人傳,圖例

Can you tell me ancient Greek legends?

可以告訴我古希臘傳說嗎?

4309

idiom [ˈɪdɪəm]

n. 成語,方言,土語,習慣用語,諺語

"No pain, no gain" is an idiom.

「沒有付出就沒有收穫」是一句諺語。

4310

dread [drɛd]

n. 恐懼,恐怖,可怕的人(或物),畏懼 v. 懼怕,擔心

I dread snakes.

我非常懼怕蛇。

4311

ancestor [ˈænsɛstɚ]

n. 祖先,祖宗

My ancestors were English.

我的祖先是英國人。

4312

conference [ˈkɑnfərəns]

n. 會議,討論會,協商會

We have a conference in Hawaii.

我們在夏威夷有會議。

4313

sob [sɑb]

v. 嗚咽,啜泣

The little boy sobbed in his room.

這個小男孩在他的房間裡啜泣。

4314

compute [kəmˈpjut]

v. 計算,估計,用電腦計算(或確定)

Final results had been computed.

決賽成績已經被計算了。

4315

agent [ˈedʒənt]

n. 代理(商)

The agent deals with the Brazilian.

那個代理商與巴西人作生意。

4316

concerning [kənˈsɝnɪŋ]

prep. 有關,涉及

There is a lot of news concerning this event.

有很多關於此事的新聞。

4317

rehearsal [rɪˈhɝsl̩]

n. 排演,演習,預演,試演

We had a rehearsal for 'Romeo and Juliet' in the afternoon. 我們下午排演羅密歐與茱麗葉。

4318

content [kən'tɛnt] ['kɑn,tɛnt]

n. (複)內容,目錄 adj. 滿意的,滿足的

Most of the museum's contents were damaged in the fire. 大部分博物館內的典藏付之一炬。

4319

gigantic [dʒaɪ'gæntɪk]

adj. 巨人般的,巨大的

There are gigantic skyscrapers in the city.
城市裡有巨大的摩天大廈。

4320

concentrate ['kɑnsn̩,tret] [-sɛn-]

vt. 集中,聚集,濃縮 vi. 集中,專心

I want to concentrate on my studies.
我要專心在課業上。

4321

spectator ['spɛktetɚ] [spɛk'tetɚ]

n. 觀賞者

The match attracted lots of spectators.
這場比賽吸引了很多觀賽者。

4322

smog [smɑg]

n. 煙霧

Cars can produce toxic smog.
車子會產生出有毒煙霧。

4323

conceal [kən'sil]

vt. 隱藏,隱瞞

Tim could barely conceal his disappointment.
提姆隱藏不住他的失望。

4324

inject [ɪn'dʒɛkt]

vt. 注射,注入

The nurse injected the drug for the patient.
護士幫病人打針。

4325

misfortune [mɪs'fɔtʃən]

n. 不幸,災禍

Typhoons cause widespread misfortune.
颱風釀成災禍。

4326

hijack ['haɪ,dʒæk]

vt. 搶劫,劫持,劫機,揩油

The airplane was hijacked by terrorists.
這班飛機被恐怖分子劫機。

4327

construction [kən'strʌkʃən]

n. 建造,施工,構築,建築物

The construction of the new airport is very good.
新機場施工良好。

4328

applause [ə'plɔz]

n. 鼓掌歡迎,歡呼

Give her a big round of applause!
給她鼓掌歡迎。

4329

mountainous ['maʊntn̩əs] [-tənəs]

adj. 多山的,山一般的,巨大的

This is the mountainous coast of Wales.
這是威爾斯的靠山的海岸。

4330

amid [ə'mɪd]

prep. 在…中

He sat amid the flowers.

他坐在花叢間。

4331

entertainment [ˌɛntɚ'tenmənt]

n. 款待,娛樂,娛樂表演

The center provides a wide choice of entertainment.

中心內提供多項娛樂選擇。

4332

foresee [fɔr'si] [for-]

vt. 預見,預知

I can't foresee any problems in the future.

我無法預知未來發生的問題。

4333

await [ə'wet]

vt. 等候

We await for the result.

我們在等結果。

4334

bribe [braɪb]

n. 賄賂 vt. 賄賂,向…行賄

Jaime wouldn't do her homework until I bribed her with some candies. 傑米不做功課直到我用糖果引誘她。

4335

conquer ['kɑŋkɚ] ['kɔŋkɚ]

vt. 征服,戰勝,佔領,克服(困難等),破(壞習慣等)

He finally conquered Jade Mountain.

他終於征服了玉山。

4336

resistant [rɪ'zɪstənt]

adj. 抵抗的,有抵抗力的

She appeared resistant.

她看起來想抵抗。

4337

applaud [ə'plɔd]

v. 拍手喝彩,稱讚,贊同

The audience applauded loudly.

觀眾大聲地拍手喝采。

4338

confine ['kɑnfaɪn]

vt. 限制,侷限,管制

Owen did not confine himself to writing only one type of article. 歐文不侷限自己只寫一種文章。

4339

participant [pɚ'tɪsəpənt] [par-]

n. 參與者,共用者 adj. 參與的

He is a participant of the meeting.

他是會議的參與者。

4340

resistance [rɪ'zɪstəns]

n. 抵抗,反抗,抵制,抵抗力,阻力

I catch colds frequently because my resistance is low.

因為我的抵抗力較弱,所以我常感冒。

4341

concrete [kɑn'krit]

adj. 具體的,有形的 v. 用混凝土修築,澆混凝土,凝結

The lack of any concrete evidence is a problem.

缺乏任何具體的證據是一個問題。

4342 constitute [ˈkɑnstəˌtjut]

vt. 制定(法律),建立(政府),組成,任命

The rise in crime constitutes a threat to society.
犯罪增加對社會造成威脅。

4343 latitude [ˈlætəˌtjud]

n. 緯度,範圍,(用複數)地區,行動或言論的自由(範圍)

The map shows the oceans of the lower latitude.
這張圖顯示低緯度的海洋。

4344 imitation [ˌɪməˈteʃən]

n. 模仿,效法,冒充,仿造物

Some researchers think that children learn a language by imitation.
部分研究者認為小孩可以藉由模仿學習語言。

4345 electrician [ˌilɛkˈtrɪʃən]

n. 電工,電學家

An electrician is a person whose job is to connect and repair electrical equipment.
電工就是連接和修理電機設備的人。

4346 habitual [həˈbɪtʃʊəl] [-ʃʊl]

adj. 習慣的,慣常的

His smoking had become habitual.
抽菸已經成為他的習慣。

4347 composition [ˌkɑmpəˈzɪʃən]

n. 構成,成分,作文,作品,樂曲,寫作,作曲

Some drinks have complex chemical compositions.
有些飲料有複雜的化學成分。

4348 revenge [rɪˈvɛndʒ]

n. 報仇,復仇 vt. 替…報仇,復仇

She took revenge on the child.
她向那個小孩報復。

4349 compose [kəmˈpoz]

vt. 組成,構成,創作

Water is composed of hydrogen and oxygen.
水由氫跟氧組成。

4350 confidence [ˈkɑnfədəns]

n. 自信

She had complete confidence in the school.
她對學校有信心。

4351 masterpiece [ˈmæstəˌpis]

n. 傑作,名著

"Hamlet" is a masterpiece by Shakespeare.
"哈姆雷特"是莎士比亞的傑作。

4352

consequence [ˈkɑnsəˌkwɛns]

n. 結果,[邏]推理,推論,因果關係,重要的地位

Poverty is a direct consequence of overpopulation.

貧窮是人口過度的結果。

4353

profitable [ˈprɑfɪtəbl̩] [ˈprɑftə-]

adj. 有利可圖的

The new building is profitable.

這棟新大樓有利可圖。

4354

commission [kəˈmɪʃən]

n. 委任,委託,代辦(權),代理(權),犯(罪),傭金

vt. 委任,任命,委託,委託製作,使服役

The government set up a commission to investigate the case.

這個政府任命委員會調查這個案子。

4355

hesitation [ˌhɛzəˈteʃən]

n. 猶豫,躊躇

He agreed without hesitation.

他毫不遲疑地同意了。

4356

slogan [ˈslogən]

n. 口號,標語

The advertising slogan is good.

這個廣告的標語很好。

4357

graceful [ˈgresfəl]

adj. 優美的

Her behaviors were graceful.

她的舉止優雅。

4358

spear [spɪr]

n. 矛,鎗

There is a spear.

那裡有一支矛。

4359

cliff [klɪf]

n. 懸崖,絕壁

We went along the cliff.

我們沿著陡壁走。

4360

destructive [dɪˈstrʌktɪv]

adj. 破壞(性)的

What is the destructive power of modern weapons?

什麼是現代武器的毀滅力量？

4361

prosper [ˈprɑspɚ]

v. 成功,興隆,昌盛,(指上帝)使成功,使昌隆,繁榮

Businesses are prospering the world.

商業讓世界繁榮。

4362

murmur [ˈmɝmɚ]

n. 低沉連續的聲音,咕噥,怨言,低語

v. 發低沉連續的聲音,發怨言,低聲說,低語說,低語

"Well done," murmured George.

「做得好」，喬治小聲的說。

4363

inspiration [ˌɪnspəˈreʃən]

n. 靈感

He draws inspiration from ordinary scenes.

他從日常的場景中獲得靈感。

4364

restriction [rɪˈstrɪkʃən]

n. 限制,約束

Japan set up restrictions on immigration.

日本設立移民的限制。

4365

manufacturer [ˌmænjəˈfæktʃərɚ]

n. 製造業者,廠商

He is a car manufacturer.

他是車子製造業者。

4366

parliament [ˈpɑrləmənt]

n. 國會,議會

The party failed to win a seat in Parliament.

這個政黨未能在國會贏得席次。

4367

messenger [ˈmɛsn̩dʒɚ]

n. 報信者,使者

Hermes is Zeus' messenger.

愛瑪仕是宙斯的信差。

4368

privacy [ˈpraɪvəsɪ]

n. 獨處而不受干擾,祕密

The book is about individual's privacy right.

這本書關於個人的隱私權。

4369

astonish [əˈstɑnɪʃ]

vt. 使驚訝

Her answer astonished me.

她的回答嚇到我了。

4370

feast [fist]

n. 節日,盛宴,筵席,宴會,酒席 vi. 參加宴會,享受

The couple went to a wedding feast yesterday.

這對夫妻昨天參加婚宴。

4371

certificate [səˈtɪfəˌket]

n. 證書,證明書 vt. 發給證明書,以證書形式授權給…

I got a degree certificate last year.

我去年得到學位文憑。

4372

shameful [ˈʃemfʊl]

adj. 不道德的,可恥的

Littering is a shameful behavior.

亂丟垃圾是一件丟臉的事。

4373

humanity [hjuˈmænətɪ]

n. 人性,人類,博愛,仁慈

He treats the dogs with humanity.

他仁慈的對待那些狗。

4374

parachute [ˈpærəˌʃut]

n. 降落傘

Planes dropped supplies by parachutes.

飛機用降落傘空投補給品。

4375

classification [ˌklæsəfəˈkeʃən]

n. 分類,分級

There are five job classifications in the newspaper.

報紙上有五種職別分類。

4376

landlady [ˈlændˌledɪ]

n. 女房東,女地主,(旅館等的)老闆娘

I paid rent to a landlady.

我付房租給房東。

4377

exceptional [ɪkˈsɛpʃənḷ]

adj. 例外的,異常的

He is an exceptional student.

他是優秀的學生。

4378

dignity [ˈdɪgnətɪ]

n. 尊嚴,高貴

He lost his dignity by the scandal.

他因為一個醜聞喪失了尊嚴。

4379

acre [ˈekɚ]

n. 英畝,地產,大片田地

They own 200 acres of farmland.

他們擁有 200 畝農田。

4380

fireplace [ˈfaɪrˌples]

n. 壁爐

I need a fireplace in my home.

我家需要壁爐。

4381

confront [kənˈfrʌnt]

vt. 使面臨,對抗

Customers are confronted with an amount of choice.

顧客面對很多選擇。

4382

endanger [ɪnˈdendʒɚ]

vt. 危及

Smoking during pregnancy endangers baby's health.

懷孕期間抽菸會危害胎兒的健康。

4383

amuse [əˈmjuz]

vt. 使發笑,使愉快

This story will amuse you.

這個故事使人發笑。

4384

congratulate [kənˈgrætʃəˌlet]

v. 祝賀

He congratulates me.

他恭喜我。

4385

fascinate [ˈfæsn̩ˌet]

vt. 使著迷,使神魂顛倒 vi. 入迷,極度迷人的

The idea of travelling fascinates me.

旅遊的念頭使我著迷。

4386

minister [ˈmɪnɪstə]

n. 部長,大臣

He is the minister of Agriculture.
他是農業部長。

4387

overthrow [ˌovəˈθro]

n. 推翻,打倒,扔得過遠得球 vt. 打倒,推翻,顛覆

They were already making plans to overthrow the government. 他們有計畫推翻政府。

4388

competition [ˌkɑmpəˈtɪʃən]

n. 競爭,競賽

He joined the violin competition.
他參加那個小提琴比賽。

4389

characteristic [ˌkærɪktəˈrɪstɪk] [ˌkærək-]

adj. 特有的,表示特性的,典型的 n. 特性,特徵

A child discovers the physical characteristics of objects. 小孩發現物體的物理特性。

4390

institute [ˈɪnstəˌtjut]

n. 學會,學院,協會

vt. 創立,開始,制定,開始(調查),提起(訴訟)

He studies in the Institute of Space Studies.
他在太空研究所學習。

4391

convey [kənˈve]

vt. 發送,傳送

The message he conveyed was friendly.
他傳送的訊息是善意的。

4392

associate [əˈsoʃɪt] [-ˌet]

v. 聯想

Red is associated with love.
紅色讓人聯想到愛。

4393

communist [ˈkɑmjʊˌnɪst]

adj. 共產主義的,共產黨的 n. 共產主義者

He studies communist ideology.
他學習共產主義思想。

4394

cargo [ˈkɑrɡo]

n. 船貨,(車,船,飛機等運輸的)貨物

A cargo plane landed in the airport.
貨機在機場降落。

4395

lighten [ˈlaɪtn̩]

v. 減輕,(使)輕鬆,(使)發亮,照

My mood gradually lightened.
我的心情逐漸開朗。

4396

endurance [ɪnˈdjʊrəns]

n. 忍耐(力),持久(力),耐久(性)

This event tests both physical and mental endurance.
這活動測試身體和心理承受能力。

4397 overflow [ˈovɚˌflo] n. 溢出,超值,泛濫,充滿,

洋溢 v. (使)泛濫,(使)溢出,(使)充溢

Plates overflowed with food.

盤子裡充滿了食物。

4398 conjunction [kənˈdʒʌŋkʃən]

n. 聯合,關聯,連接詞

Please use conjunction to connect two sentences.

請用連接詞連接這兩個句子。

4399 indication [ˌɪndəˈkeʃən]

n. 指出,指示,跡象,暗示

He gave no indication of his story.

他沒有提到他的故事。

4400 concentration [ˌkɑnsn̩ˈtreʃən] [-sɛn-]

n. 集中,集合,專心,濃縮,濃度

I lost my concentration and fell asleep in class.

我在課堂中失去注意力並且睡著了。

4401 destruction [dɪˈstrʌkʃən] n. 破壞,毀滅

The government has to face the problem of the destruction of the rainforest.

政府必須要面對雨林毀壞的問題。

4402 catalog [ˈkætl̩ˌɔg] [-ˌɑg]

n. 目錄,目錄冊 v. 編目錄

A catalog record for this book is available.

你可以取得這本書的目錄。

4403 perfume [ˈpɝfjum] [pɚˈfjum]

n. 香味,芳香,香水 vt. 使發香,灑香水於,發香味

She was wearing perfume.

她噴香水。

4404 boast [bost]

vi. 自誇,誇耀(of, about) n. 自吹自擂

Amy boasted that her son was smart.

艾美誇耀她的兒子很聰明。

4405 pirate [ˈpaɪrət]

n. 海盜,盜印者,盜版者,侵犯專利權者

vt. 盜印,盜版,掠奪,翻印

Pirates live on the sea.

海盜們過著海上生活。

4406 nourish [ˈnɝɪʃ]

vt. 滋養,使健壯,懷有(希望,仇恨等)

The cream nourishes the skin.

這個乳霜可滋養皮膚。

4407 chemist [ˈkɛmɪst]

n. 化學家,藥劑師

Take this prescription to the chemist.

拿處方給藥師。

4408
drought [draʊt]
n. 乾旱,缺乏
You can see one of the worst droughts on record.
你可以在紀錄上看到最糟的乾旱之一。

4409
conduct [kən'dʌkt]
vt. 處理,管理,指揮,傳(熱,點) n. 舉止,行為
We are conducting a survey of consumer attitude towards food. 我們正在進行消費者對食物的態度調查。

4410
edible ['ɛdəbl̩]
adj. 可食用的
These berries are not edible.
這些莓子不可以食用。

4411
distinction [dɪ'stɪŋkʃən]
n. 區別,差別,級別,特性,聲望,顯赫
Can you tell me the distinction between formal and informal languages?
可以告訴我正式與非正式用語的差別嗎?

4412
extinct [ɪk'stɪŋkt]
adj. 熄滅的,滅絕的,耗盡的 vt. (古)使熄滅
Pandas could become extinct in the wild.
野生熊貓變得很稀有。

4413
mistress ['mɪstrɪs]
n. 主婦,女主人,情婦
She is the mistress of the mansion.
她是這間豪宅的女主人。

4414
slavery ['slevərɪ]
n. 奴隸身分,奴隸制度,苦役,束縛
The president attempts to abolish slavery.
總統試圖廢除奴隸制。

4415
comparative [kəm'pærətɪv]
adj. 比較的,相當的
He conducts a comparative study of the US and British steel industries.
他進行美國跟英國鋼鐵工業的比較研究。

4416
rival ['raɪvl̩]
n. 競爭者,對手 v. 競爭,對抗,相匹敵
He beats his chief rival for the job.
他打敗了工作上主要的競爭者。

4417
patriotic [ˌpetrɪ'ɑtɪk]
adj. 愛國的,有愛國心的
They sang patriotic songs.
他們唱愛國歌曲。

4418

eyesight [ˈaɪˌsaɪt]

n. 視力,目力

Eagles have very keen eyesight.

老鷹有非常銳利的眼睛。

4419

deputy [ˈdɛpjətɪ]

n. 代理人,代表

He is the Deputy Secretary of State.

他是國務卿的職務代理人。

4420

warfare [ˈwɔrˌfɛr] [-ˌfær]

n. 戰爭,作戰,衝突,競爭

USA engaged in warfare.

美國加入了這場戰爭。

4421

equivalent [ɪˈkwɪvələnt]

adj. 相等的,相當的,同意義的 n. 等價物,相等物

Eight kilometres is roughly equivalent to five miles.

八公里約等於五哩。

4422

discard [dɪsˈkɑrd]

vt. 丟棄,拋棄 v. 放棄

Please discard old cleaning materials.

請丟掉舊的清潔用品。

4423

deceive [dɪˈsiv]

v. 欺騙,行騙

He tried to deceive the public.

他欺騙社會大眾。

4424

trademark [ˈtredˌmɑrk]

n. 商標

The striped T-shirt became the man's trademark.

斜紋襯衫成了這個人的商標。

4425

extensive [ɪkˈstɛnsɪv]

adj. 廣大的,廣闊的,廣泛的

Fire has caused extensive damage to the forests.

火災導致森林極大的損害。

4426

fluent [ˈfluənt]

adj. 流利的,流暢的

She was fluent in English.

她英文很流利。

4427

courteous [ˈkɜtɪəs]

adj. 有禮貌的,謙恭的

The staff are always courteous.

員工總是有禮貌的。

4428

craft [kræft]

n. 工藝,手藝

He is good at arts and crafts.

他精於手工藝。

4429

grammar [ˈgræmɚ]

n. 文法,有關原理的書,入門的書

Check your spelling and grammar in your article.

檢查你文章的拼字跟文法。

4430

digestion [də'dʒɛstʃən] [dɪ-]

n. 消化力,領悟

Too much suger is bad for your digestion.

太多的糖對你的消化不好。

4431

flee [fli]

vt. 逃避,逃跑,逃走 vi. 消散,逃,消失

He fled to Japan after an argument with his family.

他在與家人爭執後就跑去日本了。

4432

globe [glob]

n. 地球儀

We export our goods all over the globe.

我們出口我們的貨品到全世界。

4433

fundamental [ˌfʌndə'mɛntl]

adj. 基本的,根本的 n.(常用複數)基本原則,基本原理

We have to tackle the fundamental problem.

我們需要解決這個根本問題。

4434

dispute [dɪ'spjut] [-'sprut-]

v. 爭論,辯論,懷疑,抗拒,阻止,爭奪(土地,勝利等)

n. 爭論,辯論,爭吵

He got into a dispute over a bus fare.

他爭論公車車資。

4435

tenant ['tɛnənt]

n. 承租人,房客,租客 v. 出租

The desk was cleaned by the previous tenant.

這個桌子被之前的房客清理過了。

4436

syllable ['sɪləbl]

n. [語]音節 vt. 分成音節

He wrote a two-syllable word.

他寫了雙音節的字。

4437

divine [də'vaɪn]

adj. 神的,神聖的,非凡的,超人的,非常可愛的 n. 牧師

That fish tasted divine!

那條魚很可口。

4438

erect [ɪ'rɛkt]

vt. 建造,建立 adj. 直立的

Martin stood erect on the ground.

馬丁直立地站在地上。

4439

petal ['pɛtl]

n. 花瓣

There are five rose petals in the pool.

有五片花瓣在游泳池裡。

4440

elaborate [ɪ'læbərɪt] [ə-]

adj. 精心製作的,詳細闡述的,精細 v. 詳細描述

Bill refused to elaborate on his reasons for resigning.

比爾拒絕細說他辭職的理由。

4441

economic [ˌikəˈnɑmɪk] [ˌɛk-]

adj. 經濟(上)的,產供銷的,經濟學的

Economic growth is slow.
經濟成長很慢。

4442

persuasion [pɚˈsweʒən]

n. 說服,說服力

After persuasion, Debbie agreed to let us in.
在勸導後,黛比同意讓我們進去。

4443

essential [əˈsɛnʃəl]

adj. 必定不可少的(to),本質的 n. (複)本質,要素

A good diet is essential for everyone.
好的飲食對每個人都很重要。

4444

consequent [ˈkɑnsəˌkwɛnt]

adj. 作為結果的,隨之發生的

Parents need to deal with the responsibilities consequent upon the arrival of a new child.
家長需負起隨著新生兒而來的責任。

4445

deserve [dɪˈzɝv]

vt. 應受,值得

I deserve this prize.
我值得這個獎項。

4446

curse [kɝs]

v. 咒罵,詛咒

The girl thought that she was under a curse.
這個女孩認為她被詛咒。

4447

discourage [dɪsˈkɝɪdʒ]

vt. 勸阻,使氣餒,阻礙

They will hold a campaign to discourage smoking among teenagers.
他們將會舉行一個勸阻青少年抽菸的活動。

4448

sportsmanship [ˈsportsmənˌʃɪp]

n. 運動家精神

His sportsmanship is refreshing.
他的運動家精神令人振奮。

4449

farewell [ˌfɛrˈwɛl] [ˌfær-]

n. 辭別,再見,再會

int. 再會,別了!(常含有永別或不容易再見面的意思)

I will have a farewell party tonight.
今晚我有道別派對。

4450

founder ['faʊndə]

n. 鑄工,翻沙工,創始人,奠基人

vi. 沉沒,摔到,變跛,倒塌,失敗

He is the founder and president of the company.

他是這家公司的創始者跟總裁。

His painting is full of tragic style.

他的畫充滿悲劇風格。

4455

dormitory ['dɔrmə,torɪ]

n. 宿舍

He lives in a dormitory.

他住在宿舍。

4451

tolerable ['tɑlərəbl] ['tɑlrə-]

adj. 可容忍的,可以的

Smoking is not tolerable here.

這裡禁止吸菸。

4456

rhyme ['raɪm] n. 韻,押韻,押韻的詞

vt. 使押韻,用韻詩表達,把…寫成詩

Can you think of a rhyme for the word?

你可以想到這個字的押韻嗎?

4452

souvenir ['suvə,nɪr]

n. 紀念品

There is a souvenir shop here.

這裡有一家紀念品店。

4457

humidity [hju'mɪdətɪ]

n. 濕氣,潮濕,濕度,(美)沼澤中的肥沃高地

Today is a day of hot sunshine and humidity.

今天是日光普照且潮濕的一天。

4453

resolution [,rɛzə'luʃən]

n. 堅定,決心,決定,決議

Carol made a resolution to study hard at school.

卡洛下定決心在學校認真讀書。

4458

bulletin ['bʊlətn̩]

n. 公告,報告

The doctor gave a bulletin on the President's health.

醫生給了總統健康的報告。

4454

tragic ['trædʒɪk]

adj. 悲慘的,悲劇的

n. (文藝作品或生活中的)悲劇因素,悲劇風格

4459

calculator ['kælkjə,letə]

n. 電腦,計算器

I need a calculator.

我需要計算機。

4460 intensify [ɪn'tɛnsə,faɪ]

vt. 加強 vi. 強化

You have to intensify this part.

你需要加強這部分。

4461 departure [dɪ'partʃɚ]

n. 啟程,出發,離開

I saw Simon shortly before his departure for the USA.

我在西門出發到美國前短暫見過他。

4462 pregnancy ['prɛgnənsɪ]

n. 懷孕

This is her third pregnancy.

這是她第三次懷孕。

4463 wrinkle ['rɪŋkl̩]

n. 皺紋 v. 使皺

Her face was full of wrinkles.

她的臉充滿皺紋。

4464 promotion [prə'moʃən]

n. 促進,發揚,提升,提拔,晉升

There will be a winter sales promotion.

將會有冬季拍賣會。

4465 cope [kop]

vi. (善於)應付,(善於)處理

I find it hard to cope with the problem.

我發現這個問題很難處理。

4466 convenience [kən'vinjəns]

n. 便利,方便,有益,有用的,方便的用具,機械,安排等

Most of us like the convenience of using credit cards.

大部分人喜歡信用卡帶來的方便。

4467 complicate ['kamplə,kɪt]

v. (使)變複雜

Don't complicate the matter.

不要使這件事變複雜。

4468 facility [fə'sɪlətɪ]

n. 容易,簡易,靈巧,熟練,便利,敏捷,設備,工具

All rooms have private facilities.

全部的房間都有私人設備。

4469 exclaim [ɪks'klem]

v. 呼喊,驚叫,大聲叫

She opened her eyes and exclaimed in delight.

她張眼並且高興地歡呼。

4470 decay [dɪ'ke]

vi. 腐爛,衰敗,衰退

Her teeth were starting to decay.

她的牙齒開始腐壞。

4471 destination [,dɛstə'neʃən]

n. 目的地,終點

We finally arrived at the destination.

我們終於到達目的地。

4472

theft [θɛft]

n. 偷,行竊,偷竊的事例,偷竊行為

Motorcycle theft is on the increase.

最近機車搶案增加。

4473

dictate ['dɪktet]

v. 口述,口授,使聽寫,指令,指示,命令,規定

n. 指示(指理智,變心)

She's dictating a letter to her secretary right now.

她正向祕書口授信稿。

4474

despair [dɪ'spɛr] [-'spær]

n. 絕望,失望,令人失望的人(事物) vi. 絕望

Despite his illness, Ron never despaired.

儘管他生病,羅恩從不絕望。

4475

extraordinary [ɪk'strɔrdn̩ˌɛrɪ]

adj. 非常的,特別的,非凡的,特派的

Chris's smile that morning was quite extraordinary.

克里斯那天早上的微笑很不尋常。

4476

editorial [ˌɛdə'torɪəl] [-'tɔr-]

n. 社論 adj. 編輯上的,主筆的,社論的

She is an editorial assistant.

她是編輯助理。

4477

declaration [ˌdɛklə'reʃən]

n. 宣布,宣言,聲明

They announced a ceasefire declaration.

他們宣稱停火。

4478

continuous [kən'tɪnjʊəs]

adj. 連續的,持續的

TV shows a continuous flow of information.

電視顯示資訊的流通。

4479

fragrance ['fregrəns]

n. 芬芳,香氣,香味

I smell the rich fragrance of a garden.

我聞到了花園的芬芳。

4480

considerate [kən'sɪdərɪt] [-'sɪdrɪt]

adj. 體貼的,考慮周到的

He was always kind and considerate.

他總是友善跟體貼。

4481

quilt [kwɪlt]

n. 棉被 vi. 縫被子

I sent a patchwork quilt to him.

我送了拼布棉被給他。

4482

earnest ['ɜnɪst] [-əst]

adj. 認真的,熱心的,重要的 n. 真摯,認真,熱心

He is an earnest young man.

他是一個勤勉的年輕人。

4483

furthermore ['fɝðɚ͵mor] ['fɝðɚ-] [-͵mor]

adv. 此外,而且

He said he had not discussed the matter with her. Furthermore, he had not even contacted her.

他說他沒有跟她討論這件事。此外,他還沒有跟她接觸。

4484

ward [wɔrd]

n. 守衛,保衛,保護,牢房,病房,行政區,監護,鎖孔

vt. 守護,保衛,防止,擋住,躲開,避免

There are other patients in the ward.

病房裡有其他病人。

4485

contrast [kən'træst] ['kɑntræst]

n. 對比,對照 vt. 對比,對照

While there are similarities in the two people, there are also great contrasts.

雖然兩個人有相似之處,也有很大的不同。

4486

consonant ['kɑnsənənt]

adj. 協調一致的,子音

There are consonants and vowels in English.

英文有子音跟母音。

4487

transplant [trænsp'lænt] ['trænsplænt]

v. 移植,移種,移民,遷移 n. 移植,被移植物,移居者

Surgeons have successfully transplanted a heart into a four-year-old boy.

外科醫生成功地移植心臟到四歲小孩的身上。

4488

vegetarian [͵vɛdʒə'tɛrɪən] [-'ter-]

n. 素食者,食草動物 adj. 素食的

He is a vegetarian.

他是素食者。

4489

maturity [mə'tjʊrətɪ] [-'tu-]

n. 成熟,完備,(票據)到期

One day you'll have the maturity to understand.

有一天你會夠成熟能瞭解。

4490

desperate ['dɛspərɪt]

adj. 不惜冒險的,拚命的,不顧一切的,拼死的,絕望的

Time was running out and we were getting desperate.

時間快用完了,我們不惜一切。

4491

contribution [ˌkɑntrə'bjuʃən]

n. 捐獻,貢獻,投稿

The school makes a contribution to society.

這間學校對社會做出貢獻。

4492

empire ['ɛmpɑɪr]

n. 帝國,帝權

I read the history about the Roman empire.

我讀有關羅馬帝國的歷史。

4493

council ['kɑʊnsḷ]

n. 政務會,理事會,委員會,參議會,討論會議,顧問團,
　立法會

She's on the local council. 她在地方議會裡任職。

4494

contrary ['kɑntrɛrɪ] [kən'trɛrɪ] [-'trɛrɪ]

adj. (to)相反的　n. 相反,對立面

It wasn't a good thing; on the contrary, it was a mistake.

這不是好事，反之是一個錯誤。

4495

dense [dɛns]

adj. 密集的,稠密的

I saw dense black smoke from the chimney.

我從煙囪中看到黑色的濃煙。

4496

determination [dɪˌtɜmə'neʃən]

n. 決心,果斷

I admire her determination to do this thing.

我讚賞她做這件事的決心。

4497

estate [ə'stet]

n. 狀態,不動產,時期,階層,財產

My father is a real estate agent.

我爸爸是房地產代理商。

4498

executive [ɪg'zɛkjʊtɪv]

adj. 實行的,執行的,行政的　n. 執行者,經理主管人員

He is a marketing executive.

他是營銷經理。

4499

dialect ['dɑɪəlɛkt]

n. 方言

The people up there speak a dialect.

那邊的人說方言。

S2 高中二年級
T1 技職學院一年級　　編號 4500～5150

4500

dim [dɪm]

adj. 暗淡的,模糊的,無光澤的,悲觀的,懷疑的

vt. 使暗淡,使失去光澤

The light is too dim to see you clearly.

光線太暗無法很清楚的看見你。

4501
exchange [ɪks'tʃendʒ]

v. 交換,調換,交流

The child cleaned the house in exchange for her allowance. 小孩以清掃房子交換零用錢。

4502
pop [pɑp]

n. 取出,砰然聲,槍擊,流行樂曲,流行藝術

adj. 流行的,熱門的,通俗的

I love pop music.

我喜歡流行音樂。

4503
rid ['rɪd]

vt. 使擺脫,使去掉

It's time we got rid of bad habits.

該是我們去除壞習慣的時候了。

4504
violence ['vaɪələns]

n. 猛烈,強烈,暴力,暴虐,暴行,強暴

There is too much violence on TV.

電視上有太多暴力的內容。

4505
parade [pə'red]

n. 遊行,炫耀,閱兵,檢閱,閱兵場

v. 遊行,炫耀,誇耀,(使)列隊行進

A military parade will be cancelled on Double Tenth Day.

雙十節將會取消軍事閱兵。

4506
drain [dren]

n. 排水溝,消耗,排水 vi. 排水,流乾

The swimming pool drains at the end of summer.

游泳池會在夏天結束後排水。

4507
structure ['strʌktʃə]

n. 結構,構造,建築物 vt. 建築,構成,組織

The structure of the brain is complicated.

腦部的構造很複雜。

4508
management ['mænɪdʒmənt]

n. 經營,管理,處理,操縱,駕駛,手段

There are management training courses in universities.

很多大學都有開管理訓練課程。

4509
hay [he]

n. 乾草

Here is a bale of hay for animals in the barn.

這裡的穀倉有大捆的乾草給動物食用。

4510
permission [pə'mɪʃən]

n. 許可,允許

They didn't have permission to enter the house.

他們沒有被允許進入房子。

4511

roast [rost]

v. 烤(肉)

I am going to roast the chicken and fish for my dinner.

我要烤雞肉和魚當晚餐。

4512

waken ['wekən]

vi. 醒來 vt. 喚醒

The loud music wakened the sleeping child.

吵雜的音樂吵醒正在睡覺的小孩。

4513

preparation [ˌprɛpə'reʃən]

n. 準備,預備

Career training is a good preparation for any workers.

職業訓練對任何要工作的人是好的準備。

4514

poster ['postɚ]

n. 海報,招貼,(布告,標語,海報等的)張貼者

This is a poster for the musician's concert.

這是一位音樂家演唱會的海報。

4515

necessity [nə'sɛsətɪ]

n. 必要性,需要,必需品

A jacket is a necessity if you go out on a cool day.

在涼快的天氣裡外出，夾克是必需品。

4516

probable ['prɑbəbḷ]

adj. 很可能的,大概的

It seems probable that he will pass the exam.

他大概會通過考試。

4517

moist [mɔɪst]

adj. 潮濕的 n. 潮濕

Some people are not used to moist air.

有些人對潮濕的空氣不適。

4518

promote [prə'mot] vt. 促進,發揚,提升,增進

The government should think of policies to promote economic growth.

政府應該要想一些促進經濟發展的政策。

4519

scholar ['skɑlɚ]

n. 學者

He was a scholar.

他曾是一個學者。

4520

spray [spre]

n. 噴霧,飛沫 vt. 噴射,噴濺

She sprayed herself with perfume before going out.

她出門前噴了香水。

4521

reality [rɪ'ælətɪ]

n. 真實,事實,本體,逼真

The reality is that you should solve the problem.

事實是你必須解決問題。

4522

loosen ['lusn̩]

vt. 解開,放鬆,鬆弛

Peter loosened his tie after going back home.

彼得回家後解開領帶。

4523

muscle [ˈmʌsl̩]

n. 肌肉,臂力,(可供食用的)瘦肉,[解]肌

You can build muscle by exercising.

你可以藉由運動來練肌肉。

4524

typical [ˈtɪpɪkl̩]

adj. 典型的,有代表性的

The typical weather here is warm.

這裡典型的天氣很溫暖。

4525

tide [taɪd]

n. 潮,潮汐,潮流,趨勢

Watching strong tides during a typhoon day is dangerous. 颱風天看潮汐很危險。

4526

hell [hɛl]

n. 地獄,苦境,陰間,地獄中的人,訓斥 vi. 狂飲,飛馳

My family made my life hell.

我的家庭使我的生活成地獄。

4527

statement [ˈstetmənt]

n. 聲明,陳述,綜述

He gave a statement to the media.

他發表聲明給媒體。

4528

politician [ˌpɑləˈtɪʃn̩]

n. 政治家,政客

He is an honest politician.

他是一個誠實的政治家。

4529

pal [pæl]

n. (口)好朋友,夥伴,同志 vi. 結為朋友

My pen pal writes me a letter twice a week.

我的筆友一個星期寫兩次信給我。

4530

jewel [ˈdʒuəl]

n. 寶石

She loves to get dressed and wear jewels.

她喜歡穿的很漂亮並穿戴珠寶。

4531

nearby [ˈnɪrˈbaɪ]

adj. 附近的 adv. 在附近

Do you live nearby?

你住附近嗎？

4532

inform [ɪnˈfɔrm]

vt. 通知,報告 vi. 告發,格舉

Please inform me if you finish doing this.

如果你做完這件事，請通知我。

4533

heel [hil]

n. 鞋後跟

She struggled with the strap of her high heel shoes.

她費力的解開高跟鞋鞋帶。

4534

sufficient [səˈfɪʃənt] adj. 足夠的,充分的

The government provides sufficient working opportunities for young people.

政府提供足夠的工作機會給年輕人。

4535

victim ['vɪktɪm]

n. 受害人,犧牲者,犧牲品

He puts each victim's personal belongings into a safety box. 他將每個受害者的個人隨身物品放到保險櫃裡。

4536

reserve [rɪ'zɜv]

vt. 保留,留存,預訂

Did you reserve tickets to the movie tonight?
你有預訂今天晚上的電影票嗎?

4537

garlic ['gɑrlɪk]

n. [植]大蒜

Add some garlic in the soup.
加一點大蒜在湯裡。

4538

knot [nɑt]

n. (繩等的)結,(樹的)節,節(船速,＝哩／小時) v. 打結

The phrase "tie the knot" means getting married.
"綁領結"這個片語表示要結婚了。

4539

greenhouse ['grin,haʊs]

n. 溫室,花房

He brought flowers from the greenhouse.
他從溫室中帶了一些花。

4540

keyboard ['ki,bord] [-,bɔrd]

n. [計]鍵盤

He bought a computer keyboard on the Internet.
他從網路上買一個電腦鍵盤。

4541

enforcement [ɪn'forsmənt]

n. 實施,執行,強制,強迫

Instead of protecting civil rights, law enforcement agencies advance financial interests of certain companies.

執法機關促進某些公司的財務權益而沒有保護公民權利。

4542

setting ['sɛtɪŋ]

n. 安裝,排字,環境,全副餐桌,落下,定位,下沉

There is an old house in a beautiful setting of this picture. 這幅畫美麗的場景中有一間老房子。

4543

server ['sɜvɚ]

n. 侍者,上菜者,餐具(叉、匙、盤等),彌撒時的助祭,
發球員,(傳票令狀等的)送達者,【電腦】伺服器

The waiter and waitress are good servers in the restaurant.

這家餐廳的服務生都是很好的侍者。

4544

reunion [ri'junjən]

n. 重聚,重新結合,統一

He is waiting for a family reunion in Chinese New Year. 他正在等著新年家族團聚。

4545
greed [grid]
n. 貪慾,貪婪

People are always motivated by greed and fear.
人總是被貪婪和恐懼所驅動。

4546
fiancee [ˌfiənˈse]
n. 未婚妻

Fiancee is a woman who is going to get married.
未婚妻就是即將結婚的女人。

4547
fiddle [ˈfɪdl]
n. 小提琴 v. 虛度時光,拉小提琴,瞎搞

He fiddles around all day.
他整天瞎混。

4548
firecracker [ˈfaɪrˌkrækɚ]
n. 爆竹,鞭炮

We happily watched a New Year's Eve fireworks display. 我們高興的看了一場除夕煙火花匯表演。

4549
foe [fo]
n. 敵人,仇敵,反對者

Cats and dogs are always foes.
貓跟狗總是敵人。

4550
robin [ˈrɑbɪn]
n. 知更鳥

He has a robin as a pet.
他有一隻寵物知更鳥。

4551
creak [krik]
v. 作輾軋聲,發出輾軋聲 n. 輾軋聲,咯咯吱吱聲

The door creaks when someone opens it.
當有人開門時,門發出軋軋聲。

4552
crocodile [ˈkrɑkəˌdaɪl]
n. 鱷,鱷魚,假善人,口蜜腹劍者

Crocodile is an animal which has sharp teeth and live in rivers. 鱷魚是有著尖銳的牙齒而且住在河裡的動物。

4553
straightforward [ˌstretˈfɔrwɚd]
adj. 筆直的,率直的,粗獷的,明確的,簡單的,直接的

This is a straightforward question.
這是一個很直接的問題。

4554
stout [staʊt]
adj. 強壯的,穩重的,勇敢的,堅定的,結實的,肥胖的

n. 肥胖的人,烈啤酒

He is a short and stout man.

他是個矮小而且強壯的男人。

4555
cooperation [koˌɑpəˈreʃən] [ˌkoɑpə-]
n. 合作,協作

Fasten your seatbelt, and thank you for your cooperation.
繫緊安全帶,謝謝你的合作。

4556

cork [kork]

n. 軟木,軟木塞 v. 用塞子塞住

Pop the cork and we will drink red wine.
將軟木塞取出,我們要喝紅酒。

4557

counterclockwise [ˌkaʊntə'klɑk,waɪz]

adj. 反時針方向的 adv. 反時針方向

The plane flied in a counterclockwise direction.
飛機以逆時鐘的方向飛行。

4558

coupon ['kjupɑn]

n. 息票,贈券,優待券

We have a coupon for 20 percent off in the department store. 我們有這家百貨公司八折的折價券。

4559

cracker ['krækə]

n. 薄脆餅乾

He bought a lot of crackers in the supermarket.
他在超市買了很多薄脆餅乾。

4560

dressing ['drɛsɪŋ]

n. 調味品,穿衣,化妝

I want vinegar dressing in my salad.
我的沙拉要油醋醬。

4561

snort [snɔrt]

v. 噴著氣弄響鼻子,哼著鼻子,嘶嘶響著排氣,噴出

They made fun of him and snorted with laughter.
他們取笑他後,哼了一聲大笑起來。

4562

doorstep ['dor,stɛp]

n. 門前的台階,門階

He stood on the doorstep, waiting for his father.
他站在門前,等他爸爸。

4563

dough [do]

n. 生麵團

Pat the dough and put it in the oven for 10 minutes.
拍打麵團後,放進烤箱十分鐘。

4564

download ['daʊn,lod]

vt.【電腦】下載

Songs can't be downloaded from the Internet without permission. 歌曲未經允許不得從網路上下載。

4565

driveway ['draɪv,we]

n. 車道(私人)

The car in the driveway is expensive.
在私人車道上的汽車是很貴的。

4566

dwelling ['dwɛlɪŋ]

n. 住處

He has been living in the dwelling for twenty years.
他住在這個地方已經二十年了。

4567

earphone ['ɪr,fon]

n. 耳機,聽筒

Please wear earphones when you listen to music in public. 在公開場合聽音樂時,請帶耳機。

4568

defensible [dɪˈfɛnsəbl]

adj. 可防衛的,可擁護的,可辯護的

The fort has a defensible location.

這個要塞位於可防衛之處。

4569

spotlight [ˈspɑtˌlaɪt]

n. 聚光燈,探照燈,視聽,注意,醒目

The campus was lit by three spotlights at night.

校園在晚上時有三盞照明燈點著。

4570

diaper [ˈdaɪəpɚ]

n. 尿布

The nanny changed the kid's diaper and fed her milk.

保母換了小孩的尿布並餵奶。

4571

sophomore [ˈsɑfm̩ˌor] [-ˌɔr]

n. 大學二年級生

Sophomore is a student who is in the second year in a college. 大二生就是大學大二年級的學生。

4572

massage [məˈsɑʒ]

n. 按摩,揉 v. 按摩,揉

Joan gave me a body massage.

喬安幫我按摩身體。

4573

mayonnaise [ˌmeəˈnez] n. 美乃滋

Gently mix together eggs, mayonnaise, garlic, salt, and pepper in a bowl.

在碗裡攪拌蛋,美乃滋,蒜,鹽和胡椒。

4574

mainstream [ˈmenˌstrim] n. 主流

The mainstream media was under serious attack because they have political bias.

這個主流媒體遭到攻擊,因為他們政治立場偏頗。

4575

mechanics [mɪˈkænɪks]

n. 機械學,技巧,力學

He studies mechanics at college.

他在大學主修機械。

4576

prairie [ˈprɛrɪ]

n. 大草原,牧場

He loves to lie on the prairie.

他喜歡躺在大草原上。

4577

mileage [ˈmaɪlɪdʒ]

n. 哩數

Check the mileage before you rent a car.

租車前檢查哩程數。

4578

piss [pɪs]

n. 小便,尿 v. 撒尿,發怒,厭煩 int. 呸!

He pissed at the toilet.

他在廁所小便。

4579

pocketbook [ˈpɑkɪtˌbʊk]

n. 袖珍本,筆記本

Her pocketbook and keys were missing.

她的筆記本跟鑰匙不見了。

4580

preservation [ˌprɛzɝˈveʃən]

n. 保存,貯藏,保護

The government is working for the preservation of the environment. 政府正在為環保努力。

4581

priceless [ˈpaɪslɪs]

adj. 無價的,極其珍貴的,貴重的

Priceless antiques should be preserved in the museum. 極貴重的古董應該被保存在博物館裡。

4582

logo [ˈlɑgo]

n. 徽標,圖形,商標

They put a logo on the product. 他們在產品上放上商標。

4583

lonesome [ˈlonsəm]

adj. 寂寞的

Beth is lonesome without any friends. 貝斯沒有朋友很孤單。

4584

lotus [ˈlotəs]

n. 蓮

There are many lotus flowers on the lake. 湖上有許多蓮花。

4585

ozone [ˈozon]

n. 新鮮的空氣,臭氧

There is a hole in the ozone. 臭氧層有破洞。

4586

overwork [ˈovɝˈwɝk]

n. 過度操勞,過度工作 v. (使)工作過度

Be careful not to overwork. 小心不要過度工作。

4587

oversleep [ˈovɝˈslip]

v. (使)睡過頭

I overslept and missed the class this morning. 今天早上我睡過頭並錯過上課。

4588

overeat [ˈovɝˈit]

v. 吃過量

Don't overeat when you get older. 當你年紀越大時,不要吃過量。

4589

overdo [ˈovɝˈdu]

v. 做得過分,過度,誇張,過火

Don't overdo soy sauce in the food. 不要在食物中加太多醬油。

4590

outskirts [ˈaʊtˌskɝts]

n. 郊外,郊區,外圍,邊緣

They live on the outskirts of Taipei. 他們住在臺北外圍。

4591

outsider [ˈaʊtˈsaɪdɝ]

n. 門外漢,局外人,圈外人

I'm an outsider of fashion. 我是時尚領域的門外漢。

4592

outgoing [aʊt'goɪŋ] ['aʊtˌgoɪnŋ]

n. 外出,開支,流出 adj. 喜歡外出的

We will hire someone with outgoing and passionate personalities. 我們將會僱用外向和熱情的人。

4593

pickpocket ['pɪkˌpakɪt]

n. 扒手

Beware of pickpockets when you travel alone.
當你單獨旅行時請小心扒手。

4594

mound [maʊnd]

n. 土堆,土墩,小山,堤 v. 築堤,用土堆防衛,積成堆

The tourists attempted to make a mound.
遊客們試著堆座小土堆。

4595

mower ['moɚ]

n. 割草的人,割草機

He used a mower to cut grass.
他使用除草機除草。

4596

nearsighted ['nɪr'saɪtɪd]

adj. 近視的,淺見的

A nearsighted person is unable to see things clearly.
近視的人無法清楚地看東西。

4597

peg [pɛg]

n. 釘,藉口,銷子 v. 釘木釘,固定,限制,堅持不懈地工作

Sophia pegged away at her thesis.
蘇菲亞努力不懈地在作她的論文。

4598

newscast ['njuzˌkæst]

n. 新聞廣播

She tried to focus on newscast while she was eating dinner. 她試著在吃晚餐時專心聽廣播。

4599

nightingale ['naɪtɪŋˌgel]

n. 夜鶯

Nightingale is a small bird that sings beautifully at night.
夜鶯是會在夜晚美妙歌唱的鳥。

4600

hi-fi ['haɪ'faɪ]

n. adj. high fidelity, 立體聲(的)音響設備

We need hi-fi speakers.
我們需要高品質(的)立體聲音響。

4601

hockey ['hakɪ]

n. 曲棍球

We play hockey in winter.
我們在冬天玩曲棍球。

4602

homosexual [ˌhomə'sɛkʃʊəl]

adj. 同性戀的 n. 同性戀

Mary's brother was homosexual.
瑪莉的弟弟是同性戀。

4603

gut [gʌt]

n. 勇氣,劇情,內容,內臟,肚子,海峽 v. 取出內臟

You must have the guts to tell Paul what happened to him. 你必須有勇氣告訴保羅他發生了什麼事。

4604

gypsy [ˈdʒɪpsɪ]

n. 吉普賽人,吉普賽語

adj. v. 像吉普賽人的,流浪

Mary dressed like a gypsy in bright-colored skirts with long hair.

瑪莉像個吉普賽人一樣有著色彩鮮豔的裙子和長頭髮。

4605

hairstyle [ˈhɛrˌstaɪl]

n. 髮型

He had a new hairstyle.

他有新的髮型。

4606

handicraft [ˈhændɪˌkræft]

n. 手工藝,手藝,技巧

Her hobby is doing handicraft.

她的嗜好是手工藝。

4607

harmonica [harˈmɑnɪkə]

n. 口琴,玻璃或金屬片的敲打樂器

The child is good at playing the harmonica.

這個小孩很擅長吹口琴。

4608

healthful [ˈhɛlθfəl]

adj. 有益健康的,使人健康的,衛生的

This is a healthful drink.

這是一個有益健康的飲料。

4609

lawmaker [ˈlɔˌmekɚ]

n. 立法者

A lawmaker is a person who makes law.

國會議員是立法的人。

4610

lifelong [ˈlaɪfˈlɔŋ]

adj. 終身的,一輩子的

He is a lifelong member of the health club.

他是這家健身俱樂部的終身會員。

4611

zoom [zum]

vi. 發出嗡嗡聲,呼嘯(而過),急昇,飛漲,(影像的)縮放

n. 嗡嗡聲,急速上升,(價格)飛漲,變焦鏡頭

(= zoom lens)

Gas prices have zoomed up this year.

油價今年提升。

4612

ivy [ˈaɪvɪ]

n. 常春藤

adj. 學院的,抽象的

The walls were covered with ivy. 牆上遍布著常春藤。

4613

interruption [ˌɪntəˈrʌpʃən]

n. 打岔,中斷,中斷之事

I plan to read a book without interruption.

我打算不要被打擾的念書。

4614
jasmine [ˈdʒæzmɪn] [ˈdʒæsmɪn]
n. 茉莉,淡黃色
I like the smell of jasmine.
我喜歡茉莉的香味。

4615
jaywalk [ˈdʒeˌwɔk]
v. 擅自穿越馬路
Jaywalking is illegal.
擅自穿越馬路是違法的。

4616
journalism [ˈdʒɜnḷˌɪzəm]
n. 新聞業,報章雜誌
Mike is a journalism professor at Columbia University.
麥克是哥倫比亞大學的新聞系教授。

4617
isle [aɪl]
n. 島,小島,群島 v. 使成為島嶼,住在島嶼上
He lives on the British isle.
他住在英國島嶼上。

4618
backpack [ˈbækˌpæk]
n. 背包 v. 背
He has a red backpack.
他有一個紅色的背包。

4619
cell-phone [ˈsɛlˌfon]
n. 攜帶式行動電話,大哥大
I talk to my mother on my cell-phone everyday.
我每天跟我媽媽講電話。

4620
Celsius [ˈsɛlsɪəs]
n. 攝氏溫度
The temperature is 12 degree Celsius today.
今天是攝氏十二度。

4621
backbone [ˈbækˈbon]
n. 脊椎,骨幹,支柱,分水嶺,書脊,主幹,骨氣,勇氣
He doesn't have the backbone to solve the problem.
他沒有勇氣解決這個問題。

4622
chairperson [ˈtʃɛəˌpɜsən]
n. 議長,主席(沒有性別歧視的字眼)
He is elected as a chairperson of the meeting.
他被選為會議的主席。

4623
upload [ʌpˈlod]
v.【電腦】上載
It takes time to upload the data.
上傳資料需要時間。

4624
barbarian [barˈbɛrɪən] [-ˈbær-]
n. 野蠻人,異邦人 adj. 野蠻的,未開化的,異邦的,異族的
The child was described as an uncivilized barbarian.
這個小孩被描述為一個野蠻人。

4625
barefoot [ˈbɛr-] [ˈbɛrˌfʊt]
adj. 赤腳的 adv. 赤腳地
Children in the mountains go barefoot because of poverty. 因為貧窮,山上的小孩赤腳走路。

4626

barbershop [ˈbɑrbɚˌʃɑp]

n. 理髮店

He goes to a barbershop and gets a cut every week.

他每個星期去理髮店剪頭髮。

4627

celery [ˈsɛlərɪ]

n. 芹菜

Mom bought a stick of celery today.

媽媽今天買了芹菜。

4628

clan [klæn]

n. 氏族,宗族,黨派

The whole clan will be here in Chinese New Year.

新年時,整個家族都會在這裡。

4629

arms [ɑrms]

n. 武器,兵器,兵種

He urges enemies to lay down their arms.

他促使敵人放下武器。

4630

awhile [əˈhwaɪl]

adj. 片刻,一會兒

He takes a break awhile.

他休息一下子。

4631

thriller [ˈθrɪlɚ]

n. 使人毛骨悚然的東西,使人毛骨悚然的小說

Thriller is my favorite type of film.

驚悚片是我最喜愛的一種電影。

4632

check-in [ˈtʃɛkˌɪn]

n. 投宿登記手續,報到,(旅客登機前)驗票並領取登機卡

Be sure to check-in two hours before boarding.

搭機前兩小時請務必報到。

4633

tug-of-war [ˈtʌg-ɑv-wɔr]

n. 拔河的競賽,戰爭中之費勁的競爭,爭戰中之較勁

There was a tug-of-war between these two schools.

這兩所學校有一個校際拔河比賽。

4634

brotherhood [ˈbrʌðɚˌhʊd]

n. 手足情誼,兄弟關係

We have the spirit of brotherhood.

我們有手足情誼。

4635

boulevard [ˈbuləˌvard] [ˈbulvar]

n. 林蔭大道

'Sunset Boulevard' is a famous movie.

日落大道是一部有名的電影。

4636

boxer [ˈbɑksɚ]

n. 拳擊手,拳師狗

My father is a boxer.

我爸爸是拳擊手。

4637

boxing [ˈbɑksɪn]

n. 拳擊

He is a boxing champion.

他是拳擊冠軍。

4638

blues [bluz]

n. (複數) [口] 傷感,憂鬱

Women get the blues after their babies are born.

女性在生完小孩後會有產後憂鬱。

4639

tribal ['traɪbl̩]

adj. 部落的,種族的

These people come from tribal societies.

這些人來自部落社會。

4640

brassiere [brə'zɪr]

n. 胸罩,奶罩

Many women wear brassiere.

很多女人穿胸罩。

4641

bodily ['bɑdɪlɪ]

adj. 身體的

The car accident did him bodily harm.

車禍造成他身體上的傷害。

4642

payment ['pemənt]

n. 付款,支付,報酬,償還,報應,懲罰

She pays a student loan in monthly payment of five thousand dollars. 她每個月付助學貸款五千元。

4643

somehow ['sʌmˌhaʊ]

adv. 不知何故

Don't worry, we'll make it somehow.

不用擔心,無論如何我們都會成功。

4644

romantic [ro'mæntɪk] [rə-]

adj. 傳奇式的,浪漫的,空想的,誇大的

The wedding is held in one of the world's most romantic places. 這個婚禮在世界上最浪漫的地點之一舉辦。

4645

pianist [pɪ'ænɪst] ['piənɪst]

n. 鋼琴家,鋼琴演奏家

I'm going to be a classical pianist someday.

我有一天會成為古典鋼琴家。

4646

participle ['partəsəpl̩]

n. 分詞

Copula must be followed by a passive participle.

過去分詞必須加在繫詞後。

4647

partnership ['partnɚˌʃɪp]

n. 合夥關係,夥伴關係

I've been in partnership with the company for six years.

我跟這家公司合夥六年了。

4648

pasta ['pɑstɑ] n. 義大利麵

She eats various foods for her meal such as bread, pasta, rice, and potatoes.

她吃各式各樣的食物例如麵包、義大利麵、飯、馬鈴薯。

4649

performer [pɚ'fɔrmɚ]

n. 執行者,表演者

He is a circus performer.

他是一個馬戲團的表演者。

4650

promising [ˈprɑmɪsɪŋ]

adj. 有希望的,前途有望的

A promising young actor died from a car accident last month. 一位有前途的年輕演員上個月死於車禍。

4651

examinee [ɪɡˌzæməˈni]

n. 受審查者,受試人

The examiner asks the examinee to summarize the article. 審查者要求受試者對文章作摘要。

4652

evergreen [ˈɛvɚˌɡrin]

n. 常青樹,常綠植物 adj. 常綠的

I like the fragrance of evergreen.
我喜歡常青樹的氣味。

4653

eyelash [ˈaɪˌlæʃ] n. 睫毛

Before putting on mascara, most of women use an eyelash curler.
大部分的女人在用睫毛膏之前會用睫毛夾。

4654

silkworm [ˈsɪlkˌwɝm]

n. 蠶

A silkworm produces silk thread.
蠶會吐絲。

4655

eel [il]

n. 鰻,鰻魚

I like to eat steamed eel.
我喜歡吃清蒸鰻魚。

4656

nominate [ˈnɑməˌnet]

vt. 提名,任命,推薦

John was nominated to represent the school at the meeting. 約翰被任命代表學校出席會議。

4657

relay [ˌriˈle] n. 驛馬,接替,[電工]繼電器

vt. (消息,貨物等)分程傳遞,使接替,轉播

He relays my instructions to the other members of staff.
他傳達我的指令給其他員工。

4658

resultant [rɪˈzʌltn̩t]

adj. 作為結果而發生的,合成的

The growing economic recession and resultant unemployment happened.

經濟衰退跟隨之而來的失業率發生了。

4659

plausible [ˈplɔzəbl̩]

adj. 貌似真實的,貌似有理的

His excuse certainly sounds plausible.
他的藉口聽起來合理。

4660

innovation [ˌɪnəˈveʃən]

n. 改革,創新

The company is interested in innovation.
公司對改革很有興趣。

4661

hamper ['hæmpɚ]

v. 妨礙,牽制

Our plan is hampered by lack of money.

我們的計畫由於缺乏經費而被牽制。

4662

comprehensive [ˌkɑmprɪ'hɛnsɪv]

adj. 全面的,廣泛的,能充分理解的,包容的

Teachers should offer students comprehensive examples. 老師應提供學生可理解的例子。

4663

bracket ['brækɪt]

n. 牆上凸出的托架,括弧,支架 v. 括在一起

Additional information is given in brackets.

括號裡有額外的資訊。

4664

ambiguity [ˌæmbɪ'gjuɑtɪ]

n. 含糊,不明確

There was an element of ambiguity in the teacher's response. 老師的回答不明確。

4665

closure ['kloʒɚ]

n. 關閉 vt. 使終止

The government should deal with the problem of school closures. 政府應處理學校關閉的問題。

4666

homogeneous [ˌhomə'dʒɪnɪəs]

adj. 同類的,相似的,均一的,均勻的

This is a homogeneous group.

這是同類的一組。

4667

magnify ['mægnəˌfaɪ]

vt. 放大,擴大,讚美,誇大,誇張 vi. 有放大能力

Don't magnify the problem.

不要誇大問題。

4668

intervene [ˌɪntɚ'vin]

vi. 干涉,干預,插入,介入,(指時間)介於其間 v. 干涉

I don't usually like to intervene in disputes.

我並不喜歡介入紛爭。

4669

peninsula [pə'nɪnsələ]

n. 半島

The Korean peninsula is next to China.

朝鮮半島緊鄰中國。

4670

prick [prɪk]

vt. 刺,戳,刺痛,豎起 n. 紮,一刺,刺痛,錐,陰莖

She pricked her finger with a pin.

她用針刺傷手指。

4671

ruby ['rubɪ]

n. 紅寶石

I have a ruby ring.

我有一個紅寶石戒指。

4672

ingenious [ɪn'dʒinjəs]

adj. 機靈的,有獨創性的,精製的,具有創造才能

She's very ingenious when it comes to art.

她對於藝術有獨創性。

4673

erupt [ɪˈrʌpt]

vt. 噴出 vi. 爆發

The volcano erupts once a year.

這座火山一年爆發一次。

4674

consciousness [ˈkɑnʃəsnɪs]

n. 意識,知覺,自覺,覺悟,個人思想

David lost consciousness and then he died.

大衛失去知覺之後就過世了。

4675

doctrine [ˈdɑktrɪn]

n. 教條,學說

He committed himself to Christian doctrine.

他遵守基督教教條。

4676

monopoly [məˈnɑpl̩ɪ]

n. 壟斷,壟斷者,專利權,專利事業

Government shouldn't have a monopoly on media.

政府不該壟斷媒體。

4677

emigrate [ˈɛməˌgret]

vi. 永久(使)移居 vt. (使)移民

He emigrated to USA one year ago.

他一年前移民去美國。

4678

hypothesis [haɪˈpɑθəsɪs]

n. 假設,假說

Further experiment will test our hypothesis.

接下來的實驗會測試我們的假說。

4679

marginal [ˈmɑrdʒɪnl̩]

adj. 記在頁邊的,邊緣的,邊際的

He shows a marginal improvement in scores.

他的成績進步不多。

4680

intuition [ˌɪntjuˈɪʃən]

n. 直覺,直覺的知識

He answers the question by intuition.

他用直覺回答問題。

4681

destiny [ˈdɛstənɪ]

n. 命運,定數

Nancy thinks it was her destiny to get married to her husband. 南西認為跟她丈夫結婚是命運的安排。

4682

punishment [ˈpʌnɪʃmənt]

n. 懲罰,處罰

I was forced to clean the yard as a punishment.

我的處罰是被要求打掃庭院。

4683

implicit [ɪmˈplɪsɪt]

adj. 暗示的,盲從的,含蓄的,固有的,不懷疑的,絕對的

His statement is seen as implicit criticism.

他的陳述被視為含蓄的批評。

4684

rotary [ˈrotərɪ]

adj. 旋轉的

She had lunch in the rotary restaurant.

她在旋轉餐廳吃午餐。

4685

expedition [ˌɛkspɪˈdɪʃən]

n. 遠征,探險隊,迅速,派遣

He went on an expedition to the Antartic.
他去南極冒險。

4686

lumber [ˈlʌmbɚ]

n. (美)木材,無用的雜物(如破舊家俱),廢物,隆隆聲
vi. 伐木,喧鬧地向前走,笨重地行動

This is a lumber room. 這是雜物間。

4687

steward [ˈstjuwɚd] [ˈstu-]

n. (輪船,飛機等)乘務員,幹事

He is a steward on a ship.
他是船務員。

4688

conversion [kənˈvɜʃən]

n. 變換,轉化

He has experienced a religious conversion lately.
他最近經歷了宗教上的轉變。

4689

innumerable [ɪnˈnjumərəbl̩]

adj. 無數的,數不清的

There are innumerable books in the library.
圖書館有無數的書。

4690

hemisphere [ˈhɛməsfɪr]

n. 半球

Our brain can be divided into left and right hemispheres.
我們的腦可以分左右半腦。

4691

erroneous [ɪˈronɪəs]

adj. 錯誤的,不正確的

He seems to be under the erroneous impression that she still loves him. 他似乎有錯覺誤以為她還愛他。

4692

signify [ˈsɪgnəˌfaɪ]

vt. 表示,意味 v. 頗為重要,表示

Hamilton shrugged to signify that he doesn't know about it. 漢米頓聳肩表示他不知道這件事。

4693

criterion [kraɪˈtɪrɪən]

n. (批評判斷的)標準,准據,規範

Appearance is not the sole criterion for choosing a husband. 外表並非選丈夫的唯一標準。

4694

overhear [ˌovɚˈhɪr]

vt. 無意中聽到,偷聽

I overheard part of their gossip about the boss.
我無意中聽到他們討論老闆的私事。

4695

snatch [snætʃ]

v. 攫取 n. 攫取

The man snatched her bag and ran away.
這個男人攫取她的包包然後跑走。

4696

distill [dɪˈstɪl]

v. 蒸餾,濃縮,吸取…的精華

I like to drink distilled water.
我喜歡喝蒸餾水。

4697 heritage [ˈhɛrətɪdʒ]

n. 遺產

One of the cultural heritages of China is the Great Wall.
萬里長城是中國重要文化遺產之一。

4698 dazzle [ˈdæzl̩]

v. (使)眼花,眩耀 n. 耀眼

We were dazzled by the woman's appearance and charm. 我們被這個女人的外表和魅力迷惑了。

4699 defy [dɪˈfaɪ]

vt. 不服從,公然反抗,藐視,挑釁,違抗,使…難於

n. 挑戰

You shouldn't openly defy the rule.
你不該公開反抗這個規定。

4700 nickel [ˈnɪkl̩]

n. [化]鎳,鎳幣,(美國和加拿大的)五分鎳幣 vt. 鍍鎳於

A nickel is worth five cents in the USA and Canada.
一個鎳幣在美國和加拿大代表五分錢。

4701 integrity [ɪnˈtɛgrətɪ]

n. 正直,誠實,完整,完全,完整性

We respect a man of great moral integrity.
我們尊敬有道德感的人。

4702 assignment [əˈsaɪnmənt]

n. 分配,委派,任務,(課外)作業

We will hand in our history assignment next week.
我們會在下星期交出我們的歷史作業。

4703 expenditure [ɪkˈspɛndɪtʃɚ]

n. 支出,花費

My mom monitors my unnecessary expenditure.
我母親監督我不必要的花費。

4704 manuscript [ˈmænjəˌskrɪpt]

n. 手稿,原稿

Fortunately, the original manuscripts have been kept.
很幸運的,原稿被保存下來。

4705 inherent [ɪnˈhɪrənt]

adj. 固有的,內在的,與生俱來的

Scuba diving is an inherently dangerous sport.
浮潛是有潛在危險的運動。

4706 dilemma [dəˈlɛmə] [daɪ-]

n. 進退兩難的局面,困難的選擇

The teacher is in a dilemma over how to tackle the child's problem.

這位老師處理這個小孩的問題上陷在進退兩難的局面。

4707

cylinder ['sɪlɪndɚ]

n. 圓柱體,圓筒

This is a gas cylinder.
這是油桶。

4708

liner ['laɪnɚ]

n. (美)班機,劃線者,襯墊

A dustbin liner can keep the dustbin clean.
垃圾桶襯墊可以保持垃圾桶乾淨。

4709

fluctuate ['flʌktʃʊˌet]

vi. 變動,波動,漲落,上下,動搖

vt. 使動搖,使波動,使起伏

Temperatures can fluctuate by 10 degrees during a day.
一天的溫差上下波動十度。

4710

intercourse ['ɪntɚˌkors] [-ˌkɔrs]

n. 交往,交流

People needs social intercourse with others.
人需要跟別人有社交互動。

4711

condense [kən'dɛns]

v. (使)濃縮,精簡

Can you condense fives pages into just one page?
你可以將五頁內容精簡成一頁嗎？

4712

appendix [ə'pɛndɪks]

n. 附錄,附屬品,[解]闌尾

You can read full details given in Appendix 3.
你可以在附錄三得到完整的細節。

4713

ornament ['ɔrnəˌmɛnt]

n. 裝飾物,教堂用品 vt. 裝飾,修飾

The Christmas tree is covered with ornaments.
這棵聖誕樹布滿著裝飾品。

4714

accumulate [ə'kjumjəˌlet]

v. 累積

Fat is likely to accumulate around the belly.
脂肪囤積在腹部。

4715

plead [plid]

vi. 辯護,懇求 vt. 為…辯護,藉口,托稱

He pleaded for his family's help.
他懇求家人的幫忙。

4716

respectful [rɪ'spɛktfəl]

adj. 恭敬的,尊敬的,尊重人的,有禮貌的

He was always respectful of my choice.
他總是尊重我的選擇。

4717

archive ['ɑrkaɪv]

vt. 存檔 n. 檔案文件

The man has an archive of the writer's unpublished work. 這個人有這個作家未出版的作品。

4718
decimal [ˈdɛsəml̩]
n. 小數

The decimal, 0.81, stands for 81 percent.

小數 0.81 代表百分之八十一。

4719
drastic [ˈdræstɪk]
adj. 激烈的,(藥性等)猛烈的

Protesters take a drastic action against the government.

抗議者採取行動對抗政府。

4720
heighten [ˈhaɪtn̩] v. 提高,升高

The campaign is intended to heighten tension between people and government.

這個活動要升起政府跟人民的緊張。

4721
silicon [ˈsɪlɪkən]
n. [化]矽,矽元素

Silicon is a chemical substance.

矽是化學物質。

4722
fishery [ˈfɪʃərɪ]
n. 漁業,水產業,漁場,養魚術

The country is famous for fishery.

這個國家以漁業為名。

4723
contend [kənˈtɛnd]
v. 鬥爭,競爭,主張

I would contend that we should reduce plastic bottles.

我主張我們應減少塑膠瓶。

4724
lessen [ˈlɛsn̩]
v. 減少,減輕

To stop smoking lessens the risk of cancer.

不抽菸可以減輕癌症的機率。

4725
statesman [ˈstetsmən]
n. 政治家

The party's elder statesman gave a speech yesterday.

這個政黨資深的政治家昨天發表演說。

4726
horizontal [ˌhɑrəˈzɑntl̩]
adj. 地平線的,水平的

This is a horizontal surface.

這是水平面。

4727
ignite [ɪgˈnaɪt]
v. 點火,點燃

Gas suddenly ignited.

汽油突然間點燃。

4728
garment [ˈgɑrmənt]
n. 外衣

She put the garment on and went out.

她把外衣穿上並出去。

4729
sorrowful [ˈsɑrofəl]
adj. 悲傷的

He talked sorrowfully about his mother's death.

他很傷心的談論他母親的過世。

4730

puff [pʌf]

n. 一陣噴煙,腫塊,蓬鬆,吹噓,宣傳廣告

v. 噴出,張開,誇張,(使)膨脹,(使)驕傲,喘息,鼓吹,吹捧

He sat puffing cigarettes. 他坐著抽菸。

4731

linger ['lɪŋgɚ]

v. 逗留,閒盪,拖延,游移

The smell of food lingered in the room.

食物味道留在房間。

4732

exemplify [ɪgˈzɛmpləˌfaɪ]

vt. 例證,例示,作為···例子

Problems are exemplified in the book.

這本書內有許多習題作為例子。

4733

descendant [dɪˈsɛndənt]

n. 子孫,後裔,後代

He is a descendant of the Ching Dynasty.
他是清朝後代。

4734

startle ['stɑrtl̩]

v. 震驚

I was startled by the news.
這則新聞讓我感到震驚。

4735

municipal [mjuˈnɪsəpl̩]

adj. 市政的,市立的,地方性的,地方自治的

A municipal election will be held next year.
市立選舉明年舉行。

4736

corrupt [kəˈrʌpt]

adj. 腐敗的,貪汙的,被破壞的,混濁的,(語法)誤用的

vi. 腐爛,墮落

We can't have a corrupt government.

我們不能有貪汙的政府。

4737

customary ['kʌstəmɛrɪ]

adj. 習慣的,慣例的

In some cultures, it is customary for people to take off

hats before entering home.

有些國家人們習慣進屋前脫帽。

4738

reel [ril]

n. (棉紗,電線等的)捲軸,(磁帶等的)一盤,旋轉,蹣跚

vt. 捲···於軸上,使旋轉

My brain was reeling, and I need to stay calm.

我的腦筋很亂,我需要冷靜。

4739
instability [ˌɪnstə'bɪlətɪ]
n. 不穩定(性)

People don't like political instability in the country.
人們並不喜歡國家的政治不穩定。

4740
architectural [ˌɑrkə'tɛktʃərəl]
adj. 建築上的,建築學的

I like this temple because of its architectural beauty.
我喜歡這個寺廟是由於它的建築之美。

4741
gloomy ['glumɪ]
adj. 黑暗的,陰沉的,令人沮喪的,陰鬱的

It was a gloomy room and no one was in it.
這是一個黑暗的房間,沒有人在裡面。

4742
infectious [ɪn'fɛkʃəs]
adj. 有傳染性的,易傳染的,有感染力的

Flu is an infectious disease.
流行性感冒是傳染性的疾病。

4743
indicative [ɪn'dɪkətɪv] [ɪn'dɪkɪtɪv]
adj. 指示的,預示的,可表示的

It's indicative of a psychological effect called 'projection'. 這在心理學的反應上稱之為反射。

4744
groan [gron]
n. 呻吟,嘆息 vt. 呻吟著說

I'm tired of his groaning and complaining.
我很厭煩他的嘆息跟抱怨。

4745
pistol ['pɪstl]
n. 手槍

He grabbed his pistol and shot the man.
他抓起手槍射了那個男人。

4746
geology [dʒɪ'ɑlədʒɪ]
n. 地質學,地質概況

He majors in geology.
他主修地質。

4747
quiver ['kwɪvɚ]
n. 震動,顫抖,箭袋,箭袋中的箭 vi. 顫抖,振動,射中

The child was quivering with fear in her mother's arms.
小孩在媽媽懷抱裡害怕發抖著。

4748
feminine ['fɛmənɪn]
adj. 婦女(似)的,嬌柔的,陰性的,女性的

Nowadays, not every woman own feminine characteristics.
現今社會,並非所有女性都具有嬌柔的特質。

4749
gathering ['gæðərɪŋ]
n. 集合,集會

The gathering of the students took place at the playground. 學生在操場上集合。

4750
invert ['ɪnvɝt]
adj. 轉化的 n. 顛倒的事物

In some countries, the meaning of body language is inverted. 有些國家,肢體語言的意義會被顛倒了。

4751

orthodox [ˈɔrθəˌdɑks]

adj. 正統的,傳統的,習慣的,保守的,東正教的

He influences the orthodox views on language learning.

他影響了傳統語言學習的觀念。

4752

safeguard [ˈsefˌgɑrd]

vt. 維護,保護,捍衛　n. 安全裝置,安全措施

The labor union safeguards against the exploitation of laborers. 工會捍衛對勞工的剝削。

4753

mule [mjul]

n. 騾,倔強之人,頑固的人,雜交種動物

Paul is as stubborn as a mule.

保羅很固執。

4754

drape [drep]

n. 窗簾　v. 遮蓋,覆蓋

She had a blanket draped around her shoulders during a long flight. 在長途飛行中,她會覆蓋毛毯在她肩膀。

4755

cola [ˈkolə]

n. 可樂樹(其子含咖啡鹼),可樂類飲料

She drinks a can of cola everyday.

她每天喝一罐可樂。

4756

buck [bʌk] n. (美口)元,雄鹿,公羊,公兔

v. (馬等)突然一躍(將騎手摔下)

He spent big bucks on this.

他在這件事上花很多錢。

4757

rocky [ˈrɑkɪ]

adj. 多岩石的,堅如岩石的,堅固的,搖搖晃晃的, 頭暈目眩的,困難的

They are in a rocky marriage. 他們的婚姻岌岌可危。

4758

playful [ˈplefəl]

adj. 好玩的,嬉戲的,十分有趣的,頑皮的

A playful little dog waves its tail to strangers.

這隻好玩的狗對陌生人搖尾巴。

4759

grassy [ˈgræsɪ]

adj. 綠色的,像草的

He walks along a grassy riverbank.

他沿著青草茂盛的河岸走路。

4760

wed [wɛd]

v. 娶,嫁,結婚

The couple plan to wed next year.

這對佳偶計畫明年結婚。

4761

disagreement [ˌdɪsəˈgrimənt]

n. 意見不同,不調和,爭執,不和,爭論

We've had few disagreement about this issue.

我們在這件事上有一些意見不合。

4762

almond [ˈɑmənd]

n. [植]杏樹,杏仁,杏仁狀物

She has almond eyes.

她有一雙杏眼。

4763

unify ['junɪˌfaɪ]

vt. 統一,使成一體

His clothes unifies traditional and modern styles.

他的衣服融合傳統跟現代風格。

4764

episode ['ɛpəˌsod]

n. 一集,[音]插曲,插話,有趣的事件

The first episode of the drama series is very fantastic.

這齣戲的第一集很棒。

4765

controversial [ˌkɑntrə'vɝʃəl]

adj. 爭論的,爭議的

He is a controversial figure in the country.

在這個國家,他是個有爭議性的人物。

4766

flunk [flʌŋk]

n. 失敗,不及格 vi. 失敗,放棄,考試不及格

If you don't study hard, you will flunk.

如果你不用功,你會不及格。

4767

disposal [dɪ'spozl]

n. 處理,處置,布置,安排,配置,支配

Tony had a lot of money at his disposal.

東尼有很多錢可以支配。

4768

unlock [ʌn'lɑk]

vt. 開…鎖,開啟,顯露,放開 vi. 開著,解開,解出鎖定

He unlocked the door and entered the house.

他開了鎖,進入屋子裡。

4769

trait [tret]

n. 顯著的特點,特性

Being open-minded is his personality trait.

心胸寬廣是他的個性特質。

4770

famine ['fæmɪn]

n. 饑荒,(古)饑餓,嚴重的缺乏

People in Africa are facing famine.

非洲的人面臨飢荒。

4771

triple ['trɪpl̩]

n. 三倍數,三個一組 adj. 三倍的 v. 增加三倍

His income tripled in three years.

他的收入三年內增加了 3 倍。

4772

fiber ['faɪbɚ]

n. 纖維,光纖

Fruit and vegetables are high in fiber.

水果跟蔬菜是高纖維。

4773

superiority [səˌpɪrɪ'ɔrɪtɪ] [su-] [-'ɑr-]

n. 優越,高傲

His sense of superiority makes pople uncomfortable.

他的優越感讓人不舒服。

4774

retirement [rɪ'taɪrmənt]

n. 退休,引退,退卻,撤退

He became a volunteer after his retirement.

他退休以後做義工。

4775

tick [tɪk]

n. 滴答聲,記號,勾號 v. 滴答地響,標以記號,作滴答聲

Put a tick in the box if the answer is right.

如果答案對的話,請在空格打勾。

4776

donor ['donə]

n. 捐贈人 n. [化]原料物質

There is a shortage of blood donors.

現在有血荒。

4777

swamp [swamp] [swɔmp]

n. 沼澤,濕地,煤層聚水 v. 陷入沼澤,淹沒,覆沒

I was swamped with emails.

我被電子郵件淹沒。

4778

trivial ['trɪvɪəl]

adj. 瑣細的,價值不高的,微不足道的

This is a trivial problem.

這是不重要的問題。

4779

convict ['kɑnvɪkt] [kən'vɪkt]

vt. 證明⋯有罪,宣告⋯有罪 n. 罪犯

The man is a convicted murderer.

這個人被宣告謀殺。

4780

ultraviolet [ˌʌltrə'vaɪəlɪt]

adj. 紫外線的,紫外的 n. 紫外線輻射

We should prevent ultraviolet radiation from the sun.

我們應避免從太陽而來的紫外線。

4781

creativity [ˌkrɪetɪvətɪ]

n. 創造力,創造

Parents believe art classes can boost children's creativity. 家長相信美術課能激發孩子的創造力。

4782

vocation [vo'keʃən]

n. 召喚,號召,天命,天職,特殊的適應性,才能,行業,職業

Jan has a vocation for art.

建有藝術天分。

4783

electron [ɪ'lɛktrɑn] [ə-]

n. 電子

Electron is a substance with a negative electric charge.

電子是帶負電荷的物質。

4784

zeal [zil]

n. 熱心,熱情,熱誠

He is a volunteer with missionary zeal.

他是個有使命感熱誠的義工。

4785

suppress [sə'prɛs]

vt. 鎮壓,抑制,查禁,使止住

You need to suppress your anger in public.

你需要在公共場所抑制你的脾氣。

4786

doorway ['dor,we]

n. 門口

My mom was waiting for me in the doorway.

我的媽媽在門口等我。

4787

warehouse ['wɛr,haʊs] ['wær-]

n. 倉庫,貨棧,大商店

vt. 貯入倉庫,(俚)[經]以他人名義購進(股票)

Can you put these things in the warehouse?

你可以將這些東西放在倉庫裡嗎？

4788

terrorist ['tɛrərɪst]

n. 恐怖分子

We don't welcome terrorists.

我們不歡迎恐怖分子。

4789

delegation [,dɛlə'geʃən]

n. 代表團,授權,委託

A delegation of teachers attended the meeting.

老師代表團出席會議。

4790

threshold ['θrɛʃold]

n. 開始,開端,極限

She stepped across the threshold in the entrance.

她走過了入口的玄關。

4791

inspection [ɪn'spɛkʃən]

n. 檢查,視察

An inspection is carried out every year.

每年都會有檢查。

4792

surpass [sə'pæs] vt. 超越,勝過

The boy surpassed his teacher's expectations and did the test well.

這個男生超越了老師的期待並把考試考的很好。

4793

subordinate [sə'bɔrdn̩,et]

adj. 次要的,從屬的,下級的 n. 下屬

A subordinate officer should ask their supervisor about what to do. 下屬應該要問主管要做什麼事。

4794

contentment [kən'tɛntmənt]

n. 滿意,知己

After eating a big meal, he has a feeling of deep contentment. 吃完了大餐，他有著滿足感。

4795

fuss [fʌs]

n. 忙亂,大驚小怪,大驚小怪的人 v. 忙亂,大驚小怪

John and Mary want a wedding without any fuss.

約翰跟瑪麗希望婚禮不要太匆促。

4796

pail [pel]

n. 桶,提桶

Salt melts in a pail of water.

鹽在一桶水中融化了。

4797

consortium [kən'sɔrʃɪəm]

n. 社團,協會,聯盟,(國際)財團,[律]配偶的權利,

(美)大學聯盟協定

A consortium of oil companies openly defies the rule.

一個石油財團公然違抗規定。

4803

versatile ['vɜsətḷ]

adj. 通用的,萬能的,多才多藝的

He is a very versatile workcr and hc can do many things.

他是一個多才多藝的員工而且他會做很多事。

4798

supervise [ˌsupəˈvaɪz]

v. 監督,管理,指導

Mr. Chang closely supervised the company.

張先生嚴格監督這家公司。

4804

roughly ['rʌflɪ]

adv. 概略地,粗糙地

There were roughly 100 people in the classroom.

教室裡大約有一百人。

4799

veil [vel]

n. 面紗

It's a tradition for brides to wear veils.

新娘戴著頭紗是一項傳統。

4805

syndrome ['sɪndrəˌmi] n. 綜合病症

People who suffer from the depression syndrome can't control their mood.

有憂鬱症狀的人無法控制他們的心情。

4800

trench [trɛntʃ]

n. 溝渠,塹壕,管溝,電纜溝,戰壕 v. 掘溝,挖戰壕

Workers were digging a trench underground.

工人在地底下挖溝渠。

4806

flourish ['flɜɪʃ]

vi. 繁榮,茂盛,活躍,手舞足蹈,興旺,處於旺盛時期

vt. 揮動,誇耀

The economy is booming and flourishing.

經濟正繁榮復甦起來。

4801

submit [səbˈmɪt]

vi. 屈服,聽從 vt. 呈送,提交

All papers must be submitted next Monday.

所有的報告必須在下星期一要繳交。

4802

exclude [ɪkˈsklud]

v. 把…排除在外,排斥

Some of the evidence was excluded from the case.

在這件案件中有些證據被排除在外。

4807

dodge [dɑdʒ]

v. 避開,躲避 v. (俗)詭計,躲藏

The girl dodged under the table to escape from the other children. 這個小女孩躲在桌子下並逃離其他小孩。

4808

furnace ['fɜnɪs] [-əs]

n. 爐子,熔爐

The furnace broke down and the entire office building has no heat. 鍋爐壞了，整棟辦公大樓沒有暖氣。

4809

stumble ['stʌmbl̩]

v. 絆倒,使困惑,蹣跚,結結巴巴地說話,躊躇

n. 絆倒,錯誤

She stumbled in a hurry and spilled the water all over the floor.

她在匆忙中絆倒並把水灑在地上。

4810

exclusively [ɪk'sklusɪvlɪ]

adv. 專門地,排除其他地

This gift is available exclusively to the guest who is the first one in the shop.

這個禮物是專門給第一位來店的客人。

4811

undermine [ˌʌndə'maɪn]

v. 逐漸削弱,破壞

Constant complaint undermines his marriage.

不斷地抱怨逐漸讓他的婚姻變差。

4812

tuck [tʌk] n. 縫摺,活力,鼓聲,船尾突出部下方,食物(尤指點心,蛋糕) vt. 打摺,捲起,擠進,塞,使隱藏

Giles tucked his bag under his arm.

基兒把他的書夾在手臂。

4813

whirl [hwɜl]

v. (使)旋轉,急動,急走 n. 旋轉,一連串快速的活動

The seagulls whirl with happiness.

海鷗快樂的迴旋。

4814

tilt [tɪlt]

v. (使)傾斜,(使)翹起,以言詞或文字抨擊

My brother tilted his head and made a face.

我弟弟歪著頭並做鬼臉。

4815

trifle ['traɪfl̩]

n. 瑣事,少量,小事 v. 開玩笑,浪費時間

I don't want to argue over trifles.

我不想為了小事爭吵。

4816

symmetry ['sɪmɪtrɪ]

n. 對稱,勻稱

This is a perfect symmetry of the house design.

這個房子設計很勻稱。

4817

faculty ['fækl̩tɪ] n. 才能,本領,能力,全體教職員,(大學的)系,科,(授予的)權力

All faculty members should attend the meeting.

全體教職員都需要出席會議。

4818

tempo ['tɛmpo]

n. (音樂)速度,拍子,發展速度

The tempo of modern life is fast.

現代生活的步調很快速。

4819

adjustment [ə'dʒʌstmənt]

n. 調整,調節,調節器

She made some adjustments to her class.

她對她的班級做了一些調整。

4820

unanimous [jʊ'nænəməs]

adj. 意見一致的,無異議的

The decision to move to Taipei was almost unanimous.

搬到臺北的決定幾乎是毫無異議的。

4821

exclusion [ɪk'skluʒən]

n. 排除,除外,被排除在外的事物

Please check the essay for exclusions of words.

請檢查文章中遺漏的文字。

4822

terminate ['tɜmə,net]

v. 停止,結束,終止

The contract must be terminated now.

這項合約必須現在終止。

4823

veto ['vito]

n. 否決,禁止,否決權 vt. 否決,禁止

The commitee vetoed the proposal.

委員會否決這個提議。

4824

velocity [və'lɑsətɪ]

n. 速度,速率,迅速,周轉率

The velocity of the car is 100km per hour.

車子時速 100 公里。

4825

exert [ɪg'zɝt]

vt. 盡(力),施加(壓力等),努力 v. 發揮,竭盡全力,盡

Parents shouldn't exert pressure on the school.

家長不該對學校施加壓力。

4826

convincing [kən'vɪnsɪŋ]

adj. 有說服力的

The police found convincing evidence of his guilt.

警方發現了他罪行的有力證據。

4827

broil [brɔɪl]

v. 烤(肉),酷熱

I like to eat broiled chicken when I take a field trip.

當我郊遊時,我喜歡吃烤雞肉 。

4828

millionaire [,mɪljən'ɛr]

n. 百萬富翁,大富豪

He became a millionaire after he won a lottery.

他中樂透後,變成百萬富翁。

4829

symposium [sɪm'pozɪəm]

n. 討論會,座談會

A symposium on language learning will be held tomorrow. 一個有關語言學習的座談會明天將會舉辦。

4830

fabric ['fæbrɪk]

n. 織品,織物,布,結構,建築物,構造

Our new range of fabrics and wallpapers are fantastic.

我們一系列新的布料和壁紙都很出色。

4831

swarm [swɔrm]

n. 蜂群,一大群 v. 湧往,擠滿,密集,成群浮游,雲集

A swarm of bees are flying north.

一群蜜蜂往北飛。

4832

thereafter [ðɛr'æftɚ]

adv. 其後,從那時以後

Mary was born in Japan but shortly thereafter she moved to the USA. 瑪莉在日本出生但之後搬到美國。

4833

wag [wæg]

vt. 搖擺,搖動,饒舌 n. 搖擺,小丑

My dog always wags its tail and waits for me.

我的狗常常搖著尾巴等著我。

4834

fleet [flit]

n. 艦隊(尤指有固定活動地區的艦隊),港灣,小河

vi. 疾馳,飛逝,掠過

The US seventh fleet will arrive in Taiwan.

美國第七艦隊將會抵達臺灣。

4835

sprain [spren]

v. 扭傷

I sprained my ankle and couldn't walk.

我扭傷腳踝,所以不能走路。

4836

discharge [dɪs'tʃɑrdʒ]

vt. 卸下,放出,清償(債務),履行(義務),解雇,開(炮),放(槍),射(箭) n. 卸貨,流出,放電

Hospitals discharge patients earlier if they recover from illness.

如果病人康復,醫院會讓他們提早出院。

4837

sulfur ['sʌlfɚ] n. [化]硫磺,硫礦 vt. 用硫磺處理

Sulfur is a common light yellow chemical substance that doesn't smell good.

硫磺是一種淡黃色,有臭味的化學物質。

4838

emit [ɪ'mɪt]

vt. 散發

When water is boiling, the kettle emits a whistle.

水滾時,水壺會噓噓作響。

4839

walnut ['wɔlnət]

n. 胡桃,胡桃木

I like coffee and walnut cake.

我喜歡咖啡跟胡桃蛋糕。

4840

warrant [ˈwɔrənt]

n. 授權,正當理由,根據,證明,憑證,委任狀,批准,許可證 vt. 保證,辯解,擔保,批准,使有正當理由

They had a warrant to arrest the person.

他們有權利逮捕這個人。

4841

treason [ˈtrizn̩]

n. 叛逆,通敵,背信,叛國罪

John is accused of committing treason.

約翰被指控判國罪。

4842

void [vɔɪd]

n. 空間,空曠,空虛,悵惘

adj. 空的,無人的,空閒的,無效的,無用的,沒有的

Shopping helped to fill the void after he broke up with his girlfriend.

購物填補他和女友分手後的空虛。

4843

enzyme [ˈɛnzaɪm] n. [生化]酵

Enzyme is a chemical substance that helps to cause natural process.

酵是一個幫助自然反應發生的化學物質。

4844

transaction [trænsˈækʃən] [trænz-]

n. 辦理,處理,會報,學報,交易,事務,處理事務

The bank charges NT$100 for each transaction.

銀行對每筆交易索取壹百元。

4845

crucial [ˈkruʃəl]

adj. 至關緊要的

English plays a crucial role in the world.

英文在世界上扮演了重要角色。

4846

tuition [tjuˈɪʃən]

n. 學費

When I studied in college, the tuition was inexpensive.

當我在大學讀書時,學費很便宜。

4847

evaluation [ɪ.væljʊˈeʃən]

n. 估價,評價,賦值

We need to carry out an evaluation of the project.

我們需要執行這計畫案的評估。

4848

testimony [ˈtɛstə.monɪ]

n. 證詞(尤指在法庭所作的),宣言,陳述

In his testimony, he denied that he killed the woman.

他的證詞中否定他殺了那女子。

4849

diagram [ˈdaɪə.græm]

n. 圖表

The results are shown in diagram A.

結果顯示在圖表 A。

4850

donation [do'neʃən]

n. 捐贈品, 捐款, 貢獻

Would you like to make a donation to our school?

你想要捐款給我們學校嗎？

4851

dealing ['dilɪŋ]

n. 分發　n. 交易, 來往

We had dealings with him in the school 5 years ago.

我們五年前在學校曾與他打過交道。

4852

valve [vælv]

n. 閥, [英]電子管, 真空管

Valve is a device for controlling the flow of a liquid or gas. 閥是一個控制水流或瓦斯的機制。

4853

thermal ['θɜ·ml̩]

adj. 熱的, 熱量的

Wearing thermal underwear in winter keeps you warm.

在冬天穿著保暖內衣讓人保暖。

4854

gobble ['gɑbl̩]

n. 狼吞虎咽, 火雞叫聲　vi. 貪食, 咯咯叫聲

He gobbles his food at lunchtime.

他在午餐時間狼吞虎咽地吃著食物。

4855

knuckle ['nʌkl̩]

n. 指節, 關節

I like to eat pork knuckle.

我喜歡吃豬蹄。

4856

derive [də'raɪv]

vt. 取得, 得到　vi. 起源, 衍生(from)

We will derive great benefit from this job.

從這個工作上，我們會得到很大利益。

4857

rejection [rɪ'dʒɛkʃən]

n. 拒絕

What are the reasons for his rejection of my application?

他拒絕我的申請的理由是什麼？

4858

vicious ['vɪʃəs] adj. 惡的, 不道德的, 惡意的,

刻毒的, 墮落的, 品性不端的, 有錯誤的

A vicious murderer was arrested yesterday.

邪惡的殺人犯昨天被逮捕。

4859

quake [kwek]

n. 地震

There was a quake this morning.

今天早上有地震。

4860

summon ['sʌmən]

v. 召集, 召喚, 號召, 鼓起, 振作

The president summoned the legislater to his office.

總統召喚立法委員到他辦公室。

4861

directly [də'rɛktlɪ]

adv. 直接地, 立即

Please say directly what you want.

請直接說你要什麼。

4862

external [ɪkˈstɜnl]

adj. 外部的,外面的

The external appearance of the building is old.
這棟建築物的外觀很古老。

4863

weary [ˈwɪrɪ]

adj. 疲倦的,厭倦的,令人厭煩的,疲勞

v. 疲倦,厭倦,厭煩

She sat down with a weary sight after working for 12 hours.

在工作十二小時之後,她帶著疲憊地眼神坐下。

4864

calorie [ˈkæləɪ]

n. 卡路里

I like to eat a low-calorie snack when I go on a diet.
當我節食時,我喜歡吃低卡點心。

4865

equation [ɪˈkweʒən] [-ʃən]

n. 方程式,等式

In the equation $2x = 8$, what is x?
在等式中 2x 等於 8,x 為多少?

4866

directive [dəˈrɛktɪv]

n. 指示

He will give you some directives in this meeting.
在這次的會面中他會給你一些指示。

4867

witty [ˈwɪtɪ]

adj. 富於機智的,詼諧的

She is very witty.
她很聰明。

4868

emission [ɪˈmɪʃən]

n. (光,熱等的)散發,發射,噴射,排出之物

The emission of the vehicles pollutes the air.
交通工具排出的廢氣汙染了空氣。

4869

execute [ˈɛksɪ͵kjut]

vt. 執行,實行,完成,處死,製成,[律]經簽名蓋章等手續
　　使(證書)生效

The criminals have been executed. 罪犯已經被處決了。

4870

embarrassment [ɪmˈbærəsmənt]

n. 困窘,阻礙

To her embarrassment, she couldn't say anything.
令她困窘的是,她無法說任何話。

4871

token [ˈtokən]

n. 表示,象徵,記號,代幣　adj. 象徵的,表意的

They gave this gift as a small token of their gratitude.
他們贈予這個禮物作為他們的感激之情 。

4872

diplomatic [͵dɪpləˈmætɪk]

adj. 外交的,老練的

The chairperson is very diplomatic.
這位主席具有外交手腕。

4873

thrill [θrɪl]

v. 發抖

I was thrilled by the story she told.

我被她講的故事嚇到。

4874

conviction [kən'vɪkʃən]

n. 深信,確信,定罪,宣告有罪

She is a woman of strong political convictions.

她是一個有強烈政治信仰的女人。

4875

wrench [rɛntʃ]

n. 扳鉗,扳手,猛扭,痛苦,扭傷,歪曲

vt. 猛扭,使扭傷,曲解,搶,折磨

The door had been wrenched open and robbers came inside.

門被扳手撬開,搶匪走進去。

4876

tanker ['tæŋkɚ]

n. 油輪

An oil tanker carries oil.

油罐車載油。

4877

vicinity [və'sɪnətɪ]

n. 鄰近,附近,接近

There is no shop in the vicinity.

附近沒有任何店。

4878

dental ['dɛntl]

adj. 牙齒的,牙科的 vt. 使齒音化

Dental care is important.

牙齒保健很重要。

4879

framework ['frem,wɝk]

n. 構架,框架,結構

The room is built on a wooden framework.

這間房是木造結構。

4880

watt [wɑt]

n. [電]瓦

Watt is a unit of power.

瓦是計算電的單位。

4881

validity [və'lɪdətɪ]

n. 有效性,合法性,正確性

The period of validity of the document has expired.

這份文件的效期已經過期。

4882

filter ['fɪltɚ]

n. 濾波器,篩檢程式,濾光器,篩選

vt. 過濾,滲透,用過濾法除去

We need coffee paper to filter unwanted substances.

我們需要咖啡濾紙來過濾不要的物質。

4883

endless [ˈɛndlɪs]

adj. 無止境的,無窮的

There is an endless round of boring meetings today.

今天有開不完的無聊會議。

4884

frustration [ˌfrʌsˈtreʃən]

n. 挫敗,挫折,受挫

People often feel a sense of frustration after their failure.

人在失敗後會常感到挫折感。

4885

withhold [wɪðˈhold]

vt. 使停止,拒給,保留,抑制 vi. 忍住

I withheld payment until they keep the promise.

我停止付款直到他們遵守承諾。

4886

discretion [dɪˈskrɛʃən]

n. 謹慎,處理權

You have the discretion to the issue.

你有這件事情的處理權。

4887

exclusive [ɪkˈsklusɪv]

adj. 排外的,孤高的,唯我獨尊的,獨佔的,唯一的,高級的

The news is exclusive.

這是則獨家新聞。

4888

deter [dɪˈtɜ]

v. 阻止

The monitor was installed to deter people from stealing.

這個監視器是為了阻止人們偷竊而設置的。

4889

torrent [ˈtɔrənt]

n. 急流

The rain came down in torrents and I was wet.

突然下起大雨,我全身濕了。

4890

ceramic [səˈræmɪk]

adj. 陶器的 n. 陶瓷製品

There will be an exhibition of ceramics in the museum.

博物館裡有陶器展。

4891

pickle [ˈpɪkl̩]

n. (醃肉,菜等用的)醃漬品,泡菜,酸黃瓜 vt. 醃,泡

I eat cheese and pickle sandwiches for my breakfast.

我吃起司和酸黃瓜三明治當我的早餐。

4892

sturdy [ˈstɝdɪ]

adj. 強健的,堅定的,毫不含糊的

That chair looks very sturdy.

那個椅子看起來很堅固。

4893

frontier [frʌnˈtɪr]

n. 邊境,邊界,邊疆

Enemies are close to the frontier.

敵人靠近邊界。

4894

diameter [daɪˈæmətɚ]

n. 直徑

He draws a circle two centimetres in diameter.

他畫了直徑兩公分的圓形。

4895

transformer [træns'fɔrmɚ]

n. [電]變壓器,使變化的人

We need a transformer to change electricity.

我們需要變壓器轉換電力。

4896

transistor [træn'zɪstɚ]

n. [電子]電晶體

A transistor is an electronic element.

電晶體是一個電子元件。

4897

endorse [ɪn'dɔrs]

v. 在(票據)背面簽名,簽註(文件),認可,簽署,背書

I endorse his remarks.

我認可他的言論。

4898

fluid ['fluɪd]

n. 流體(液體和氣體的總稱),流動性

adj. 流動的,不固定的,可改變的,可另派用場的,流暢的

I was told by the doctor to drink plenty of fluids.

醫生告訴我要多喝流質。

4899

supersonic [ˌsupɚ'sɑnɪk]

adj. 超音波的 n. 超聲波,超聲頻

Supersonic aircraft is faster than the speed of sound.

超音波的飛機比音速還快。

4900

sleigh [sle]

n. 雪橇 v. 乘雪橇,用雪橇運輸

A sleigh ride is pulled by a horse.

馬拉著雪橇。

4901

vegetation [ˌvɛdʒə'teʃən]

n. [植]植被,(總稱)植物,草木,(植物的)生長,呆板單調的生活

The city has little vegetation. 城市內少有綠色植物。

4902

unfold [ʌn'fold]

vt. 打開,顯露,開展,闡明 vt. 放(羊)出欄

He unfolds a map to look for the city.

他打開地圖找城市。

4903

mustache ['mʌstæʃ] [mə'stæʃ]

n. 髭,鬍子

Men have to shave their mustache everyday.

男人必須每天刮鬍子。

4904

involvement [ɪn'vɑlvmənt]

n. 連累,包含

Harris cannot get rid of his involvement with the crime.

哈瑞無法擺脫與這項犯罪的關聯。

4905

timely ['taɪmlɪ]

adj. 及時的,適時的

The quarrel ended with the timely arrival of their mother. 這場爭吵適時的在他們母親來到結束。

4906
verbal ['vɝbḷ]

adj. 口頭的

They have a verbal agreement.

他們口頭上同意了。

4907
testify ['tɛstə,faɪ]

v. 證明,證實,作證

Some witnesses will testify for the crime.

有些目擊者將為這項犯罪作證。

4908
conversely [kən'vɝslɪ]

adv. 相反地

She likes beef; conversely, I like pork.

她喜歡牛肉,但是相反地,我喜歡豬肉。

4909
underestimate ['ʌndɚ'ɛstə,met]

vt. 低估,看輕　n. 低估

We underestimated the cost of the skirt.

我們低估了這件裙子的費用。

4910
immigrate ['ɪmə,gret]

vi. 移來　vt. 使移居入境

She immigrated to the United States one year ago.

她一年前移民去美國。

4911
expressive [ɪk'sprɛsɪv]

adj. 表現的,表達…的,有表現力的,富於表情的

The expressive power of his music impressed the audience. 他音樂的感染力使觀眾印象深刻。

4912
chirp [tʃɝp]

n. 喳喳聲,唧唧聲　v. 吱喳而鳴,尖聲地說

The sparrows were chirping.

麻雀吱喳而鳴。

4913
throne [θron]

n. 王座,君主

In 1913, Victoria was on the throne.

在一九一三年,維多莉亞繼承王位。

4914
wreath [riθ]

n. 花圈,花冠,圈狀物

The president laid a wreath at the war memorial.

總統在戰爭紀念碑上放了一個花圈。

4915
taboo [tə'bu]

n. (宗教)禁忌,避諱,禁止接近,禁止使用

adj. 禁忌的,忌諱的

The topic is still a taboo in our family.

這個主題在我們家仍是禁忌。

4916
sue ['su]

vt. 控告,向…請求,請願　vi. 提出訴訟,提出請求

She was suing the nanny for abusing her child.

她控告保母虐待她小孩。

4917
traitor ['tretɚ]
n. 叛逆者,叛國者
She is a traitor.
她是叛國者。

4918
comma ['kɑmə]
n. 逗點,逗號
A comma is the mark that separates things in a list.
逗號是分隔兩件事的符號。

4919
disciplinary ['dɪsəplɪnˌɛrɪ]
adj. 紀律的,學科的
The govenment will be taking disciplinary action against the company.
政府會採取紀律措施對抗這家公司。

4920
fruitful ['frutfəl] [frɪut-]
adj. 果實結得多的,多產的,富有成效的,豐富的
A library provides a fruitful source of information.
圖書館提供很豐盛的資訊。

4921
unemployment [ˌʌnɪm'plɔɪmənt]
n. 失業,失業人數
The unemployment rate is high.
失業率很高。

4922
transmission [træns'mɪʃən] [trænz-]
n. 播送,發射,傳動,傳送,傳輸,轉播
The transmission of disease is fast.
疾病傳播很快。

4923
desirable [dɪ'zaɪrəbl]
adj. 值得要的,合意的,令人想要的,悅人心意的
It is desirable that you should finish your work as soon as possible. 你應當要盡快完成工作。

4924
dispose [dɪ'spoz]
vi. 處理,丟掉 vt. 安排
Trash is disposed in the trash bin.
垃圾被放置在垃圾桶裡。

4925
density ['dɛnsətɪ]
n. 密度
This is the area of high population density.
這是高密度人口的區域。

4926
deliberate [dɪ'lɪbəˌret]
adj. 深思熟慮的,從容不迫,故意的,預有準備的 v. 商討
She spoke with deliberate steps.
她說話從容不迫。

4927
conservation [ˌkɑnsə'veʃən]
n. 保存,保持,守恆
She devotes herself in wildlife conservation.
她致力奉獻於野生動物保育上。

4928

screwdriver [ˈskruˌdraɪvɚ]

n. 螺絲起子

I need a screwdriver.
我需要螺絲起子。

4929

uphold [ʌpˈhold]

vt. 支援,贊成,捍衛

We agree to uphold the law.
我們同意支持這項法律。

4930

grasshopper [ˈgræsˌhɑpɚ]

n. 蚱蜢,蝗蟲,小型偵察機

I saw a grasshopper in the grass.
我在草地裡看到一隻蚱蜢。

4931

victorious [vɪkˈtorɪəs]

adj. 獲勝的,勝利的

They are the victorious team.
他們是獲勝的隊伍。

4932

grammatical [grəˈmætɪkl]

adj. 文法的,合乎文法的

When you use English, you need to obey grammatical rules. 當你使用英文,你需要遵守文法規則。

4933

queer [kwɪr]

n. 同性戀者 adj. 奇怪的,可疑的,不舒服的

His face was queer pale.
他的臉出奇的蒼白。

4934

tar [tɑr]

n. 焦油,柏油

It is useless spoiling the ship for a haporth of tar.
節省少量的油而毀掉一艘船(意指因小失大)。

4935

controversy [ˈkɑntrəˌvɝsɪ]

n. 論爭,辯論,論戰

His statement causes controversy.
他的言論導致爭議。

4936

detention [dɪˈtɛnʃən]

n. 拘留,禁閉,阻止,滯留,留堂

She was always put in detention because of her bad behavior. 她常因為行為失當而關禁閉。

4937

sincerity [sɪnˈsɛrətɪ]

n. 誠摯,真實,真摯

He showed his sincerity in the speech.
他的演說流露真摯的情感。

4938

creditor [ˈkrɛdɪtɚ]

n. 債權人

You need to pay off the debt from your creditor.
你需要償還債權人的債務。

4939

decent [ˈdisṇt]

adj. 正派的,端莊的,有分寸的,(服裝)得體的,大方的
adj. (口)相當好的,像樣的

This is a decent salary. 這個薪水還不錯。

4940

counsel [ˈkaʊnsl]

n. 討論,商議,辯護律師 vt. 勸告,忠告

She counseled them to do this.
她建議他們這樣做。

4941

descend [dɪˈsɛnd]

vi. 下來,下降,遺傳(指財產,氣質,權利),突擊,
出其不意的拜訪 v. 下去

Our plane started to descend and landed.

我們的飛機開始下降並降落。

4942

successor [səkˈsɛsɚ]

n. 繼承者,接任者,後續的事物

I'm sure she will be a good successor.
我確定她會是好的繼承者。

4943

detection [dɪˈtɛkʃən]

n. 察覺,發覺,偵查,探測,發現

Early detection of the disease improves the chances of
treatment. 早期發現疾病可以增加治療的機會。

4944

transition [trænˈzɪʃən] [trænsˈɪʃən]

n. 轉變,轉換,躍遷,過渡,變調

The society is in transition now.
社會正在轉變中。

4945

thorn [θɔrn]

n. [植]刺,棘,荊棘

He's been a thorn in the side of the class for years.
他好幾年來一直是班上的大麻煩。

4946

sled [slɛd]

n. 雪橇,摘棉 v. 乘雪橇,用雪橇運,用摘棉機摘

The girl's father is pulling the sled with the girl on it.
小女孩坐在雪橇中被她的父親拉著。

4947

versus [ˈvɝsəs]

prep. 對(指訴訟,比賽等中),與…相對

It was a choice of better job opportunities versus

leaving her friend far away.

這是一個好的工作機會與離開她朋友兩者之間的選擇。

4948

beautify [ˈbjutəˌfaɪ]

v. 美化,變美,修飾

We should grow some plants to beautify the house.
我們應該種一些植物美化房子。

4949

undoubtedly [ʌnˈdaʊtɪdlɪ]

adj. 無疑,必定

Undoubtedly, this is a true story.
毫無疑問的,這是一個真實故事。

4950

understandable [ˌʌndɚˈstændəbl̩]

adj. 可以理解的

It is understandable that she left her home after fighting with her mother.

她跟她母親吵架後離家是可以理解的。

4951

carton [ˈkɑrtn̩]

n. 硬紙盒,紙箱 v. 用紙箱裝

I drink a carton of fruit juice everyday.

我每天喝一盒果汁。

4952

batter [ˈbætɚ]

vt. 連擊,重擊. 打擊,搗毀,貶低

n. 打擊手,糊狀物,(鉛字的)磨損

When she made a mistake, she was battered by her father.

當她犯錯時,她被父親打了一頓。

4953

belongings [bəˈlɔŋɪŋz]

n. 財產,攜帶物品,家眷,親戚

Watch out for your belongings when you leave your office. 當你離開辦公室時,注意你的私人物品。

4954

caretaker [ˈkɛrˌtekɚ]

n. 管理者,看管者,看守人

The baby's mother is a good caretaker.

這小孩的媽媽是好的照顧者。

4955

website [ˈwɛbˌsaɪt]

n.【電腦】網站(全球資訊網的主機站)

We can look for information on this website.

我們可以在這個網站找資訊。

4956

advertiser [ˈædvɚˌtaɪzɚ]

n. 登廣告者,廣告客戶

The Stockport Advertiser is one of the biggest companies. 史克伯廣告商是最大的公司之一。

4957

wheelchair [ˈhwilˌtʃɛr]

n. 輪椅

He'll be in a wheelchair for many years.

他將會坐很多年的輪椅。

4958

whereabouts [ˈhwɛrəˌbaʊts]

n. 下落,所在之處 adj. 在何處

Whereabouts do you live?

你住何處?

4959

whisk [hwɪsk]

n. 掃帚,毛撢子,攪拌器,打蛋器

v. 掃,拂,揮動,迅速移動,攪拌,飛奔

Whisk the egg whites until stiff and put it in the oven.

攪拌蛋白直到凝固後放入烤箱。

4960

airway ['ɛr,we]

n. (礦井的)風道,風巷,(肺的)氣道,(麻醉時用的)
導氣管,航空路線,航空公司

The airway is the passage in your throat.

氣管就是喉嚨的通道。

4961

abortion [ə'bɔrʃən]

n. 流產,小產,墮胎,失敗,夭折,發育不全

She will have an abortion.

她將會做墮胎手術。

4962

yoga ['jogə]

n. 瑜珈

Mary joined a fitness yoga class at the health club.

瑪莉在健身中心參加健身瑜珈課。

4963

computerize [kəm'pjutə,raɪz]

v. 用電腦處理,電腦化

The school has been fully computerized.

這間學校已經完全電腦化了。

4964

ace [es]

n. (紙牌的)一點,能手,好手,高手,少許 adj. v. 一流的,
傑出的,卓越的,優秀的,受崇敬的,以發球贏一分

I've got a pair of aces when I played cards.

我玩牌時拿到了一對紅心。

4965

teller ['tɛlə]

n. 講話者,告訴者,出納員

A bank teller's job is to receive and pay out money.

銀行出納員的工作就是收錢和付錢。

4966

complexity [kəm'plɛksətɪ]

n. 複雜(性),複雜的事物,複雜性

I was confused at the complexity of the problem.

我對這個問題的複雜性感到困惑。

4967

brochure [bro'ʃʊr]

n. 小冊子

We carry a brochure with us when we travel.

旅遊時我們攜帶小冊子。

4968

chronic ['krɑnɪk]

adj. 慢性的,延續很長的

The man has a chronic heart disease.

這個人有慢性心臟病。

4969
socialism [ˈsoʃəlˌɪzəm]

n. 社會主義

Socialism means public ownership of the country.

社會主義指社會共同擁有國家。

4970
alleviate [əˈlivɪˌet]

vt. 使(痛苦等)易於忍受,減輕

There will be a new medicine to alleviate the symptoms of stomachache. 將會有減輕胃痛症狀的新藥物出現。

4971
socialist [ˈsoʃəlɪst]

adj. 社會主義的 n. 社會主義者

Socialists are people that believe in socialism.

社會主義者是指相信社會主義的人。

4972
anticipation [ænˌtɪsəˈpeʃən]

n. 預期,預料

She waited in eager anticipation for her father.

她急切的期待她爸爸的出現。

4973
absurd [əbˈsɝd]

adj. 荒謬的,可笑的

It's an absurd idea.

這是一個荒謬的主意。

4974
avert [əˈvɝt]

v. 避開,移開

He averted a car accident.

他避開了一場車禍。

4975
acute [əˈkjut]

adj. 敏銳的,[醫]急性的,劇烈

I have an acute pain in my back.

我有劇烈的背痛。

4976
anonymous [əˈnɑnəməs]

adj. 匿名的

I received an anonymous phone call yeasterday.

我昨天接到一通匿名的電話。

4977
apt [æpt]

adj. 易於⋯的,有⋯傾向的,靈敏的,靈巧的,適當的,切題的,敏捷,傾向是

The staff are apt to have a day off on Mondays.

員工傾向於星期一放假。

4978
administrator [ədˈmɪnəˌstretɚ]

n. 管理人,行政官

He is a good administrator.

他是很好的管理者。

4979
blunder [ˈblʌndɚ]

v. 跌跌撞撞地走,犯大錯,做錯 n. 大錯,失誤

The company had blundered in its handling of the matter. 公司在處理這件事上犯了錯。

4980 cavalry [ˈkævl̩rɪ]

n. 騎兵

The Emperor led the cavalry and charge against enemies. 帝王帶著一隊騎兵對抗敵人。

4981 allocate [ˈæləˌket]

vt. 分派,分配

You should allocate candy to each child.
你應該分糖果給每位小孩。

4982 ambiguous [æmˈbɪgjuəs]

adj. 曖昧的,不明確的

The sentence is ambiguous.
這個句子意思不明確。

4983 compensation [ˌkɑmpənˈseʃən]

n. 補償,賠償

She received compensation from the company for her damage. 她收到公司寄來的賠償費。

4984 assess [əˈsɛs]

vt. 估定,評定

You need to assess a patient's needs.
你需要評估病人的需求。

4985 chaos [ˈkeɑs]

n. 混亂,混沌(宇宙未形成前的情形)

The room was in chaos.
房間很亂。

4986 alliance [əˈlaɪəns] n. 聯盟,聯合

People are in alliance with local charities, trying to help the children.
人們為了幫助小朋友跟當地慈善機關合作。

4987 blunt [blʌnt]

adj. 鈍的

I can't write with a blunt pencil.
我無法用鈍的鉛筆寫字。

4988 bleak [blik]

adj. 寒冷的,陰冷的,荒涼的,淒涼的,黯淡的

The future looks bleak.
未來看起來很悽涼。

4989 coherent [koˈhɪrənt]

adj. 黏在一起的,一致的,連貫的

This is a coherent composition.
這是一篇有連貫性的文章。

4990 clarity [ˈklærətɪ]

n. 清楚,透明

He has clarity of thought.
他有清楚的思緒。

4991 biological [baɪəˈlɑdʒɪkl̩]

adj. 生物學的

He is the child's biological father.
他是這小孩的生父。

4992

complement [ˈkɑmpləˌmɛnt]

n. 補足物,[文法]補語,[數]餘角,互補色 vt. 補助,補足

The complement or opposite color of red is green.
紅色的互補色是綠色。

4993

accordingly [əˈkɔrdɪŋlɪ]

adv. 因此,從而

Katherine still loves him and takes care of him
accordingly. 凱薩琳仍然愛著他,因此照顧他。

4994

boost [bust]

v. 推進

A great cheer boosted the team's confidence.
歡呼聲鼓舞了團隊的士氣。

4995

antibody [ˈæntɪˌbɑdɪ]

n. 抗體

It was an antibody that protected the immune system
from the virus's attack.

抗體保護了免疫系統免受病毒攻擊。

4996

certify [ˈsɝtəˌfaɪ]

vt. 證明,證實,發證書(或執照)給

The police certified that he had been killed in the
accident. 警方證實他在車禍中喪生。

4997

anticipate [ænˈtɪsəˌpet]

vt. 預期,期望,過早使用,先人一著,佔先

v. 預訂,預見,可以預料

We anticipate that we can make lots of money.

我們期待能賺很多錢。

4998

captive [ˈkæptɪv]

n. 俘虜,被美色或愛情迷住的人 adj. 被俘的,被迷住的

Those captives tried to escape last Friday.

那些俘虜試圖在上週五逃走。

4999

amplify [ˈæmpləˌfaɪ]

vt. 放大,增強 v. 擴大

Would you like to amplify that statement?
你可以擴大那個論點嗎?

5000

collide [kəˈlaɪd]

vi. 碰撞,抵觸

A car and a truck collided on the highway.
一輛車子跟卡車在高速公路上碰撞。

5001

coincide [ˈkɔɪnˌsaɪd]

vi. 一致,符合

His meeting coincided with his vacation.
他的會議跟他的假期撞期。

5002

analogy [ə'næləZdʒɪ]

n. 類似,類推

There is no analogy between China and those countries.
中國和那些國家並無相似之處。

5003

compensate ['kɑmpənˌset]

v. 償還,補償,付報酬

Her effort compensates for her lack of experience.
她的努力彌補了她的經驗不足。

5004

accounting [ə'kaʊntɪŋ]

n. 會計學

His major is accounting.
他主修會計。

5005

compile [kəm'paɪl]

vt. 編譯,編輯,彙編

The document was compiled by the secretary.
祕書編輯了文件。

5006

Antarctic [æn'tɑrktɪk]

adj. 南極的,南極區的 n. 南極區,南極圈

The Antarctic is the coldest place in the world.
南極是世上最冷的地方。

5007

articulate [ɑr'tɪkjəlet]

adj. 有關節的,發音清晰的

vt. 用關節連接,接合,清晰明白地說

He can articulate English words.

他能很清楚地說英文。

5008

betray [bɪ'tre]

vt. 背叛,出賣,對…不忠,洩漏,透露,(無意中)暴露,
顯示,把…引入歧途

He betrays his company for money.

他因為錢背叛了他的公司。

5009

component [kəm'ponənt]

n. 成分 adj. 組成的,構成的

Exercise is one of the components of a healthy life.
運動是健康生活的一部分。

5010

aviation [ˌevɪ'eʃən]

n. 飛行,航空,航空學,航空術

NASA is in the aviation industry.
NASA 是在航太工業內。

5011

capsule ['kæpsl̩]

n. 膠囊,太空艙

The medicine can be taken in a capsule form.
這種藥可以膠囊的形式服用。

5012
assert [ə'sɜt]

v. 斷言,聲稱

He asserted that this thing will happen.
他聲稱這件事將會發生。

5013
Arctic ['ɑrktɪk]

adj. 北極的,北極區的　n. 北極,北極圈

TV news showed the view of Arctic.
電視新聞播放北極的景色。

5014
bias ['baɪəs]

n. 偏見,偏愛,斜線　vt. 使存偏見

He showed political bias in the press conference.
他在記者會上有政治偏見。

5015
brisk [brɪsk]

adj. 敏銳的,凜冽的,輕快的,活潑的　vt. 使活潑

He walks at a brisk walking pace.
他走路時步伐輕快。

5016
compatible [kəm'pætəbl̩]

adj. 諧調的,一致的,相容的

Their idea is compatible with yours.
他們的想法跟你一致。

5017
oppress [ə'prɛs]

vt. 壓迫,壓抑

The atmosphere in her family oppressed her.
家庭的氣氛使她感到壓迫。

5018
extinguish [ɪk'stɪŋgwɪʃ]

vt. 熄滅,消滅,壓制,使黯然失色,償清

Before you enter the office, please extinguish your cigarette. 進辦公室以前,請熄滅你的香菸。

5019
stern [stɜn]

adj. 嚴厲的,苛刻的　n. 船尾

Her voice is stern and we are afraid of her.
她的語氣很嚴苛,我們都怕她。

5020
fragile ['frædʒəl]

adj. 易碎的,脆的

Be careful with that fragile vase.
請小心那個易碎的花瓶。

5021
reliability [rɪˌlaɪə'bɪlətɪ]

n. 可靠性

His words are of high reliability.
他的話是高度可靠的。

5022
obscure [əb'skjʊr] [-'skɪʊr]

adj. 暗的,朦朧的,模糊的,晦澀的　vt. 使暗,使不明顯

The reason of his death still remains obscure.
關於他的死因仍然是模糊不清的。

5023
manifest ['mænəˌfɛst]

adj. 顯然的,明白的,清楚的　n. 載貨單,旅客名單

vt. 表明,證明

His tension was manifested in the fight with his coworkers.

他的緊張情緒在跟他同事吵架中看的出來。

Your suggestions have been incorporated in the plan.

你的建議已經被納入這個計畫裡。

5024

dedicate ['dɛdə,ket]

vt. 獻(身),致力,題獻(一部著作給某人)

She dedicates herself to charity.

她致力於慈善事業。

5025

detain [dɪ'ten]

v. 拘留,留住,阻止

He was detained in Washington because of the heavy rain. 因為大雨,他被留在華盛頓。

5026

conception [kən'sɛpʃən]

n. 觀念,概念

They have no conception of how a child grows.

他們對於小孩成長沒有概念。

5027

statistical [stə'tɪstɪkl]

adj. 統計的,統計學的

The research needs some statistical evidence.

這個研究需要統計證據。

5028

incorporate [ɪn'kɔrpərɪt]

adj. 納入的,合併的,結社的,一體化的

vt. [律]結社,使成為法人組織

5029

conspicuous [kən'spɪkjuəs]

adj. 顯著的

I felt very conspicuous in my red coat.

我的紅色外套讓我覺得很顯目。

5030

exceedingly [ɪk'sidɪŋlɪ]

adv. 非常地,極度地

You are exceedingly friendly.

你非常地友善。

5031

aggression [ə'grɛʃən] n. 進攻,侵略

The research shows that some TV programes may cause aggression in children.

研究顯示有些電視節目會導致兒童有侵略傾向。

5032

heir [ɛr]

n. 繼承人,後嗣

The man is the heir to the throne.

這個人是王位繼承人。

5033

locomotive [,lokə'motɪv]

n. 機車,火車頭 adj. 運動的

Steam locomotives are very rare now.

蒸氣火車現在很少見。

5034

dismay [dɪs'me]

n. 沮喪,驚慌 v. 使沮喪,使驚慌

To her dismay, she flunked the test.

讓她失望的是她考試不及格。

5035

pneumonia [nju'monjə]

n. [醫]肺炎

She stayed in a hospital, suffering from pneumonia.

因為罹患肺炎,她待在醫院。

5036

fossil ['fɑsl]

n. 化石,僵化的事物 adj. 化石的,陳腐的,守舊的

I saw fossils of early reptiles in the museum.

我在博物館看到早期爬蟲類的化石。

5037

resemblance [rɪ'zɛmbləns]

n. 相似,相貌相似,相似點,相似程度,相似物,畫像,
　　肖像,類同之處

Tina bears a resemblance to her mother.

蒂娜跟她母親相似。

5038

despise [dɪ'spaɪz]

v. 輕視

She despised her classmates.

她輕視同學。

5039

royalty ['rɔɪəltɪ]

n. 皇室,王權

The meeting was attended by royalty.

皇室出席這個會議。

5040

eclipse [ɪ'klɪps] n. 食,日蝕,月蝕,蒙蔽,衰落

vt. 引起日蝕,引起月蝕,超越,使黯然失色

I saw an eclipse of the sun on TV.

我在電視上看到日蝕。

5041

fling [flɪŋ]

n. 投,擲,猛衝,暴躁的行動,急衝,嘲弄,譏笑
vi. 猛衝,直衝,急行

He flung the ring into the river. 他將戒指丟進河裡。

5042

shutter ['ʃʌtɚ]

n. 關閉者,百葉窗,快門

vt. 關上,裝以遮門,以百葉窗遮閉

Mary opened the shutters and gazed at the mountains

far away.

瑪麗打開百葉窗凝視遠處的山景。

5043

mourn [morn]

v. 哀悼

He was mourning his mother's death.

他在哀悼他母親的過世。

5044

drawback ['drɔ,bæk]

n. 缺點,障礙,退還的關稅,退稅(指進口貨物再出口時退還其進口時的關稅)

The main drawback to the product is that it can't be opened easily.

這項產品的主要缺點是它無法容易地被打開。

5045

applicable ['æplɪkəbḷ]

adj. 可適用的,可應用的

The new remedy had widely applicable methods to the disease. 新的治療法對於這項疾病有很多可應用的方法。

5046

conquest ['kɑŋkwɛst]

n. 征服 n. 戰利品

The government is proud of the conquest of inflation. 政府對於戰勝了通貨膨脹感到滿意。

5047

reptile ['rɛptḷ]

n. 爬蟲動物,卑鄙的人 adj. 爬行的,爬蟲類的,卑鄙的

Snakes and crocodiles are reptiles. 蛇跟鱷魚都是爬蟲類。

5048

qualitative ['kwɑlə,tetɪv]

adj. 性質上的,定性的

I am conducting a qualitative research. 我正在做質化研究。

5049

extravagant [ɪk'strævəgənt]

adj. 奢侈的,浪費的,過分的,放縱的

John has an extravagant lifestyle.

約翰有奢侈的生活型態。

5050

sideways ['saɪd,wez]

adv. 向一旁,向側面地 adj. 一旁的,向側面的

She sat sideways on the chair and fell down. 她斜坐在椅子上,然後從椅子上掉下來。

5051

diffuse [dɪ'fjus] v. 散播,傳播,漫射,擴散,

(使)慢慢混合 adj. 散開的,彌漫的

The pollutants diffuse into the air. 汙染物擴散在空氣裡。

5052

certainty ['sɜtṇtɪ]

n. 確定,確實的事情

She knew with absolute certainty that she couldn't go out. 她確定她無法出去。

5053

consolidate [kən'sɑlə,det]

v. 鞏固

The manager has consolidated his position as a leader. 經理已經鞏固他領導者的地位。

5054

mobilize ['mobḷ,aɪz]

v. 動員

The party launched a campaign to mobilize support for the strike. 這個政黨發動員支持罷工的行動。

5055
expire [ɪk'spaɪr]

v. 期滿,終止,呼氣,斷氣,屆滿

The librarian informed that loan of my book will expire next week. 圖書館員通知我的書下星期到期。

5056
grease [gris]

n. 油脂,賄賂 vt. 塗脂於,(俗)賄賂

Her hands were covered with oil and grease after eating roast chicken. 她的手在吃完烤雞後,沾滿了油脂。

5057
necessitate [nə'sɛsə,tet]

v. 成為必要

Suffient money necessitates a plan to have a baby. 想養育一個孩子,充足的錢是必要的。

5058
duplicate ['djuplə,ket]

adj. 複製的,副的,雙重的,兩倍的,完全相同

n. 複製品,副本

The video can't be duplicated.

這個錄影帶不能被拷貝。

5059
directory [də'rɛktərɪ]

n. 姓名地址錄,目錄

I can find his phone number in the telephone directory. 我可以在電話冊上發現他的電話號碼。

5060
corrode [kə'rod]

v. 使腐蝕,侵蝕

Acidic water will corrode the metal. 酸水會腐蝕金屬。

5061
boom ['bum]

n. 繁榮,隆隆聲 v. 發隆隆聲,興隆,大肆宣傳

There is a sudden boom in the stock market. 股票市場突然大漲。

5062
eject [ɪ'dʒɛkt]

vt. 逐出,攆出,驅逐,噴射 n. 推斷的事物

She was ejected from her family. 她被家人逐出。

5063
confer [kən'fɜ]

vt. 授予(稱號,學位等),贈與,把…贈與,協定

v. 協商,交換意見

He wanted to confer with his colleagues before his boss came back.

他想在他老闆回來以前跟他同事討論。

5064
mutton ['mʌtn̩]

n. 羊肉,(謔)綿羊

I like to eat mutton. 我喜歡吃羊肉。

5065

formulate [ˈfɔrmjəˌlet]

vt. 用公式表示,明確地表達,作簡潔陳述 v. 闡明

She has difficulty formulating her ideas.

她表達意見有困難。

5066

quarterly [ˈkwɔrtəˌlɪ]

n. 季刊 adj. 一年四次的,每季的

You have to pay the rent quarterly.

你必須每季付房租。

5067

shipment [ˈʃɪpmənt]

n. 裝船,出貨

The grain is ready for shipment.

這些穀類是要出貨的。

5068

shriek [ˈʃrik]

v. 尖聲叫喊,聳人聽聞地報導,尖聲喊叫
n. 尖叫,尖聲,尖聲喊叫

He shrieked in anger. 他生氣的尖叫。

5069

soluble [ˈsɑljəbl]

adj. 可溶的,可溶解的

The medicine does not seem soluble.

這些藥似乎不能溶解。

5070

daring [ˈdɛrɪŋ]

adj. 大膽的,勇敢的,魯莽的,前衛的 n. 大膽,勇敢,魯莽

There are daring exhibitions in the gallery.

美術館有前衛的展覽。

5071

paralyze [ˈpærəˌlaɪz]

vt. 使癱瘓,使麻痺

Her body was partly paralyzed in the car accident.

她的身體在車禍中部分癱瘓。

5072

eloquent [ˈɛləkwənt]

adj. 雄辯的,有口才的,動人的

He delivers an eloquent speech in public.

他在公開場合發表強而有力的演說。

5073

hinge [hɪndʒ]

n. (門,蓋等的)鉸鏈,樞鈕,關鍵 v. 裝以鉸鏈,依⋯而轉移

The hinge of the door is broken.

門鉸鏈壞了。

5074

narrate [næˈret]

v. 敘述,講述,作解說,講故事

The film was narrated by David.

這個電影是由大衛解說。

5075

crossing [ˈkrɔsɪŋ]

n. 十字路口,交叉點

Turn left at the crossing nearby.

在附近的十字路口左轉。

5076

smuggle [ˈsmʌgl̩]

n. 走私,偷帶 v. 走私

The drugs were smuggled into the USA.

毒品被走私到美國。

5077 intricate [ˈɪntrəkɪt]

adj. 複雜的,錯綜的,難以理解的

I like the intricate patterns on the scarf.

我喜歡這條圍巾上複雜的圖案。

5078 contradict [ˌkɑntrəˈdɪkt]

vt. 同…矛盾,同…抵觸

Your behavior flatly contradicts your claims.

你的行為很明顯跟你說的互相矛盾。

5079 proclaim [proˈklem]

vt. 宣布,聲明,顯示,顯露

Protesters proclaimed that the man was innocent.

抗議者宣稱這個人是無辜的。

5080 elite [eˈlit]

n. (法)[集合名詞]精華,精銳,精英

The team was made up of elites.

這個團隊由精英們組成。

5081 distract [dɪˈstrækt]

v. 轉移

Don't distract attention from the teacher in class.

上課不要分心。

5082 periodical [pɪrɪˈɑdɪkl]

adj. 周期的,定期的 n. 期刊,雜誌

You should read this periodical.

你應該閱讀這本期刊。

5083 equator [ɪˈkwetɚ]

n. 赤道,赤道似的圓圈

The country is twenty degrees north of the equator.

這個國家位於赤道以北二十度。

5084 propeller [prəˈpɛlɚ]

n. 推進者,推進物,尤指輪船,飛機上的螺旋推進器

Grant hit the start button and the propeller revolved afterward. 格蘭按下開始鍵之後螺旋運轉了。

5085 deficient [dɪˈfɪʃənt]

adj. 缺乏的,不足的,不完善的

You are deficient in vitamin C and you need to eat more fruit. 你缺維他命 C,所以你需要吃更多水果。

5086 perish [ˈpɛrɪʃ]

vi. 毀滅,死亡,腐爛,枯萎 vt. 毀壞,使麻木

Hundreds of people perished when the car accident happened. 這車禍造成上百人死亡。

5087 friction [ˈfrɪkʃən]

n. 摩擦,摩擦力

There is friction between every object.

任何物體間都有摩擦力。

5088 assimilate [əˈsɪmlˌet]

v. 吸收

Immigrants need time to assimilate into the community.

移民者需要時間融入新社區。

5089

fuse [fjuz]

n. 保險絲,熔絲　v. 熔合

Please teach me how to change a fuse.
請教我如何換保險絲。

5090

disastrous [dɪz'æstrəs]

adj. 損失慘重的,悲傷的

Her first marriage is disastrous.
她第一個婚姻是多災多難的。

5091

dispatch [dɪ'spætʃ]

vt. 分派,派遣　n. 派遣,急件

I was dispatched to mail a letter.
我被派遣去寄信。

5092

category ['kætə,gorɪ]

n. 種類,別,[邏]範疇

There are five categories of vegetable here.
這裡有五種蔬菜。

5093

reclaim [rɪ'klem] vt. 要求歸還,收回,開墾

Please go to the police station to reclaim your wallet within three days.
請在三天內去警察局拿回你的皮夾。

5094

incur [ɪn'kɜ]

v. 招致

If you incur a debt, you have to pay money back.
如果你欠債就必須要還錢。

5095

quart ['kwɔrt]

n. 夸脫(容量單位)

He drinks a quart of milk.
他喝一夸脫的牛奶。

5096

gaseous ['gæsɪəs]

adj. 氣體的,氣態的

In the gaseous state, CO_2 molecules move at great speeds. 二氧化碳的分子在氣狀時高速移動。

5097

merchandise ['mɝtʃən,daɪz]

n. 商品,貨物

There is a wide selection of merchandise in the department store. 百貨公司有很多商品。

5098

repay [rɪ'pe]

v. 償還,報答,報復

I will repay what I owe you.
我會償還我欠你的。

5099

overwhelm [,ovɚ'hwɛlm]

vt. 淹沒,覆沒,受打擊,制服,壓倒

I am overwhelmed by stress.
我被壓力淹沒。

5100

affirm [ə'fɝm]

v. 斷言,確認,肯定

The teacher affirmed that he will be the champion next year. 老師斷言他明年會成為冠軍。

5101

slum [slʌm]

n. 貧民窟 vi. 訪問貧民區

These children came from a slum in India.

這群小孩來自印度貧民窟。

5102

replacement [rɪˈplesmənt]

n. 歸還,重定,交換,代替者,補充兵員,置換,移位

The boss needs a replacement for the position.

老闆需要這個職位的代替者。

5103

motorway [ˈmotɚˌwe]

n. 汽車高速公路

The motorway is full of cars.

高速公路上充滿車子。

5104

dart [dɑrt]

n. 標槍,鏢,(昆蟲的)刺,飛快的動作 v. 飛奔,投擲

He plays darts in British pubs everyday.

他每天在英國酒吧玩飛鏢。

5105

differentiate [ˌdɪfəˈrɛnʃɪˌet]

v. 區別,區分

It's hard to differentiate the twins.

分辨這一對雙胞胎是很難的。

5106

spontaneous [spɑnˈtenɪəs]

adj. 自發的,自然產生的

The crowd gave a spontaneous applause.

群眾自動自發的鼓掌。

5107

hasten [ˈhesn̩]

v. 催促,趕緊,促進,加速

I hastened to hand in my English assignment.

我趕著繳交我的英文作業。

5108

plaster [ˈplæstɚ]

n. 石膏,灰泥,膏藥,橡皮膏

vt. 塗以灰泥,敷以膏藥,減輕,黏貼,重創

She broke her legs yesterday, and they are in plaster.

她摔斷了腿,現在她的腳上了石膏。

5109

foremost [ˈforˌmost]

adj. (位置或時間)最先的,最初的,最重要的

adv. 首要地,首先

Educational concerns are foremost on parents' mind.

教育問題是家長最關心的。

5110

activate [ˈæktəˌvet]

vt. 刺激,使活動 vi. 有活力

This month's growth is activated by dramatic rises in consumption. 巨大的消費加速了這個月的成長。

5111

migrate ['maɪgret]

vi. 移動,移往,移植,隨季節而移居,(鳥類的)遷徙

vt. 使移居,使移植

Fewer and fewer swallows migrate south in winter nowadays.

現在愈來愈少的燕子在冬季遷徙到南方。

5112

displease [dɪs'pliz]

v. 使不快,使(人)生氣,冒犯,惹怒

He looked extremely displeased, and tended to lose his temper soon. 他看起來很不高興而且快生氣了。

5113

skeleton ['skɛlətn̩]

n. (動物之)骨架,骨骼,基幹,綱要,萬能鑰匙

The human skeleton consists of 206 bones.
人類的骨骼包含兩百零六根骨頭。

5114

notorious [no'torɪəs]

adj. 聲名狼籍的

He is a notorious computer hacker.
他是惡名昭彰的電腦駭客。

5115

breakdown ['brek,daʊn]

n. 崩潰,衰弱,細目分類

Family breakdown can lead to mental problems in children. 家庭破碎會導致小孩的心理問題。

5116

disable [dɪs'ebl̩]

v. 使殘廢,使失去能力,喪失能力

He was disabled in an accident.
他在一場事故中變成殘障。

5117

scrap [skræp]

n. 小片,廢料,剪下來的圖片,文章,殘餘物,廢料,打架

vt. 扔棄,敲碎,拆毀

Please write your number on a scrap of paper.

請在這一小張紙上寫下你的號碼。

5118

integral ['ɪntəgrəl]

adj. 完整的,整體的,[數學]積分的,構成整體所需要的

n. [數學]積分,完整,部分

Water is an integral part of our lives.

水是我們生活不可或缺的一部分。

5119

refute [rɪ'fjut]

vt. 駁倒,反駁

Some scientists refute Darwin's theories.
有些科學家反駁達爾文的理論。

5120

revolve [rɪ'vɑlv]

v. (使)旋轉,考慮,迴圈出現

The wheel revolved fast.

輪胎快速的旋轉。

5121

slit [slɪt]

vt. 切開,撕裂 n. 裂縫,狹長切口

She slits an envelope open with a knife.

她用拆信刀切開信封封口。

5122

porch ['pɔrtʃ]

n. 門廊,走廊

He sat on the porch, crying sadly.

他坐在門廊傷心地哭。

5123

enlighten [ɪn'laɪtn]

vt. 啟發,啟蒙,教導,授予…知識,開導,(古)照耀

I was enlightened by the speech.

我被這場演講啟發了。

5124

precede [pri'sid]

v. 領先(於),在…之前,先於

Lunch will be preceded by an English class.

午餐在英文課之後。

5125

radiate ['redɪˌet]

vt. 放射,輻射,傳播,廣播 adj. 有射線的,輻射狀的

The fire radiated and glowed.

火散發輻射與光。

5126

impetus ['ɪmpətəs]

n. 推動力,促進

Your support will give an impetus to my project.

你的支持將推動我的計畫。

5127

commodity [kə'mɑdətɪ]

n. 日用品

Commodity prices are stable.

生活用品的價格很穩定。

5128

sponge [spʌndʒ]

n. 海綿,海綿體 v. 用海綿等洗滌,揩拭,擦拭或清除,用海綿吸收(液體),(俗)依賴某人生活

He uses a bath sponge when he takes a bath.

他使用海綿球洗澡。

5129

perpetual [pə'pɛtʃʊəl]

adj. 永久的

I like this little girl with a perpetual smile.

我喜歡這個笑口常開的女生。

5130

condemn [kən'dɛm]

vt. 判刑,處刑,聲討,譴責

He was condemned to death.

他被判死刑。

5131

doom [dum]

n. 厄運,毀滅,死亡,世末日 v. 註定,判決

The plan is all doomed to fail in the end.

這個計畫註定要失敗。

5132

deteriorate [dɪ'tɪrɪə,ret]

v. (使)惡化

Ethel's toothache has deteriorated, so he went to a dentist. 艾得的牙痛惡化,所以他去看醫生。

5133

sly [slaɪ]

adj. 狡猾的

He looked at me with a sly smile.

他看著我,狡猾地笑著。

5134

advocate ['ædvə,ket]

n. 提倡者,鼓吹者 vt. 提倡,鼓吹

The report advocated that we should avoid going to public places. 這個報導鼓吹我們避免去公共場所。

5135

accordance [ə'kɔrdn̩s]

n. 一致,和諧

The system may be used in accordance with my computer. 這個系統可能可以跟我的電腦相符。

5136

distort [dɪs'tɔrt]

vt. 弄歪(嘴臉等),扭曲,歪曲(真理,事實等),誤報

Reporters often distort the truth.

記者通常扭曲事實。

5137

remainder [rɪ'mendɚ]

n. 殘餘,剩餘物,其他的人,[數]餘數

adj. 剩餘的,出售剩書的

I kept some of his pictures and gave away the remainder.

我保留了一些他的照片,並送走了剩下的。

5138

affiliate [ə'fɪlɪet]

v. (使…)加入,接受為會員,附屬

The hospital is affiliated with the school.

這家醫院附屬於學校之下。

5139

scent [sɛnt]

n. 氣味,香味,香水,線索,嗅覺,臭跡

vt. 聞出,嗅,發覺,循著遺臭追蹤,使充滿氣味

I like yellow roses with a lovely scent.

我喜歡芬芳的黃色玫瑰。

5140

communism ['kɑmjʊ,nɪzəm]

n. 共產主義

The collapse of communism in some countries occurred. 有些共產主義的國家已經垮掉了。

5141

fellowship [ˈfɛloˌʃɪp]

n. 夥伴關係,交情,團體,獎學金,友誼

The fellowship is for graduates only.

這個獎學金只提供給研究生。

5142

rectify [ˈrɛktəˌfaɪ]

vt. 矯正,調整,[化]精餾

We must take steps to rectify the situation before the damage. 我們必須在受到損害之前矯正目前情況。

5143

epoch [ˈɛpək]

n. 新紀元,時代,時期,時間上的一點,[地質]世

The president's resignation marked the end of an epoch.

這位總統辭職是一個時代的結束。

5144

odds [ɑdz]

n. 可能的機會,成敗的可能性,優勢,不均,不平等,差別

The odds are that he will resigned from the job soon.

有可能他將會辭職。

5145

beloved [bɪˈlʌvɪd]

adj. 心愛的　n. 所愛的人,愛人

He never forgets his beloved ex-wife.

他從未忘記他摯愛的前妻。

5146

essence [ˈɛsn̩s]

n. 基本,[哲]本質,香精

The essence of roses is expensive.

玫瑰香精十分昂貴。

5147

porcelain [ˈpɔrslɪn]

n. 瓷器,瓷

He bought a porcelain.

他買了一個瓷器。

5148

relic [ˈrɛlɪk]

n. 遺物,遺跡,廢墟,紀念物

The vases are relics from the Ming Dynasty.

這些花瓶是明朝的遺跡。

5149

reconcile [ˈrɛkənˌsaɪl]

vt. 使和解,使和諧,使順從

Finally Jonah and his son were reconciled.

最後瓊納跟他兒子和解。

5150

latent [ˈletn̩t]

adj. 潛在的,潛伏的,隱藏的　n. 隱約的指印

The virus remains latent in public.

病毒潛伏在公共場所。

S2 高中二年級
T2 技職學院二年級　編號 5151～5413

5151

prey [pre]

n. 被掠食者,犧牲者,掠食　vi. 捕食,掠奪,折磨

The tiger often stalk its prey for hours before hunting it.

老虎在獵殺前通常悄悄貼近獵物數小時。

5152 patent ['petṇt] n. 專利權,執照,專利品

adj. 特許的,專利的,顯著的,明白的,新奇的

He applied for a patent for the product.

他為產品申請專利。

5153 simulate ['sɪmjə,let]

vt. 類比,模仿,假裝,冒充

Role-playing simulates real-life situations.

角色扮演模仿真實情境。

5154 compulsory [kəm'pʌlsərɪ]

adj. 必需做的,必修的,被強迫的,被強制的,義務的

Students have 9 years of compulsory education.

學生有九年義務教育。

5155 proposition [,prɑpə'zɪʃən]

n. 主張,建議,陳述,命題

I will put a business proposition to you tomorrow.

明天我將會給你生意上的建議。

5156 parameter [pə'ræmətə]

n. 參數,參量,(口)起限定作用的因素

The researchers set the parameters of the experiment.

研究者為這個實驗設立參數。

5157 invalid ['ɪnvəlɪd]

n. 病人,殘廢者 adj. 有病的,殘廢的

She is an invalid person and her family takes care of her.

她是一位殘障人士,她的家人照顧她。

5158 respectable [rɪ'spɛktəbḷ]

adj. 可敬的,有名望的,高尚的,值得尊敬的

He is a respectable married man.

他是有名望的已婚男子。

5159 junction ['dʒʌŋkʃən]

n. 連接,接合,交叉點,匯合處

This is the junction of Greenland Road and Mill Street.

這是格林蘭路跟米勒路的交接處。

5160 conform [kən'fɔrm]

vt. 使一致,使遵守,使順從 adj. 一致的,順從的

He conforms to the local customs when he travels abroad. 當他旅遊海外時須遵守當地規定。

5161 sociology [,soʃɪ'ɑlədʒɪ]

n. 社會學

I am interested in sociology.

我對社會學有興趣。

5162 intermittent [,ɪntə'mɪtṇt]

adj. 間歇的,斷斷續續的

I noted intermittent spelling errors in her essay.

我在她的文章中發現斷斷續續的拼字錯誤。

5163 sensation [sɛn'seʃən]

n. 感覺,感情,感動,聳人聽聞的

Caroline had the sensation that she would be fired.

卡洛琳有感覺她會被開除。

5164
discern [dɪ'zɜn]

v. 目睹,認識,洞悉,辨別,看清楚

We could just discern a town far away.

我們可以看到遠處的城鎮。

5165
consent [kən'sɛnt]

n. 同意,贊成 vi. 同意

He took my pen without my consent.

沒有我的許可,他拿走我的筆。

5166
shear [ʃɪr]

v. 修剪

Her long fair hair should be shorn.

她該修剪頭髮。

5167
oar [or]

n. 槳,櫓

Mary and Jon took one oar each and rowed to the shore.

瑪莉跟強划槳到岸邊。

5168
expel [ɪk'spɛl]

v. 驅逐,開除,排出,發射

Two girls were expelled from school for cheating in the exam. 兩個女生因為作弊被學校開除。

5169
explicit ['ɛksplɪsɪt]

adj. 外在的,清楚的,直率的,(租金等)直接付款的

He gave me a very explicit direction to get there.

他給我明確的指示到那邊。

5170
confession [kən'fɛʃən]

n. 供認,承認,招供

She made a full confession for theft.

她坦承犯下竊盜案。

5171
rebellion [rɪ'bɛljən]

n. 謀反,叛亂,反抗,不服從

The country rose in rebellion against the government.

該國反對政府的聲浪高漲。

5172
domain [do'men]

n. 領土,領地,(活動,學問等的)範圍,領域

This problem is within the domain of science.

這個問題在自然科學領域。

5173
cubic ['kjubɪk]

adj. 立方體的,立方的

How many cubic meters is the box?

這個盒子有多少立方公尺?

5174
moss [mɔs]

n. 苔,蘚

The walls were covered with moss.

這個牆壁長滿了苔。

5175
irritate ['ɪrə,tet]

vt. 激怒,使急躁 v. 刺激

He irritated me and I lost my temper.

他激怒我而我生氣了。

5176
kindle ['kɪndl̩]
vt. 點燃,使著火,引起,照亮 vi. 著火,煽動,激起,發亮
We kindled a fire.
我們點燃了火。

5177
henceforth [ˌhɛns'forθ]
adv. 自此以後,今後
Henceforth, all staff need to show their ID cards before entering his office.
自此以後,全部員工進入他的辦公室前需出示身分證。

5178
notwithstanding [ˌnɑtwɪθ'stændɪŋ]
prep. 雖然,儘管 conj. 雖然,儘管
Fame and fortune notwithstanding, Donna helps poor children. 儘管她擁有財富跟名聲,多娜幫助窮小孩。

5179
novelty ['nɑvl̩tɪ]
n. 新穎,新奇,新鮮,新奇的事物
He has the novelty of ideas.
他有新奇的點子。

5180
aerial ['ɛrɪəl]
adj. 航空的,生活在空氣中的,空氣的,高聳的 n. 天線
Bees have aerial dances to indicate where to find nectar.
蜜蜂在空中飛舞指示蜜的位置。

5181
counterpart ['kaʊntɚ,pɑrt]
n. 副本,極相似的人或物,配對物
Their secretary of state is the counterpart of our foreign minister. 他們的國務卿相當於我們的外交部長。

5182
disregard [ˌdɪsrɪ'gɑrd]
v. 不理漠視 n. 漠視,忽視
Mark disregarded my advice.
馬克漠視我的意見。

5183
flaw [flɔ]
n. 缺點,裂紋,瑕疵,一陣狂風 vi. 生裂縫,變的有缺陷
There is a flaw in the software.
這個軟體有缺點。

5184
embody [ɪm'bɑdɪ]
vt. 具體表達,使具體化,包含,收錄
She embodies everything I admire in a mother.
她擁有我所景仰的母親特質。

5185
diagnose ['daɪəgnoz]
v. 診斷
She was diagnosed with cancer.
她被診斷出癌症。

5186
advisable [əd'vaɪzəbl̩]
adj. 可取的,明智的
It is advisable to add your autobiography in your resume. 將自傳加入履歷內是明智之舉。

5187
assumption [əˈsʌmpʃən]

n. 假定,設想,擔任,承當,假裝,作態

A lot of people make the assumption that ghosts exist.
很多人假設鬼是存在的。

5188
oath [oθ]

n. 誓言,宣誓,詛咒

He swears an oath of loyalty to his wife.
他對他的太太宣示忠誠。

5189
stability [stəˈbɪlətɪ]

n. 穩定性

Politics may influence the economic and social stability.
政治會影響經濟跟社會的穩定性。

5190
designate [ˈdɛzɪɡ,net]

vt. 指明,指出,任命,指派 v. 指定,指派

She has been designated to represent her company.
她被指派代表她的公司。

5191
probability [,prɑbəˈbɪlətɪ]

n. 可能性,或然性,概率

There's a high probability that we change different jobs in life. 我們一生會換不同工作的機率很高。

5192
reap [rip]

v. 收割,收穫

You reap what you sow.
要怎麼收穫先怎麼栽。

5193
encyclopedia [ɪn,saɪkləˈpidɪə]

n. 百科全書

I have reference books such as a dictionary and an encyclopedia.

我有一些參考書,例如字典跟百科全書。

5194
profound [prəˈfaʊnd]

adj. 深刻的,意義深遠的,淵博的,造詣深的

TV has a profound impact on the developing child.
電視對發展中的兒童有很深的影響。

5195
offspring [ˈɔf,sprɪŋ]

n. (單複數同形)兒女,子孫,後代,產物

The kangaroo takes care of its offspring.
袋鼠照顧牠的後代。

5196
cordial [ˈkɔrdʒəl]

n. 果汁,甜香酒 adj. 熱忱的,誠懇的,興奮的

She promised herself she would be cordial because the appointment was important.

她保證她會很熱忱,因為會議很重要。

5197

specimen [ˈspɛsəmən]

n. 範例,標本,樣品,樣本,待試驗物

The doctor needs the patient's blood specimen.
醫生需要病人的血液樣本。

5198

prolong [prəˈlɔŋ]

vt. 延長,拖延

I was trying to prolong the conversation with the stranger. 我試著延長和陌生人的對話。

5199

pastime [ˈpæsˌtaɪm]

n. 消遣,娛樂

Shopping was her favorite pastime.
購物曾是她最喜歡的消遣。

5200

fixture [ˈfɪkstʃɚ]

n. 固定設備,預定日期,比賽時間,[機]裝置器,工作夾具

The brochure covers a list of this season's fixtures.
這本小冊子包含本賽季的比賽時間。

5201

paddle [ˈpædl]

v. 划槳

Can you go for a paddle with me?
你可以跟我去划槳嗎?

5202

embark [ɪmˈbɑrk]

v. 上船,上飛機,著手,從事,裝於船上,登上

He embarked on a new job as a firefighter.
他開始了新的消防員工作。

5203

plague [pleg]

n. 瘟疫,麻煩,苦惱,災禍 vt. 折磨,使苦惱,使得災禍

The plague caused thousands of deaths in London.
這場災禍導致倫敦很多傷亡。

5204

fragrant [ˈfregrənt]

adj. 芬芳的,香的

He sent me fragrant flowers.
他送我芬芳的花。

5205

collective [kəˈlɛktɪv] adj. 集體的 n. 集體

The whole staff should have collective responsibility for the company.
整個員工都應對公司有集體責任。

5206

antenna [ænˈtɛnə]

n. 天線

It's a antenna that transmits a radio signal.
這是個可以傳輸收音機信號的天線。

5207

carrier [ˈkærɪɚ]

n. 運送者,郵遞員,帶菌者,(自行車等)行李架,搬運器,航空母艦 n. [電]載波(信號)

He is a mobile-phone carrier. 他是手機營運商。

5208

hospitality [ˌhɑspɪˈtælətɪ]

n. 好客,宜人,盛情

Thanks for your hospitality.
謝謝你的好客。

5209

establishment [ə'stæblɪʃmənt]

n. 確立,制定,設施,公司,軍事組織

The establishment of the company was in 1980.
公司建立在 1980 年。

5210

incidence ['ɪnsədəns]

n. 落下的方式,影響範圍,發生率,[物理]入射

Keep away from areas with a high crime incidence at night. 晚上遠離高度犯罪的地方。

5211

plateau [plæ'to]

n. 高地,高原(上升後的)穩定水平(或時期,狀態)

Her house is on a plateau in China.
她的房子在中國平原上。

5212

forthcoming ['fɔrθ'kʌmɪŋ] ['forθ-]

adj. 即將來臨的 n. 來臨

The forthcoming elections will be in March.
即將來臨的選舉在三月。

5213

inland ['ɪnlənd]

adj. 內陸的,國內的 n. 內地

The largest inland country in the world is Kazakhstan.
世界上最大的內陸國是哈薩克。

5214

denote [dɪ'not]

vt. 指示,表示,意指

Family denotes mother, father and children.
家人意指母親,父親,和小孩。

5215

immune [ɪ'mjun]

adj. 免疫的

You'll become immune to the disease.
你將會對這疾病免疫。

5216

deviate ['divɪ,et]

vi. 背離,偏離 v. 偏離

Don't deviate from your original plan.
不要偏離你原本的計畫。

5217

ecology [ɪ'kɑlədʒɪ]

n. 生態學,[社會]環境適應學,均衡系統

You will learn the natural ecology of the Earth in science class. 你將會在自然課學到地球科學。

5218

bolt [bolt]

n. 門閂,螺釘,閃電,跑掉 v. 上門閂,囫圇吞下,逃跑

The gate bolts are inside the gate.
門的螺釘在裡面。

5219

purify ['pjʊrəfaɪ]

vt. 使純淨 v. 淨化

Can you find chemicals to purify the water?
你可以找到用來淨化水的化學物質嗎?

5220

appraisal [ə'prezl]

n. 評價,估價(尤指估價財產,以便徵稅),鑒定

The appraisal of the vase is 200,000 dollars.
那只花瓶的估價為二十萬元。

5221 deadly [ˈdɛdlɪ]

adj. 致命的,勢不兩立的,死一般的,極度的,必定的

They are deadly enemies forever.

他們永遠是死對頭。

5222 advertising [ˈædvɚˌtaɪzɪŋ]

n. 廣告業,做廣告

We need a good advertising campaign to increase our sales. 我們需要好的廣告活動增加銷售量。

5223 instantaneous [ˌɪnstənˈtenɪəs]

adj. 瞬間的,即刻的,即時的

Danger is instantaneous.

危險是瞬間發生的。

5224 hinder [ˈhɪndɚ]

adj. 後面的 v. 阻礙,打擾

His career has been hindered by a disease.

他的事業被疾病擔擱。

5225 pasture [ˈpæstʃɚ]

n. 牧地,草原,牧場 v. 放牧,牧(牛,羊)等,吃草

The cattle and sheep were put out to pasture.

羊群和牛群被趕去牧場。

5226 monetary [ˈmʌnəˌtɛrɪ]

adj. 貨幣的,金錢的

The government's monetary policy needs to be corrected. 政府的貨幣政策需要被修正。

5227 flare [ˈflɛr]

n. 閃光,閃耀 vi. 閃光,突然燒起來,閃耀

The house flared up and the fire fighters arrived afterward. 這間房子突然燒起來,消防隊隨後到了。

5228 facilitate [fəˈsɪləˌtet]

vt. (不以人作主語的)使容易,使便利,推動,幫助,使容易,促進

Telephones can be used to facilitate communication.

電話可以加速溝通。

5229 confusing [kənˈfjuzɪŋ]

adj. 令人困惑的

The statement was really confusing.

這個陳述很令人困惑。

5230 gasp [gæsp]

vi. 喘息,氣喘 vt. 氣吁吁地說

He climbed upstairs, gasping for breath.

他爬上樓,喘息一下。

5231 manipulate [məˈnɪpjəˌlet]

vt. (熟練地)操作,使用(機器等),操縱(人或市價,市場),利用,應付,假造 vt. (熟練地)操作,巧妙地處理

He likes to manipulate people. 他喜歡操控人。

5232

gross [gros]

adj. 總的,毛的,粗俗的

He earns a gross profit of $5 million every year.

他每年大約獲利五百萬元。

5233

rim [rɪm]

n. 邊,輪緣,籃框 vt. 鑲邊,為⋯裝邊,沿⋯邊緣滾動

The rim of his glasses is dirty.

他眼鏡邊緣很髒。

5234

miniature [ˈmɪnɪətʃɚ]

n. 縮小的模型,縮圖,縮影 adj. 微型的,縮小的

It looks like a miniature version of a house.

這看起來像房子的縮小版。

5235

displace [dɪsˈples]

vt. 移置,轉移,取代,置換 v. 轉移

Factory workers have been displaced by machines.

工廠的工人已經被機器取代。

5236

elevation [ˌɛləˈveʃən]

n. 上升,高地,正面圖,海拔,提高,仰角,崇高,莊嚴

The city is at an elevation of 200 meters.

這城市位在海拔兩百公尺。

5237

immerse [ɪˈmɜs]

vt. 沉浸,使陷入

She immersed herself in music.

她將自己沉浸在音樂中。

5238

eternal [ɪˈtɜnl̩]

adj. 永恆的,永遠的,不滅的,沒完沒了的

She's an eternal optimist and she always looks on the bright side. 她是永遠的樂觀者,她總是看光明面。

5239

consensus [kənˈsɛnsəs]

n. 一致同意,多數人的意見,輿論

There is a consensus that the plan should be carried out.

大家一致同意該進行這個計畫。

5240

pipeline [ˈpaɪplaɪn]

n. 管道,傳遞途徑

The water pipeline is under construction.

這條水管還在建造中。

5241

dubious [ˈdjubɪəs]

adj. 可疑的,不確定的

I was dubious about the whole plan.

我對整個計畫有所懷疑。

5242

convert [ˈkɑnvɜt] [kənˈvɜt]

n. 皈依者 vt. 使轉變,轉換⋯,使⋯改變信仰

They converted to Buddhism.

他們改信佛教。

5243

stationary [ˈsteʃənˌɛrɪ]

adj. 固定的

The country has a stationary population.

這個國家有固定的人口。

5244

petition [pə'tɪʃən]

n. 請願,情願書,訴狀,陳情書 v. 請求,懇求,請願

They signed a petition against children abuse.

他們簽署反對虐待小孩的陳情書。

5245

accessory [æk'sɛsərɪ]

n. 附件,零件,附加物,從犯,同謀者
adj. 附屬的,補充的,同謀的,副的

She likes fashion accessories. 她喜歡流行飾品。

5246

monstrous ['mɑnstrəs]

adj. 巨大的,畸形的,怪異的,恐怖的,兇暴的
adj. (口)難以置信的,荒謬的

It's monstrous to do this thing. 做這件事很怪異。

5247

decisive [dɪ'saɪsɪv]

adj. 決定性的

Women play a decisive role in their families.
女人在家庭中扮演決定性的角色。

5248

shaft [ʃæft]

n. 軸,桿狀物

An elevator shaft goes through the building.
電梯軸貫穿整個建築。

5249

expertise [ˌɛkspə'tiz]

n. 專家的意見,專門技術

He has expertise in management.
他有管理的專長。

5250

overlap ['ovəˌlæp]

v. (與…)交疊

They have overlapping interests.
他們有相同興趣。

5251

forum ['forəm]

n. 古羅馬城鎮的廣場(或市場),論壇,法庭,討論會

The school will hold an international forum on linguistics.
學校將會舉辦國際語言學論壇。

5252

nominal ['nɑmənl̩]

adj. 名義上的,有名無實的,名字的,[語]名詞性的

We only pay a nominal bill.
我們只付名義上的帳單。

5253

stainless ['stenlɪs]

adj. 純潔的,無瑕疵的,不鏽的

My cup is made of stainless steel.
我的杯子是用不鏽鋼做的。

5254

indignant [ɪn'dɪgnənt]

adj. 憤怒的,憤慨的

She was very indignant at him.
她對他很生氣。

5255

offset ['ɔfˌsɛt] n. 偏移量,分支,平版印刷,膠印

vi. 偏移,形成分支,抵銷,彌補

His diligence offsets his weakness.
他的勤奮彌補了他的弱點。

5256

enrich [ɪnˈrɪtʃ]

vt. 使富足,使肥沃,裝飾,加料於,濃縮

Travel can greatly enrich your life.

旅遊可以豐富你的生命。

5257

lame [lem]

adj. 跛足的,僵痛的,不完全的,金屬薄片,不知內情
的人,(辯解,論據等)無說服力的

vt. 使成殘廢

Stephen made some lame excuses for not coming.

史蒂芬為了他的缺席編造出無說服力的藉口。

5258

radioactive [ˌredɪoˈæktɪv]

adj. 放射性的,有輻射能的

We need to solve the problem of how to dispose of
radioactive waste. 我們需要解決輻射廢料的問題。

5259

combat [ˈkɑmbæt]

n. 戰鬥,格鬥 v. 戰鬥,搏鬥,抗擊

To combat inflation, the government should think of a
solution. 為了對抗通貨膨脹,政府應該想辦法。

5260

ruthless [ˈruθlɪs]

adj. 無情的,殘忍的

Qin Shi Huang was a ruthless emperor.

秦始皇是殘忍的獨裁者。

5261

reciprocal [rɪˈsɪprəkl]

adj. 互惠的,相應的,倒數的,彼此相反的

n. 倒數,互相起作用的事物

The couple has a reciprocal arrangement.

這對夫妻有互相的安排。

5262

confidential [ˌkɑnfəˈdɛnʃəl]

adj. 祕密的,機密的

Please keep the confidential report in a safe place.

請將這份機密報告放置安全的地方。

5263

indignation [ˌɪndɪgˈneʃən]

n. 憤慨,義憤

To his indignation, Charles found that he wasn't informed.

讓他生氣的是,查爾斯發現他沒被通知。

5264

presume [prɪˈzum]

vt. 假定,假設,認為

I presume we'll be there soon.

我認為我們很快就會到那裡。

5265

materialism [məˈtɪrɪəlˌɪzəm]

n. 唯物主義

He believes in materialism.

他相信唯物主義。

5266

regime [rɪ'ʒim]

n. 政體,政權,政權制度

The regime was built in 1900.

這個政權在 1900 年建立。

5267

haul [hɔl]

n. 用力拖拉,拖,拉,捕獲物,努力得到的結果,(尤指)一
網捕獲的魚量,拖運距離

vi. 拖,拉,改變方向,改變主意

The dog hauled a toy.

這隻狗拖著一個玩具。

5268

commute [kə'mjut]

v. 交換,抵償,減刑,(電工)整流

Jim commutes to his office everyday.

吉姆每天通勤去辦公室。

5269

hail [hel]

n. 冰雹,致敬,招呼,一陣 vi. 招呼,下雹,歡呼

The fans hailed their idol.

粉絲們為偶像歡呼。

5270

resent [rɪ'zɛnt]

v. 憤恨,怨恨

I resented doing such a work.

我討厭做這種工作。

5271

literally ['lɪtərəlɪ]

adv. 照字面意義,逐字地

The meaning of his name literally means 'smart'.

他的名字字面上來說是「聰明」。

5272

quantitative ['kwɑntə,tetɪv] ['kwɒn-]

adj. 數量的,定量的

We need to do a quantitative analysis of the reseach.

我們需要做研究的量化分析。

5273

perplex [pə'plɛks]

v. 困惑

Her problem perplexed me.

她的問題使我困惑。

5274

collision [kə'lɪʒən]

n. 碰撞,衝突

The truck was in collision with a motorbike.

卡車跟機車碰撞。

5275

endeavor [ɪn'dɛvɚ]

n. 努力,盡力 vi. 盡力,努力

We always endeavor to achieve our goal.

我們總是很努力達到目標。

5276

acquisition [,ækwə'zɪʃn]

n. 獲得,獲得物

The acquisition of language happens in context.

語言習得發生在語境下。

5277
dictator [ˈdɪkˌtetɚ]
n. 獨裁者,獨裁政權執政者,口授令他人筆錄者

Qin Shi Huang was a dictator and everyone was afraid of him. 秦始皇是獨裁者,每個人都怕他。

5278
finite [ˈfaɪnaɪt]
adj. 有限的,[數]有窮的,限定的

We should cherish the earth's finite resources.
我們應該珍惜地球的有限資源。

5279
radius [ˈredɪəs]
n. 半徑,範圍,輻射光線,有效航程,範圍,界限

He lives within a 10-mile radius of the school.
他住在學校十英哩範圍內。

5280
discriminate [dɪˈskrɪməˌnet]
v. 歧視,區別,區別待遇

It is bad to discriminate against minorities and women.
歧視女人跟少數族群是不好的。

5281
prescription [prɪˈskrɪpʃən]
n. 指示,規定,命令,處方,藥方

We need a prescription for sleeping pills.
我們需要安眠藥的處方。

5282
muscular [ˈmʌskjələ]
adj. 肌肉的,強健的

He's very muscular and tall.
他很強壯並高大。

5283
inclusive [ɪnˈklusɪv]
adj. 包含的,包括的

The rent is 120 a week, inclusive of utility.
房租每星期 120 元包含水電費。

5284
fracture [ˈfræktʃɚ]
n. 破裂,骨折 v. (使)破碎,(使)破裂

He fractured his right leg during a car accident.
他右腳在車禍中骨折。

5285
physiology [ˌfɪzɪˈɑlədʒɪ]
n. 生理學

Can I borrow a book on physiology?
我可以借生理學的書嗎?

5286
mock [mɑk] [mɔk]
v. 嘲笑,騙,挫敗,嘲弄 n. 嘲弄,模仿,仿製品

He mocks my French accent.
他嘲笑我的法國口音。

5287
outbreak [ˈautˌbrek]
n. (戰爭的)爆發,(疾病的)發作

There will be an outbreak of flu in fall.
秋天將會有流感爆發。

5288
hierarchy [ˈhaɪəˌrɑrkɪ]
n. 層次,層級

India has a social hierarchy.
印度保有社會階級。

5289

hillside [ˈhɪlˌsaɪd]

n. 山坡,山腹

Our house was on the hillside overlooking the city.

我們的房子在山坡上,鳥瞰這個城市。

5290

excessive [ɪkˈsɛsɪv]

adj. 過多的,過分的,額外

Excessive eating can lead to obesity.

過度的吃會導致肥胖。

5291

approximate [əˈprɑksəmət]

adj. 近似的,大約的 vi. 近似,接近

I will be coming in approximately 20 minutes.

我將會在二十分鐘內來。

5292

minimize [ˈmɪnəˌmaɪz]

vt. 將···減到最少 v. 最小化

We must minimize the problem of air pollution.

我們必須將空氣汙染問題減到最小。

5293

fabricate [ˈfæbrɪˌket]

vt. 製作,構成,捏造,偽造,虛構

The children were fabricating stories.

這些小孩在杜撰故事。

5294

lever [ˈlɛvə]

n. 桿,槓桿,控制桿 v. 抬起

Pull the lever towards you to open the door.

把拉桿拉向你自己來打開門。

5295

contrive [kənˈtraɪv]

v. 發明,設計,圖謀

She contrived to spend one hour with him every evening.

她計畫每天晚上要花一小時跟他在一起。

5296

longitude [ˈlɑndʒəˌtjud]

n. 經度,經線

The country lies at longitude 30 degrees east.

該國位於東經 30 度。

5297

inertia [ɪnˈɜʃə]

n. 慣性,慣量

You must throw off this feeling of inertia.

你必須要扔掉慣有的想法。

5298

outfit [ˈaʊtˌfɪt]

n. 用具,配備,機構,全套裝配 vt. 配備,裝備

She wore a new outfit for the party.

她穿新的套裝去舞會。

5299

deficiency [dɪˈfɪʃənsɪ]

n. 缺乏,不足

There is a deficiency of safe area for children here.

這裡小孩的安全空間不足。

5300

erosion [ɪˈroʒən]

n. 腐蝕,侵蝕

Scientists should deal with the problem of soil erosion.

科學家應該要處理泥土侵蝕的問題。

5301
initiate [ɪˈnɪʃɪˌet]
vt. 開始,發動,傳授 v. 開始,發起
Many children initiated learning English at an early age. 很多小孩在很小的年紀開始學英文。

5302
empirical [ɛmˈpɪrɪkḷ]
adj. 完全根據經驗的,經驗主義的,[化]實驗式
The police found empirical evidence for the crime. 警方發現這個犯罪的實驗證據。

5303
dome [dom]
n. 圓屋頂
The dome of St Paul's Cathedral is famous. 聖保羅教堂的屋頂很有名。

5304
handbook [ˈhændˌbʊk]
n. 手冊,便覽,旅遊指南
I like to use a handbook when I travel abroad. 當我出國時,我喜歡使用旅遊指南。

5305
notable [ˈnotəbḷ]
adj. 值得注意的,顯著的,著名的
The city is notable for its night markets. 這個城市以夜市聞名。

5306
radiator [ˈredɪˌetɚ]
n. 散熱器,水箱,冷卻器,電暖爐,暖氣裝置,輻射體
I want to rent a suite with a radiator. 我想租一間有暖氣的套房。

5307
apparatus [ˌæpəˈretəs]
n. 器械,設備,儀器
Carpenters need fixing apparatus to cut wood. 木匠需要固定的裝置來砍木頭。

5308
quench [kwɛntʃ]
vt. 結束,熄滅,淬火 vi. 熄滅,平息
We stopped at the convenience store to quench our thirst. 我們停在便利商店解渴。

5309
depict [dɪˈpɪkt]
vt. 描述,描寫
He was depicted as a stingy man. 他被描述成一個吝嗇的人。

5310
attain [əˈten]
vt. 達到,取得
He is eager to attain fame. 他渴望成名。

5311
astronomy [əˈstrɑnəmɪ]
n. 天文學
The boy is interested in astronomy. 這個男生對天文有興趣。

5312
mutter [ˈmʌtɚ]
n. 咕噥,嘀咕 v. 咕噥,嘀咕
What is he muttering about? 他在嘀咕什麼?

5313

accustom [ə'kʌstəm]

vt. 使習慣於

It took years to accustom myself to a new life.

我花了好多年適應新生活。

5314

comparable ['kɑmpərəbḷ]

adj. 可比較的,比得上的

Patty isn't comparable in appearance to Kelly.

佩蒂在外表上比不上凱莉。

5315

invaluable [ɪn'væljəbḷ] [-'væljʊəbḷ]

adj. 無價的,價值無法衡量的

Your help is invaluable to us.

你的幫忙對我們很珍貴。

5316

mute [mjut]

n. 啞巴,啞音字母,[律]拒不答辯的被告,弱音器

adj. 啞的,無聲的,沉默的

The child sat mute on the chair.

這個小孩沉默的坐在椅子上。

5317

concession [kən'sɛʃən]

n. 讓步

I am not prepared to make any concessions.

我還沒準備好要讓步。

5318

induce [ɪn'djus]

vt. 勸誘,促使,導致,引起,感應

Nothing would induce me to take her advice.

沒有事情能使我接受她的建議。

5319

constituent [kən'stɪtʃʊənt]

n. 委託人,要素

adj. 有選舉權的,有憲法制定【修改】權的

She hopes her constituents to vote for her.

她希望她的選民能投票給她。

5320

seam [sim]

n. 接縫,線縫,縫合線,銜接口,傷疤,層 vi. 裂開,發生裂痕

Join the pants' seams together.

把褲子的線縫起來。

5321

proficiency [prə'fɪʃənsɪ]

n. 熟練,精通,熟練程度

He has high level of proficiency in English.

他英文程度很高。

5322

predominant [prɪ'dɑmənənt]

adj. 卓越的,支配的,主要的,突出的,有影響的

We tried not to favor any predominant culture.

我們試著不要偏袒任何強勢文化。

5323 generalize [ˈdʒɛnərəlˌaɪz]

vt. 歸納,概括,推廣,普及

Can the findings be generalized to other researches?

這個結果可以適用至其他研究嗎？

5324 aerospace [ˈɛrəˌspes]

n. 航空宇宙

Russia develops aerospace industry.

俄國發展航空工業。

5325 monotonous [məˈnɑtn̩əs]

adj. 單調的,無變化的

I don't want to have a monotonous life.

我不想過單調的生活。

5326 conscientious [ˌkɑnʃɪˈɛnʃəs]

adj. 盡責的

A conscientious teacher does things right.

一個盡責的老師做對的事。

5327 commonplace [ˈkɑmənˌples]

n. 平凡的事,平常話 adj. 平凡的

Robbers are commonplace in this city.

這個城市搶匪很多。

5328 magnitude [ˈmæɡnəˌtjud]

n. 大小,數量,巨大,廣大,量級

We realize the magnitude of the problem.

我們瞭解到這個問題的重要性。

5329 deem [dim]

v. 認為,相信

They deemed that he was capable of doing his job.

他們認為他可以做他的工作。

5330 preach [pritʃ]

v. 布道,宣講,鼓吹

She preached to the congregation about love.

她向教徒宣導愛。

5331 sacred [ˈsekrɪd]

adj. 神的,宗教的,莊嚴的,神聖的

I attended a sacred ceremony yesterday.

昨天我參加一場神聖的典禮。

5332 apprehension [ˌæprɪˈhɛnʃən]

n. 理解,憂懼,拘捕

He looked at me with apprehension.

他以帶有憂懼的表情看著我。

5333 deduce [dɪˈdjus]

vt. 推論,演繹出

What did he deduce from the hypothesis?

他從假設中推斷出什麼？

5334 opaque [oˈpek]

n. 不透明物 adj. 不透明的,不傳熱的,遲鈍的

This is an opaque glass.

這是一個不透明的玻璃杯。

5335
agitate [ˈædʒəˌtet]
v. 攪動,搖動,煽動,激動
His friends are agitating to get him angry.
他的朋友正在煽動他想讓他生氣。

5336
preside [prɪˈzaɪd]
v. 主持
I would like to preside at your meeting.
我想主持你的會議。

5337
disgrace [dɪsˈgres]
n. 恥辱,失寵,丟臉的人(或事) v. 玷汙
He disgraced us in the meeting.
他在會議中讓我們受辱。

5338
cosmic [ˈkɑzmɪk]
adj. 宇宙的
Do you believe in cosmic space?
你相信宇宙空間嗎?

5339
patron [ˈpetrən]
n. (對某人,某種目標,藝術等)贊助人,資助人
He is a wealthy patron.
他是富有的資助人。

5340
gallop [ˈgæləp]
n. 疾馳,飛奔 vt. 使飛跑,迅速運輸
I watched a horse gallop away.
我看著馬疾馳。

5341
pamphlet [ˈpæmflɪt]
n. 小冊子
Here is a pamphlet with some information.
這裡有一本提供一些資訊的小冊子。

5342
detach [dɪˈtætʃ]
vt. 分開,分離,分遣,派遣(軍隊)
You can detach the label from the jacket.
你可以把標籤從夾克上拆開。

5343
concede [kənˈsid]
vt. 勉強,承認,退讓 vi. 讓步
I conceded that I had made some mistakes.
我承認我犯了一些錯。

5344
Fahrenheit [ˈfærənˌhaɪt] [ˈfɑrən-]
adj. 華氏溫度計的 n. 華氏溫度計,華氏溫度計
Today is 72 degrees Fahrenheit.
今天是華氏七十二度。

5345
accusation [ˌækjəˈzeʃn] [ˌækjʊ-]
n. 譴責,[律]指控
He faces accusations of corruption now.
他現在面臨貪汙的指控。

5346
quartz [ˈkwɔrts]
n. 石英
This is a quartz crystal.
這是石英的晶體。

5347

impair [ɪmˈpɛr]

v. 削弱,妨害

His appearance impaired his chances of finding a girlfriend. 他的外表降低了他找女友的機會。

5348

premier [ˈprimɪɚ]

adj. 第一的,首要的 n. 總理

The Irish Premier visited our country last weekend.
愛爾蘭總理上周末拜訪了我們國家。

5349

insulate [ˈɪnsəˌlet]

vt. 使絕緣,隔離

The hands in the gloves are insulated from heat.
戴著手套的手與熱隔絕。

5350

galaxy [ˈgæləksɪ]

n. 星系,銀河,一群顯赫的人,一系列光彩奪目的東西

I like reading about a galaxy of Hollywood stars in the magazine.

我喜歡讀雜誌上有關好萊塢明星的事情。

5351

moan [mon]

n. 呻吟,哀悼,呼嘯 vt. 呻吟

My mom likes moaning at me.
我媽媽喜歡對我抱怨。

5352

sober [ˈsobɚ]

adj. 冷靜的 v. 鎮定

John is a sober and hard-working young man.
約翰是一個溫和且努力的年輕人。

5353

glare [glɛr]

n. 眩目的光,顯眼,怒目而視,(冰等的表面)光滑的表面

v. 閃耀

She glared at him instead of shouting.

她瞪著他卻沒有大聲喊叫。

5354

petty [ˈpɛtɪ]

adj. 小的,不重要的,小規模的,小型的,細微的,小器的,卑鄙的

Why can she be so petty? 為何她那麼小器？

5355

inlet [ˈɪnˌlɛt]

n. 進口,入口,水灣,小港,插入物

A fuel inlet is the part of a machine through which liquid flows in.

燃料入口就是在機械中可以讓水流入的一個入口。

5356

denial [dɪ'naɪəl]

n. 否認,否定,謝絕,拒絕

The school issued a denial of the proposal.

學校否決這項提議。

5357

salute [sə'lut]

n. (尤指軍隊等之)舉手禮,升降旗致敬,鳴禮炮等,敬禮

v. 行禮致敬,敬禮

The soldiers jumped to their feet and saluted.

軍人踏步並行舉手禮。

5358

documentary [ˌdɑkjə'mɛntərɪ]

n. 記錄片 adj. 文件的

This is a television documentary about aborigines.

這是關於原住民的電視紀錄片。

5359

epidemic [ˌɛpə'dɛmɪk]

adj. 流行的,傳染的,流行性

n. 時疫,疫疾流行,(風尚等的)流行,流行病

Over 100 people died during the flu epidemic.

超過一百人死於流行性感冒。

5360

diversion [daɪ'vɝdʒən]

n. 轉移,轉換,牽制,解悶,娛樂,迂迴路

Reading is his favorite diversion.

閱讀是他最喜歡的娛樂。

5361

intact [ɪn'tækt]

adj. 完整無缺的,尚未被人碰過的,(女子)保持童貞的,(家畜)未經閹割的

Most of the houses remained intact after years.

大部分的房子在好幾年後依然保持完整。

5362

likelihood ['laɪklɪˌhʊd]

n. 可能,可能性

There is high likelihood of her getting married.

她結婚的可能性非常高。

5363

reign [ren]

vi. 統治,支配,盛行,佔優勢 n. 統治,統治時期,支配

He is successful in business during his reign in the company. 在他掌管公司時期,他生意很成功。

5364

deprive [dɪ'praɪv]

vt. 剝奪,使喪失

A lot of people have been deprived of lives during the war. 很多人在戰爭中被剝奪生命。

5365
inaccessible [ˌɪnəkˈsɛsəbl̩] [ˌɪnækˈsɛsəbl̩]

adj. 達不到的,難以接近

The amusement park is now inaccessible to people.

遊樂園現在不開放給民眾。

5366
multitude [ˈmʌltəˌtjud] [-ˌtrud] [-ˌtud]

n. 多數,群眾

I had never seen such a multitude of people before.

我以前沒有看過這麼多人。

5367
attendance [əˈtɛndəns]

n. 出席,出席的人數,伺候,照料

Today's class saw an attendance figure of 10.

今天班上出席人數有十人。

5368
incidentally [ˌɪnsəˈdɛntl̩ɪ]

adv. 附帶地,順便提及

Incidentally, have you heard from them?

順便提及,他們有跟你聯絡嗎?

5369
realization [ˌrɪələˈzeʃən] [ˌrɪəl-] [-aɪˈz-]

n. 實現,現實

There is a realization that she recovered from the illness.

她從病中康復得以實現。

5370
obedience [oˈbidɪəns]

n. 服眾,順從

He lived in obedience to his parents.

他順從他的父母。

5371
lounge [laʊndʒ]

n. 閒逛,休閒室,長沙發 vt. 虛度光陰

The television lounge is in the corner.

電視休閒室在角落。

5372
feeble [ˈfibl̩]

adj. 虛弱的,衰弱的,無力的,微弱的,薄弱的

This is a feeble excuse.

這是很薄弱的理由。

5373
impulse [ɪmˈpʌls]

n. 推動,刺激,衝動,推動力 vt. 推動

Most women impulse buying things that they don't need in the department store.

大部分女生會在百貨公司內衝動購物。

5374
odor [ˈodɚ]

n. 氣味,名聲

I smell obnoxious odors from a factory.

我聞到來自工廠的臭味。

5375
disclose [dɪsˈkloz]

vt. 揭露,透露

He refused to disclose the scandal.

他拒絕透露這件醜聞。

5376

commonwealth [ˈkɑmənˌwɛlθ]

n. 國民整體,共和國,聯邦

The city and commonwealth have a good fame.

城市跟全體國民有很好的名聲。

5377

lubricate [ˈlubrɪˌket]

vt. 潤滑 v. 加潤滑油

The mechanic lubricates the engine with grease.

技工用油潤滑引擎。

5378

liability [ˌlaɪəˈbɪlətɪ]

n. 責任,義務,傾向,債務,負債

Passengers have legal liability for any damage here.

旅客需對這裡的任何損失負責。

5379

pendulum [ˈpɛndʒələm] [ˈpɛndl̩əm] [ˈpɛndjələm]

n. 鐘擺,搖錘

The pendulum keeps swinging back and forth.

鐘擺持續前後擺盪。

5380

inhabit [ɪnˈhæbɪt]

vt. 居住於,存在於,佔據,棲息

This is an inhabited island.

這是有人居住的島。

5381

extract [ˈɛkstrækt]

n. 精,汁,榨出物,摘錄,選粹
vt. 拔出,榨取,開方,求根,摘錄,析取,吸取

Salt is extracted from sea. 鹽從海粹取。

5382

ore [or]

n. 礦石,含有金屬的岩石

An ore is a kind of rock.

礦石是一種石頭。

5383

curriculum [kəˈrɪkjələm]

n. 課程

Computer is an essential part of the school curriculum.

電腦是學校課程裡很重要的部分。

5384

tentative [ˈtɛntətɪv]

n. 試驗,假設 adj. 試驗性的,試探的,嘗試的,暫定的

We made a tentative arrangement to arrive on Monday.

我們暫定安排星期一會到。

5385

zinc [zɪŋk]

n. 鋅 vt. 塗鋅於

They built a home out of zincs.

他們用鋅來建房子。

5386

upgrade [ˈʌpˈgred]

n. 升級,上升,上坡 vt. 使升級,提升,改良品種

You'll need to upgrade your hard drive.

你需要升級你的硬碟。

5387

synthesis [ˈsɪnθəsɪs]

n. 綜合,合成

The clothes are a synthesis of cotton and silk.

這件衣服是棉跟絲合成。

5388

wholesome ['holsəm]

adj. 益於健康的,健康的

You should eat more wholesome food.

你需要吃健康食品。

5389

equilibrium [ˌɪkwə'lɪbrɪəm]

n. 平衡,平靜,均衡,保持平衡的能力,沉著,安靜

We hope to achieve an equilibrium in the economy.

我們希望達到經濟平衡。

5390

triumphant [traɪ'ʌmfənt]

adj. 勝利的,成功的,狂歡的,洋洋得意的

After fighting, she gave me a triumphant smile.

在爭吵過後,她對我作出勝利的微笑。

5391

tramp [træmp]

n. v. 重步行走,踏,踐,踐踏

I tramped through the heavy snow to get to work.

我在雪中踩著沉重的步伐去上班。

5392

subscribe [səb'skraɪb]

v. 捐款,訂閱,簽署(文件),贊成,預訂

You can subscribe to the newspaper for a year.

你可以訂閱報紙一年。

5393

franchise ['fræntʃaɪz]

n. 特權,公民權 v. 賦予特權,賦予公民權,經銷權

Southern Television lost their franchise after negotiation.

南方電視台在協商後失去特權。

5394

verdict ['vɜdɪkt]

n. [律](陪審團的)裁決,判決,判斷,定論,結論

There was sufficient evidence for a guilty verdict.

在這個有罪的判決裡有足夠的證據。

5395

intonation [ˌɪnto'neʃən]

n. 語調,聲調

There's no intonation in his reading.

他唸書時語氣平淡。

5396

ventilate ['vɛntlˌet]

vt. 使通風,給…裝通風設備

This is a well-ventilated room.

這是一間通風良好的房間。

5397

trolley ['trɑlɪ]

n. 電車,(電車)滾輪,手推車,手搖車,台車

vt. 用手推車運

He put food in a supermarket trolley.

他把食物放在超市手推車裡。

5398

contradiction [ˌkɑntrə'dɪkʃən]

n. 反駁,矛盾

There is a contradiction between his idea and statement. 他的想法跟陳述中有矛盾。

5399

structural [ˈstrʌktʃərəl]

adj. 結構的,建築的

Storms have caused structural damage.

暴風雨造成結構上的損害。

5400

copyright [ˈkɑpɪˌraɪt]

n. 版權,著作權

She owns the copyright of this book.

她擁有這本書的版權。

5401

weakness [ˈwiknɪs]

n. 缺點,弱點,衰弱

Do you know your own weaknesses?

你知道你的弱點嗎?

5402

update [ʌpˈdet]

v. 使現代化,修正,校正,更新 n. 現代化,更新

The system needs to be updated.

這個系統需要更新。

5403

exterior [ɪkˈstɪrɪɚ]

adj. 外部的,外在的,表面的,外交的,[建](適合)外用的

n. 外部,表面,外型

The exterior walls need more colors.

外牆需要多點顏色。

5404

uncertainty [ʌnˈsɝtn̩tɪ]

n. 無常,不確定,不可靠,半信半疑

I feel an uncertainty about my future.

我對未來感到不確定。

5405

electoral [ɪˈlɛktərəl] [ə-]

adj. 選舉的

We should update an electoral system.

我們需要更新選務系統。

5406

verge [vɝdʒ]

v. 瀕臨 n. 邊緣

The ant is on the verge of the table.

那隻螞蟻在桌子的邊緣。

5407

turbulent [ˈtɝbjələnt]

adj. 狂暴的,吵鬧的

There is a turbulent crowd coming.

一群暴民來了。

5408

tariff [ˈtærɪf]

n. 關稅,關稅表,稅則,(旅館,飯店等的)價目表,價格表

vt. 課以關稅

The government may impose tariffs on these cigarettes.

政府可能會施加關稅在香菸上。

5409

diligence [ˈdɪlədʒəns]

n. 勤奮

She shows great diligence at work.

她在工作上很勤奮。

5410

cop [kɑp]

n. [俚]警察

He is a local cop.

他是一位當地的員警。

5411

lone [lon]

adj. 孤獨的,獨立的

A lone sailor stood on the ship.

一個孤獨的水手站在船上。

5412

pavement [ˈpevmənt]

n. 人行道,公路

Can you wait on the pavement outside her house?

你可以在她房子外的人行道等嗎？

5413

fearful [fɪrfəl]

adj. 可怕的,嚇人的,恐怕的,嚴重的

I don't like fearful stories.

我不喜歡嚇人的故事。

S3 高中三年級
V2 高職二年級　編號 5414～5484

5414

yearly [ˈjɪrlɪ]

adj. 每年的 adv. 每年

We pay the fee yearly.

我們每年付費。

5415

embarrass [ɪmˈbærəs]

vt. 使窘迫,使為難

She was embarrassed by his praise.

她對他的讚美感到難為情。

5416

decrease [dɪˈkris]

v. 減小,減少

The average house prices decreased last year.

去年的平均房價下降了。

5417

weekly [ˈwiklɪ]

adj. 每星期的,一周的 adv. 每周一次

The book is published weekly.

這本書每個星期出版。

5418

monthly [ˈmʌnθlɪ]

adj. 每月一次的 adv. 每月一次

Her mother visits her monthly.

她母親每個月來拜訪她。

5419

genius ['dʒinjəs]

n. 天才,天賦,天才人物

He is a genius.

他是天才。

5420

sportsman ['sportsmən] ['sɔrtsmən]

n. 運動家,冒險家

He's a very keen sportsman.

他是個嚴格的運動員。

5421

junior ['dʒunjə]

adj. 年少的,資歷較淺的 n. 年少者,晚輩

This is the second semester of my junior year in college.

這是我大學低年級的第二學期。

5422

ignorant ['ɪgnərənt]

adj. 無知的

Don't be an ignorant and uneducated man.

不要做一個無知而沒學識的人。

5423

negotiate [nɪ'goʃɪet]

v. (與某人)商議,談判,磋商,買賣,讓渡(支票,債券等),
   通過,越過

The government refuses to negotiate with the

protesters.

政府拒絕跟抗議者溝通。

5424

intend [ɪn'tɛnd]

vt. 想要,打算,意指,意謂

I intend to spend the day on the beach.

我想要在海灘上度過一天。

5425

prime [praɪm]

adj. 首要的,主要的,最好的 n. 青春,壯年,全盛時期

Smoking is the prime cause of cancer.

抽菸是致癌的主要原因。

5426

singular ['sɪŋgjələ]

n. 單數 adj. 單一的,非凡的,異常的,持異議的

Can you tell me the singular form of the noun?

你可以告訴我這個名詞的單數嗎？

5427

eliminate [ɪ'lɪmə,net] vt. 消除,排除

How to eliminate learners' anxiety to English is an

important issue.

如何消除學生對英文的學習焦慮是個重要議題。

5428

objective [əb'dʒɛktɪv]

n. 目標,目的,(顯微鏡的)(接)物鏡,[語法]賓格

adj. 客觀的,[語法]賓格的

He vowed to achieve certain objectives.

他發誓要達到某種目標。

5429

manufacture [ˌmænjəˈfæktʃɚ]

vt. 製造,加工 n. (大量)製造,製造業,製造品

The pharmaceutical factory manufactured drugs.

這家藥廠製造藥品。

5430

nevertheless [ˌnɛvɚðəˈlɛs]

adv. 然而,不過

Our defeat was expected but it is disappointing nevertheless.

我們的失敗是意料中的事,然而,還是令人失望。

5431

infant [ˈɪnfənt]

n. 嬰兒,幼兒 adj. 嬰兒的,幼稚的

An infant's skin is very soft.

嬰兒的皮膚很軟。

5432

transfer [ˈtrænsfɚ]

vi. 轉移,調動,轉學,轉車,換船

vt. 搬,轉移,調動,使轉學,轉讓,過戶

The film studio has transferred to Hollywood.

電影工業已轉移到好萊塢。

5433

mere [mɪr]

adj. 僅僅的,起碼的,純粹的

She lost the election by a mere 1 vote.

她以一票之差輸了選舉。

5434

economics [ˌikəˈnɑmɪks] [ˌɛk-]

n. 經濟學

He is a Harvard professor of economics.

他是哈佛經濟學教授。

5435

guilt [gɪlt]

n. 罪行,內疚

Don't you have any feelings of guilt about stealing money? 難道你偷錢不會有任何罪惡感嗎?

5436

genuine [ˈdʒɛnjʊɪn]

adj. 真的,非人造的,真誠的,真心的

She is the most genuine person I've ever met.

她是我見過最真誠的人。

5437

tension [ˈtɛnʃən]

n. 緊張(狀態),不安,拉緊,壓力,張力,牽力,電壓

vt. 拉緊,使緊張

Exercise is the ideal way to relieve tension.

運動是一個理想的解除壓力的方法。

5438

mysterious [mɪsˈtɪrɪəs]

adj. 神秘的,難以理解的

Bill disappeared in mysterious circumstances.

比爾在神祕的環境中消失。

5439

gratitude [ˈɡrætəˌtjud]

n. 感謝的心情

The teacher expressed her gratitude for their contribution.

那位老師表達她對他們的貢獻的感激。

5440

laboratory [ˈlæbrəˌtori]

n. 實驗室

He works in a laboratory.

他在實驗室工作。

5441

rebel [rɪˈbɛl] n. 造反者,叛逆者,反抗者,叛亂者

v. 造反,反叛,反抗,叛亂

Anti-government rebels attacked the city.

反政府的叛軍攻擊這座城市。

5442

prompt [prɑmpt]

n. 提示,付款期限 adj. 敏捷的,迅速的,即時的

Please be prompt when attending these meetings.

參加這些會議時請準時。

5443

offend [əˈfɛnd]

vt. 冒犯,得罪,使厭惡

His remarks deeply offended many Scottish people.

他的言論深深地激怒了很多蘇格蘭人。

5444

technician [tɛkˈnɪʃən]

n. 技術員,技師

He works as a laboratory technician.

他在實驗室當技術員。

5445

senior [ˈsinjɚ]

adj. 資格老的,地位較高的,年長的

He is more senior than me.

他比我資深。

5446

recreation [ˌrɛkriˈeʃən]

n. 消遣,娛樂

The government built a recreation area for children to play. 這個政府建造了娛樂區域給小孩玩。

5447

enormous [ɪˈnɔrməs]

adj. 巨大的,龐大的,(古)極惡的,兇暴的

He sent me an enormous bunch of flowers.

他送我一束很大束的花。

5448

innocence [ˈɪnəsn̩s]

n. 清白,天真,幼稚,純真

People lose their innocence as they grow older.

當人們愈來愈老時,他們失去了天真。

5449

elsewhere [ˈɛlsˌhwɛr]

adv. 在別處

She is becoming famous in the country and elsewhere.

她在這個國家和其他地方變得很有名。

5450
outcome [ˈaʊtˌkʌm]
n. 結果,成果
It was hard to predict the outcome of the election.
很難去預測選舉的結果。

5451
obtain [əbˈten]
vt. 獲得,得到
You will need to obtain information from the Internet.
你需要從網路上得到資訊。

5452
regulate [ˈrɛgjəˌlet]
vt. 管制,控制,調節,校準
The company are regulated by law.
這間公司受到法律的規範。

5453
explore [ɪkˈsplor] [-ˈsplɔr]
v. 探險,探測,探究
I'm going to explore Sahara desert.
我要去探索撒哈拉沙漠。

5454
emerge [ɪˈmɝdʒ]
vi. 出現,湧現,(問題)冒出
The flowers emerge in spring.
這些花在春天出現。

5455
honorable [ˈɑnərəbl]
adj. 可敬的,榮譽的,光榮的
This is an honorable job.
這是一個光榮的工作。

5456
refugee [ˌrɛfjʊˈdʒi]
n. 難民,流亡者
There are many refugee camps here.
這裡有很多難民營。

5457
impression [ɪmˈprɛʃən]
n. 印象
She left a good impression for the class.
她讓課堂上的同學留下了好印象。

5458
hopeful [ˈhopfəl]
adj. 懷有希望的,有希望的
Everyone's feeling pretty hopeful about the game.
每個人對這場比賽抱有希望。

5459
keen [kin]
adj. 熱心的,渴望的,強烈的,敏銳的
He told me that he was keen to support me.
他告訴我他很熱心支持我。

5460
depress [dɪˈprɛs]
vt. 使沮喪,使消沉
It depresses me that she hurt me.
她傷害我使我沮喪。

5461
hatred [ˈhetrɪd]
n. 憎恨,仇恨
He showed his intense hatred of foreigners.
他表現出對外國人深深的敵意。

5462
economy [ɪˈkɑnəmɪ]
n. 經濟,節約,節約措施,經濟實惠,系統,機體,
經濟制度的狀況
The economy is in recession. 經濟在衰退。

5463
insurance [ɪnˈʃʊrəns]
n. 保險
Do you have insurance on your car?
你車子有保險嗎？

5464
remark [rɪˈmɑrk]
vt. 說,評論說 vi. 評論,議論
The minister denied making the remarks.
部長否認說過這番言論。

5465
offense [əˈfɛns]
n. 進攻,罪過,冒犯
No offense, but you look pale in the dress.
我無意冒犯，但你穿這件洋裝看起來臉色蒼白。

5466
prosperous [ˈprɑspərəs]
adj. 繁榮的
He is a prosperous landowner.
他是有錢的地主。

5467
economist [ɪˈkɑnəmɪst]
n. 經濟學家
He is an economist.
他是經濟學家。

5468
technological [tɛknəˈlɑdʒɪkl]
adj. 科技的
The world is in a technological change.
這個世界正在進行科技上的改變。

5469
imaginary [ɪˈmædʒəˌnɛrɪ]
adj. 假想的,想像的,虛構的
I had an imaginary friend.
我曾有一位想像的朋友。

5470
wit [wɪt]
n. 智力,才智,智慧
I wanted to be a woman of great wit and charm.
我想要做一個有智慧和魅力的女子。

5471
fertile [ˈfɜtl]
adj. 肥沃的,富饒的,豐產的
This is a fertile region.
這是一塊肥沃的區域。

5472
reception [rɪˈsɛpʃən]
n. 接待處,接受,接納,歡迎會
Please leave your key at the reception desk.
請將你的鑰匙放在櫃檯。

5473
psychologist [saɪˈkɑlədʒɪst]
n. 心理學者
Courtney is a psychologist.
康納是心理學家。

5474

orchestra ['ɔkɪstrə]

n. 管弦樂隊,樂隊演奏處

I am a leader of the school orchestra.

我是學校管絃樂團的首席。

5475

protest ['protɛst] v. 抗議,反對

Thousands of people blocked the street, protesting against the new government.

成千上百的人封鎖這條街以抗議新政府。

5476

learned [lɜnd]

adj. 有學問的,學術上的

He is a learned professor.

他是個博學多聞的教授。

5477

pessimistic [ˌpɛsə'mɪstɪk]

adj. 悲觀的,厭世的

He has a pessimistic view of life.

他對生命看法很悲觀。

5478

procedure [prə'sidʒɚ]

n. 程式,手續

What's the procedure for applying for an ID card?

申請身分證的流程是什麼?

5479

harmony ['hɑrmənɪ]

n. 協調,融洽

We need to be in harmony with our environment.

我們需要與環境和諧共處。

5480

protein ['protin]

n. [生化]蛋白質 adj. 蛋白質的

Protein exists in food such as meat, eggs, and beans.

蛋白質在食物裡,例如肉、蛋跟豆子。

5481

harden ['hɑrdn]

vt. 使變硬,使堅強,使冷酷 vi. 變硬,變冷酷,漲價

It takes a short time for the glue to harden.

膠水凝固僅需很短時間。

5482

relieve [rɪ'liv]

vt. 減輕,救濟

Exercises help to relieve the pain.

運動有助於減輕疼痛。

5483

oxygen ['ɑksədʒən]

n. [化]氧

Oxygen is in the air.

氧在空氣裡。

5484

gene [dʒin]

n. [遺傳]因數,[遺傳]基因

Scientists discover unknown human genes.

科學家們發現未知的人類基因。

S3 高中三年級
V3 高職三年級 編號 5485～5919

5485

vendor ['vɛndɚ]

n. 攤販

He bought a drink from a vendor.

他從攤販那邊買飲料。

5486

underline [ˌʌndɚ'laɪn]

vt. 在…下面劃線,作…的襯裡,加下劃線,強調

n. 下劃線

Please underline the first three sentences.

請把前三行加下劃線為重點。

5487

purchase ['pɜtʃəs]

vt. 買,購買 n. 買,購買

You can purchase the T-shirt on-line.

你可以上網買 T-shirt.

5488

liter ['litɚ]

n. 公升

I drank a liter of water.

我喝了一升水。

5489

newscaster ['njuzˌkæstɚ]

n. 新聞廣播員

He is a newscaster.

他是新聞播報員。

5490

analyst ['ænlɪst]

n. 分析家,分析者

Political analysts expect the party to win.

政治分析員期待這個政黨會贏。

5491

inevitable [ɪn'ɛvətəbl̩]

adj. 不可避免的

It's inevitable that everyone will make occasional mistakes.

無可避免的是每個人將會犯偶爾的錯誤。

5492

license ['laɪsn̩s]

n. 許可(證),執照 v. 許可

I got a driver license yesterday.

我昨天拿到了汽車駕照。

5493

inherit [ɪn'hɛrət]

vt. 繼承,遺傳而得

He inherited a fortune from his grandmother.

他從他的祖母那邊繼承遺產。

5494

sneak [snik]

vi. 鬼鬼祟祟做事

n. 鬼鬼祟祟的人,偷偷摸摸的行為,(美口)帆布膠底
  運動鞋

She snuck out of the house when her parents were
asleep.

當她父母睡覺時,她偷溜出去。

5495

launch [lɔntʃ]

vt. 發射,投射,發動,發起,使(船)下水 n. 發射,(船)下水

The spaceship will be launched in 5 minutes.

太空船將在五分鐘後發射。

5496

ridiculous [rɪ'dɪkjələs]

adj. 荒謬的,可笑的

That's a ridiculous idea!

那真是一個荒謬的主意。

5497

inquire [ɪn'kwaɪr]

v. 打聽,詢問,調查

'Why are you doing that?' the boy inquired.

「你為什麼要那樣做?」男孩問。

5498

witness ['wɪtnɪs]

n. 目擊者,證人 vt. 目擊,作…的證人

There is no witness of the accident.

這意外沒有任何目擊者。

5499

split [splɪt]

v. 劈開,(使)裂開,分裂,分離 n. 裂開,裂口,裂痕

The party is split over the issue.

這個政黨因為這個議題分裂。

5500

paragraph ['pærə,græf]

n. (文章)段,節,段落

Can you read the opening paragraph of the novel?

你可以讀這本小說開始的第一段嗎?

5501

route [rut] [raʊt]

n. 路線,路程,通道 v. 發送

What's the best route to Taipei?

到臺北最好的路線是什麼?

5502

interpretation [ɪn,tɜprɪ'teʃən]

n. 解釋,闡明,口譯,通譯

It's difficult to put an interpretation on the survey results.

解讀研究結果很難。

5503

rage [redʒ]

n. v. 盛怒

Sam became quite violent when he was in a rage.

當山姆在生氣時變得很暴力。

5504

suggestion [sə'dʒɛs-]

n. 提議,意見,暗示,微量

May I make a suggestion?

我可以提個建議嗎?

5505

immigrant ['ɪməgrənt]

adj. (從外國)移來的,移民的,移居的 n. 移民,僑民

He is an illegal immigrant.

他是非法居民。

5506

enterprise ['ɛntɚ‚praɪz] ['ɛntə-]

n. 企業,事業,計劃,事業心,進取心

He is the boss of the enterprise.

他是這家企業的老闆。

5507

confrontation [‚kɑnfrən'teʃən]

n. 面對,面對面,對質,對抗

She had stayed in her room to avoid another confrontation. 她待在她的房間避免再一次的對質。

5508

container [kən'tenɚ]

n. 容器(箱,盆,罐,壺,桶,罈子),集裝箱

I have ice cream in plastic containers.

我有冰淇淋在塑膠盒裡。

5509

software ['sɔft‚wɛr]

n. 軟體

She installed the new software.

她裝了新的軟體。

5510

glimpse [glɪmps]

n. 一瞥,一看 v. 瞥見

They caught a glimpse of a beautiful girl.

他們看了一眼一位美麗的女生。

5511

suspension [sə'spɛnʃən]

n. 吊,懸浮,懸浮液,暫停,中止,懸而未決,延遲

He received a six-month suspension for such a behavior. 他因為這樣的行為得暫停職務六個月。

5512

superb [sʊ'pɜb]

adj. 莊重的,堂堂的,華麗的,極好的

The food was superb.

這個食物很棒。

5513

downwards ['daʊnwɚdz]

adv. 向下

Nina glanced downwards.

妮娜往下看。

5514

qualification [‚kwɑləfə'keʃən] [‚kwɒl]

n. 資格,條件,限制,限定,賦予資格

They have the academic qualifications needed for university entrance. 他們入學需要有學歷資格。

5515

disapprove [‚dɪsə'pruv]

v. 不贊成

Her family strongly disapproved of her excuses.

她的家人強烈反對她的理由。

5516

comedian [kə'midɪən]

n. 喜劇演員

He's a real comedian.

他是真的喜劇演員。

5517

spokesman ['spoksmən]

n. 發言人,代表者

He is a White House spokesman.

他是白宮發言人。

5518

jury ['dʒʊrɪ]

n. [律]陪審團,評判委員會,陪審員 adj. [海]臨時應急的

The jury found the prisoner guilty of killing Albert.

陪審團認為殺害艾伯特的囚犯有罪。

5519

skim [skɪm]

v. 撇去,去除,瀏覽,略讀

Julie skimmed the page.

茱莉略讀了這一頁。

5520

sympathize ['sɪmpəˌθaɪz]

vi. 同情,共鳴,同感,同意,吊唁

I can sympathize with those who have lost their health.

我能同情那些失去健康的人。

5521

injection [ɪn'dʒɛkʃən]

n. 注射,注射劑,(毛細血管等的)充血,(人造衛星,
    太空船等的)射入軌道

Children hate having injections. 小孩討厭打針。

5522

radiation [ˌredɪ'eʃən]

n. 發散,發光,發熱,輻射,放射,放射線,放射物

There is a link between exposure to radiation and

childhood cancer. 暴露在輻射之下與小孩癌症有關連。

5523

federal ['fɛdərəl]

adj. 聯邦的,聯合的,聯邦制的,同盟的

n. (南北戰爭時期)北部聯邦同盟盟員

You must obey the federal law. 你必定遵守聯邦法律。

5524

scheme [skim]

n. 安排,配置,計劃,陰謀,方案,圖解,摘要

v. 計劃,設計,圖謀,策劃

Do you have a retirement scheme? 你有退休計畫嗎？

5525

entitle [ɪn'taɪtl̩]

vt. 給…權利(或資格),給…題名,給…稱號 v. 授權,授權

Full-time employees are entitled to receive insurance.

全職的員工應該有保險。

5526

imperial [ɪm'pɪrɪəl]

adj. 帝國的,宏大的,英制的

His imperial family is famous in history.

他的皇族在歷史上很有名。

5527

torch [tɔrtʃ]

n. 火把,啟發之物,手電筒 vi. 像火炬一樣燃燒

Shine the torch on the lock while I try to get the key in.

當我拿鑰匙進門時，請將手電筒照明在鎖把上。

5528

meantime ['min,taɪm]

n. 其間,其時 adv. 其間

The doctor will be here soon. In the meantime, please have a drink.

醫生將會不久後會到，在等待的時候，請喝茶。

The manufacturing sector becomes more and more important.

製造業變得愈來愈重要。

5529
treaty ['tritɪ]

n. 條約,談判

Both sides have disagreed to sign the treaty.

兩邊都不同意這個條約。

5534
intruder [ɪn'trudɚ]

n. 侵入者,干擾者,妨礙者

The police thinks an intruder got into the house.

員警認為入侵者闖入房子裡。

5530
stimulate ['stɪmjəˌlet]

vt. 激勵,刺激

Her interest in art was stimulated by her parents.

她對藝術的興趣是受她的父母啟發。

5535
alcoholic [ˌælkə'hɔlɪk]

adj. 酒精的,含酒精的,酗酒的 n. 酗酒者,酒鬼, 酒精中毒者

I like alcoholic drinks. 我喜歡喝含酒精的飲料。

5531
worthy ['wɝðɪ]

adj. 值得的,配得上的,可尊敬的

He is a worthy opponent.

他是可敬的對手。

5536
interval ['ɪntɚvl̩]

n. 間隔,間距,幕間(或之間)休息

He left the room, returning after a short interval.

他離開這間房間，在短暫時間後回來。

5532
fertilizer ['fɝtl̩ˌaɪzɚ]

n. 肥料(尤指化學肥料),[動]受精媒介物

I bought a bag of fertilizer.

我買了一包肥料。

5537
sponsor ['spɑnsɚ]

n. 發起人,主辦者,保證人,主辦人 v. 贊助

We are looking for corporate sponsors.

我們在找贊助商。

5533
sector ['sɛktɚ]

n. 部門,扇形,尺規,函數尺

v. 把…分成部門,把…分成扇形

5538
issue ['ɪʃju]

n. 問題,爭論點(書刊的)期號 v. 發行,頒布

This is a highly controversial issue.

這是一個高度爭議的議題。

5539
cultivate ['kʌltə,vet]
vt. 培養,耕作
The land was impossible to cultivate.
這塊土地不可能耕作。

5540
terminal ['tɜmən!]
n. 終點(站),末端,終端　adj. 末端的,終點的
He got terminal cancer.
他得了末期癌症。

5541
symptom ['sɪmptəm]
n. [醫][植]症狀,徵兆
Common symptoms of flu are coughing and a running
nose. 流感的症狀是咳嗽跟流鼻水。

5542
imply [ɪm'plaɪ]
vt. 暗示
Are you implying that I am wrong?
你在暗示我是錯的嗎？

5543
summarize ['sʌmə,raɪz]
v. 概述,總結,摘要而言
The authors summarize their views in the book.
作者歸納這本書的觀點。

5544
vague [veg]
adj. 含糊的,不清楚的,茫然的,曖昧的
Julia was vague about where she had been.
茱莉亞對於她去了哪裡交代得不清不楚。

5545
limitation [,lɪmə'teʃən]
n. 限制,局限性
It's a good little car, but it has its limitations.
這是一部好的小車，但有所限制。

5546
corridor ['kɔrədə]
n. 走廊
We had to wait outside in the corridor.
我們必須在外面走廊等。

5547
spiritual ['spɪrɪtʃʊəl]
adj. 精神上的
These are spiritual values.
這些是精神性的價值。

5548
impose [ɪm'poz]
vt. 把強加於(on),徵(稅等)
The government imposed a ban on the sale of wild
animals. 政府禁止野生動物的買賣。

5549
correspondent [,kɔrə'spandənt]
n. 通訊記者,通信者　adj. 一致的,符合的
I'm not a very good correspondent.
我並不是好的通訊記者。

5550
repetition [,rɛpɪ'tɪʃən]
n. 重複,背誦,迴圈,複製品,副本
Children used to learn by repetition.
孩子曾透過背誦來學習。

5551

elementary [ˌɛləˈmɛntərɪ]

adj. 基本的,初級的

You've made a very elementary mistake.
你犯了基本的錯誤。

Do you have a remedy for colds?
你有感冒的治療方法嗎？

5552

surrender [səˈrɛndɚ]

vi. 投降,屈服,讓步 vt. 交出,放棄

He surrendered himself to the authorities.
他屈服於權威。

5557

extension [ɪkˈstɛnʃən]

n. 延長,擴充,範圍 n. 副檔名

This money can be used for extension of the system.
這個錢可用來作為系統的擴充。

5553

steer [stɪr]

v. 駕駛,掌舵

Teachers try to steer pupils away from drugs.
老師嘗試教導學生遠離毒品。

5558

tough [tʌf]

adj. 堅韌的額,堅強的,頑強的,棘手的,(食物)老的,
困難的

It was a tough race. 這是一場困難的比賽。

5554

presentation [ˌprɛznˈteʃən] [ˌprizɛnˈteʃən]

n. 介紹,陳述,贈送,表達,呈現,上演

I have a presentation ceremony.
我有一場演說典禮。

5559

shelter [ˈʃɛltɚ]

n. 掩蔽處,身避處,掩蔽,保護,庇護所,掩體 v. 掩蔽,躲避

They are in need of food and shelter.
他們需要食物跟避難所。

5555

highly [ˈhaɪlɪ]

adv. 高地,非常

He is a highly successful businessman.
他是非常成功的生意人。

5560

pacific [pəˈsɪfɪk]

adj. 和平的,平靜的 n. 太平洋,中太平洋

I live in a pacific community.
我住在平和的社區裡。

5556

remedy [ˈrɛmədɪ]

n. 藥物,治療法,補救,賠償

vt. 治療,補救,矯正,修繕,修補

5561

recognition [ˌrɛkəgˈnɪʃən]

n. 讚譽,承認,重視,公認,賞識,識別

All he wanted was recognition for his work.
他所想要的只是工作上的認同。

5562

restore [rɪ'stor] [-'stor]

vt. 恢復,使回復,歸還,交還,修復,重建

The government promises to restore the economy.
政府承諾要恢復經濟。

5563

ounce [aʊns]

n. 盎司,少量,[動]雪豹

Every ounce of attention was focused on our common goal. 所有的注意力都集中在我們的共同目標。

5564

economical [ˌikə'namɪkl] [ˌɛk-]

adj. 節約的,經濟的

A small car is more economical.
小型車比較節約。

5565

passive ['pæsɪv]

adj. 被動的

Kathy takes a very passive role in the relationship.
凱西在關係中扮演被動角色。

5566

imitate ['ɪmə,tet]

vt. 模仿,仿效,仿製

You can eat vegetarian products which imitate meat.
你可以吃仿製肉的素食產品。

5567

largely ['lardʒlɪ]

adv. 主要地,大量地,很大程度上

It had been a tiring day, largely because of waiting.
真是累人的一天,主要是因為等待。

5568

reluctant [rɪ'lʌktənt]

adj. 不情願的,勉強的

He was reluctant to talk about it.
他不想談這件事。

5569

memorial [mə'mɔrɪəl] [mə'morɪəl]

n. 紀念物,紀念館,紀念議事,請願書 adj. 紀念的,記憶的

A memorial service will be held on Saturday.
星期六將會有追悼會。

5570

decline [dɪ'klaɪn] vi. 下傾,下降,下垂

n. 下傾,下降,下垂,斜面,斜坡,衰敗,衰落

We have to face the decline of manufacturing.
我們必須面對製造業的衰退。

5571

extend [ɪk'stɛnd]

v. 擴充,延伸,伸展,擴大,[軍]使疏開,給予,提供,
演化出的全文,(英)[律]對(地產等)估價

The teacher agreed to extend the deadline.
老師同意延長期限。

5572

evolution [ˌɛvə'luʃən]

n. 進展,發展,演變,進化

Do you know the evolution of mammals?
你知道哺乳動物的演化嗎?

5573

hook [hʊk]

n. 掛鉤

Tom hung his coat on the hook behind the door.
湯姆把他的外套掛在門後的掛鉤裡。

5574

sow [saʊ] [so]

n. 大母豬 vt. 播種,散布,使密布

You reap what you sow.
要怎麼收穫,先怎麼栽。

5575

merit ['mɛrɪt]

n. 優點,價值,法律依據 v. 有益於

The great merit of the project is its low cost.
這個計畫的優點是花費很低。

5576

digest [daɪ'dʒɛst]

n. 分類,摘要 vt. 消化,融會貫通

I tried to digest the news.
我試著消化這些新聞。

5577

inhabitant [ɪn'hæbətənt]

n. 居民,居住者

New York is a city of six million inhabitants.
紐約市有六百萬居民。

5578

violinist [ˌvaɪə'lɪnɪst]

n. 小提琴演奏者,小提琴家

A violinist has a concert tonight.
一位小提琴家今晚有演奏會。

5579

stroke [strok]

n. 擊,敲,報時的鐘聲,(網球等)一擊,(划船等)一划,(繪畫等)一筆,一次努力,打擊,中風 vt. 撫摸

I looked after my father after he had a stroke.
在父親中風後,我照顧父親。

5580

curiosity [ˌkjʊrɪ'ɑsətɪ]

n. 好奇心

I opened the door just to satisfy my curiosity.
我為了滿足我的好奇心而開門。

5581

constitution [ˌkɑnstə'tjuʃən]

n. 憲法,構造,體質,體格,國體,章程,慣例

The right to speak freely is written into the Constitution.
憲法裡記載著言論自由。

5582

nursery ['nɝsərɪ]

n. 托兒所

Her youngest child is at nursery now.
她最小的小孩現在在托兒所。

5583

embassy ['ɛmbəsɪ]

n. 大使及其隨員,大使的派遣,大使館

The American Embassy is in Paris.
美國大使館在巴黎。

5584
shortage [ˈʃɔrtɪdʒ]

n. 不足,缺乏

The factory has a shortage of skilled labor.
工廠缺乏有技能的勞工。

5585
publicity [pʌbˈlɪsətɪ]

n. 公開

It's important to gain good publicity for the company.
對公司來說獲得好的名聲很重要。

5586
pilgrim [ˈpɪlgrɪm]

n. 聖地朝拜者,朝聖

Pilgrims visit a holy shrine every year.
朝聖者每年拜訪聖殿。

5587
formula [ˈfɔrmjələ]

n. 公式,規則,客套語

We're still searching for a formula.
我們還在找公式。

5588
violate [ˈvaɪəˌlet]

v. 違反

34 protesters were arrested for violating the law.
34 位抗議者因為違反法律被逮捕。

5589
supreme [səˈprim]

adj. 極度的,極大的,至高的,最高的

This is a matter of supreme importance.
這件事情很重要。

5590
contest [ˈkɑntɛst]

n. 論爭,競賽 v. 爭論,爭辯,競賽,爭奪

I entered the contest in July.
我在七月進入比賽。

5591
margin [ˈmɑrdʒɪn]

n. 頁邊空白,邊緣,餘地,餘裕

Someone had taken a note in the margin.
有人在空白處做了筆記。

5592
panel [ˈpænl̩]

n. 面板,嵌板,儀錶板,座談小組,全體陪審者 vt. 嵌鑲板

A panel of experts discussed the proposal.
一群專家討論這個提議。

5593
mainland [ˈmenlənd]

n. 大陸,本土

Terrorist attacks mainland China.
恐怖分子攻擊中國大陸。

5594
substitute [ˈsʌbstəˌtjut]

n. 代用品,代替者 vt. 用⋯代替

He is a substitute goalkeeper.
他是替代的守門員。

5595
mostly [ˈmostlɪ]

adv. 主要地,大部分,通常

Green tea is mostly from China.
綠茶主要來自中國。

5596

rhythm [ˈrɪðəm]

n. 節奏,韻律

I like the rhythm of it.
我喜歡它的節奏。

5597

insert [ˈɪnsɜt]

vt. 插入,嵌入 n. 插入物

He inserted the key into the lock.
他將鑰匙插入鎖裡。

5598

invade [ɪnˈved]

vt. 侵入,侵略,侵犯

The United States invaded Iraq on March 20, 2003.
2003 年 3 月 20 日美國侵略伊拉克。

5599

shortcoming [ˈʃɔrtˌkʌmɪŋ]

n. 缺點,短處

Peter was aware of his own shortcomings.
彼得意識到自己的缺點。

5600

investment [ɪnˈvɛstmənt]

n. 投資,可獲利的東西

The project is about Japanese investment in American real estate this year.

這個計畫是關於今年日本在美國房地產投資。

5601

forbid [fɚˈbɪd]

vt. 不許,禁止

He was forbidden to leave the house.
他被禁止離開家裡。

5602

telescope [ˈtɛləˌskop]

n. 望遠鏡 v. 壓縮

A bird in the sky can only be seen clearly through a telescope. 你只能透過望遠鏡將天上的鳥看清楚。

5603

publication [ˌpʌblɪˈkefən]

n. 出版物,出版,發行,公布,發表

She is here for the publication of her new book.
她在這裡是為了出版她的新書。

5604

crush [krʌʃ]

vt. 壓碎,碾碎,壓服,壓垮,粉碎,(使)變形

The car was crushed in the accident.
這輛車在一場意外中被撞碎。

5605

idle [ˈaɪdl]

adj. 空閒的,閒著的,無所事事的 vi. 懶散

Sometimes he just idled.
有時候他無所事事的。

5606

ministry [ˈmɪnɪstrɪ]

n. (政府的)部門

The Ministry of Agriculture is here.
農業部在這裡。

5607

overhead ['ovɚ'hɛd]

adj. 在頭上的,高架的 n. 企業一般管理費用,天花板
adv. 在頭頂上,在空中,在高處

A bird flew overhead. 一隻鳥飛過頭上。

5608

regardless [rɪ'gɑrdlɪs]

adj. 不管,不顧,不注意

The law requires equal treatment for all, regardless of race. 法律需要不論種族,公平地對待全體人民。

5609

continual [kən'tɪnjʊəl]

adj. 連續的,頻繁的,持續不斷的

There are five weeks of continual rain.
連續下了五週的雨。

5610

radical ['rædɪkl]

adj. 根本的,基本的,激進的 n. 激進分子

The government has a radical reform to the tax system.
政府對於稅務制度有很大的改革。

5611

severe [sə'vɪr]

adj. 嚴重的,嚴厲的,艱難的,嚴峻的

She's suffering from severe depression.
她正承受嚴重的憂鬱症。

5612

virtue ['vɝtʃʊ]

n. 美德,優點,長處

Honesty is the virtue of being honest.
誠信是誠實的美德。

5613

surgery ['sɝdʒərɪ]

n. 外科,外科學,手術室,診療室

She required surgery on her right foot.
她右腳需要作手術。

5614

terror ['tɛrɚ]

n. 恐怖,可怕的人,恐怖時期,恐怖行動

I hate the terrors of war.
我討厭戰爭的恐怖。

5615

rehearse [rɪ'hɝs]

vt. 預演,排演,使排練,複述,練習,背誦,作假

vi. 排練,練習,演習

The band was rehearsing for their concert.

樂團在為他們演唱會彩排。

5616

peculiar [pɪ'kjuljɚ]

adj. 奇怪的,特殊的

There was a peculiar smell in the bathroom.
浴室有奇怪的味道。

5617

naval ['nevl]

adj. 海軍的

He is a naval officer.
他是海軍官員。

5618

moreover [mor'ovɚ]

adv. 而且,此外

The rent is reasonable and, moreover, the location is perfect. 房租很合理而且地點很好。

5619

detergent [dɪ'tɜdʒənt]

n. 清潔劑,去垢劑

I need detergent for washing clothes.
我需要清潔劑來洗衣服。

5620

constructive [kən'strʌktɪv]

adj. 建設性的

The meeting was very constructive.
該會議很有建設性。

5621

evolve [ɪ'vɑlv]

v. 發展,進化,淡化

Scientists think that birds probably evolved from reptiles.
科學家認為鳥類有可能是從爬行類動物進化而來的。

5622

infect [ɪn'fɛkt]

vt. [醫]傳染,感染

More and more people were infected with H1N1.
愈來愈多人感染 H1N1。

5623

laser ['lezɚ]

n. 雷射

I had a laser surgery yesterday.
我昨天做了一個雷射手術。

5624

manual ['mænjʊəl]

n. 手冊,指南

adj. 手的,手動的,手工的,體力的,手冊(性質)的,
　　[律]實際佔有的

This is a manual for the camera.

這是一本相機的使用手冊。

5625

dusk [dʌsk]

n. 黃昏

I left at dusk.
我在傍晚離開。

5626

wilderness ['wɪldɚnɪs]

n. 荒野,雜草叢生處,茫茫一片,大量,荒地

The garden was a wilderness.
這個花園是雜草叢生處。

5627

prospect ['prɑspɛkt]

n. 景色,前景,前途,期望

He is a student with good prospect.
他是位有前途的學生。

5628

loan [lon]

n. 暫借,貸款　vt. 供…以臨時住宿

I had to take out a loan to buy a house.
我必須貸款買房子。

5629

phenomenon [fə'nɑmə,nɑn]

n. 現象(複)

A rainbow is a natural phenomenon.

彩虹是自然現象。

5630

mislead [mɪs'lid]

vt. 誤導

Politicians have misled the public over the dangers of the war. 政客們誤導了公眾對戰爭的危險。

5631

stock [stɑk]

n. 庫存,現貨,樹幹,股票,公債(英式英語) v. 儲備

He keeps a stock of snacks in the cupboard.

他放了很多零食在櫥櫃裡。

5632

ensure [ɪn'ʃʊr]

vt. 保證,擔保

I ensure you the safety of the car.

我向你保證這輛車子的安全。

5633

grind [graɪnd]

v. 磨(碎),碾(碎),折磨

I need a stone for grinding knives and scissors.

我需要一塊用來磨刀子和剪刀的石頭。

5634

stake [stek]

n. 樹樁,股份

He holds a 50% stake in the firm.

他在公司有一半的股份。

5635

systematic [,sɪstə'mætɪk]

adj. 系統的,體系的

Can you tell me a systematic approach to solving the problem?

可以告訴我一個有系統解決這個問題的方法嗎?

5636

grave [grev]

n. 墓穴,墳墓 adj. 嚴重的,(顏色)黯淡的,(聲音)低沉的

He took that secret to the grave.

他帶著祕密死去。

5637

shrug [ʃrʌg]

n. 聳肩 v. 聳肩

Kathy shrugged and laughed.

凱西聳肩並微笑。

5638

exaggerate [ɪg'zædʒə,ret]

v. 誇大,誇張

He likes to exaggerate problems.

他喜歡將問題誇大。

5639

volunteer [,vɑlən'tɪr]

n. 志願者,志願兵 adj. 志願的,義務的,無償的

I need some volunteers to help with the work.

我需要一些志願者幫我這個工作。

5640
precise [prɪˈsaɪs]

adj. 精確的,準確的 n. 精確

It was important to get precise information.

得到精確的資料是很重要的。

5641
exception [ɪkˈsɛpʃən]

n. 除外,例外,反對,異議

We all laughed, with the exception of her.

我們都笑了,除了她以外。

5642
persist [pɚˈsɪst]

vi. (in)堅持不懈,執意,持續

She persisted with her opinion.

她堅持她的主見。

5643
peer [pɪr]

n. 同等的人,貴族 vt. 與…同等,封為貴族,凝視

Staff are trained by their peers.

員工被他們的同事訓練。

5644
session [ˈsɛʃən]

n. 會議,開庭

We have a training session for teachers about computers.

我們有一個開給老師的電腦課程。

5645
preferable [ˈprɛfərəbl̩]

adj. 更可取的,更好的,更優越的

For this dish, fresh herbs and garlic are preferable.

以這道菜來說,新鮮香料和大蒜是比較好的組合。

5646
triumph [ˈtraɪəmf]

n. 勝利,成功 v. 獲得勝利

Graduating is a great personal triumph.

畢業是個人極大的勝利。

5647
mechanical [məˈkænɪkl̩]

adj. 機械的,機械製的,機械似的,呆板的,技巧上的

The plane had to make a landing because of mechanical problems. 因為技術上的問題,這架飛機必須降落。

5648
reference [ˈrɛfərəns]

n. 提及,涉及,參考,參考書目,證明書(人),介紹信(人)

There is a reference to the Bible in the novel.

在小說中,她引用聖經作為例子。

5649
undertake [ˌʌndɚˈtek]

vt. 承擔,著手做,從事,承諾

Dr. Johnson undertook the task of writing a comprehensive English article.

約翰遜博士承擔了編寫英語文章的全面任務。

5650
overcome [ˌovɚˈkʌm]

vt. 戰勝,克服,勝過,征服 vi. 得勝

He struggled to overcome his shyness.

他嘗試克服他的害羞。

5651

consume [kən'sjum]

vt. 消耗,消費,消滅,大吃大喝,吸引 vi. 消滅,毀滅

Before he died, he had consumed a lot of food.

他去世前已經消耗了大量的食物。

5652

recall [rɪ'kɔl]

vt. 回憶,回想,召回,撤消

He seems to recall that I've met him before somewhere.

他似乎回想到我以前在哪裡見過他。

5653

logic ['lɑdʒɪk]

n. 邏輯,邏輯學,邏輯性

It's hard to understand his logic.

很難瞭解他的邏輯。

5654

percentage [pə'sɛntɪdʒ]

n. 百分數,百分率,百分比

Tax is paid as a percentage of total income.

稅是按照收入的百分比繳納。

5655

expose [ɪk'spoz]

vt. 暴露,揭露,使處於…作用之下

The report revealed that workers had been exposed to high levels of harmful materials.

報告顯示工人暴露在高度有害的物質中。

5656

prohibit [prə'hɪbɪt]

vt. 禁止,不准

They are prohibited from revealing details about the candidates. 他們被禁止透露候選人的細節。

5657

literary ['lɪtəˌrɛrɪ]

adj. 文學(上)的,從事寫作的,文藝的,精通文學的,書本的

He won a literary prize.

他獲得文學獎。

5658

consumer [kən'sjumə]

n. 消費者

Consumers will soon be paying lower airfares.

顧客即將付較便宜的飛機票。

5659

intermediate [ɪnt'əmidɪət]

adj. 中間的 n. 媒介

The book aimed at students at the intermediate level.

這本書是針對中級學生的程度。

5660

gravity ['grævətɪ]

n. 地心引力,重力,嚴重性

Newton's law of gravity has great influence to the world.

牛頓的地心引力對世界造成很大的影響。

5661

opera [ˈopərə]

n. 歌劇

He is an opera singer.

他是歌劇演唱家。

5662

sympathetic [ˌsɪmpəˈθɛtɪk]

adj. 有同情心的,合意的,贊成的

n. [解]交感神經,容易感受的人

I have a sympathetic attitude.

我有同情心。

5663

enhance [ɪnˈhæns]

vt. 提高,增強 v. 提高

You should enhance your English speaking ability.

你應該加強英文口說能力。

5664

theme [θim]

n. (談話,寫作等的)題目,主題,學生的作文,作文題,[音樂]主題,主題曲,主旋律

Her bedroom is decorated in a Victorian theme.

她的臥室以維多利亞風為主題布置而成。

5665

contemporary [kənˈtɛmpəˌrɛrɪ]

n. 同時代的人 adj. 當代的,同時代的

There is an exhibition of contemporary Japanese painting in July. 七月時有一個當代日本繪畫展。

5666

mild [maɪld]

adj. 和緩的,溫和的

I like the mild climate here.

我喜歡這裡溫和的氣候。

5667

recovery [rɪˈkʌvərɪ]

n. 恢復,痊癒,防禦,重獲

Ann made a quick recovery from her operation.

安很快的從手術中復原。

5668

liquor [ˈlɪkɚ]

n. 液體,汁,酒精飲料,[藥]溶液 vt. 浸水

She drinks liquor.

她喝酒。

5669

usage [ˈjusɪdʒ]

n. 使用,用法

I bought a book on modern English usage.

我買了一本關於現代英語用法的書。

5670

tendency [ˈtɛndənsɪ]

n. 趨向,傾向

The drug has a tendency to cause headaches.

這個藥物可能導致頭痛。

5671

assassinate [əˈsæsṇˌet]

vt. 暗殺,行刺

President Kennedy was assassinated in 1963.

甘迺迪總統於 1963 年遭暗殺。

5672

series [ˈsiriz]

n. 一系列,連續,叢書

There's been a whole series of accidents on this road.

這條路上發生了一連串的意外。

5673

enlarge [ɪnˈlɑrdʒ]

v. 擴大,放大

She had an operation to enlarge her breasts.

她做了一個隆乳手術。

5674

overlook [ˈovɚˌlʊk]

vt. 俯瞰,眺望,看漏,忽略

It is easy to overlook small details.

很容易忽略小細節。

5675

duration [djʊˈreʃən]

n. 持續時間,為期

The course is three years' duration.

這項課程為期三年。

5676

volcano [vɑlˈkeno]

n. 火山

Pompeii was destroyed by the volcano.

龐貝城被火山毀壞。

5677

herd [hɝd]

n. 獸群,牧群 v. 把…趕在一起放牧,成群

He raised a herd of cattle in the farm.

他在農場裡養了一群牛。

5678

occupy [ˈɑkjəˌpaɪ]

vt. 佔用,佔領,使忙碌

He occupies the house without paying any rent.

他佔用這個房子而沒有付房租。

5679

simplify [ˈsɪmpləˌfaɪ]

vt. 單一化,簡單化

The rule needs to be simplified.

這個規則需要被簡化。

5680

urgent [ˈɝdʒənt]

adj. 緊要的,急迫的

He was in urgent need of medical attention.

他急需醫療照顧。

5681

microscope [ˈmaɪkrəˌskop]

n. 顯微鏡

Each insect was examined through a microscope.

每一隻昆蟲都透過顯微鏡的檢查。

5682

withdraw [wɪðˈdrɔ]

vt. 收回,撤銷 vi. 縮回,退出

I'd like to withdraw $500 from my current account.

我想要從我現有的帳戶中領 500 元。

5683
qualify ['kwɑləˌfaɪ]

v. (使)具有資格,(使)勝任

He finally qualified as a pilot.

他終於勝任駕駛員這份工作。

5684
evidence ['ɛvədəns]

n. 明顯,顯著,明白,跡象,根據,[物]證據,證物

We have no evidence of it.

我們沒有這件事的證據。

5685
vigorous ['vɪgərəs]

adj. 精力旺盛的,有力的,健壯的

He is a vigorous young man.

他是個有活力的年輕人。

5686
spark [spɑrk]

n. 火花,火星,閃光,情郎,花花公子,活力,電信技師,瞬間放電 vt. 發動,鼓舞,使有朝氣,求婚

A discarded cigarette sparked a small fire.

一個被丟棄的香菸引發了一場小火 。

5687
legendary ['lɛdʒəndˌɛrɪ]

n. 傳奇故事書,傳奇文學 adj. 傳說中的

He is a legendary man in our department.

他是本系的傳奇人物。

5688
minimum ['mɪnəməm]

adj. 最低的,最小的 n. 最低限度,最少量

The minimum age for retirement is 60.

退休的最低年齡是 60 歲。

5689
retire [rɪ'taɪr]

v. 退休

Most people retire at 65.

大多數的人在 65 歲退休。

5690
iceberg ['aɪsˌbɜg]

n. 冰山,冷冰冰的人

The ship struck an iceberg in the ocean.

船撞到在海洋中的一座冰山。

5691
cruelty ['kruəltɪ]

n. 殘忍,殘酷

The children had suffered cruelty.

小孩遭受殘酷的對待。

5692
tiptoe ['tɪpˌto]

n. 腳尖,趾尖 vi. 用腳尖走

She stood on tiptoe to get a book.

她墊著腳尖拿書。

5693
reservation [ˌrɛzɚ'veʃən]

n. 保留,(旅館房間等)預定,預約

I have a dinner reservation tonight.

我今晚有預約晚餐。

5694

knowledgeable [ˈnɑlɪdʒəbl̩]

adj. 知識淵博的,有見識的

George's very knowledgeable about history.

喬治非常熟悉歷史。

5695

slight [slaɪt]

adj. 輕微的,微小的

He has a slight improvement.

他有一點進步。

5696

stem [stɛm]

n. 莖,幹,詞幹,莖幹 v. 滋生,阻止

You should put on a tight bandage to stem the blood.

你應該貼上很緊的繃帶阻止流血。

5697

revolutionary [ˌrɛvəˈluʃənˌɛrɪ] [-ˈlɪu-]

adj. 革命的,巨變的   [ˌrɛvl̩ˈjuʃənˌɛrɪ]

This is a revolutionary new drug.

這是革命性的新藥。

5698

inflation [ɪnˈfleʃən]

n. 脹大,誇張,通貨膨脹,(物價)暴漲

Inflation is now over 16%.

通貨膨脹超過 16%。

5699

distribute [dɪˈstrɪbjʊt]

vt. 分發,分配,分布

Clothes and blankets have been distributed among the refugees in winter. 衣服跟毯子已經在冬天發給難民。

5700

immigration [ˌɪməˈgreʃən]

n. 外來的移民,移居入境

The government set up a new policy on immigration.

政府設定新移民政策。

5701

vigor [ˈvɪgɚ]

n. 精力,活力

He works with vigor.

他精神飽滿的工作。

5702

impact [ˈɪmpækt] [ɪmˈpækt]

n. 碰撞,衝擊,影響,效果

vt. 擠入,撞擊,壓緊,對…發生影響

We need to assess the impact on climate change.

我們需要評估對氣候改變的影響。

5703

retain [rɪˈten]

vt. 保持,保留

The government wants to retain control of food imports.

政府想要保持對食物進口的控制。

5704

refresh [rɪˈfrɛʃ]

v. (使)精力恢復,(使)涼爽,(使)想起

He refreshed himself with a glass of ice tea.

他用一杯冰茶讓自己涼爽些。

5705
hydrogen [ˈhaɪdrədʒən] [ˈhaɪdrədʒɪn]

n. 氫

Hydrogen combines with oxygen to form water.
氫跟氧形成水。

5706
secure [sɪˈkjʊr] [səˈkjʊr]

adv. 安全的,可靠的　vt. 得到,保衛,使安全

We want our children to be secure in the future.
我們希望我們的小孩有一個安全穩當的未來。

5707
inference [ˈɪnfərəns]

n. 推論

What inferences have you drawn from this article?
你可以從這個文章中有什麼推論？

5708
obstacle [ˈɑbstəkl]

n. 障礙,妨害物

Fear of changing is an obstacle to success.
害怕改變是成功的障礙。

5709
continental [ˌkɑntəˈnɛntl]

adj. 大陸的,大陸性的　n. 歐洲人

I drink coffee in a continental-style cafe.
我在歐陸風格的咖啡店喝咖啡。

5710
vowel [ˈvaʊəl]

n. 母音　adj. 母音的

Each language has a different vowel system.
每個語言有不同的母音系統。

5711
misunderstand [ˌmɪsʌndɚˈstænd]

vt. 誤解,誤會

I misunderstood her intentions.
我誤解她的意圖。

5712
penalty [ˈpɛnl̩tɪ]

n. 處罰,罰款,壞處

Drug dealers face death penalties.
毒品交易商面臨死刑。

5713
urban [ˈɝbən]

adj. 城市的,市內的,城鎮的

The unemployment rate is higer in urban areas.
失業率在都會區比較高。

5714
corporation [ˌkɔrpəˈreʃən]

n. [律]社團,法人,公司,企業,(美)有限公司,
(市,鎮的)自治機關,(口)大肚皮

He works for a large corporation. 他在大公司上班。

5715
venture [ˈvɛntʃɚ]

n. 冒險,投機,風險　v. 冒險,冒昧,膽敢(謙語)

When it is dark, he would venture out.
當天氣變黑時，他要出去冒險。

5716
rescue [ˈrɛskjʊ]

vt. 營救,援救　n. 救援行動,搶救,援救

It is too late for rescue.
已經來不及救援了。

5717

observation [ˌɑbzɚˈveʃən]

n. 觀察,觀測,觀察資料(或報告),評論

He spent two nights under observation in hospital.

他花了兩晚在醫院觀察。

5718

guilty [ˈgɪltɪ]

adj. 內疚的,有罪的

I feel really guilty about her.

我對她感到罪惡感。

5719

photography [fəˈtɑgrəfɪ]

n. 攝影,攝影術

I visit the National Museum of Photography.

我參觀國家攝影博物館。

5720

magnificent [mægˈnɪfəsn̩t]

adj. 華麗的,高尚的,宏偉的,值得讚賞的

He has a magnificent performance.

他有一場值得讚賞的演出。

5721

parallel [ˈpærəˌlɛl]

adj. 平行的,相應的,同時發生的

v. 與…相似,與…同時發生

n. 極相似的人事物(不同時地下),相似處,緯線

Lines AB and CD are parallel.

直線 AB 跟 CD 是平行的。

5722

tornado [tɔrˈnedo]

n. 旋風,龍捲風,大雷雨,具有巨大破壞性的人(或事物),

[軍](狂風)英國,德國,義大利三國合作研製的雙座

雙發超音速變後掠翼戰鬥機

She burst into the room like a tornado.

她像龍捲風一樣突然出現在房間。

5723

drift [drɪft]

n. 漂流物,觀望,漂流,主旨

v. (使)漂流,漂移,無意間發生,不知不覺中陷入

The boat drifted out to sea.

船漂流出海。

5724

evident [ˈɛvədənt]

adj. 明顯的,顯然的

It soon became evident that the outcome of the
experiment was bad. 很明顯的研究成果很糟。

5725

reward [rɪˈwɔrd]

n. 酬勞,獎賞,報答 v. 給以獎賞或酬勞

The club's directors rewarded him with a free season
ticket. 俱樂部的領導人給他一張免費的票當獎勵。

5726

expansion [ɪk'spænfən]

n. 擴充,開展,膨脹,擴張物,遼闊,浩瀚

We have an expansion in student numbers.

我們擴充學生的數量。

5727

objection [əb'dʒɛkʃən]

n. 異議,缺陷,妨礙,反對之理由

Lawyers raised no objections to the plan.

律師在這個計畫沒有異議。

5728

disturb [dɪ'stɜb]

vt. 打擾,使不安,擾亂

Sorry to disturb you.

很抱歉打擾你。

5729

miserable ['mɪzrəbl̩] [-zərə-]

adj. 痛苦的,悲慘的,可憐,令人難受的,乖戾的

What a miserable life.

如此痛苦的生活。

5730

input ['ɪnˌpʊt]

n. 輸入,投入(時間,資源等) v. 輸入

Farmers contributed most of the input into the farm.

農夫投入了大部分的資源在農田裡。

5731

caption ['kæpʃən]

n. 標題,說明,字幕 vt. 加上標題,加上說明

The cartoon was captioned 'The English World'.

卡通標題是英國世界。

5732

scratch [skrætʃ]

n. 亂寫,刮擦聲,抓痕,擦傷

vt. 亂塗,勾抹掉,擦,刮,搔,抓,挖出

He stood scratching his head. 他站著抓著頭。

5733

neglect [nɪ'glɛkt]

vt. 忽視,忽略,疏忽,疏於看照 n. 忽視

This is a neglected garden.

這是座疏於照顧的花園。

5734

intrude [ɪn'trud]

vi. 闖入,侵入 vt. 強擠入,把(自己的思想)強加於人

Would I be intruding if I entered the room?

如果我闖入房間會冒失嗎？

5735

formation [fɔr'meʃən]

n. 形成,構成,編隊

The formation of a new government is a process.

新政府的形成是一個過程。

5736

halt [hɔlt]

n. 停止,暫停,中斷 vi. 立定,停止,躊躇

The government has to halt economic decline.

政府必須停止經濟衰退。

5737

urge [ɜdʒ]

vt. 催促,力勸 n. 強烈慾望,迫切要求

I got a letter from Jo urging me to get in touch.

我收到一封喬的信，要求我要保持聯絡。

5738

rod [rɑd]

n. 桿,棒,手槍(美式)

I need a measuring rod.
我需要一個測量棒。

5739

preserve [prɪˈzɝv]

vt. 保護,維持,保存 n. 專門領域,保留地

He was anxious to preserve his reputation.
他很緊張維護他的名聲。

5740

mercy [ˈmɝsɪ]

n. 仁慈,寬恕,憐憫,恩惠

God have mercy on us.
上帝寬恕我們。

5741

nutrient [ˈnjutrɪənt] [ˈnu-]

adj. 有營養的

Children suffer from a serious nutrient deficiency.
小孩受缺乏營養之苦。

5742

reflection [rɪˈflɛkʃən]

n. 反射,映像,倒影,反省,沉思,反映

Can you see your reflection in the river?
你可以看你在河裡的倒影嗎?

5743

option [ˈɑpʃən]

n. 選項,選擇權,[經]買賣的特權

We have two options.
我們有兩個選擇。

5744

delegate [ˈdɛləˌget]

n. 代表 vt. 委派…為代表

Around 350 delegates attended the conference.
大約 350 名代表出席會議。

5745

primitive [ˈprɪmətɪv]

adj. 原始的,遠古的,粗糙的,簡單的,落後的,本能的

n. 文藝復興前的藝術家(或作品),原始派畫家或作品

This is a primitive society.
這是原始社會。

5746

harsh [hɑrʃ]

adj. 粗糙的,荒蕪的,苛刻的,刺耳的,刺目的

He had harsh words for the Government.
他對政府有嚴厲的描述。

5747

influential [ˌɪnfluˈɛnʃəl]

adj. 有影響的,有勢力的

He had influential friends.
他有一些具影響力的朋友。

5748

physician [fɪˈzɪʃən]

n. 醫師,內科醫師

His father is a physician.
他的父親是內科醫生。

5749

sacrifice ['sækrə,faɪs] [-,faɪz]

vt. 獻祭,犧牲 n. 供奉,犧牲

Her parents made sacrifices so that she could have a good education.

她的父母犧牲所有使她能有一個良好的教育。

5750

explosion [ɪk'sploʒən]

n. 爆發,發出,爆炸,[礦]煤氣爆炸,猛增,(感情上的,
尤指憤怒)爆發

We heard a loud explosion.

我們聽到巨大的爆炸聲。

5751

magnetic [mæg'nɛtɪk]

adj. 磁的,有磁性的,有吸引力的

I need magnetic materials.
我需要有磁性的材料。

5752

publish ['pʌblɪʃ]

v. 出版,刊印 vt. 公布,發表

The first edition was published this year.
第一版在今年出版。

5753

defensive [dɪ'fɛnsɪv]

adj. 防禦性的,戒備的 n. 採取戒備

Don't ask him about his plans—he just gets defensive.
不要問他計畫,他很有防衛心。

5754

voluntary ['vɑlən,tɛrɪ]

adj. 自願的,志願的

I do some voluntary work at the community.
我在社區做些慈善工作。

5755

twinkle ['twɪŋkl̩]

v. 閃爍,閃耀,(使)閃光 n. 閃爍,發光,欣喜的神情

I saw stars twinkling in the sky.
我在天空上看到星星閃爍。

5756

alternative [ɔl'tɜnətɪv]

n. 二中擇一,可供選擇的辦法,事物

adj. 選擇性的,二中擇一的

There are alternatives for paying bills.

有不同的選擇去付款。

5757

shift [ʃɪft]

v. 移動,轉移,改變 n. 轉換,轉變,輪班,換班

The White House hopes to shift the media's attention away from the scandal.

白宮希望能轉移媒體在這件醜聞上的焦點。

5758

reflect [rɪ'flɛkt]

v. 反射,反映,思考,考慮

She could see her face reflected in the mirror.

她可以看到她的臉在鏡中反映出來。

5759

privilege ['prɪvlɪdʒ] ['prɪvlɪdʒ]

n. 特權,特別待遇,基本公民權力,特免,榮幸

vt. 給與…特權

Education should not be a privilege.

教育不應該是特權。

5760

dynamic [daɪ'næmɪk]

adj. 動力的,動力學的,動態的,充滿活力的

n. 力學,動力,動態

Learning is a dynamic and unstable process.

學習是動態的和不穩定的過程。

5761

hardship ['hɑrdʃɪp]

n. 困苦,艱難,辛苦

Many students are suffering severe hardship.

很多學生遭受嚴重的困難。

5762

oval ['ovl]

adj. 卵形的,橢圓的 n. 卵形,橢圓形

I bought an oval mirror.

我買了一個橢圓的鏡子。

5763

prominent ['prɑmənənt]

adj. 卓越的,顯著的,突出的,著名的

He is a prominent Russian scientist.

他是一位著名的俄羅斯科學家。

5764

decoration [,dɛkə'reʃən]

n. 裝飾,裝飾品

Th school have Christmas decorations.

這間學校有聖誕節的裝飾品布置。

5765

construct [kəns'trʌkt] ['kɑnstrʌkt]

vt. 建造,構造,創立 n. 構想,結構

There are plans to construct a new bridge across the river. 有計畫建造跨過河流的新橋。

5766

sketch [skɛtʃ]

n. 略圖,草圖,素描 vt. 素描,概述,應付

Karl drew a rough sketch of his house.

卡爾畫了房子的草圖。

5767
distinct [dɪ'stɪŋkt]
adj. (from)不同的,清楚的
Chinese and English are two distinct languages.
中文跟英文是兩個不同的語言。

5768
tolerate ['tɑlə,ret]
vt. 容忍,忍受,容許
I can't tolerate boring work.
我無法容忍無聊工作。

5769
invasion [ɪn've3ən]
n. 入侵,侵犯
I read the history about the invasion of Normandy.
我讀有關諾曼帝佔領的歷史。

5770
outward ['aʊtwəd]
adj. 外面的,外表的,公開的,向外的,外出的
adv. 向外,在外,表面上,外表,周圍世界
n. 外在
Mark showed outward signs of distress.
馬克顯出失望的表情。

5771
machinery [mə'ʃinərɪ] [mə'ʃinrɪ]
n. [總稱]機器,機械,系統,體制
The use of heavy machinery has damaged the place.
使用重型機器對這個地方造成危害。

5772
psychology [saɪ'kɑlədʒɪ]
n. 心理學,心理狀態
He is an expert in the field of psychology.
他是心理學的專家。

5773
digital ['dɪdʒɪtl]
adj. 數字的,數字的,手指的 n. 數字,數字式
I bought a digital TV.
我買了一台數位電視。

5774
thorough ['θ3o]
adj. 徹底的,完全的,仔細周到的,精心的
The doctor gave me a thorough check-up.
醫生徹底的給我全身檢查。

5775
overall ['ovə,ɔl]
adj. 全部的,全面的
The overall cost of the exhibition was over a million.
這個展覽全部的花費超過一百萬元。

5776
overtake [,ovə'tek]
vt. 趕上,追上,(暴風雨,麻煩等)突然來襲,壓倒
Television soon overtook the cinema.
電視很快地超越了劇院。

5777
identify [aɪ'dɛntə,faɪ]
vt. 認出,鑒定,認為…等同於(with)
He was too far away that we couldn't identify his face.
他太遠了以致於我們無法辨別他的臉。

5778

signature [ˈsɪgnətʃɚ] [ˈsɪgnɪ-]

n. 簽名,署名,信號

Her signature is not very clear.

她的簽名不太清楚。

5779

vain [ven]

adj. 徒勞的,無效的,自負的,虛榮的

Police searched in vain for the missing criminal.

員警徒勞無功的尋找消失的罪犯。

5780

numerous [ˈnjumərəs] [ˈnu-]

adj. 眾多的,許多的

The two parties have worked together on numerous occasions. 這兩個政黨在很多場合中一起合作過。

5781

oppose [əˈpoz]

vt. 反對,反抗

He is opposed by two other candidates.

他被其它兩個候選人反對。

5782

spacecraft [ˈspesˌkræft]

n. 太空船

A spacecraft travels in space.

太空船在太空中飛行。

5783

organic [ɔrˈgænɪk]

adj. 器官的,有機的,組織的,建制的

Organic farming is better for the environment.

有機栽種對環境比較好。

5784

motivate [ˈmotəˌvet]

vt. 作為…的動機,促動,激勵

Was he motivated solely by a desire?

他單純被慾望鼓舞嗎？

5785

modest [ˈmɑdɪst]

adj. 謙虛的,謙讓的,適度的

He made some modest improvements.

他做了適度的改善。

5786

landscape [ˈlændskep] [ˈlænskep]

n. 風景,山水畫,地形,前景 v. 美化

We can expect changes in the political landscape.

我們可以預期政治格局的變化。

5787

sanction [ˈsæŋkʃən]

n. 批准,同意,支援,制裁,認可

v. 批准,同意,支援,鼓勵,認可

USA has a resolution to impose sanctions on North Korea.

美國決心要抵制北韓。

5788

suspend [səˈspɛnd]

vt. 吊,懸掛 v. 延緩

Dave was suspended from school for a month.

大衛被學校停學一個月。

5789
plentiful ['plɛntɪfəl]
adj. 許多的,大量的,豐富的,豐饒的

The man provides a plentiful supply of food.

這個人提供大量的食物供給。

5790
naturalist ['nætʃərəlɪst] ['nætʃrəl-]
n. 自然主義者,博物學者

He is a naturalist.

他是自然主義者。

5791
resign [rɪ'zaɪn]
vi. 辭職　vt. 放棄,辭去,使順從(to)

Two members resigned from the job.

兩名成員辭去了這份工作。

5792
portable ['portəbl]
adj. 輕便的,手提(式)的,攜帶型的

I bought a portable TV.

我買了可攜帶的電視。

5793
context ['kɑntɛkst]
n. 上下文,文章的前後關係

The meaning of 'happy' depends on its context.

"happy"這個字的意思,取決在上下內文。

5794
guarantee [ˌgærən'ti]
n. 保證,保證書,擔保,抵押品　vt. 保證,擔保

I guarantee you'll love this shirt.

我保證你會愛上這件襯衫。

5795
literature ['lɪtərətʃə] [-ˌtʃʊr]
n. 文學(作品),文藝,著作,文獻

He likes Italian literature.

他喜歡義大利文學。

5796
dissolve [dɪ'zɑlv]
v. 溶解,解散,消散

Suger dissolves in water.

糖溶解在水裡。

5797
sympathy ['sɪmpəθɪ]
n. 同情,同情心

I have no sympathy for Kevin.

我對凱文沒有同情心。

5798
pregnant ['prɛgnənt]
adj. 懷孕的,重要的,富有意義的,孕育的

I was too old to get pregnant.

我太老以致於不能懷孕。

5799
noun [naʊn]
n. 名詞

Names or things are nouns.

名字或是事物都是名詞。

5800
philosopher [fə'lɑsəfə]
n. 哲學家,哲人

He is a philosopher.

他是哲學家。

5801

presidential [ˌprɛzə'dɛnʃəl]

adj. 總統的,總裁的

A presidential election is coming soon.

總統選舉要到了。

5802

predict [prɪ'dɪkt]

v. 預言,預測

It is very difficult to predict weather.

預測天氣很困難。

5803

gear [gɪr]

n. 齒輪,傳動裝置 v. 調整,(使)適合,換檔

His mountain bike had 18 gears.

他的登山腳踏車有 18 個齒輪。

5804

interference [ˌɪntəˈfɪrəns]

n. 衝突,干涉

I resent his interference in my life.

我討厭他干涉我的生活。

5805

philosophy [fə'lɑsəfɪ]

n. 哲學,哲學體系,達觀,冷靜

Emma studies philosophy at university.

艾瑪在大學研讀哲學。

5806

reform [rɪ'fɔrm]

n. 改革,改善,改良運動,感化 vt. 改革,革新,重新組成

A reform of public traffic transportation is developing.

大眾交通運輸工具正在改革中。

5807

troublesome ['trʌbl̩səm]

adj. 麻煩的,討厭的,棘手的

He is a troublesome child.

他是麻煩的小孩。

5808

foundation [faʊn'deʃən]

n. 基礎,根本,建立,創立,地基,基金,基金會

The builders lay the foundations of the new school.

建築者展示新學校的基礎。

5809

intention [ɪn'tɛnʃən]

n. 意圖,目的

Please describe the intention of your choice.

請你說明為什麼做這個決定。

5810

psychological [ˌsaɪkə'lɑdʒɪkl̩]

adj. 心理(上)的

He has a psychological problem.

他有心理的問題。

5811

rural ['rʊrəl]

adj. 鄉下的,田園的,鄉村風味的,生活在農村的

I like a rural setting.

我喜歡鄉村的環境。

5812

version ['vɝʒen] [-ʃen]

n. 譯文,譯本,版本

They were the early version of department stores.

這些是百貨公司早期的版本。

5813

punctual [ˈpʌŋktʃʊəl] [ˈpʌŋktʃʊl]

adj. 嚴守時刻的,準時的

Be punctual, please.

請準時。

5814

correspond [ˌkɔrəˈspɑnd] [ˌkɑr-]

vi. 相符合(with),相當(to),通信(with)

The numbers correspond to data in the study.

這些數字對應研究中的資料。

5815

resident [ˈrɛzədənt]

n. 居民,定居者 adj. 居住的,住校的

They are the residents of Taipei.

他們是台北的居民。

5816

significance [sigˈnɪfəkəns]

n. 意義,重要性

Can you tell me the significance of climate change?

你可以告訴我氣候變化的重要性嗎?

5817

forecast [ˈforˌkæst] [ˈfɔr-]

n. 預報 v. 預報

The weather forecast is good for tomorrow.

天氣預報說明天天氣很好。

5818

tragedy [ˈtrædʒədɪ]

n. 悲劇,慘案,悲慘,災難

The tragedy happened as they were returning home.

悲劇在他們回家時發生了。

5819

interpret [ɪnˈtɝprɪt]

v. 解釋,說明,口譯,通譯,認為是…的意思

They spoke good Spanish, and promised to interpret for me. 他們說流利的西班牙文,並且承諾為我口譯。

5820

isolate [ˈaɪsˌlet] [ˈɪsˌlet]

vt. 使隔離,使孤立,使絕緣,離析 n. 隔離種群

The town was isolated by the floods.

這座城鎮被洪水阻隔。

5821

transform [trænsˈfɔrm]

vt. 使變形,使改觀,改造,改善,變換

A new color scheme will transform your bedroom.

新的色彩將會使你的臥室改觀。

5822

orbit [ˈɔrbɪt]

n. 軌道,勢力範圍,生活常規,眼眶 vt. 繞…軌道而行

The earth orbits the sun.

地球繞太陽。

5823

intellectual [ˌɪntḷˈɛktʃʊəl] [ˌɪntḷˈɛktʃʊl]

adj. 智力的,有智力的,顯示智力的 n. 知識分子

Mark's very intellectual.

馬克很聰明。

5824

germ [dʒɝm]

n. 微生物,細菌

Dirty hands can be a place for germs.

髒的手可以是讓菌繁殖的地方。

5825 distrust [dɪs'trʌst]

n. 不信任　vt. 不信任

She distrusts him.

她不相信他。

5826 nightmare ['naɪt,mɛr] ['naɪt,mær]

n. 夢魘,惡夢,可怕的事物

I still have nightmares about it.

我仍然有些夢魘。

5827 nowhere ['no,hwɛr] [-,hwær]

adv. 無處,到處都無

A vagrant has no job and nowhere to live.

遊民沒有工作而且沒有地方住。

5828 nonsense ['nɑnsɛns]

n. 胡說,廢話

He talks all this nonsense about health foods.

他講關於健康食品都是廢話。

5829 supervisor [,supɚ'vaɪzɚ] [,sɪu-] [,sju-]

n. 監督人,管理人,檢查員,督學,主管人

Mr.Wang is a supervisor.

王先生是主管。

5830 typist ['taɪpɪst]

n. 打字員

I'm a fast typist.

我是快速的打字員。

5831 tense [tɛns]

adj. 緊張的,拉緊的　v. (使)緊張,(使)拉緊

You look a little tense.

你看起來有點緊張。

5832 rear [rɪr]

n. 後部,尾部　adj. 後方的,後部的　v. 培養,飼養

There are toilets at both front and rear of the train.

在火車前後方都有廁所。

5833 porter ['portɚ] ['portɚ]

n. 守門人,門房,行李搬運工

He is the night porter.

他是飯店夜間門房。

5834 namely ['nemlɪ]

adv. 即,也就是

We need to focus on older students, namely seniors.

我們需注意年紀大點的學生,也就是大四生。

5835 curl [kɝl]

v. (使)捲曲　n. 捲狀物

The cat curled into a ball and went to sleep.

貓捲成一團睡覺。

5836 voyage ['vɔɪɪdʒ] ['vɔjɪdʒ]

n. 航程,航空,航海記,旅行記　vt. 渡過,飛過

The voyage from England to India took six months.

從英國到印度的旅程花了六個月。

5837

gaze [gez]

vi. 凝視

Patrick sat gazing into space.

派翠克直視著天空。

5838

liberate ['lɪbəˌret]

v. 解放,釋放

The book is about the liberating power of education.

這本書是關於教育的解放力量。

5839

thoughtful ['θɔtfəl]

adj. 考慮周到的,體貼的,深思的

It was very thoughtful of you to send the card.

你送卡片真體貼。

5840

solar ['solə]

adj. 太陽的,日光的

I saw a solar eclipse on TV.

我在電視上看到日蝕。

5841

intimate ['ɪntəˌmet]

adj. 親密的,隱私的,詳盡的,密切的 n. 熟友

He is an intimate friend of his.

他是他的密友之一。

5842

grant [grænt]

n. 撥款 vt. 授予,同意,准予

The bank finally granted me a loan.

銀行最後准許我貸款。

5843

consult ['kɑnsʌlt] [kən'sʌlt]

v. 商量,商議,請教,參考,考慮

Have you consulted your lawyer?

你請教過你的律師嗎?

5844

experimental [ɪkˌspɛrə'mɛntl]

adj. 實驗的,根據實驗的

The hypothesis is now confirmed by experimental evidence. 這項假設現在已有實驗結果證實。

5845

implication [ˌɪmplɪ'keʃən]

n. 牽連,含意,暗示,可能的影響,作用或結果

What are the implications of these researches?

這些研究的作用是什麼?

5846

poultry ['poltrɪ]

n. 家禽

He eats plenty of fish and poultry.

他吃很多魚和家禽。

5847

invention [ɪn'vɛnʃən]

n. 發明,創造

The washing machine is a wonderful invention.

洗衣機是很棒的發明。

5848

pace [pes] n. (一)步,速度,步調,步法,步態

vt. 用步測,踱步於,(馬)溜花蹄

The pace of life is very slow here.

這裡的生活步調很慢。

5849
potential [pə'tɛnʃəl]
adj. 有潛力的,有可能性的,潛在的
He thinks of new ways of attracting potential customers.
他想了新的方法吸引潛在顧客。

5850
resemble [rɪ'zɛmbl]
vt. 像,類似
He resembles his father.
他像他的父親。

5851
scenery ['sinərɪ]
n. 風景,景色
I like the fantastic scenery here.
我喜歡這裡的美麗風景。

5852
opponent [ə'ponənt]
adj. 對立的,對抗的 n. 對手,反對者
In debate, he was an opponent.
在辯論中他是對手。

5853
worthwhile ['wɝθ'hwaɪl]
adj. 值得做的,值得出力的
He wanted to look for a worthwhile job.
他想要找值得他做的工作。

5854
monument ['mɑnjəmənt]
n. 紀念碑,歷史遺跡,古跡,永久的典範
Ancient monuments are protected by the government.
政府保護古蹟。

5855
industrialize [ɪn'dʌstrɪəl‚aɪz]
vt. 使工業化 vi. 工業化
The country was slow in industrializing.
這個國家很慢地在工業化。

5856
commitment [kə'mɪtmənt]
n. 委託事項,許諾,承擔義務
Are you ready to make a commitment?
你準備好做出承諾了嗎?

5857
prosperity [prɑs'pɛrətɪ]
n. 繁榮
Can you foresee the future prosperity of the country?
你可以預知這個國家未來的繁榮嗎?

5858
photographic [‚fotə'græfɪk]
adj. 照相的
I have photographic equipment.
我有照相裝備。

5859
memorable ['mɛmərəbl]
adj. 值得紀念的,難忘的
The city is memorable for its beautiful scenery.
這個城市以美的風景令人難忘。

5860
initial [ɪ'nɪʃəl]
adj. 開始的,最初的 n.(常複)(姓名或組織等的)首字母
These are the initial stages of the disease.
這些是這個疾病的開始階段。

5861

ingredient [ɪnˈgridɪənt]

n. 成分,因素,材料

Combine all the ingredients in a bowl.

請將碗裡的材料結合。

5862

therapy [ˈθɛrəpɪ]

n. 治療,療法

He thinks of new drug therapies.

他想到新的藥物治療方法。

5863

profession [prəˈfɛʃən]

n. 職業,專業,表白,宣布,專業人員

They are members of the teaching profession.

他們是教學專業的會員。

5864

nuclear [ˈnjuklɪɚ] [ˈnɪu-] [ˈnu-]

adj. [核]核子的,原子能的,核的,中心的

He is interested in the nuclear industry.

他對核能產業有興趣。

5865

workshop [ˈwɜkˌʃɑp]

n. 車間,工場,研討會,講座

They held a number of workshops.

他們舉辦很多研討會。

5866

symbolize [ˈsɪmblˌaɪz] vt. 象徵,用符號表現

vi. 作為…的象徵,採用象徵,使用符號

Crime often symbolizes a social problem.

犯罪是社會問題的表徵。

5867

negotiation [nɪˌgoʃɪˈeʃən]

n. 商議,談判,流通

The negotiations with the company haven't finished.

跟這家公司的談判還沒結束。

5868

waterproof [ˈwɔtɚˌpruf]

adj. 防水的,不透水的

I bought a waterproof jacket.

我買了件防水的外套。

5869

sharpen [ˈʃɑrpən]

v. 削尖,磨快,尖銳,使提高改善,(使感覺或感情)更明顯

Anne sharpened her pencil and did her homework.

安削了鉛筆並寫了功課。

5870

durable [ˈdjʊrəbl̩] [ˈdɪʊr-] [ˈdʊr-]

adj. 持久的,耐用的

Paper is not a durable material.

紙張並不是一個持久的材料。

5871

rifle [ˈraɪfl̩]

n. 來福槍,步槍,來福線,膛線

vt. 快速搜尋,用步槍射擊,搶奪

She rifled through her clothes for something suitable to wear in the meeting.

她在匆忙中翻找適合會議穿的衣服。

5872

hence [hɛns]

adv. 因此,從此,此後

The consequences will only be known several years hence. 這個結果在數年後才會被知道。

5873

browse [braʊz]

v. 瀏覽,吃草,放牧 n. 瀏覽,吃草,放牧

Jon was browsing through the album.
強尼正在瀏覽相簿。

5874

interfere [ˌɪntəˈfɪr] vi. 干涉,介入(with, in),

妨礙,干擾,意圖性侵犯,弄壞,干預,介入

Anxiety can interfere with students' performance at school. 焦慮會干擾學生在學校的表現。

5875

widespread [ˈwaɪdˌsprɛd]

adj. 分布廣泛的,普遍的

The table shows the widespread use of chemicals in agriculture. 這個圖表顯示農業大量使用化學藥劑。

5876

polish [ˈpolɪʃ]

n. 磨光,光澤,上光劑,優雅,精良 n. 波蘭人

I spent all afternoon polishing the shoes.
我花了一整個下午擦亮鞋子。

5877

loyal [ˈlɔɪəl] [ˈlɔjəl]

adj. 忠誠的,忠心的

The army is loyal to the government.
這個軍隊對政府效忠。

5878

lag [ˈlæg]

n. 落後,囚犯,遲延,桶板,防護套 vi. 緩緩而行,滯後

She stopped to call out to Ian who was lagging behind.
她停下來呼叫落後的依恩。

5879

surroundings [səˈraʊndɪŋz]

n. [複]周圍的事物,環境,周圍的,附近的

I need to work in cheerful surroundings.
我需要在愉快的環境中工作。

5880

institution [ˌɪnstəˈtjuʃən] [-ˈtru-] [-ˈtu-]

n. 社會公共機構,制度,習俗

He works in the Institution of Electrical Engineering.
他在電子工程機構工作。

5881

scan [skæn]

v. 細看,審視,瀏覽,掃描 n. 掃描

I scanned the page for her name.
我在頁面上搜尋她的名字。

5882

favorable [ˈfevrəbl] [ˈfevərəbl]

adj. 贊成的,有利的,贊許的,良好的,討人喜歡的,
起促進作用的

These are favorable film reviews.

這些都是好的電影影評。

5883

moderate ['mɑdə,ret]

adj. 中等的,適度的,適中的 v. 緩和

Even moderate amounts of alcohol can be dangerous.

即使適度的酒精也可能是危險的。

5884

plot [plɑt]

n. 地區圖,圖,祕密計劃(特指陰謀),(小說的)情節,結構

vt. 密謀,策劃

They have a plot to bomb the building.

他們密謀炸掉建築物。

5885

intense [ɪn'tɛns]

adj. 強烈的,劇烈的,熱切的,熱情的,激烈的

The pain was so intense that I couldn't sleep.

疼痛如此強烈,以致於我無法睡覺。

5886

feedback ['fid,bæk]

n. [無]回授,反饋,反應

How can I provide feedback?

我該如何提供回饋。

5887

incident ['ɪnsədənt]

n. 發生的事,事件,事變

A spokesman said it was an isolated incident.

發言人說這是單一事件。

5888

tremendous [trɪ'mɛndəs]

adj. 巨大的,極大的

She was making a tremendous effort to show up.

她花了很大力氣出現。

5889

visual ['vɪʒʊəl]

adj. 看的,視覺的,形象的,栩栩如生的

Artists translate their ideas into visual images.

藝術家將想法轉為視覺影像。

5890

wreck [rɛk]

vt. 毀壞,使遇難 n. 失事,(船,飛機的)殘骸

Somebody threatened to wreck his career.

有人威脅要破壞他的職業生涯。

5891

infer [ɪn'fɝ]

vt. 推論,推斷,推理,間接地提出,暗示,意指

From the evidence we can infer that this is true.

從這個證據我們可以斷言這是對的。

5892

progressive [prə'grɛsɪv]

n. 改革論者,進步論者

adj. 前進的,(稅收)累進的,進步的

The graph shows the progressive increase in population.

這個圖表顯示人口持續增加。

5893

orphanage [ˈɔrfənɪdʒ]

n. 孤兒院,孤兒身分

He was raised in an orphanage.

他在孤兒院被養大的。

5894

residence [ˈrɛzədəns]

n. 居住,住處,住所,住房,宅第,豪宅,居住權,居留許可,有正式職位,常駐

The ambassador's official residence is nearby.

大使館的官邸在附近。

5895

dependent [dɪˈpɛndənt]

adj. 依靠的,依賴的,由…決定的,隨…而定的

Norway's economy is heavily dependent on trading.

挪威的經濟主要依靠貿易。

5896

insult [ˈɪnsʌlt]

n. 侮辱,凌辱 vt. 侮辱,凌辱,辱罵,冒犯

I hope Andy won't be insulted if I don't come.

我希望安迪不會因為我沒來而覺得受委屈。

5897

definite [ˈdɛfənɪt]

adj. 明確的,一定的

It's easy for me to give you a definite answer.

對我來說給你一個確定的答案很容易。

5898

grateful [ˈgretfəl]

adj. 感激的,感謝的

I'm so grateful for all your help.

我很感激你的幫忙。

5899

loyalty [ˈlɔɪəltɪ] [ˈlɔjəl-]

n. 忠誠,忠心

They swore their loyalty to the king.

他們對國王宣示忠實。

5900

reputation [ˌrɛpjəˈteʃən]

n. 名譽,名聲

Judge Charles has a reputation for being honest.

法官查理斯有一個誠實的聲譽。

5901

dye [daɪ]

n. 染料,染色 v. 染

His hair was dyed black.

他的頭髮被染黑。

5902

consultant [kənˈsʌltənt]

n. 顧問 n. 顧問醫生,會診醫生

He is a management consultant.

他是管理諮詢員。

5903

oral [ˈɔrəl] [ˈorəl]

adj. 口頭的

They have an oral agreement.

他們有口頭約定。

5904

lean [lin]

vi. 傾斜,屈身,靠,依(against)

adj. 脂肪少的,精幹的,貧乏的

They were leaning and facing each other.

他們身體彎曲並面向彼此。

5905

crystal [ˈkrɪstḷ]

adj. 結晶狀的 n. 水晶,水晶飾品,結晶,晶體

I bought a set of six crystal glasses.

我買了一組六個的水晶杯。

5906

sparrow [ˈspæro]

n. 麻雀

I saw a sparrow in the farm.

我在農場上看到麻雀。

5907

offensive [əˈfɛnsɪv]

adj. 討厭的,無禮的,攻擊性的 n. 進攻,攻勢

His comments were deeply offensive to me.

他的言論對我來說相當無禮。

5908

vessel [ˈvɛsḷ]

n. 船,容器,器皿,脈管,導管

The doctor checked a burst blood vessel in my body.

醫生檢查我身體內爆開的血管。

5909

overnight [ˈovɚˌnaɪt]

n. 頭天晚上

adv. 在前一夜,整夜,昨晚一晚上

adj. 夜間的,只供一夜的(旅店等)

Pam's staying overnight at my house.

潘在我房子待整晚。

5910

proceed [prəˈsid]

vi. 進行,繼續進行,接著做

Sammy took off his coat and proceeded to sleep.

山姆把外套脫掉並繼續睡覺。

5911

slang [slæŋ]

n. 俚語,行話 v. 用粗話罵,用俚語說

This is a schoolboys' slang.

這是學校男孩的俚語。

5912

hardware [ˈhɑrdˌwɛr] [-ˌwær]

n. 五金器具,(電腦的)硬體,(電子儀器的)部件

This is a hardware shop.

這是五金行。

5913

physical [ˈfɪzɪkḷ]

adj. 身體的,物質的,自然的,物理的 n. 體格檢查

She was in physical pain.

她有生理上的痛。

5914

tolerance ['tɑlərəns] [-lrəns]

n. 公差,寬容,忍受,容忍,(食物中殘存殺蟲劑的)(法定)容許量 vt. 給(機器零件等)規定公差

They have tolerance towards religious minorities.

他們對少數宗教有容忍性。

5915

implement ['ɪmpləˌmɛnt]

n. 工具,器具 v. 執行

We have decided to implement the committee's recommendations. 我們已經決定要執行會議的建議。

5916

welfare ['wɛlˌfɛr] [-ˌfær]

n. 福利,安寧,幸福,福利事業,社會安全 adj. 福利的

Our only concern is the children's welfare.

我們唯一在乎的是小孩福利。

5917

intensive [ɪn'tɛnsɪv]

adj. 強烈的,精深的,透徹的,[語法]加強語氣的

n. 加強器

We have a one-week intensive course in English.

我們有一個星期的英文密集課。

5918

province ['prɑvɪns]

n. 省(一個國家的大行政區)

Xinjiang is a Chinese province.

新疆是中國一省。

5919

prediction [prɪ'dɪkʃən]

n. 預言,預報

Can you make a useful economic prediction?

你可以做有用的經濟預測嗎?

VQC

單字力 B Rank

S3 高中三年級
T2 技職學院二年級（編號5920～6446）

S3 高中三年級
T3 技職學院三年級（編號6447～6948）

S3 高中三年級（編號6949～6984）

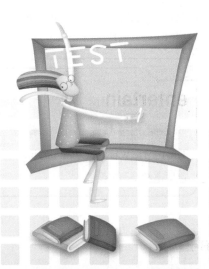

S3 高中三年級
T2 技職學院二年級　編號 5920～6446

5920

retreat [rɪ'trit]

vt. 退卻,撤退,離去,退去,後退,退縮,隱退,逃避,
　　躲避,跌價,退卻

n. 退卻,退避,退縮,靜僻處

The enemies retreated to the mountains.

敵人撤退到山裡。

5921

frame [frem]

n. 結構,體格　n. 幀,畫面,框架　v. 給…做框(邊),制定

Put the picture in its wooden frame.

把照片放到木框裡。

5922

layer [lɛr] ['leɚ]

n. 層,階層　v. 把～分層

There is a thick layer of dust on the furniture.

傢俱上有一層厚厚的灰塵。

5923

entertain [ˌɛntɚ'ten]

vt. 娛樂,招待,接受,懷抱　vi. 款待

The movie was very entertaining.

這個電影很有娛樂性。

5924

vital ['vaɪtl]

adj. 生死攸關的,極其重要的,有生命的

It is vital that you should be honest.

極其重要的是你要誠實。

5925

distinguish [dɪ'stɪŋgwɪʃ]

v. 區別,辨別

You must distinguish between being right and wrong.

你必須分辨對或錯。

5926

satellite ['sætlˌaɪt]

n. 衛星,人造衛星

We watch satellite television.

我們看衛星電視。

5927

invest [ɪn'vɛst]

v. 投(資),購買(有用之物)～,授予,投入(時間或精力等)

He invested money in the stock market.

他在股票市場投資金錢。

5928

output ['aʊtˌpʊt]

n. 產量,輸出,輸出量

Agricultural output is up 10% on last year.

農業輸出比去年增長了 10%。

5929

reduction [rɪ'dʌkʃən]

n. 減少,縮影,變形,縮減量,約簡

Do you have any strategies for noise reduction?

你有任何策略減少噪音汙染嗎？

5930

exploit [ɪk'splɔɪt] vt. 剝削,利用,開拓,開發

n. 功績,功勳,輝煌的成就,英勇的行為

Laborers can easily be exploited by employers.

勞工很容易被雇主剝削。

5931

intelligence [ɪn'tɛlədʒəns]

n. 智力,聰明,智慧

John showed high intelligence in math.

約翰在數學上表現出高度的智慧。

5932

landlord ['lænd,lɔrd] ['læn-]

n. 房東,地主,(旅館等的)老闆

We pay rent to a landlord.

我們付房租給房東。

5933

identical [aɪ'dɛntɪkl]

adj. 相同的,相等

The sisters were identical in personality.

兩個姐妹有相同個性。

5934

register ['rɛdʒɪstə]

n. 登記,註冊 vi. 登記,註冊

How many students did they register for the new semester? 新的學期有多少學生註冊？

5935

illustrate ['ɪləstret] [ɪ'lʌstret]

vt. 舉例說明,圖解,加插圖於,闡明 vi. 舉例

Can you give an example to illustrate the point?

你可以舉例說明這個論點嗎？

5936

presently ['prɛzṇtlɪ]

adv. 目前,不久

Presently, I am busy.

現在我很忙。

5937

refusal [rɪ'fjuzl] [-'fɪu-]

n. 拒絕,推卻,優先取捨權,優先取捨的機會

His refusal to do the job is not wise.

他拒絕做這個工作是不明智的。

5938

recommend [,rɛkə'mɛnd]

vt. 推薦,介紹

I recommend that the food in the restaurant is famous.

我推薦這家餐廳食物很有名。

5939

salary ['sælərɪ]

n. 薪水

She's on a salary of $10,000 each month.

她每個月薪水一萬元。

5940

unexpected [,ʌnɪk'spɛktɪd]

adj. 想不到的,意外的,未預料到

Her coming was totally unexpected.

她的到來是意料外的。

5941

household ['haʊs,hold] ['haʊs,old]

n. 家庭,戶 adj. 家庭的,家常的

Most households are now in debt.

很多家庭現在都負債。

5942

physicist [ˈfɪzəsɪst]

n. 物理學者,唯物論者

He is a famous physicist.

他是有名的物理學者。

5943

recession [rɪˈsɛʃən]

n. 撤回,退回,退後,工商業之衰退,不景氣

The economy is in deep recession nowadays.

現在經濟嚴重衰退。

5944

orderly [ˈɔrdəlɪ]

adj. 有秩序的,整齊的,整潔的 n. 傳令兵,勤務兵

She needs to organize her room in an orderly way.

她需要整理房間。

5945

enthusiasm [ɪnˈθjuzɪˌæzəm] [ˈθɪuz-] [ˈθuz-]

n. 狂熱,熱心,積極性,激發熱情的事物

He shows his enthusiasm for music.

他對音樂有熱情。

5946

starvation [starˈveʃən]

n. 饑餓,餓死

Fewer and fewer people are dying of starvation nowadays. 現今愈來愈少人死於飢餓。

5947

luxury [ˈlʌkʃərɪ]

n. 奢侈,華貴

He was leading a life of luxury when he was young.

當他年輕時,他過著奢侈生活。

5948

virus [ˈvaɪrəs]

n. [微]病毒,濾過性微生物,毒害,惡毒

Children get infected by H1N1 virus easily.

小孩容易得到 H1N1 病毒。

5949

plural [ˈplʊrəl] [ˈplɪʊrəl]

adj. 複數的

In English, 'we' is a plural pronoun.

在英文裡,we 是複數代名詞。

5950

unknown [ʌnˈnon]

adj. 不知道的,未知的 n. 不知名的

The secret remains unknown.

這個祕密仍然未知。

5951

regulation [ˌrɛgjəˈleʃən]

n. 規則,規章,調節,校準

Under the new regulations, everyone should be on time.

在一些新規定底下,每個人必須準時。

5952

possess [pəˈzɛs]

vt. 擁有特質,感覺,情緒,攫住,支配,控制,使言行失常,佔用,擁有

Modern people possess at least one credit card.

現在人至少擁有一張信用卡。

5953

judgment [ˈdʒʌdʒmənt]

n 審判,裁判,判決,判斷,鑑定,評價,判斷力,辨別力,
意見,看法,批評,指責,神的審判,天譴

You should make a wise judgment.

你應該有明智的判斷。

5954

draft [dræft]

n. 草稿,草案 v. 起草,草擬

I revise the draft of the article.

我修改文章的草稿。

5955

unusual [ʌnˈjuʒʊəl] [-ˈjuʒʊl] [-ˈjuʒəl]

adj. 不平常的,與眾不同的,不尋常的

It's unusual for Dave to do this.

對於大衛做這件事是不尋常的。

5956

telegraph [ˈtɛləˌgræf]

n. 電報

People send messages though telegraph.

人們以電報傳送訊息。

5957

preview [priˈvju] [-ˈvɪu]

n. 事先查看,[計]預覽 vt. 事先查看,預展,預演

You should preview the course before the class.

你該在課前預習。

5958

nylon [ˈnaɪlɑn]

n. 尼龍

The hat was made of nylon.

這頂帽子用尼龍做的。

5959

mutual [ˈmjutʃʊəl]

adj. 相互的,彼此的,共有的

We have a mutual interest in music.

我們在音樂上有共同的興趣。

5960

universal [ˌjunəˈvɜsl]

adj. 普遍的,全體的,通用的,萬能的,宇宙的,世界的

This is a universal truth.

這是普遍的事實。

5961

sociable [ˈsoʃəbl]

adj. 好交際的,友善的,增進友誼的,喜歡群居的

She's a sociable person.

她是喜歡社交的人。

5962

postman [ˈpostmən]

n. 郵差

Postmen collect and deliver letters.

郵差收集跟送信。

5963

strengthen [ˈstrɛŋkθən] [ˈstrɛŋθ-]

v. 加強,鞏固,增強

The exercises are designed to strengthen your heart.

這些運動設計來強化你的心臟。

5964 explosive [ɪk'splosɪv]

adj. 爆炸(性)的,爆發(性)的,暴露 n. 爆炸物,炸藥

Because the gas is highly explosive, you should be careful. 因為瓦斯容易爆炸,你應該要小心。

5965 status ['stetəs] ['stætəs]

n. 身分,地位,情形,狀況

What is your marital status? Are you single or married? 你的婚姻狀況是什麼?你單身或是已婚?

5966 logical ['lɑdʒɪkl]

adj. 合乎邏輯的,合理的

He drew a logical conclusion from the report. 他從這份報告中推出合理結論。

5967 instinct ['ɪnstɪŋkt]

n. 本能,直覺,本能反應

His first instinct was to escape. 他第一個反應是逃跑。

5968 opposition [ˌɑpə'zɪʃn]

n. 反對,敵對,相反,反對派,[天]衝,[邏]對當法

There was no opposition to the war. 對於戰爭沒有反對派。

5969 resolve [rɪ'zɑlv]

v. 決心,決定,解決 n. 決心,決定

After the argument, she resolved never to talk to him. 在吵架後,她下定決心不要再跟他說話。

5970 qualified ['kwɑlə,faɪd] ['kwɒl-]

adj. 有資格的

Dawn is well qualified for her new job. 唐在這份工作上很具資格。

5971 translation [træns'leʃən] [trænz-]

n. 翻譯,譯文,轉化,調任,轉換,[物][數]平移

This is a new translation of the novel. 這是小說新的翻譯。

5972 multiple ['mʌltəpl]

adj. 多樣的,多重的 v. 成倍增加 n. 倍數

We need multiple copies of this document. 我們需要這份文件的大量副本。

5973 exposure [ɪk'spoʒɚ]

n. 暴露,揭露,曝光,揭發,位向,方向,陳列

Prolonged exposure to computer will cause nearsightedness. 暴露在電腦前過長時間將導致近視。

5974 gulf [gʌlf]

n. 海灣,深淵,漩渦,隔閡 vt. 吞沒,使深深捲入

The gulf of Mexico is at the northern part. 墨西哥灣在北部。

5975 site [saɪt]

n. 地點,場所,遺址 n. 站點

Birds are looking for a nesting site. 鳥在找築巢地點。

5976
whichever [hwɪtʃˈɛvɚ]

pron. 無論那一個,任何一個

It is no use, whichever method you choose.

不論你試何種方法都沒用。

5977
horizon [həˈraɪzn̩]

n. 地平線,(常複)眼界,見識

The sun rises from the horizon.

太陽從地平線昇起。

5978
emigrant [ˈɛməgrənt]

n. (向外)移民,僑民 adj. (向外)移民的,移居的

They are emigrant workers.

他們是移民者。

5979
short-term [ˈʃɔrtˈtɝm]

adj. 短期的

This is a short-term plan.

這是短期計畫。

5980
shooting [ˈʃutɪŋ]

n. 發射,獵場,射擊,放射,開(槍),放砲,射出光線等,
射中,射傷,射死

His brother died in a shooting incident last year.

他的兄弟去年被槍殺過世。

5981
shocking [ˈʃɑkɪŋ]

adj. 可怕的,過分的,不正當的

His reaction was shocking.

他的反應很驚人。

5982
separatist [ˈsɛpəˌretɪst]

n. 分離主義者,獨立派

The government tries to take control of the separatists.

政府試著要控制分離主義者。

5983
shining [ˈʃaɪnɪŋ]

adj. 光亮的,華麗的

The sun was shining.

太陽很光亮。

5984
EQ [ˈiˈkju]

n. (Emotional Quotient 縮寫)情緒商數

People with good EQ get along well with others.

有好的情緒商數跟別人相處很好。

5985
encouraging [ɪnˈkɝɪdʒɪŋ]

adj. 獎勵的,可獎勵的,令人鼓舞的

The encouraging news is that the typhoon isn't coming.

令人鼓舞的新聞是颱風不會來。

5986
sherry [ˈʃɛrɪ]

n. 雪利酒,葡萄酒,雪莉(女子名)

I would like to order a cup of sherry.

我想點一杯雪利酒。

5987
engaged [ɪnˈgedʒd]
adj. 忙碌的,使用中的,已訂婚
He is now engaged in his final research.
他現在正在忙他的期末研究。

5988
shaped [ʃept]
adj. (常用於複合詞中)成某種形狀的,合適的,有計劃的
She has almond-shaped eyes.
她有雙杏眼。

5989
sexuality [ˌsɛkʃʊˈælətɪ]
n. 性別,性方面的事情,性慾,性徵
His sexuality is attractive.
他的性感很吸引人。

5990
settled [ˈsɛtl̩d]
adj. 固定(下來)的,確定不變的,(對住所,工作,新環境等)感到自在的
I don't like a settled job. 我不喜歡不太有變化的工作。

5991
serving [ˈsɝvɪŋ]
n. 服務,招待,上菜,一份(食物),一客
This recipe is not enough for four servings.
這個食譜對四個人來說不夠。

5992
serviceman [ˈsɝvɪsˌmæn]
n. 軍人,維修人員
He is a British serviceman.
他是英國軍人。

5993
fascist [ˈfæʃɪst]
n. 法西斯黨員,法西斯主義者
My boss is a real fascist.
我的老闆是法西斯黨員。

5994
shipping [ˈʃɪpɪŋ]
n. 船舶(總稱),船舶噸數,船運,裝貨,裝運,運送,航運業,海運業,運輸業,[廢]航行
The port is for all shipping. 這個港口是給所有的船隻。

5995
GMO [dʒəˈnɛtɪkl̩ɪ ˈmɑdəˌfɪd ˈɔrgənˌɪzəm]
n. (genetically modified organism 縮寫)基因改造生物
GMO crops are common.
基因改造食品很普遍。

5996
scattered [ˈskætɚd]
adj. 散亂的,散布的,分散的,疏疏落落的,散慢的
Salt lay scattered over the floor.
鹽散落在地板上。

5997
fumes [ˈfjumɪz]
vi. (有害,濃烈,或難聞的)煙,氣,汽,憤怒,煩惱
n. 冒煙(或氣,汽),(煙,汽等)冒出,發怒
vt. (用香)薰,煙薰,憤怒地說(話)
I was overcome by smoke and fumes in the factory.
我因為工廠的煙和難聞的臭氣失去知覺。

5998

fundamentalism [ˌfʌndə'mɛntl̩ˌɪzəm]

n. 正統派基督教,原理主義,基本教義論

He knows everything about religious fundamentalism.

他知道基督教正統派的所有教義。

5999

fundamentalist [ˌfʌndə'mɛntl̩ɪst]

n. 基要主義者 adj. 基要主義的

You can visit the fundamentalist website of Christians.

你可以拜訪基督教基要主義者的網站。

6000

right-wing ['raɪt ˌwɪŋ]

adj. 右翼的,右派的

The party is very right-wing.

這個政黨是右派。

6001

right-hand ['raɪt-ˌhænd]

adj. 用右手的,得力的,右側的

The right-hand side of his body can't move.

他身體的右半邊不能動。

6002

funding ['fʌndɪŋ]

n. 資金,基金

The school will allocate funding for each department.

學校將會分配基金給各科系。

6003

gel [dʒɛl]

n. 膠化體,凝膠 v. 膠化,成凝膠狀

I bought shower gel in the supermarket.

我在超市買了沐浴乳。

6004

ghetto ['gɛto]

n. 猶太人區,貧民區,少數民族居住區

There are many poor people in the ghetto.

貧民窟有很多窮人。

6005

gilt [gɪlt] n. 鍍金,表面的裝飾,小母豬

adj. 鍍金的,gild 的過去式和過去分詞

He saw faded gilt letters on the envelope.

他在信封上看到褪色鍍金字.

6006

given ['gɪvən]

adj. 贈予的,沉溺的,約定的,指定的,規定的,

give 的過去分詞

prep. 鑒於

n. 假設事實

You can come here at any given time.

你可以在任何指定的時間來。

6007

glassware ['glæsˌwɛr] [-ˌwær]

n. 玻璃器皿

I like crystal glassware.

我喜歡水晶玻璃器皿。

6008

front-page ['frʌnt'pedʒ]

adj. 頭版的,重要的

Front-page news is shocking.

頭版新聞很嚇人。

6009
frankly [ˈfræŋklɪ]
adv. 坦白地,直率地

Please answer these questions frankly.
請坦白回答這些問題。

6010
retrospection [ˌrɛtrəˈspɛkʃən]
n. 回顧,追憶,考慮

From her retrospection, she writes her first book.
她用回憶寫了第一本書。

6011
go-ahead [ˈɡoˌəhɛd]
adj. 前進著的,有進取心的 n. 進取心,許可

He is a go-ahead student.
他是位有進取心的學生。

6012
goalkeeper [ˈɡolˌkipɚ] n. 守門員

A goalkeeper's job is to stop the ball from going into his or her own team's goal.
守門員的工作是阻止球進入他隊上的球門裡。

6013
going [ˈɡoɪŋ]
n. 去,離去,工作情況,行為
adj. 進行中的,流行的,現存的

His going will be our loss. 他的離去對我們是損失。

6014
good-looking [ˈɡʊdˈlʊkɪŋ]
adj. 好看的

He is a really good-looking guy.
他長的很好看。

6015
retired [riˈtaɪrd]
adj. 退休的,退職的

My mother is a retired teacher.
我媽媽是退休老師。

6016
retailer [ˈritaɪlɚ]
n. 零售商,轉述者

The shop is one of the largest clothing retailers.
這家店是最大服飾零售商之一。

6017
guerrilla [ɡəˈrɪlə]
n. 游擊隊

The troop crossed the guerrilla camps.
軍隊跨過遊擊隊的營地。

6018
restructure [riˈstrʌktʃɚ]
v. 更改結構,重建構造,調整

The department store is undergoing a major restructuring. 百貨公司現在整修中。

6019
restricted [rɪˈstrɪktɪd]
adj. 受限制的,限於內部傳閱的,最低保密級的

I don't like to work in such a restricted space.
我不喜歡在限制的空間工作。

6020
revealing [rɪˈvilɪŋ]
adj. 有啟迪作用的,(衣服)袒胸露肩的

She wears a very revealing dress.
她穿袒胸露肩的衣服。

6021

fitting [ˈfɪtɪŋ]

adj. 適合的,恰當的 n. 配件,附件,裝配,安裝

The award was a fitting tribute to her.

這個獎項對她來說是很恰當的禮物。

6022

sit-down [ˈsɪtˌdaun]

n. 靜坐抗議

There will be a sit-down protest tomorrow.

明天將會有靜坐抗議。

6023

fatty [ˈfætɪ]

adj. 脂肪的,含脂肪的,脂肪狀的

Don't eat too much fatty food.

不要吃太多脂肪的食物。

6024

federation [ˌfɛdəˈreʃən]

n. 聯邦,聯合,聯盟

I read the history about the Russian Federation.

我讀有關俄羅斯聯邦的事情。

6025

Saudi [saˈudɪ]

n. 沙烏地阿拉伯(國名,在西亞)

Saudi Arabia is a country rich in natural resources.

沙烏地阿拉伯是天然資源豐富的國家。

6026

satisfying [ˈsætɪsˌfaɪɪŋ]

adj. 滿意的,充分的,足可相信的

This is a satisfying meal.

這是一頓令人滿意的餐點。

6027

feeder [ˈfidɚ]

n. 餵食者,飼養員,食客,支流,支脈

He is an animal feeder in the zoo.

他在動物園是動物餵食者。

6028

finding [ˈfaɪndɪŋ]

n. 發現,發現物,調查的結果

These findings suggest that there is no direct link between the two variables.

結果顯示這兩個變數沒有直接關係。

6029

firefighter [ˈfaɪrˌfaɪtɚ]

n. (美)消防隊員

The man is a firefighter.

這個人是消防隊員。

6030

salon [səˈlɑn]

n. 客廳,上流社會,接待室,沙龍

She goes to a beauty salon everyday.

她每天去美容沙龍。

6031

full-time [ˈfʊlˈtaɪm]

adj. 全部工作日的,專職的

I have a full-time job.

我有一份全職工作。

6032

first-class ['fɜst'klæs]

adj. 頭等的,第一流的

This is a first-class painting.

這是一流的畫。

6033

fixed [fɪkst]

adj. 固定的,固著的,安裝好,不變的,穩定的,一定的,確定的,既定的,(視線等)全神貫注的,出神的,準備好的,[化] (酸油)凝固的,不易揮發的,[化] 被化合物吸收了的,(氮等)固定的,[口] 處境…的,[口] 勝負已內定的,預先安排好結果的,被賄賂的,[占星] 不易相的(cardinal, mutable, zodiac)(與金牛、獅子、天蠍、寶瓶四宮有關的)

The dress is fixed price. 這件洋裝不二價。

6034

run-up ['rʌn ˌʌp]

n. 前期準備,助跑

There will be a run-up to the election.

選舉的起跑快開始了。

6035

runner-up ['rʌnɚ'ʌp]

n. 亞軍,亞軍隊

The runners-up will all receive 500 dollars.

亞軍將會得到五百元。

6036

ruling ['rulɪŋ]

n. 判決,裁定,統治 adj. 統治的,支配的,流行的

Democratic Party is the ruling party.

民主黨是統治黨。

6037

rugby ['rʌgbɪ]

n. 英式橄欖球

We play rugby after school.

我們放學後玩英式橄欖球。

6038

follow-up ['falo,ʌp]

adj. 作為重複的,繼續的,接著的

You have to conduct a follow-up study on the issue.

你必須在這個議題上接著作研究。

6039

footage ['fʊtɪdʒ]

n. 以尺計算長度,尺數,影片的鏡頭

I found an old footage from the First World War.

我發現第一次世界大戰影片的鏡頭。

6040

forbidden [fɚ'bɪdn̩]

adj. 被禁止的,嚴禁的,forbid 的過去分詞

It is forbidden to drink alcohol here.

在這裡喝酒是犯法的。

6041

franc [fræŋk]

n. 法郎

Franc is one of the standard units of money.

法郎是標準貨幣單位之一。

6042

fireproof ['faɪr'pruf]

adj. 耐火的,防火的 v. 變成有耐火性

We need a fireproof dish.

我們需要耐火的碗盤。

6043

cutting [ˈkʌtɪŋ]

n. 切斷,切下,開鑿

She likes to collect newspaper cuttings.

她喜歡收集報紙剪報。

6044

starter [ˈstɑrtɚ]

n. 開端者,發令員,啟動器,開胃菜

We had salad as a starter.

我們開胃菜是沙拉。

6045

crap [kræp]

n. 賭輸的一注,廢物,廢話 v. 擲骰子

Greg's full of crap.

格雷格講很多廢話。

6046

crib [krɪb]

n. 嬰兒床,食槽,柵欄 v. 抄襲,拘禁,關入柵欄

The baby was sleeping in the crib.

嬰兒在嬰兒床睡覺。

6047

strained [strend]

adj. 緊張的,做作的,矯飾的

There was a strained atmosphere in the classroom.

教室裡有緊張的氣氛。

6048

crooked [ˈkrʊkɪd]

adj. 彎的,彎曲的,歪的,畸形的,腰彎的,不誠實的,不正直的,不正派的,[口] 不正當的,用不正當手段獲得的,[俚] 祕密製造[出售]的,(手杖)有彎柄的,[澳·紐俚]令人不滿意的,發怒的

His lips curled into a crooked smile and seemed very happy. 他的嘴型彎曲至微笑狀,似乎很高興。

6049

cross-country [ˈkrɔsˌkʌntrɪ]

adj. 越野的,橫過田野的

We took a cross-country route.

我們越過田野的路徑。

6050

striker [ˈstraɪkɚ]

n. 打擊者,罷工者

The strikers call a strike on Monday.

罷工的人星期一罷工。

6051

striking [ˈstraɪkɪŋ]

adj. 醒目的,驚人的,打擊的,罷工的

There is a striking finding in the survey.

在這個研究裡有驚人發現。

6052

stimulating [ˈstɪmjəˌletɪŋ]

adj. 刺激的,有刺激性的

The stimulating effects of coffee and tea are harmful.

咖啡跟茶的刺激性有害身體。

6053

sterling [ˈstɜlɪŋ] n. 英國貨幣,標準純銀

adj. 英國貨幣的,標準純銀的,純正的

Sterling silver is at least 92% pure.

純銀至少有百分之九十二純度。

6054

daffodil ['dæfə,dɪl]

n. 水仙,水仙花,達弗蒂兒(女子名) adj. 水仙花色的

I like daffodil.

我喜歡水仙花。

6055

dame [dem]

n. 夫人,(英)女爵

Dame Maggie Smith lives nearby.

瑪姬史密斯夫人住在附近。

6056

damned [dæmd]

adv. adj. [口]該死的,可惡的,(加強語氣)完全的

It's damned shame he made such a big mistake.

他犯這種錯誤真是太可惡了。

6057

dandruff ['dændrəf]

n. 頭皮屑

I wash my hair with an anti-dandruff shampoo.

我用去頭皮屑洗髮精洗頭。

6058

statistics [stə'tɪstɪks]

n. 統計,統計數字

Statistics show that 50% of people are not happy.

統計顯示有百分之五十的人不快樂。

6059

statistician [,stætə'stɪʃən]

n. 統計員,統計學家

A statistician is good at statistics.

統計學家擅長統計。

6060

daybreak ['de,brek]

n. 黎明,拂曉,破曉,天亮

We arrived in Taipei at daybreak.

我們在破曉時抵達臺北。

6061

simultaneous [,saɪml'tenɪəs] [,sɪml-] [-njəs]

adj. 同時的,同時發生的

We need simultaneous translation at the meeting.

我們在會議中需要同步翻譯。

6062

cruiser ['kruzɚ] ['krɪuzɚ]

n. 巡洋艦,巡航飛機,警察巡邏車

A cruiser passed by.

員警巡邏車經過附近。

6063

stylistic [star'lɪstɪk]

adj. 格式上的,體裁上的

There are stylistic features in the novel.

小說有格式上的特色。

6064

connected [kə'nɛktɪd] adj. 連續的,連貫的,有關係[聯絡]的,有親戚關係的,有門路的

The computer is connected to the timer.

這台電腦跟計時器連在一起。

6065

consuming [kən'sjumɪŋ]

adj. 消費的,消耗(精力或時間)的,強烈的

Only 27% of the trash we consume is useless.

我們所消耗的垃圾只有百分之二十七是沒用的。

6066

contractor [ˈkɑntræktɚ]

n. 立契約的人,承包商

Johnny's dad is a building contractor.
強尼的爸爸是建築承包商。

6067

substitution [ˌsʌbstəˈtjuʃən] [-ˈtrʊ-] [-ˈtu-]

n. 代理,替換,交換

This is the substitution of low-fat diet for greasy food.
這是取代油膩食品的低脂減肥。

6068

substantially [səbˈstænʃəlɪ]

adv. 本質上,實質上,大體上,相當多地,大大地

The price of the dress has risen substantially in recent years. 這件洋裝價格近幾年已經大大地漲價。

6069

coordinate [koˈɔrdn̩ˌet] n. 同等者,同等物,

座標(用複數) vt. 調整,整理,使協調,使配合

Her movements coordinate her goal.
她的行動跟她的目標一致。

6070

submersion [səbˈmɝʃən]

n. 下沉,淹沒,沉沒

TV news reported submersion accidents.
電視新聞報導沉沒事件。

6071

cosmetic [kɑzˈmɛtɪk]

n. 化妝品 adj. 化妝用的

We will buy cosmetic products in the shop.
我們會在這家店買化妝品。

6072

starch [stɑrtʃ]

n. 澱粉,漿糊,刻板 v. 漿硬,使拘泥

We should eat less starch when we go on a diet.
減肥時應該吃少一點澱粉。

6073

councilor [ˈkaʊnslɚ] [-slɚ]

n. 議員,評議員,顧問,參事

He is a councilor of the city.
他是市議員。

6074

counseling [ˈkaʊnslɪŋ] [-slɪŋ]

n. 個別輔導,商議,審議,忠告,勸告,計劃,決策

More and more modern people need a debt counseling service. 愈來愈多現代人需要債務諮商服務。

6075

stunning [ˈstʌnɪŋ]

adj. 足以使人暈倒的,極好的

You look absolutely stunning in those clothes.
你穿那件衣服很好看。

6076

countless [ˈkaʊntlɪs]

adj. 數不盡的,無數的

The new treatment could save countless lives.
新的治療方法可以拯救無數生命。

6077

stuck [stʌk]

stick 的過去式和過去分詞

They got stuck in a traffic jam yesterday.
他們昨天卡在車陣中。

6078 coverage [ˈkʌvərɪdʒ] [ˈkʌvrɪdʒ]

n. 覆蓋的範圍,保險總額,新聞報導

Health care coverage is important to you.
健康保險對你很重要。

6079 crackdown [ˈkræk,daʊn]

n. 壓迫,鎮壓,痛擊

The government launched a crackdown on crime.
政府掃蕩犯罪。

6080 corpse [krɔrps]

n. 屍體

The corpse was found near the house.
屍體在房子旁被發現。

6081 day-to-day [ˈde tə ˈde]

adj. 按日計劃的,逐日的,每天的,日常工作的,例行的,
日常的

We do housework on a day-to-day basis.
我們每天都會做家事。

6082 snorkel [ˈsnɔrkl̩]

n. 潛艇換氣裝置

I need to use a snorkel when I dive.
我潛水時都會用換氣裝置。

6083 smallpox [ˈsmɔl,pɑks]

n. 天花

Smallpox is a serious disease.
天花是嚴重的疾病。

6084 smack [smæk]

n. 風味,滋味,少量,拍擊聲,咂嘴聲,小漁船,海洛因
v. 咂嘴,摑,打

Should parents smack their children?
家長應該打小孩嗎?

6085 doom [ˈdum]

adj. 命中注定的,天數已盡的,注定失敗的

We are all doomed to fail finally.
我們註定最後要失敗。

6086 dosage [ˈdosɪdʒ]

n. 劑量,用量,配藥

He takes a high dosage of sleeping pills everyday.
他每天服用高劑量的安眠藥。

6087 distributor [dɪˈstrɪbjətə]

n. 分配者,批發商

He's the largest clothing distributor.
他是最大的衣服批發商。

6088

line-up ['laɪnˌʌp]

n. 人(或物)之列隊,選手陣容,(警察要見證人指出誰為嫌疑犯而讓數人排成的)行列,電視節目時間表

There is a wonderful line-up of programs today.

今天有很棒的節目表。

6089

distributed [dɪ'strɪbjətɪd]

adj. 分發,分配,散布,分布,把…分類,[統] 分布成…的

Clothes and blankets have been distributed in the shelter.

衣服跟毯子在避難所發放。

6090

outing ['aʊtɪŋ]

n. 郊遊,遠足 adj. 遠足適用的

We will have an outing to the beach.

我們要去海灘遠足。

6091

slash [slæʃ]

v. 砍,猛砍,亂砍,削減 n. 猛砍,亂砍,斜杠

We should slash some costs.

我們應該刪減一些開支。

6092

dub [dʌb]

v. 配音,輕點,授予稱號,打擊 n. 一下擊鼓聲,笨蛋

This British film was dubbed into Chinese.

這部英國影片有中文配音。

6093

DVD ['drəkɛt-vju-'drvas]

n. (Digital Video Disc/Disk 縮寫)數位視訊影碟

We need a DVD player.

我們需要數位元視訊影碟放影機。

6094

skipper ['skɪpɚ]

n. 船長,主將,正駕駛

One skipper is in charge of one ship.

一位船長負責一艘船。

6095

situated ['sɪtʃʊˌetɪd]

adj. 位於…的,座落在…的

The house is situated near the city.

這棟房子座落於城市附近。

6096

sit-in ['sɪtˌɪn]

n. 室內靜坐抗議,室內靜坐罷工

He once staged a sit-in to protest the government.

他曾發起靜坐向政府抗議。

6097

gunman ['gʌnˌmæn]

n. 槍手,持槍的歹徒,製造槍械者

Two gunmen opened fire.

兩個持槍的歹徒開火。

6098

draught [dræft]

n. 草稿,氣流,匯票,通風,拉,牽引 v. 起草,徵兵,選派

There's a draught in the classroom.

教室裡有一股氣流。

6099

developed [dɪ'vɛləpt]

adj. (國家等)高度發展的,極發達的,工業化了的,先進的

There are fewer poor people in the developed world.
在高度發展的國家比較少有窮人。

6100

dedicated ['dɛdəˌketɪd]

adj. 致力於主義[理想,目的]的,(裝備等)用於特定目的的,專用的

She is a dedicated teacher. 她是一個有理想的老師。

6101

stand-up ['stænd-ˌʌp]

adj. 站立的,直立的,衣領挺的

There is a stand-up cafe near the train station.
火車站附近有一間站立式的咖啡店。

6102

definitely ['dɛfənətlɪ]

adv. 一定地,肯定地,明確地,確切地

I am definitely late.
我一定遲到了。

6103

demonstrator ['dɛmənˌstretə]

n. 論證者,證明者,指示者,示威者

There are anti-smoking demonstrators here.
這裡有反菸的示威者。

6104

deployment [dɪ'plɔɪmənt]

n. 部署,調度

The country made a decision on missiles deployment.
這個國家決定部署飛彈。

6105

squad [skwɑd]

n. 班,小隊,小集團 v. 編成班

The Italian World Cup squad wins the game.
義大利世界盃隊贏得這場比賽。

6106

destined ['dɛstɪnd]

adj. 命中注定的,(場所)預定的

She seemed destined for the guy.
她似乎命中注定要嫁給他。

6107

sporting ['sportɪŋ]

adj. 喜好運動的,運動用的,冒險性的

One of the major sporting events of the year was
broadcasted live. 今年最重要的運動項目之一有現場直播。

6108

sponsorship ['spɑnsəˌʃɪp]

n. 保證人(或教父、教母)的地位,資助,贊助

The company is looking for sponsorship.
這家公司在找贊助商。

6109

detached [dɪ'tætʃt]

adj. 分離的,不受他人影響的,(房屋)不與其他房舍連接的,分遣的

Take a more detached view about the matter.

試著用不受他人影響的觀點看這件事。

6110

disturbed [dɪ'strɜbd]

adj. 精神[情緒]障礙(者)的,不安[擔心]的,
　　心理不正常的,混亂的,騷動的

Parents are very disturbed about video games.

父母對於電動玩具很不安。

6111

devastating ['dɛvəs,tetɪŋ]

adj. 破壞力極大的,摧毀一切的,毀滅性的

Drugs have a devastating effect on people.

毒品對人有毀滅性影響。

6112

sperm [spɜm]

n. 精液,精蟲,鯨油 comb. 表示「種子」「精子」「精液」

Conception occurs when a single sperm fuses with an egg.

受孕的發生是精子與卵子結合。

6113

developer [dɪ'vɛləpə]

n. 開發商,開發公司,新產品的開發者,研製者,開發者,
　　顯影劑,顯色劑

He is a software developer.

他是軟體研發者。

6114

specification [,spɛsəfə'keʃən]

n. 規格,詳述,詳細說明書

The house was built to our specifications.

這個房子是以我們具體要求所建。

6115

soundtrack ['saʊnd,træk]

n. 聲帶,電影配音,電影音樂磁帶(或唱片),
　　電影對白磁帶或唱片

The soundtrack to the movie is not very clear.

這電影的配音不是很清楚。

6116

sophisticated [sə'fɪstɪ,ketɪd]

adj. 深明人情世故的,通情達理的,老練的,富有經驗的

Mark is smart and sophisticated.

馬克很聰明並深明人情世故。

6117

disgraceful [dɪs'gresfəl]

adj. 可恥的,不名譽的,不光彩的

It is disgraceful that you stole money.

你偷了錢是不名譽的事。

6118

distraction [dɪ'strækʃən]

n. 娛樂,分心的事物,分心

There are too many distractions here.

這裡有太多令人分心的事物。

6119

socialize ['soʃə,laɪz]

v. 交往,交際,使變成社交性,使適應社會

People should socialize with their neighbors as much as they used to.

人們應該跟以前年代一樣跟鄰居多彼此交流。

6120

devalue [di'vælju]

vi. 實行貨幣貶值,(貨幣)貶值,貶低

The country devalued the importance of education.
這個國家貶低教育的重要性。

6121

medication [,mɛdɪ'keʃən]

n. 藥物治療,藥物處理,醫藥

He's on medication for cancer.
他現在作癌症藥物治療。

6122

piercing ['pɪrsɪŋ]

adj. 刺骨的,刺穿的,諷刺的

For him, it's piercing pain.
對他來說,那是刺骨般的痛。

6123

potter ['pɑtɚ]

n. 陶工 v. 鬼混,閒逛,吊兒郎當

I spent the morning pottering in the park.
我在公園閒逛了一整個早上。

6124

malaria [mə'lɛrɪə] [mə'lɛrɪə] [mə'lærɪə]

n. 瘧疾,瘴氣

He gets malaria.
他得到瘧疾。

6125

post-war ['post-,wɔr]

adj. 戰後的

There is a baby boom in the post-war years.
戰後時期有嬰兒潮。

6126

pore [pɔr] [por]

n. 孔,毛孔,小孔,氣孔 v. 熟讀,熟視,細想,鑽研,沉思

She was poring over a book when her father came home. 當她爸爸回家時她正在鑽研一本書。

6127

mare [mɛr] [mær]

n. 母馬,母驢,月球表面陰暗部

Money makes the mare go.
有錢能使鬼推磨。(諺語)

6128

marketing ['mɑrkɪtɪŋ]

n. 行銷,買賣

She works in a marketing department.
她在行銷部門工作。

6129

polytechnic [,pɑlə'tɛknɪk]

adj. 各種工藝的,綜合技術的 n. 工藝學校

This is a polytechnic institute.
這是工藝學校。

6130

poised [pɔɪzd]

adj. 泰然自若的,準備好的,蓄勢待發,沉著自信的

He was poised to become a president in Europe.

他已準備好要成為歐洲的總統。

6131

pointed ['pɔɪntɪd]

adj. 尖的,有尖頭的

He has a pointed chin.

他有尖下巴。

6132

mellow ['mɛlo] ['mɛlə]

adj. 成熟的,醇的,熟練的

David's certainly grown mellower.

大衛更加成熟了。

6133

mentality [mɛn'tælətɪ]

n. 精神力,智力,頭腦作用,思想,心態

I cannot understand the mentality of the protesters.

我無法理解抗議者的心態。

6134

mercury ['mɝkjərɪ] ['mɝkərɪ] ['mɝkrɪ]

n. 汞,水銀,水星,使者,墨丘利神

Temperature on Mercury is high.

水星的溫度很高。

6135

merely ['mɪrlɪ]

adj. 僅僅,只不過

We're merely good friends, not close friends.

我們只是好朋友不是親密朋友。

6136

middle-aged ['mɪdl̩-ˌedʒd]

adj. 中年的,有中年人特點的,適合中年人的

He is a middle-aged businessman.

他是中年的生意人。

6137

mining ['maɪnɪŋ]

n. 採礦,採礦業

The coal mining industry was booming.

煤礦業曾經蓬勃發展。

6138

ministerial [ˌmɪnəs'tɪrɪəl]

adj. 部長的,內閣的,執政的

A ministerial meeting will be held.

內閣會議即將舉辦。

6139

pimple ['pɪmpl̩]

n. 丘疹,面皰,疙瘩,粉刺,小膿包

There is a pimple on her chin.

她下巴有一顆青春痘。

6140

miscarriage [mɪs'kærɪdʒ]

n. 失敗,誤送,流產

She had two miscarriages but she still wanted to have a baby. 她有過兩次流產但是她仍想要有小孩。

6141

pro [pro]

n. 選手,從事某職業的人,職業選手 adj. 職業的

He is a tae kwon do pro.

他是跆拳職業選手。

6142

guild [gɪld]

n. 公會,協會,行會,行業協會

She is the leader of the Women's Guild.

她是婦女會領袖。

6143

privatize ['praɪvətaɪz]

vt. 使私有(民營)化

Utilities have been privatized.

公用事業已經私有民營化。

6144

live-in ['lɪv͵ɪn]

adj. 住在受僱之處的,(未婚而)同居的

She is a live-in nanny.

她是住在受僱處的保母。

6145

living ['lɪvɪŋ]

adj. 活的,活著的,現存的,逼真的,生活的,維持生活的

n. 生活,生計

English is a living language in the world now.

英文現在是世界通行的語言。

6146

previously ['privɪəslɪ]

adv. 從前,過去

Six months ago, he got married.

六個月前他結婚了。

6147

llama ['lɑmə]

n. 產於南美的美洲駝

Llamas are very social animals and like to live with other llamas as a herd.

美洲駝是非常社會性的動物而且喜歡與其他美洲駝群共同生活。

6148

loaded ['lodɪd]

adj. 裝滿東西的

Here comes a truck loaded with bananas.

來了一輛裝滿香蕉的卡車。

6149

prevailing [prɪ'velɪŋ]

adj. 盛行很廣的,一般的,最普通的,流行的

The prevailing color is red.

現在流行的顏色是紅色。

6150

making ['mekɪŋ]

n. 形成,形成的要素,素質,製造

The company is involved in the making of cosmetics.

這家公司參與化妝品的製造。

6151

presidency ['prɛzədənsɪ]

n. 總統職位,總統任期,統轄,主宰,支配

There were few economic reforms during his presidency. 在總統任內有一些經濟改革。

6152

mixed [mɪkst]

adj. 混合的,混成的,混雜的

There is a mixed group of women in the club.

俱樂部裡有混合的女性團體。

6153

loving ['lʌvɪŋ]

adj. 親愛的,鐘情的,忠誠的

He's very loving to his sister.

他非常愛他的妹妹。

6154

predominantly [prɪ'dɑmɪnətlɪ] [prɪ'dɑmɪnəntlɪ]

adv. 佔主導地位地,佔優勢地,顯著地,主要的

The wall is predominantly white.

這面牆以白色為主。

6155

predictable [prɪ'dɪktəbḷ]

adj. 可預言的,可預見的,可預料的,老套乏味的

The air pollution had a predictable effect on health.

空氣汙染對健康的影響是可預見的。

6156

lunchtime ['lʌntʃ͵taɪm]

n. 午餐時間

Did you have a meal with her at lunchtime?

你和她在午餐時間一起吃飯嗎？

6157

made-up ['med'ʌp]

adj. 作成的,製成的,捏造的,化了妝的

The actress became a made-up Juliet in the play.

女演員在劇裡裝扮成茱麗葉。

6158

precisely [prɪ'saɪslɪ]

adv. 精確地,明確地

Can you tell me precisely when you will arrive here?

你可以精確的告訴我你何時會抵達嗎？

6159

mafia ['mɑfɪ͵ɑ]

n. 黑手黨,祕密政黨,幫派

The city was controlled by the Mafia.

這個城市被黑手黨控制。

6160

preceding [prɪ'sidɪŋ]

adj. 在先的,在前的,前面的

You will see the diagram in the preceding chapter.

你可以在前一章看到這個圖表。

6161

president-elect ['prɛzɪdənt-ɪ'lɛkt]

n. 總統當選人

He is the president-elect.

他是總統當選人。

6162

overwhelming [͵ovɚ'hwɛlmɪŋ]

adj. 勢不可擋的,佔壓倒優勢的

He felt an overwhelming desire to kiss her.

他無法抗拒的想要親吻她。

6163

mistaken [mə'stekən]

adj. 犯錯的,錯誤的,弄錯的

You must be mistaken.

你一定弄錯了。

6164 notation [no'teʃən]

n. 記號法,表示法,註釋

He is learning musical notation.

他正在學樂譜。

6165 passing ['pæsɪŋ]

n. 通過,逝去,死 adj. 經過的,目前的,短暫的,及格的

The passing years have changed her.

過去的幾年改變了她。

6166 part-time ['pɑrt'taɪm]

adj. 兼任的,半工半讀的,部分時間的

adv. 部分時間,兼任地

He has a part-time job. 他有一份兼職的工作。

6167 noted ['notɪd]

adj. 有名的,知名的,著名的,顯著的,[樂]帶音符的

He is a noted author.

他是一個知名作家。

6168 parsley ['pɑrslɪ]

n. 香菜,荷蘭芹,巴西利

I ordered a fish with parsley sauce.

我點巴西利醬汁魚。

6169 parliamentary [pɑrlə'mɛntrɪ]

adj. 國會的,議會的,議會制度的

The world's oldest parliamentary democracy is in Greece. 世界上最古老的議會民主制在希臘。

6170 paperback ['pepɚ,bæk]

n. 平裝本,紙面本

His shelf is full of paperbacks.

他的書架上充滿紙面裝訂的書本。

6171 packing ['pækɪŋ]

n. 包裝,填墊材料,襯墊,封函,行李

I can do my packing before the trip.

我可以在旅遊前打包。

6172 packed [pækt]

adj. 充滿…的,塞滿了…的

The hotel was packed with tourists.

這家旅館充滿遊客。

6173 nostril ['nɑstrəl] ['nɔs-] [-trɪl]

n. 鼻孔

He was bleeding from one nostril.

他一個鼻孔在流鼻血。

6174 opposed [ə'pozd]

adj. 反對的,對抗的,敵對的,對立的,對面的

Most of us are opposed to the punishment.

我們大部分反對這項懲罰。

6175 opt [ɑpt]

v. 選擇

Some people opt for finding a job.

有些人選擇找工作。

6176

organized [ˈɔrgənˌaɪzd]

adj. 安排有序的,整齊的,有組織的,參加組織的,
有組織結構的,[俚]喝醉了的

I joined a carefully organized association.

我參加了一個有系統的組織。

6177

oriented [ˈɔrɪɛntɪd] [ˈo-]

adj. 以…為方向的,以…為目的的

This is a process-oriented plan.

這是過程導向的計畫。

6178

outnumber [aʊtˈnʌmbɚ]

v. 數目超過,比…多

Women outnumber men by two to one nowadays.

現在男女比例是一比二。

6179

one-time [ˈwʌnˌtaɪm]

adj. 從前的,一度的,過去的 adv. 從前,一度

The coal mining industry was one-time popular.

礦業曾經一度很流行。

6180

pensioner [ˈpɛnʃənɚ]

n. 領年金者,受雇者,僱傭

There are old age pensioners nowadays.

現在有老年領年金者。

6181

picturesque [ˌpɪktʃəˈrɛsk]

adj. 生動的,如畫的,獨特的

This is a fishing village with a picturesque harbor.

漁村附近有獨特的港口。

6182

pick-up [ˈpɪk-ʌp]

n. 收集,整理,拾得物

Here is a trash pick-up.

這裡有垃圾收集。

6183

pharmacy [ˈfɑrəmsɪ]

n. 藥房,配藥學

I went to a pharmacy yesterday.

我昨天去藥局。

6184

motorist [ˈmotərɪst]

n. 乘汽車者,常坐汽車的人

A motorist died in the accident.

一位乘客在意外中過世。

6185

mounted [ˈmaʊntɪd]

adj. 騎在馬[腳踏車等]上的

Look at the mounted police.

看一下這個騎在馬上的員警。

6186

mouthpiece [ˈmaʊθˌpis]

n. 發話筒,代言人,電話筒對嘴的一端

He was the mouthpiece of the company.

他是公司發言人。

6187

moving [ˈmuvɪŋ]

adj. 動的,鼓動的,動人的,使感動的

The Kite Runner is a fascinating and deeply moving story.

《追風箏的孩子》是一個精彩且感人的故事。

6188

multinational [ˌmʌltɪˈnæʃən]

adj. 多國的,跨國公司的 n. 跨國公司

He works in a multinational company.

他在跨國的公司上班。

6189

nationalist [ˈnæʃənlɪst] [ˈnæʃnəlɪst]

n. 國家主義者,民族主義者

Nationalists believe their country is the best.

民族主義者相信他們的國家最好。

6190

nationwide [ˈneʃənˌwaɪd]

adj. 全國性的

This is a nationwide activity.

這是全國性的活動。

6191

penis [ˈpinɪs]

n. 陰莖

Penis is a sex organ of men and male animals.

陰莖是男性和雄性動物的性器官。

6192

neighboring [ˈnebərɪŋ]

adj. 附近的,鄰近的,鄰接的

The hundreds of people from the neighboring towns and villages came here.

數以百計的人從鄰近鄉鎮來到這裡。

6193

newlywed [ˈnjulɪˌwɛd]

n. 新婚者,新婚夫婦

The newlyweds are on their honeymoon.

這些新婚者在度蜜月。

6194

newsreel [ˈnjuzˌril] [ˈnɪuz-] [ˈnuz-]

n. 新聞(短)片

There is an old newsreel of the Olympics.

這是奧林匹克的新聞短片。

6195

peacekeeping [ˈpisˌkipɪŋ]

adj. 維持和平的

They adopt peacekeeping operations.

他們採用維持和平的機制。

6196

PDA

n. (Personal Digital Assistant 縮寫)個人數位掌上型電腦,個人數位助理

PDA is useful. 個人數位掌上型電腦很有用。

6197

nightclub [ˈnaɪtˌklʌb]

n. 夜總會

The hotel had a nightclub.

這家飯店有夜總會。

6198

nationalism [ˈnæʃənlˌɪzəm] [ˈnæʃnəlˌɪzəm]

n. 民族主義,民族之特性

A strong sense of nationalism emerged during the war.

強烈的民族主義在戰爭中油然而升。

6199

inhibited [ɪnˈhɪbɪtɪd]

adj. 受抑制的,受禁制的,自我約束的,內省的

Many people are inhibited about death.

很多人對於死亡感到壓抑。

6200

remaining [rɪˈmenɪŋ]

adj. 剩餘的,剩下的

The few remaining guests were in the lobby.

剩下的客人在大廳。

6201

heavyweight [ˈhɛvɪˌwet]

n. 重量級

He is a heavyweight boxer.

他是重量級的拳擊手。

6202

relaxed [rɪˈlækst]

adj. 放鬆的,(法律等)鬆懈的,不嚴格的,輕鬆自在的,悠閒的

I'm feeling more relaxed. 我覺得很放鬆。

6203

heroin [ˈhɛroˌɪn]

n. 海洛因,嗎啡

Using heroin is illegal.

使用海洛因不合法。

6204

regulator [ˈrɛgjəˌletɚ]

n. 調整者,校準者,調整器,標準鐘

This is a heat regulator.

這是熱調整器。

6205

reggae [ˈrɛge]

n. 雷鬼(西印度群島的一種節奏強勁的流行音樂)

Bob Marley is the father of reggae music.

鮑勃馬利是雷鬼音樂之父。

6206

regain [rɪˈgen]

v. 重新獲得,奪回,恢復

The mayor has regained control of the city.

這位市長已經重新控制了該城市。

6207

refund [ˈriˌfʌnd]

n. 償還 v. 付還,償還借款,換回新公債,歸還

You will receive a full refund of the price of the clothes.

你將會收到這件衣服全額退費。

6208

heating [ˈhitɪŋ]

n. 加熱,暖氣(裝置)

Can you turn the heating off?

你可以將暖器關掉嗎?

6209

holding ['holdɪŋ]

n. 把持,支持,保持,私有財產

I heard that this company has large land holdings.

我聽說這家公司有很多的持有土地。

6210

heated ['hitɪd]

adj. 熱的,加了熱的

There is a heated swimming pool nearby.

附近有熱水游泳池。

6211

honorary ['ɑnə‚rɛrɪ]

adj. 榮譽的,名譽的,道義上的

He received an honorary doctorate last year.

他去年收到榮譽博士學位。

6212

hospitalize ['hɑspɪtḷ‚aɪz] ['hɒs-]

v. 把⋯送入醫院治療

Eight people were hospitalized after the accident.

八個人在車禍後送入醫院治療。

6213

hysterical [hɪs'tɛrɪkḷ]

adj. 歇斯底里的,異常興奮的

Janet became hysterical and got angry.

珍妮特變得歇斯底里而且生氣。

6214

ideological [‚aɪdɪo'lɑdʒɪkḷ]

adj. 觀念學的,空論的,意識形態的

Everyone has ideological differences.

每個人都有意識形態的差異。

6215

recur [rɪ'kɜ]

v. 重新出現,再發生,復發,依賴,借助於⋯

The disease may recur.

這個疾病有可能再發生。

6216

recording [rɪ'kɔrdɪŋ]

adj. 記錄的,記錄用的 n. 錄音,錄影,記錄

We have a video recording of the interview.

我們有面談的影像記錄。

6217

imposing [ɪm'pozɪŋ]

adj. 令人難忘的,壯麗的,威風的

Taipei 101 is an imposing building.

台北 101 是氣勢宏偉的建築物。

6218

inclined [ɪn'klaɪnd]

adj. 傾向於⋯的,有⋯意向的,傾斜的

Andy has different ideas from me, but I'm inclined to agree with him.

安迪跟我意見不同,但是我傾向於支持他。

6219

rating ['retɪŋ]

n. 等級,額定值,評分,收視率,責罵

The hotel has the best rating.

這家飯店擁有最好的酒店評等。

6220
privileged ['prɪvlɪdʒd] ['prɪvlɪdʒd]

adj. (享)有特權的,特許的,特免的

She comes from a privileged family.

她來自享有特權的家庭。

6221
refreshing [rɪ'frɛʃɪŋ]

adj. 使清爽的,有精神的,爽快的

This is a refreshing drink.

這是使人有精神的飲料。

6222
hardwood ['hɑrd,wʊd]

n. 硬木,硬木材,落葉樹

She was sleeping on the hardwood floor.

她睡在硬木材的地板上。

6223
dressed ['drəsɪd]

adj. 穿衣服的,(雞等宰殺的,放了血的,完全弄乾淨的家禽)供烹調用的,裝飾的

Are you dressed? 你穿衣服了嗎?

6224
respectively [rɪ'spɛktɪvlɪ]

adv. 各自地,各個地,分別地,依序為

They are Mary and John respectively.

他們分別是瑪莉和約翰。

6225
hacker ['hækɚ]

n. 破解(者),駭客

A hacker got into the system.

駭客進入系統。

6226
half-time ['hæf,taɪm]

adj. 半工制的

He works half-time everyday.

他每天工作半天。

6227
resigned [rɪ'saɪnd]

adj. 斷念的,順從的

She's resigned to go there on her own.

她認命的自己去。

6228
residential [,rɛzə'dɛnʃəl]

adj. 住宅的,與居住有關的

He prefers a quiet residential district.

他比較喜歡安靜的住宅區。

6229
reserved [rɪ'zɝvd]

adj. 保留的,留作專用的,預備的

A separate room is reserved for VIP.

這個分離的房間是要留給貴賓的。

6230
remains [rɪ'menz]

n. 剩餘物,廢墟,殘餘

My mother always eats the remains of the evening meal.

我的媽媽總是吃每餐的剩菜。

6231
hardliner [,hɑrdlɪnɚ]

n. (主張)強硬路線者,強硬派

He is a hardliner in such situation.

在這種情況下他是個強硬派。

6232 ranking [ˈræŋkɪŋ]

n. 等級,順序 adj. 上級的,幹部的,超群的

She is now second in the class rankings.

她在班上排名是第二名。

6233 reportedly [rɪˈpɔrtɪdlɪ]

adv. 根據傳說,根據傳聞

The couple has reportedly decided to break up.

這對夫妻根據傳聞決定要分手。

6234 replay [riˈple]

v. 重新比賽,重演 n. 重賽

The match will be replayed tomorrow.

明天將會重新比賽。

6235 repeated [rɪˈpitɪd]

adj. 反覆的,再三的

The boss was angry at his repeated absences from work.

老闆對他再三缺席感到生氣。

6236 repayment [rɪˈpemənt]

n. 付還,報恩,報復

This is the repayment of debt.

這是償還債務。

6237 reorganize [riˈɔrgəˌnaɪz]

v. 改組,再編制,改造,整頓

Our office is completely reorganized.

我們的辦公室被重新整頓。

6238 reopen [riˈopən] [-ˈopm̩]

v. 重開,再開始,再開

The department store will reopen in May.

這家百貨公司將會在五月重新開放。

6239 renowned [rɪˈnaʊnd]

adj. 有名的,著名的

He's a renowned speaker.

他是位有名的演講者。

6240 heading [ˈhɛdɪŋ]

n. 上標題,標題,起始字,方向

Chapter headings are on the top of pages.

章節標題在頁面上方。

6241 head-on [ˈhɛdˈɑn] [-ˈɒn] [-ˈɔn]

adj. 頭朝前的,正面的,迎面的,直接的

adv. 頭朝前地,迎頭,正面針對地

There is a head-on crash between two trains.

兩台火車迎面撞上。

6242 hearing [ˈhɪrɪŋ]

n. 聽,聽見,聽到,聽說,聽取,聽力,聽證會,訴訟,審訊

He is a child with a hearing disability.

他是一個有聽力障礙的小孩。

6243

hardline [ˌhɑrdˈlaɪn]

adj. 強硬的,不妥協的

A politician deals with political problems in a hardline way. 政治人物用強硬的手段處理政治問題。

6244

liberalize [ˈlɪbərəlˌaɪz] [-brəl-]

v. 寬大,使自由主義化

The government liberalizes society.
政府使社會自由化。

6245

rape [rep]

n. 搶奪,掠奪,強姦,破壞,葡萄渣,油菜 v. 掠奪,搶奪,強姦

The village was raped.
這個村子遭到掠奪。

6246

landing [ˈlændɪŋ]

n. 登陸,碼頭,降落

Can you tell me the procedures for take-off and landing?
你可以跟我說起飛跟降落的步驟?

6247

large-scale [ˈlɑrdʒˈskel]

adj. 大規模的,大型的

There will be a large-scale employment of young people. 將會有大規模的年輕人就業機會。

6248

provided [prəˈvaɪdɪd]

conj. 假若,如果

He can come with us, provided he comes here on time.
如果他準時的話,他便可以加入我們。

6249

lasting [ˈlæstɪŋ]

adj. 永久的,永恆的,持久的 n. 厚實斜紋織物

The love between them will be lasting forever.
他們之間的愛將會持久下去。

6250

prostitution [ˌprɑstəˈtjuʃən] [-ˈtrut] [-ˈtut-]

n. 賣淫,墮落

Prostitution is illegal.
賣淫是非法。

6251

prostitute [ˈprɑstəˌtjut] [-ˌtrut] [-ˌtut]

n. 妓女,男娼 adj. v. 使淪為妓女,賣淫的,墮落的

Being a prostitute is illegal.
做妓女是非法。

6252

LCD [ˈlɪkwɪd ˌkrɪstl̩ ˈdɪˈsple]

n. (Liquid Crystal Display 縮寫)液晶顯示

Nate glanced at a small LCD monitor.
奈特瞥了一眼小螢幕液晶顯示。

6253

lead-in [ˈlidˌɪn]

n. 引入線,介紹,開場白

The lead-in is made by someone to introduce a radio or television show.

開場白就是在收音機跟電視開場前有介紹的前言。

6254

left-hand ['lɛft'hænd]

adj. 左邊的,左手的

We walk on the left-hand side.

我們走在左邊。

6255

left-wing ['lɛft,wɪŋ]

n. 左翼

This is a left-wing newspaper.

這是左翼報紙。

6256

prowl [praʊl]

n. (為覓食而)潛行,徘徊,悄悄踱步
v. 潛行以覓食,徘徊,逡巡於

Teenagers prowl the streets. 青少年徘徊在街上。

6257

lesser ['lɛsɚ]

adj. 較少的,較小的,次要的

They were all involved to a lesser degree.

他們以比較小的程度牽涉在裡面。

6258

killing ['kɪlɪŋ]

n. 謀殺,殺戮 adj. 殺害的,疲憊的,迷人的

There are a series of killings on the street.

街上有許多殺戮。

6259

prolonged [prə'lɔŋd]

adj. 延長的,拖延的,特別長的

Don't expose yourself under the sun for a prolonged period of time. 不要將自己暴露在太陽底下太久時間。

6260

lifestyle ['laɪf,staɪl]

n. (反映個人或團體之態度及價值觀的)生活方式

Eating vegetable and fruit is part of a healthy lifestyle.

吃蔬果是健康生活型態一部分。

6261

lighting ['laɪtɪŋ]

n. 照明,光線的明暗,舞台燈光

The building needs good lighting.

這棟建築物需要好的照明。

6262

limited ['lɪmɪtɪd]

adj. 狹窄的,見識不廣的,有限的

The school has very limited resources.

這間學校資源有限。

6263

abandoned [ə'bændənd]

adj. 被拋棄的,自甘墮落的,無恥的,放縱的

The child was found abandoned.

發現一個遭遺棄的小孩。

6264

processor ['prɑsɛsɚ]

n. (農產品)加工業者,[電腦] 資訊處理機,中央處理機,[電腦] 處理程式 (把程式語言翻譯成機器語言的程式),概念藝術家

The processor power of the whole institute is very strong.

整個機構的中央處理器很強。

6265

proceeding [prə'sidɪŋ]

n. 進行,程序,行動,訴訟程序,事項

Proceedings of divorce are complicated.
離婚程序繁瑣複雜。

6266

lining ['laɪnɪŋ]

n. 襯裡,內層,襯套

I have a jacket with a silk lining.
我有一件有絲內襯的夾克。

6267

lesbian ['lɛzbɪən]

adj. 同性戀的 n. 女同性戀者

She is a lesbian.
她是女同性戀者。

6268

inmate ['ɪnmet]

n. 住院者,入獄者,同住者,居民

The jail has 100 inmates.
這個監獄有一百個入獄者。

6269

inning ['ɪnɪŋ]

n. 一局,發展的機會,好時機,圍墾

During the seventh inning, Leo suddenly dropped his
baseball mitt. 在第七局,李歐突然掉了棒球手套。

6270

insurer [ɪn'ʃʊrə]

n. 承保人,保險公司

The insurer may cover your loss when you have
accidents. 當你有意外時保險公司會承擔您的損失。

6271

racing ['resɪŋ]

n. 賽馬,賽跑,賽艇

He is a car racing driver.
他是賽車駕駛。

6272

intriguing [ɪn'trigɪŋ]

adj. 吸引人的,有趣的

He found her intriguing and wanted to make friends
with her. 他發現她很吸引人並且想跟她做朋友。

6273

investigator [ɪn'vɛstə,getə]

n. 調查者,研究者,審查者,私人偵探

The police investigators will report the result.
警方調查員將會報告結果。

6274

inviting [ɪn'vaɪtɪŋ]

adj. 引人動心的,有魅力的

The food has an inviting smell.
這食物有一種令人心動的味道。

6275

IQ ['aɪ'kju]

n. (Intelligence Quotient 縮寫)智力商數

Her brother has a genius IQ.
她弟弟很聰明。

6276

irrespective [ˌɪrɪ'spɛktɪv] [ˌɪrrɪ-]

adj. 不顧的,無關的,沒關係的

Everyone is equal, irrespective of age and race.
每個人都是平等的,無關年紀跟種族。

6277 qualifier ['kwɑləˌfaɪə]

n. 給與資格的人,限定物,限定句

He's among the qualifiers for the World Cup.
他有參加世界盃的資格。

6278 know-how ['noˌhaʊ]

n. 技術,實際知識,技能,本事,竅門

Those who have the know-how can deal with the disaster. 那些知道技術的人可以處理這場災難。

6279 restrained [rɪ'strend]

adj. 受約束的,克制的

The decoration is quite restrained.
這個裝飾相當受限。

6280 putt [pʌt]

v. 擊球入洞,擊高爾夫球 n. 輕輕一擊(入洞)

I was practicing putting.
我在練習擊高爾夫球。

6281 put-down ['pʊtˌdaʊn]

n. 令人難堪的言語或行動

She doesn't like his put-downs.
她不喜歡他不尊重別人的發言。

6282 punk [pʌŋk]

n. 廢物,半朽的木頭 adj. 無用的,腐朽的

He picked up the punk in the forest.
他在森林裡撿起半朽的木頭。

6283 jersey ['dʒɝzɪ]

n. 運動衫

This is a 100% cotton jersey.
這是純綿的運動衫。

6284 jobless ['dʒɑblɪs]

adj. 失業的

The number of jobless young men is increasing.
失業年輕人的數字正在增加。

6285 jumper ['dʒʌmpɚ]

n. 跳躍者,跳躍運動員,跳蟲(如蚤等),跳越障礙的馬,卡車司機送貨助手,短外衣

He's a good jumper. 他是好的跳躍運動員。

6286 psychiatrist [saɪ'kaɪətrɪst]

n. 精神科醫師

Psychiatrists study mental illnesses.
精神科醫師研究心理疾病。

6287 justified ['dʌstəfaɪd]

adj. 有正當理由的,情有可原的

She felt fully justified in divorcing.
她認為有離婚的充分理由。

6288 killer ['kɪlɚ]

n. 殺人者,嗜殺成性的人,殺手

He is a cruel killer.
他是殘忍殺手。

6289

unpredictable [ˌʌnprɪˈdɪktəbl]

adj. 不可預知的

Future is unpredictable.

未來是不可預知的。

6290

unrest [ʌnˈrɛst]

n. 不安的狀態,動盪的局面

There is growing unrest in the class.

班上有一種不安的狀態。

6291

time-out [ˈtaɪmˈaʊt]

n. [體] (比賽) 暫停,休息時間

With 15.7 seconds left, the judge called time-out.

隨著剩下 15.7 秒,裁判宣布暫停。

6292

unusually [ʌnˈjuʒʊəlɪ] [-ˈjuʒʊlɪ] [-ˈjuʒəlɪ]

adv. 顯著地,異常地,不尋常地

This year has an unusually cold winter.

今年有不尋常的寒冬。

6293

unveil [ʌnˈvel]

v. 揭開,揭幕,除去面紗

The company has unveiled plans to build a new branch.

這家公司揭開計畫要建分部。

6294

unwanted [ʌnˈwɑntɪd] [-ˈwɔntɪd]

adj. 不必要的,空閒的

These children feel unwanted and isolated.

這些小孩感覺不受關心跟被遺棄。

6295

ballot [ˈbælət]

n. 投票,投票用紙,選票,投票總數,投票權,抽籤

vi. 不記名投票,抽籤 vt. 拉票,以抽籤選出

200 voters cast their ballots.

兩百名投票者投票。

6296

centered [ˈsɛntəd]

adj. 在中心的,有中心的

The teacher adopted a student-centered approach.

這個老師採取以學生為主的方法。

6297

upbringing [ˈʌpˌbrɪŋɪŋ]

n. 教養

Mike has a good upbringing.

麥克有好的教養。

6298

challenger [ˈtʃælɪndʒɚ]

n. 挑戰人,挑戰物

His challenger was claiming victory.

他的挑戰者宣布勝利。

6299

timeless [ˈtaɪmlɪs]

adj. 無時間限制的,長期的,永恆的

We have a timeless universe.

我們有永恆的宇宙。

6300

unidentified [ˌʌnaɪˈdɛntəˌfaɪd] [ˌʌnə-]

adj. 沒有辦認出來的,身分不明的

An unidentified man was spotted on the ground.

身分不明的人在地面上被發現。

6301

bash [bæʃ]

vt. 重擊,毆打 n. 重擊

I bashed into the car in front at a high speed.

我以高速重擊前面的車。

6302

barrack [ˈbærək]

n. 兵營,軍營,供多人住的簡陋房屋

vt. 使駐兵營內,喝采,喝倒采

vi. 居於兵營,喝采,喝倒采

Inside the barrack in a narrow room, the soldiers talk and laugh.

在兵營裡的房間裡,軍人在談笑。

6303

tollway [ˈtolˌwe]

n. (美)收費公路

There are many cars on the tollway.

在收費公路上有很多車。

6304

tollbooth [ˈtolˌbuθ]

n. 過路收費亭

The tollbooth is where you pay to drive on a road.

過路收費站是你付費使用公路的地方。

6305

timing [ˈtaɪmɪŋ]

n. 適時,時間測定,定時,調速

Please check your flight timings.

請檢查你航班時間。

6306

celebrated [ˈsɛləˌbretɪd]

adj. 馳名的,著名的

She is a celebrated actress.

她是著名的女演員。

6307

tinkle [ˈtɪŋkl̩]

v. 使發出清脆的聲響,叮噹地發出,叮噹作響

n. 清脆的金屬音,叮噹聲

There is a tinkling bell on the wall.

牆上有一個叮噹作響的鈴鐺。

6308

unofficial [ˌʌnəˈfɪʃəl]

adj. 非正式的,非公認的,無許可的

The President made an unofficial visit to the USA.

總統在美國有非正式的訪問。

6309

unpack [ʌnˈpæk]

v. 卸下,打開,解除,打開包裹

She unpacked her suitcase and took a rest.

她卸下旅行箱並休息。

6310

toddler ['tɑdlə]

n. 幼兒

This is a toddler's toy.

這是幼兒的玩具。

6311

toddle ['tɑdl]

v. 幼兒蹣跚行走,東倒西歪地走,蹣跚學步,散步

n. 東倒西歪的走路,剛學走步的小孩

I have to watch the kid when he is toddling.

我必須在這小孩學步時看著他。

6312

banking ['bæŋkɪŋ]

n. 銀行業務,銀行業,銀行家的職業

They are recovering the huge problems in the banking system. 他們正在修復銀行系統出現的大問題。

6313

tint [tɪnt]

n. 色彩,淺色,淡色 v. 染色於

She has red tints in her hair.

她染了紅頭髮。

6314

ceasefire ['sisˌfaɪr]

n. 停火,休戰期

The company has called a temporary ceasefire.

公司已經暫時休戰。

6315

clover ['klovə]

n. 三葉草,苜蓿

Clover is a small plant.

苜蓿是一個小植物。

6316

challenging ['tʃælɪndʒɪŋ]

adj. 有[帶,具]挑戰性的,考驗能力的,
　　　引起爭論[興趣]的,意味深長的,有魅力的

Please solve this challenging problem.

請解決這個挑戰性的問題。

6317

textual ['tɛkstʃʊəl]

adj. 本文的,原文的

Here is a textual analysis of the novel.

這裡有小說的文本分析。

6318

birdie ['bɜdɪ]

n. 小鳥

A birdie appeared in front of the house.

一隻小鳥在房子前方出現。

6319

clean-up ['klin-ʌp]

n. 大掃除

The clean-up of the house took days.

房子大掃除需要好幾天。

6320

clearance ['klɪrəns]

n. 清除,解除,間隙,森林開拓

They began a clearance of the trash to make way for a new park. 他們開始清除垃圾為了要為新公園開路。

6321

closed [klozd]

adj. 關閉的,完結了的,不公開的,排他性的,自足的,
獨立的,(跑道)同起點同終點的

Before you go out, make sure all the windows are closed.

你出去之前,請確認窗戶關好。

6322

assured [ə'ʃʊrd]

adj. 有保證的,確定的,確實的,確信的,自信的
n. [英]被保險人

She shows an assured manner. 她表現出自信的態度。

6323

thermos ['θɜrməs]

n. 熱水瓶

I bring a thermos of steaming coffee to my office.
我帶一壺熱咖啡到辦公室。

6324

armored ['ɑrməd]

adj. 裝甲的,穿著護具的

The mayor takes an armored car for safety.
市長為了安全搭裝甲車。

6325

veterinarian [ˌvɛtrə'nɛrɪən] [-tərə-] [-'ner-]

n. 獸醫

A veterinarian gives medical care to animals.
獸醫給動物醫療照顧。

6326

appalling [ə'pɔlɪŋ]

adj. 震驚的,可怕的,駭人的,拙劣的

The weather was really appalling.
天氣真的很糟。

6327

anymore ['ɛnɪmɔr]

adv. 再也(不)

I won't talk to you anymore.
我再也不想跟你說話了。

6328

cocaine [ko'ken] ['koken]

n. 古柯鹼

Taking cocaine is illegal.
吸食古柯鹼是不合法的。

6329

cockpit ['kɑkˌpɪt]

n. (飛機駕駛員)座艙,戰場

The cockpit slammed down into the water and people died. 駕駛艙墜落水中且人員傷亡。

6330

vend [vɛnd]

v. 出售,販賣

They vend T-shirts and stickers.
他們販賣襯衫跟貼紙。

6331

chartered ['tʃɑrtɚd]

adj. 訂有租船契約的,(公共汽車、飛機)包租的,特許的,持有特許狀的,有特權的,享有破格自由的

He is a chartered accountant.

他是一個授予許可證照的會計師。

6332

topping ['tɑpɪŋ]

adj. 高聳的,傑出的,一流的

n. 除頂部,修剪樹稍,剪落之小樹枝,頂部

I ordered baked vegetables with a cheese topping.

我點的烤蔬菜上面有起司。

6333

uprising ['ʌp,raɪzɪŋ] [ʌp'raɪzɪŋ]

n. 起義,升起

The government suppresses an uprising.

政府鎮壓起義。

6334

awesome ['ɔsəm]

adj. 令人敬畏的,可怕的

They had an awesome task.

他們有可怕的任務。

6335

urine ['jʊrɪn]

n. 小便,尿

It smells like urine.

這聞起來像尿味。

6336

chapped [tʃæpt]

adj. [醫] (皮膚)凍裂

I get chapped lips on a cold day.

我在冷天氣嘴唇會凍裂。

6337

assuming [ə'sumɪŋ]

adj. 傲慢的,僭越的,不遜的,狂妄的

He is assuming.

他很傲慢。

6338

chariot ['tʃærɪət]

n. 二輪戰車,四輪輕馬車,(華麗的)馬車

He goes to a party with a chariot and three horses.

他搭馬車去舞會。

6339

champagne [ʃæm'pen]

n. 香檳,香檳酒,香檳色

There are a number of fine champagnes here.

這裡有很多好香檳。

6340

checked [tʃɛkt]

adj. 有格子圖案的,有格子的,[音] (音節)以輔音結尾的,閉音節的,封閉的

I have a checked blouse. 我有一件格子的短衫。

6341

attempted [ə'tɛmptɪd]

adj. 未遂的,意圖的

His attempted suicide shocked us.

他自殺未遂嚇到我們。

6342

attached [ə'tætʃt]

adj. 附加的,附屬的,愛慕的,結了婚的

This photo is attached to my resume.

這張照片附在我的履歷表上。

6343

check-up ['tʃɛk ʌp]

n. 檢查,核對,體格檢查

I have regular check-ups every year.

我每年都有身體檢查。

6344

chilli ['tʃɪlɪ]

n. 紅辣椒

I like to eat chili con carne.

我喜歡吃墨西哥辣豆。

6345

cholesterol [kə'lɛstərɔl]

n. 膽固醇

Too much cholesterol can cause health problems.

太多的膽固醇會導致健康問題。

6346

ATM

n. (Automatic Teller Machine 縮寫)自動存提款機

I get money from ATM.

我從自動存提款機提錢。

6347

utterly ['ʌtəlɪ]

adj. 完全,全然,絕對

You look utterly wrong.

你絕對錯的。

6348

two-thirds ['tu‚θɜdz]

n. 三分之二

Two-thirds of people are missing.

三分之二的人不見了。

6349

binding ['baɪndɪŋ]

n. 捆扎,裝訂,裝幀 adj. 有約束力的

There are rare books in leather bindings.

很少書是皮裝訂的。

6350

blot [blɑt]

n. 汙點,墨水漬,缺點

v. 亂塗,使模糊,吸乾,弄上墨漬,吸墨水

There is a blot on the skirt. 裙子上有墨水漬。

6351

brew [bru] [brɪu]

v. 釀造,醞釀,圖謀 n. 釀造酒,醞釀

Beck beer was brewed in Germany.

貝克啤酒在德國釀造。

6352

briefing ['brifɪŋ]

n. 簡報,簡令

John gave his coworkers a full briefing.

強給他的同事完整的簡報。

6353

bloc [blɑk]

n. 集團

The former Soviet bloc doesn't exist anymore.

前任蘇維埃集團現在已經不存在。

6354

broadcaster [ˈbrɔdˌkæsɚ]

n. 廣播電臺, 電視臺, 廣播(或電視)公司, 廣播員, 播種機, 播種者

He is a well-known broadcaster.

他是有名的廣播員。

6355

turnover [ˈtɜnˌovɚ]

n. 翻覆, 翻折, 半圓卷餅, 營業額, 流通量, 周轉
adj. 翻折的領子

There is a high turnover of staff. 人員流動的比例很高。

6356

tumor [ˈtjumɚ] [ˈtɪu-] [ˈtu-]

n. 腫脹, 腫, 腫瘍, 瘤

The doctor told him he has a brain tumor.

醫生告訴他腦部有瘤。

6357

broadly [ˈbrɔdlɪ]

adv. 寬闊地, 寬廣地, 廣泛地, 概括地, 大約地

She knows broadly what it is about.

她大致知道那是什麼。

6358

typically [ˈtɪpɪkl̩ɪ] [ˈtɪpɪkɪlɪ]

adv. 典型地, 通常地

I typically take a walk everyday.

我通常每天散步。

6359

dried [draɪd]

adj. 乾燥的, 乾縮的

These are dried herbs.

這是乾草藥。

6360

broth [brɔθ] [brɒθ]

n. 肉湯

I have broth for my dinner.

我晚餐吃肉湯。

6361

transit [ˈtrænsɪt] [-zɪt]

n. 經過, 通行, 運輸, 運輸線, 轉變 v. 橫越, 通過, 經過

Taipei has rapid transit networks.

臺北有快速的運輸網絡。

6362

buffer [ˈbʌfɚ]

n. 緩衝(區) v. 緩衝

He is a buffer between his wife and mother.

他是他太太跟媽媽的緩衝。

6363

biochemistry [ˌbaɪoˈkɛmɪstrɪ]

n. 生物化學

He majors in biochemistry.

他主修生物化學。

6364

ton [tʌn]

n. 公噸

The steel weighs a tonne!

鋼重一公噸！

6365

broadcasting ['drɔd,kæstɪŋ]

n. 廣播

The British Broadcasting Corporation is the biggest company. 英國廣播公司是最大的公司。

6366

troubled ['trʌbḷd]

adj. [英]煩惱的,不安的,困惑的,擾亂的,動亂的,騷擾的

Benson looked troubled when the teacher asked him a question. 老師問班森問題時，他看起來很困擾。

6367

bowel ['baʊəl] ['baʊl]

n. 腸

He got bowel cancer.

他得了大腸癌。

6368

borrowing ['baroɪŋ]

n. 借,借入,借用,借用之事物(如語言等)

He wants to reduce bank borrowings as soon as possible.

他想要盡快減少銀行借款。

6369

bowler ['bolɚ]

n. 玩滾球的人,玩球戲的人,投手

They wear bowler hats.

他們帶著投手帽子。

6370

trigger ['trɪgɚ]

n. 板機,觸發器,制滑機 v. 觸發,發射,引起,鬆開板柄

He kept his finger on the trigger and squeezed it.

他將手放在板機上，然後緊壓著。

6371

bulky ['bʌlkɪ]

adj. 龐大的

This is a bulky parcel.

這是一件龐大的包裹。

6372

brandnew ['bræn'nju] ['brænd-] [-'nɪu] [-'nu]

adj. 全新的,嶄新的,新製的

He bought a brandnew car.

他買了全新的車。

6373

bomber ['bɑmɚ]

n. 轟炸機,轟炸員

He was killed by a bomber.

他被轟炸機炸死了。

6374

boiling ['bɔɪlɪŋ]

adj. 沸騰的,激昂的 adv. 沸騰

It was a boiling hot day.

真是很熱的一天。

6375

bob [bɑb]

n. v. 男子名,髮髻,微不足道的東西,懸掛的飾品,剪短,敲擊,急拉,振動,上下跳動

She always wears her hair in a bob. 她總是用髮髻。

6376

break-in [ˈbrek-ˌɪn]

n. 非法侵入

Because of the break-in, we've called the police.

由於遭到非法侵入，我們已經通知員警。

6377

break-up [ˈbrek ˌʌp]

n. 中斷,中止,分離,分散,分裂,崩潰,解體

The break-up of their marriage made them sad.

婚姻分離讓他們傷心。

6378

booking [ˈbʊkɪŋ]

n. 記入,預約,登台契約

I made a booking for two rooms.

我訂了兩個房間。

6379

township [ˈtaʊnʃɪp]

n. 鎮區,鄉

Our township is along the river.

我們的鄉鎮沿著河流。

6380

mansion [ˈmænʃən]

n. 大廈,官邸,公寓(用複數,用於專有名詞中)

This is a beautiful country mansion.

這是一個漂亮的大廈。

6381

permanent [ˈpɝmənənt]

adj. 永久的,固定的

He is looking for a permanent job.

他在找固定的工作。

6382

republican [rɪˈpʌblɪkən]

adj. 共和國的,共和政體的,共和主義的,有關共和的
n. 共和黨人

This is a republican government. 這是共和政府。

6383

cue [kju] [kɪu]

n. 暗示,線索,提示,球桿

I think that's my cue to explain the mistake.

我想這是我解釋這個錯誤的線索。

6384

parking [ˈpɑrkɪŋ]

n. 停車,停機,停放

I couldn't find a parking space.

我找不到停車場。

6385

one-sided [ˈwʌnˈsaɪdɪd]

adj. 單方面的,片面的,不公平的

This is a one-sided game.

這是單方面的遊戲。

6386

colored [ˈkʌlɚd]

adj. 染色的,有色人種的,黑人的

There are many colored balloons here.

這裡有很多彩色的汽球。

6387

powerless [ˈpaʊɚlɪs]

adj. 無力的,無權的,無效能的

I was powerless to help him.

我無能為力幫助他。

6388

properly [ˈprɑpəlɪ]

adv. 適當地,正當地,嚴格地

The radio isn't working properly.

這台收音機無法適當運作。

6389

coming [ˈkʌmɪŋ]

n. 來臨 adj. 就要來的,將來的

The exam is coming soon.

考試即將到來。

6390

newcomer [ˈnjuˌkʌmɚ] [ˈnɪu-] [ˈnu-]

n. 新來者,初學者

He is a newcomer in the company.

他在這個公司是新進人員。

6391

smoky [ˈsmokɪ]

adj. 冒煙的,似煙的,燻髒的,嗆人的,煙霧瀰漫

I can't stay in a smoky room for too long.

我無法待在煙霧瀰漫的房間太久。

6392

separatism [ˈsɛpərəˌtɪzəm] [-ˈsɛprə]

n. 分離主義

There is no separatism in our country.

我們國家沒有分離主義。

6393

sentimental [ˈsɛntəˈmɛntl̩] adj. 感傷性的,

感情脆弱的,傷感的,充滿柔情的,多愁善感的

He has a strong sentimental attachment to the school.

他對學校有強烈的眷戀之情。

6394

established [əsˈtæblɪʃt]

adj. 已建立的,已確立的,已確定的,已證實的

He adopted well-established methods.

他採用通行的方法。

6395

eternity [ɪˈtɜnətɪ]

n. 永恆,無窮,不朽

Most people believe eternity.

大多數人相信永恆的真理。

6396

senate [ˈsɛnɪt]

n. 參議院,上議院,評議會

The Senate approved the law.

參議院同意這項法律。

6397

ethics [ˈɛθɪks]

n. 道德規範,倫理學

Doctors should have medical ethics.

醫生要有醫學道德規範。

6398

semi-final [ˈsɛmɪˌfaɪnl̩]

n. 準決賽 adj. 準決賽的

He joins the semi-final of the game.

他參加這場比賽準決賽。

6399

self-esteem [ˌsɛlfəˈstim]

n. 自尊,自負,自大

He has a low self-esteem.

他的自尊心不足。

6400
congressman ['kɑŋgrəsmən]

n. 國會議員,眾議院議員

We heard that Congressman Bill will come here.
我們聽說眾議院議員比爾要來這裡。

6401
segregated ['sɛgrɪ͵getɪd]

adj. 分離的,被隔離的,實行種族隔離的,
　　某一種族專用的,種族歧視的

This school used to be racially segregated.

該校曾經實行種族隔離。

6402
seriously ['sɪrɪəslɪ]

adv. 嚴肅地,認真地,嚴重地

He is seriously ill.
他生病的很嚴重。

6403
seeming ['simɪŋ]

adj. 表面上的 n. 外觀

She handled the matter with seeming passionate.
她表面上很熱情的處理這件事。

6404
seduction [sɪ'dʌkʃən]

n. 慫恿,誘惑,誘惑物,誘餌

Keep away from the seduction of money.
遠離金錢的誘惑。

6405
secretary-general ['sɛkrə͵tɛrɪ-'dgɛnərəl]

n. 祕書長,總書記

The UN Secretary General is in charge of a large
organization. 聯合國祕書長是負責這個大型組織。

6406
secondly ['sɛkəndlɪ]

adj. 第二,其次

Firstly, you need to get up early and secondly, you need
to exercise. 首先你要早點起床,其次你需要運動。

6407
seasoned ['siznd]

adj. 調過味的,(木材等)風乾[曬乾]的,
　　(人、動物)習慣的,老練的

He is a seasoned musician. 他是很有經驗的音樂家。

6408
experienced [ɪk'spɪrɪənst]

adj. 有經驗的,經驗豐富的,閱歷多的,老練的

She is experienced and passionate.
她是閱歷豐富並充滿熱情的人。

6409
extremist [ɪk'strimɪst]

n. 極端主義者,過激分子 adj. 極端主義的

They are political extremists.
他們是政治極端分子。

6410
farming ['fɑrmɪŋ]

n. 農業,農事,耕作

The apple is from organic farming.
這顆蘋果來自有機農場。

6411

Fascism [ˈfæʃɪzəm]

n. 法西斯主義,極端的國家主義

Fascism is an extreme right-wing political system.

法西斯主義是極端右翼政治系統。

6412

segregation [ˌsɛgrɪˈgeʃən]

n. 隔離,種族隔離

The country adopted racial segregation.

這個國家採用種族隔離。

6413

shilling [ˈʃɪlɪŋ]

n. 先令(貨幣單位)

An egg costs a shilling.

一顆蛋值一先令。

6414

edged [ɛdʒd]

adj. 具有…刃的,有…邊的

Hatred is often a double-edged sword.

敵意通常是雙面刃。

6415

educated [ˈɛdʒəˌketɪd] [ˈɛdʒʊ-]

adj. 受過(高等)教育的,有教養的,受過訓練的,熟練
的,高級知識分子的,高等文化者的,基於知識
[經驗]的

She is a highly educated woman.

她是受高等教育的。

6416

simmer [ˈsɪmɚ]

v. 慢慢地煮,燉,內心充滿

n. 即將沸騰的狀態,滿腔怒火即將發作

He was left simmering with anger.

他憋著怒氣被留下。

6417

side-effect [ˈsaɪdɪˈfɛkt]

n. 邊際效應,附帶效果,副作用

The natural remedy has no side effects.

這個自然療法沒有副作用。

6418

electorate [ɪˈlɛktərɪt] [ə-] [-trɪt]

n. 選民,有選舉權者,選區

A majority of the electorate support him.

大部分選民支持他。

6419

elevated [ˈɛləˌvetɪd]

adj. 抬高的,(比地面、基準面)高的,高架的,
(知識、道德水準)高的,高尚的,高雅的,高潔的

He has elevated blood pressure. 他的血壓偏高。

6420

binoculars [bɪˈnɑkjələs]

n. 雙筒望遠鏡

He watched stars with binoculars.

他用雙筒望遠鏡看星星。

6421
trade-off ['tred,ɔf]

v. 交換,交易,交替使用

They must trade-off between quality and quantity.

他們必須在質與量間權衡。

6422
trade-in ['tred,ɪn]

n. 折價物

She is going to give her Ford as a trade-in.

她即將要將福特車當作折價物。

6423
beating ['bitɪŋ]

n. 打,挫敗,搏動

He gave me a brutal beating.

他給我重重一擊。

6424
caring ['kɛrɪŋ]

adj. 有愛心的

He is a warm and caring man.

他很溫暖和富有愛心。

6425
underway [ˌʌndɚ'we]

adj. 進行中

The project is underway.

這個計畫在進行中。

6426
cartel ['kɑrtl̩] [kɑr'tɛl] n. 企業聯合,俘虜交換

條約書,決鬥挑戰書,政治集團,集團

An illegal drug cartel made a lot of profits.

非法毒品集團獲得很多利潤。

6427
battlefield ['bætl̩,fild]

n. 戰場,沙場

He's already on the battlefield.

他已經上戰場了。

6428
casino [kə'sino]

n. 賭場,供表演跳舞賭博的地點,一種牌戲

That club has a casino.

這家俱樂部有賭場。

6429
touching ['tʌtʃɪŋ]

n. 觸摸 adj. 動人的,悲慘的

The story is touching.

這個故事很感人。

6430
catering ['ketərɪŋ]

n. 承辦酒席,提供飲食及服務

The restaurant did the catering for your son's wedding party. 這家餐廳承辦你兒子的婚宴。

6431
associated [ə'soʃɪˌetɪd]

adj. 聯合的,聯營的,相關的

The book is associated with the risks of taking drugs.

這本書在說明吸毒的風險。

6432
unemployed [ˌʌnɪm'plɔɪd]

adj. 失業的,未被利用的

I've been unemployed for a few months.

我已經失業好幾個月。

6433
campaigner [kæm'penə]

n. 出征軍人,老兵,從事社會運動的人

He is a campaigner on political issues.

他是從事政治運動的人。

6434
transcript ['træn,skrɪpt]

n. 抄本,副本,謄本,正式文本,成績單

A transcript of the tapes is here.

錄音帶的副本在這裡。

6435
bunker ['bʌnkə]

n. 燃料庫,煤倉,沙坑,暗堡 v. 擊入沙坑,陷入窮境

I have a secret bunker.

我有一個祕密隱匿處。

6436
bureaucrat ['bjʊrə,kræt]

n. 官僚作風的人,官僚,官僚政治論者

He acts as a government bureaucrat.

他表現的像官僚作風的人。

6437
burning ['bɜnɪŋ]

adj. 燃的,燒的,像燃燒一樣的 n. 燒,燃燒

She was saved from a burning building.

她從燃燒的建築物中被救出。

6438
unbeaten [ʌn'bitṇ]

adj. 未搗碎的,未走過的,未被擊敗的

The team was always unbeaten.

這個隊伍從未被打敗。

6439
byte [baɪt]

n. (電腦的)位元組

A computer's memory is stored in bytes.

電腦的記憶體儲存在位元組。

6440
tranquilizer ['træŋkwɪ,laɪzə]

n. 鎮定劑

She's taking tranquillizers.

她服用鎮定劑。

6441
calculated ['kælkjə,letɪd]

adj. 被計算出來的,打算的,精心策劃的,蓄意的

He made a calculated attempt to deceive his mother.

他蓄意欺騙他的母親。

6442
topical ['tɑpɪkl] adj. 論題的,題目的時事問題
的,局部的,當前關注的,熱門話題的

He told some topical jokes.

他說了些當前熱門的笑話。

6443
traitorous ['tretərəs] ['tretrəs]

adj. 叛逆的,不忠的,口蜜腹劍的

I don't like his traitorous behaviour.

我不喜歡他叛逆的行為。

6444
unchanged [ʌn'tʃendʒd]

adj. 無變化的

The result remains unchanged.

這個結果保持不變。

6445
unclear [ʌnˈklɪr]

adj. 不易了解的,不清楚的,含混的

Our plans are unclear.

我們的計畫不清楚。

6446
uncomfortable [ʌnˈkʌmfətəbl]

adj. 不舒服的,不合意的,不安的

I felt uncomfortable here.

我感覺這裡不舒服。

S3 高中三年級
T3 技職學院三年級　編號 6447～6948

6447
captivity [kæpˈtɪvətɪ]

n. 囚禁,被關

The criminals were released from captivity.

罪犯從監獄中釋放。

6448
underlying [ˈʌndəˌlaɪɪŋ]

adj. 在下面的,基本的,根本的

The underlying cause of her depression is that she can't forgive him.

她憂鬱的基本原因是她無法原諒他。

6449
tranquilize [ˈtræŋkwɪˌlaɪz]

v. 使安靜,使平靜

A zookeeper tried to tranquilize the tiger.

動物園管理員試著使老虎安靜。

6450
takeover [ˈtekˌovə]

n. 接管,接收,接任

Tom has announced a takeover bid of the company.

湯姆已經宣布要接管這家公司。

6451
wee [wi]

adj. 很小的,微小的　n. 一點點

She looked a wee bit happy.

她看起來有點開心。

6452
well-being [ˈwɛlˈbiŋ]

adj. 安寧,福利,幸福感

I have a sense of well-being.

我感覺幸福的。

6453
tax-free [ˈtæks-fri]

adj. 免稅的,不付稅的　adv. 免稅地

These are tax-free cigarettes.

這些是免稅的香菸。

6454
companionship [kəmˈpænjənʃɪp]

n. 交誼,友誼,陪伴

When my dog died, I missed his companionship.

當我的狗死掉時,我想念他的陪伴。

6455

aesthetics [ɛsˈθɛtɪks]

n. 美學

I appreciate the aesthetics of this building.

我欣賞這棟建築的美學。

6456

takeaway [ˈtekəˌwe]

n. (從餐館)帶出去吃的簡便食物,外賣餐館

We can buy something from the Chinese takeaway.

我們可以在中國料理餐館外帶。

6457

tailor-made [ˈteləˌmed]

adj. 裁縫製的,特製的,訂製的

The dress is tailor-made.

這件裙子是訂製的。

6458

tactics [ˈtæktɪks]

n. 戰術,策略,兵法,用兵學

He uses harsh tactics on the enemy.

他對敵人使用嚴格的策略。

6459

admiral [ˈædmərəl]

n. 艦隊司令,海軍上將,旗艦

The admiral visited the ships.

這個海軍上將參觀了艦艇。

6460

taco [ˈtɑko]

n. 炸玉米餅(或捲)

Taco is a type of Mexican food.

炸玉米餅是墨西哥食物之一種。

6461

addicted [əˈdɪktɪd]

adj. 上癮的,沉迷於

Many people are addicted to computer games.

很多人沉迷於電腦遊戲。

6462

advancement [ədˈvænsmənt]

n. 前進,進步,增進,促進,升級,晉升

There are good opportunities for advancement in English. 有提升英文的良機。

6463

columnist [ˈkɑləmɪst] [ˈkɑləmnɪst]

n. 專欄作家

He is a newspaper columnist.

他是報紙專欄作家。

6464

alleged [əˈlɛdʒd]

adj. 被指(控)做,被說成是,可疑的,真偽難辨的,聲稱的

It is alleged that he abused dogs.

他被指控虐待狗。

6465

voucher [ˈvaʊtʃɚ]

n. 消費券,商品券,證人,保證人,證明者,憑證,憑單,證書

v. 證實…的可靠性

The voucher can be used at the supermarket.

這張消費券可以在超市使用。

6466
tattoo [tæˈtu]

n. 小馬,歸營號,得得的連敲聲,紋身
v. 得得地連敲,刺花紋於

He has a tattoo on his back. 他在背上有紋身。

6467
alarming [əˈlɑrmɪŋ]

adj. 驚人的,嚇人的

The graphics show an alarming increase in violent crime.
這個圖表顯示犯罪率驚人的提升。

6468
tasteless [ˈtestlɪs]

adj. 沒味道的,無鑒賞力的,沒品味的,俗氣的

The soup is tasteless.
這碗湯沒味道。

6469
way-out [ˈweˌaʊt]

adj. 抽象的,不清楚的,非傳統的,擺脫困境的途徑,解決難題的辦法,出路

This is the only way out. 這是唯一的出路(解決方法)。

6470
airlift [ˈɛrˌlɪft]

n. 空運,空運物資,空中補給 vt. 空運

Over 200 refugees were airlifted off the island.
超過兩百多位難民被空運離開這座島。

6471
communicative [kəˈmjunəˌketɪv] [-ˈmɪun-]

adj. 毫無隱諱交談的,愛說話的,暢談的

Students' communicative skills are good.
學生的溝通技巧很好。

6472
wallpaper [ˈwɔlˌpepɚ]

n. 壁紙,牆紙 v. 貼牆紙

There is a roll of wallpaper here.
這裡有一卷壁紙。

6473
tasteful [ˈtestfəl]

adj. 懂得風趣的,風雅的,雅觀的,有鑒賞力的

I like the tasteful furnishings in his home.
我喜歡他家風雅的傢俱。

6474
AI [eˈɑɪ]

n. (artificial intelligence 縮寫)人工智慧

In the future, AI will not be just science fiction.
在未來,人工智慧將不只是科幻。

6475
aging [ˈedʒɪŋ]

n. 老化,(酒、乳酪)成熟

There are aging movie stars.
有一些老電影明星。

6476
warring [ˈwɔrɪŋ]

adj. 相爭的,敵對的

Warring parties fight against each other.
敵對的政黨吵架。

6477
wartime [ˈwɔrˌtaɪm]

n. 戰時

In wartime, people feel helpless.
在戰時人們感到無助。

6478

winger [ˈwɪŋɚ]

n. (足球等的)邊鋒球員

Winger plays on the left or right side of the field in a game.

邊鋒球員是在比賽中擔任左翼或右翼的位置。

6479

absent-minded [ˈæbsntˈmaɪndɪd]

adj. 心不在焉的,茫然的,恍惚的

He is getting absent-minded.

他逐漸心不在焉。

6480

windshield [ˈwɪndˌʃild] [ˈwɪn-]

n. (摩托車的)擋風玻璃,[美](汽車的)擋風玻璃

The driver removed the bugs on the windshield.

駕駛把蟲子從擋風玻璃上清掉。

6481

supportive [səˈportɪv]

adj. 支持的,(尤指)用以維持患者體力的

He was strongly supportive of my essay.

他強烈支持我的論文。

6482

accountable [əˈkaʊntəbl]

adj. 負有責任的,應負責的,可說明的,能解釋的

You should be accountable to your family.

你應該為你的家人負責。

6483

supplier [səˈplaɪɚ]

n. 供應者

A shop needs to deal with both customers and suppliers.

一家店需要處理消費者和供應商的問題。

6484

confederation [kənˌfɛdəˈreʃən]

n. 同盟,聯盟,組織聯盟

The Confederation of British Industry warned that this situation will get worse.

英國工業聯合會警告這個狀況會越發嚴重。

6485

would-be [ˈwʊdˌbi]

adj. 佯裝的,本來打算的,想要成為,自充的

The would-be models were on the stage.

即將成為模特兒的人站在舞臺上。

6486

accomplished [əˈkɑmplɪʃt] adj. 完成的,實現的,有造詣的,有教養的,有才藝的,技藝高超的

He is a highly accomplished designer.

他是一個技藝高超的設計師。

6487

surgical [ˈsɝdʒɪkl]

adj. 外科的,外科醫生的,手術上的

The book shows surgical techniques.

這本書顯示手術上的技巧。

6488

superstitious [ˌsupɚˈstɪʃəs] [ˌsɪu-] [ˌsju-]

adj. 迷信的

I'm superstitious about this color.

我對這個顏色很迷信。

6489

worrying [ˈwɝɪɪŋ]

adj. 麻煩的,憂慮的

The situation is worrying.

這個情況很麻煩。

6490

confined [kənˈfaɪnd]

adj. 被限制的,狹窄的,在分娩中的,坐月子的

He keeps dogs in confined spaces.

他在狹窄的地方養狗。

6491

yoke [jok] n. 軛,牛軛,束縛,統治

v. 給…上軛,連接,結合,使成配偶,配合

We should get rid of the yoke of tradition.

我們必須屏除傳統的束縛。

6492

zip [zɪp] n. 拉鏈,(子彈飛過的)尖嘯聲

vt. 拉拉鍊 vi. 呼嘯而過,加速

Zip up your coat! It's windy outside.

拉上你的外套拉鍊！外面風大。

6493

superpower [ˌsupɚˈpaupɚ]

n. 極巨大的力量,超強大國,國際組織

USA is a global superpower.

美國是全球超大國家。

6494

written [ˈrɪtn̩]

adj. 書面的,寫成文字的,write 的過去分詞

This is a written test.

這是書面考試。

6495

woo [wu]

v. 求愛,追求,懇求,吸引

Clothes are being sold at a low price to woo customers into the store. 衣服以半價賣出為了要吸引顧客。

6496

whatsoever [ˌhwɑtsoˈɛvɚ] [hwɒt-]

pron. 無論什麼

Whatsoever you do, be a good man.

無論你做什麼，做個好人。

6497

tablespoon [ˈteblˌspun] [-ˌspʊn]

n. 大湯匙

Put two tablespoons of sugar into the soup.

放兩大匙糖在湯裡。

6498

systematical [ˌsɪstəˈmætɪkl]

adj. 有系統的,成體系的

This is a systematical approach.

這是有系統的方法。

6499

competing [kəmˈpitɪŋ]

adj. 只能選其中之一的,不能同時接受的

This is a competing situation that you must make a decision. 這是只能擇一的狀況，而後必須做決定。

6500

winning [ˈwɪnɪŋ]

n. 勝利,獲得,成功,贏得物 adj. 得勝的,勝利的

The winning team celebrated their success.

贏的那支隊伍慶祝他們的成功。

6501

activist [ˈæktəvɪst]

n. 行動主義者,實踐主義者,活躍分子

They are activist groups.

他們是行動主義者。

6502

acting [ˈæktɪŋ]

n. 演戲,行為,假裝 adj. 代理的,臨時的,演出用的

She started her acting career after she graduated.

在學校畢業後,她開始她的演戲職業。

6503

condom [ˈkɑndəm]

n. 保險套(套在男性陰莖上,用來避孕及防止性病),
陰莖套

Make sure you wear a condom during sex.

確定你在性行為中戴上保險套。

6504

compelling [kəmˈpɛlɪŋ] adj. 強制的,
強迫性的,令人注目的,非常強烈的,不可抗拒的

I have a compelling need to do it.

我有一個強制的欲望做這件事。

6505

computing [kəmˈpjutɪŋ]

n. 使用電腦,從事電腦工作

We use computing facilities for research.

我們為了研究使用電腦器材。

6506

con [kɑn]

adv. 反對地,從反面 adj. 反對的,詐欺的

v. 精讀,學習,默記 n. 反對者,反對票,肺病

pref. 連同(= with),一起(= together)

He's a con man.

他是詐欺犯。

6507

woodland [ˈwʊdˌlænd] [-ˌlənd]

n. 森林地,林地

The house is surrounded by woodlands.

這個房子被森林圍繞。

6508

workforce [wɜk ˈfors]

n. 全體工作人員,勞動力,工作小組

Two thirds of the workforce is female.

三分之二的工作人員是女性。

6509

concerned [kənˈsɜnd]

adj. 擔心的,掛慮的

I was concerned about her.

我很擔心她。

6510

workplace [ˈwɜkˌples]

n. 工作場所,工場,作坊

The law applies to all workplaces.

這項法律適用全部工作場所。

6511 alternatively [ɔl'tɜnə,tɪvlɪ]

adv. 二選一地,或者

You can relax on the beach or alternatively go to the department store.

你可以在海灘上放鬆或是去逛百貨公司。

6512 telecommunication

[,tɛləkə,mjunə'keʃn]

n. (通過電話、電報、無線電、電視等的)遠距離通信,電信學

The book is about the telecommunications industry.

這本書關於電信產業。

6513 teaspoon ['ti,spun] [-,spʊn] ['tis,p-]

n. 茶匙

Add a teaspoon of salt to your soup.

加一茶匙鹽巴在你湯裡。

6514 teamwork ['tim,wɜk]

n. 聯合作業,協力

We want to encourage good teamwork in our company.

在公司中我們鼓勵好的團隊合作。

6515 angler ['æŋglə]

n. 釣魚者,琵琶魚

An angler catches a fish.

一位釣魚者釣了一隻魚。

6516 team-mate ['tim,met]

n. 隊友,同隊隊員

He is one of my team-mates.

他是我的同隊隊員之一。

6517 teens [tinz]

n. 十多歲,青少年時期

She shows a talent for writing in her teens.

她在青少年時顯示出她在寫作的天分。

6518 ammunition [,æmjə'nɪʃən]

n. 彈藥,軍火

The army bombarded the place with ammunition.

軍隊用炸藥炸那個地方。

6519 vocals ['vokl̩z]

n. 聲樂作品,聲樂節目

The album is on vocals.

這張唱片是聲樂。

6520 vintage ['vɪntɪdʒ]

n. 採葡萄,釀酒,酒,葡萄收穫期,釀葡萄酒的時間
adj. (特指葡萄酒)上佳的,採葡萄,古典的,老式的

1990 was a fine vintage. 1990 年是葡萄酒最好的時間。

6521

tempted ['tɛmptɪd]

adj. 有興趣的,很想要做的

I'm tempted to eat cakes.

我想要吃蛋糕。

6522

collected [kə'lɛktɪd]

adj. 集中的,收集成的

Data was collected from the school.

資料是從學校蒐集的。

6523

villager ['vɪlɪdʒɚ]

n. 村民,鄉下人

Some of the villagers have lived here for a long time.

有些村民住在這裡很久。

6524

amends [ə'mɛndz]

n. (複數)賠償,補償,道歉

She tried to make amends for what she had said to her boyfriend by giving him a gift.

她試圖藉由送禮物的方式彌補她跟男朋友說過的話。

6525

animated ['ænə,metɪd]

adj. 栩栩如生的,生氣勃勃的,活躍的

We have an animated discussion.

我們有熱烈的討論。

6526

visualize ['vɪʒʊəl,aɪz]

v. 使看得見,使具體化,想像,設想,顯現

I tried to visualize the building when he talked about it.

當他談到這棟建築時,我試著想像它。

6527

taxpayer ['tæks,peɚ]

n. 納稅人

The proposal could cost the taxpayers 1 million dollars.

這項提議可能花納稅人一百萬元。

6528

vineyard ['vɪnjɚd]

n. 葡萄園

I own a vineyard at the foothills of the mountains in France. 我在法國山丘上有一個葡萄園。

6529

carnival ['kɑrnəvl̩]

n. 狂歡節,飲宴狂歡

There is a carnival atmosphere in the class.

班上有狂歡的氣氛。

6530

prevail [prɪ'vel]

vi. 流行,盛行,獲勝,成功

Those beliefs still prevail among some people.

那些信仰在某些人群中還盛行。

6531

expiration [,ɛkspə'reʃən]

n. 滿期,呼出,呼氣,(古)終止,到期,截止

Conor diagnoses his own expiration everyday.

康納每天檢查他自己呼吸狀況。

6532 continuity [ˌkɑntə'nuətɪ] [-'nɪu-] [-'nju-]

n. 連續性,連貫性

There are obvious continuities between beauty and personality. 在個性跟美貌之間有明顯的連續性。

6533 velvet ['vɛlvɪt]

n. 天鵝絨,柔軟,光滑 adj. 天鵝絨的,柔軟的,光滑的

I have a velvet dress.
我有一件天鵝絨的禮服。

6534 missionary ['mɪʃənˌɛrɪ]

adj. 傳教的,傳教士的 n. 傳教士

This is a missionary work.
這是傳教的工作。

6535 soften ['sɔfən] ['sɒf-]

v. (使)變柔軟,(使)變柔和,使溫和,削弱

Use warm water to soften your skin.
使用溫水柔軟你的皮膚。

6536 beckon ['bɛkən]

v. 招手,召喚

I could see my father beckoning me.
我可以看到我父親在召喚我。

6537 grope [grop]

v. 摸索 n. 摸索

Gina groped for her cellphone in her purse.
吉娜在皮包裡找手機。

6538 throng [θrɔŋ]

v. 群集 n. 人群

The children thronged into the school.
這群小孩群集進入學校。

6539 dwarf [dwɔrf]

n. 矮子,侏儒 v. (使)變矮小

Snow White and the Seven Dwarfs is a famous tale.
白雪公主跟七個小矮人是有名的童話。

6540 subscription [səb'skrɪpʃən]

n. 捐獻,訂金,訂閱,簽署,同意,[醫]下標處方

Are you interested in taking out a subscription to the magazine? 你對於訂閱這本雜誌有興趣嗎？

6541 sneer [snɪr]

v. 冷笑,譏笑,嘲笑 n. 冷笑,嘲笑

She sneered at Tom's hairstyle.
她嘲笑湯姆的髮型。

6542 abbreviation [əˌbrɪvɪ'eʃən]

n. 節略,縮寫,縮短

'Prof.' is the written abbreviation of 'Professor'.
Prof 是 Professor 的縮寫。

6543 script [skrɪpt]

n. 手稿,手跡,劇本,考生的筆試卷,原本

He has a film script.
他有電影腳本。

6544

contemplate ['kɑntəm,plet] [kən'tɛmplet]

v. 凝視,沉思,預期,企圖,考慮

He contemplated resigning but his parents objected to it.

他考慮要辭職但是他的父母反對。

6545

legitimate [lɪ'dʒɪtə,met]

adj. 合法的,合理的,正統的 v. 合法

That's a perfectly legitimate solution.

這是一個完全合法的方案。

6546

boyhood ['bɔɪhʊd]

n. 少年時代

I have little boyhood memories.

我有一點點少年時代的回憶。

6547

snarl [snɑrl]

vi. 纏結,混亂,吠,咆哮,怒罵
n. 咆哮,吼叫,怒罵,纏結,混亂

The dog snarled at me. 這隻狗對我吠。

6548

fascination [,fæsn̩'eʃən]

n. 魔力,入迷,魅力,迷戀,強烈愛好,吸引力

Egypt always holds a great fascination for me.

埃及對我來說有很大的吸引力。

6549

honk ['hɑŋk] ['hɔŋk]

v. 雁鵝叫,按(喇叭) n. 雁鵝叫聲,喇叭聲

Honk is a loud noise.

喇叭聲很吵。

6550

quest [kwɛst]

n. 尋求,探索 v. 追求,探求

Everyone has the quest for human happiness.

每個人都有追求快樂的需求。

6551

wither ['wɪðɚ]

vt. 使凋謝,使消亡,使畏縮 vi. 枯萎,衰退,感到羞愧

The flower had withered in the warm sun.

花在太陽下凋謝。

6552

fury ['fjʊrɪ] ['fɪʊrɪ]

n. 狂怒,狂暴,激烈,狂怒的人

I was looking at her with fury.

我生氣地看著她。

6553

retrieve [rɪ'triv]

v. 重新得到,取回,換回 n. 找回

She bent down to retrieve her money.

她彎下腰找回錢。

6554

ironic [aɪ'rɑnɪk]

adj. 說反話的,諷刺的

It's ironic that he is robbed in front of the police station.

很諷刺的是他在警察局前被搶。

6555

radish ['rædɪʃ]

n. [植]蘿蔔

He grows a bunch of radishes.

他種一堆蘿蔔。

6556

radiant ['redɪənt] ['redjənt]

adj. 發光的,輻射的,容光煥發的

He has a radiant smile.

他有容光煥發的笑容。

6557

degrade [dɪ'gred]

v. (使)降級,(使)墮落,(使)退化

Don't degrade yourself by doing this.

不要做這樣的事情來使你自己墮落。

6558

tyranny ['tɪrənɪ]

n. 暴政,苛政,專治

People fight against tyranny.

人們對抗暴政。

6559

bombard ['bɑmbɑrd]

vt. 炮轟;轟擊,質問,提供過多資訊或信息

The enemy bombarded this city yesterday.

敵軍昨天炮轟了這城市。

6560

stimulus ['stɪmjələs]

n. 刺激物,促進因素,刺激,刺激

Books provide a stimulus for knowlegde.

書提供知識的刺激。

6561

plantation [plæn'teʃən]

n. 耕地,種植園,大農場,森林,人造林,殖民

There is a banana plantation on the farm.

農場上種植香蕉。

6562

peddler ['pɛdlɚ]

n. 小販,傳播者

I saw a street peddler selling drinks.

我看見小販賣飲料。

6563

rattle ['rætl̩]

v. 發出卡嗒卡嗒聲,喋喋不休,急忙地做

n. 嚇吱聲,喋喋不休的人

Nancy rattled on for hours about her son.

南西喋喋不休的談論她兒子。

6564

rejoice [rɪ'dʒɔɪs]

v. (使)欣喜,(使)高興,喜悅

I rejoiced at the news.

我很高興聽到這個新聞。

6565

legislative ['lɛdʒɪs,letɪv]

adj. 立法的,立法機關的 n. 立法機關

There will be legislative elections coming.

將會有立法機構的選舉舉行。

6566

supervision [,supɚ'vɪʒən] [,sɪu-] [,sju-]

n. 監督,管理

The company needs constant supervision.

這家公司需要時常監督。

6567

cocoon [kə'kun] [ku'kun]

n. 繭

She was surrounded by the cocoon of love.
她被愛圍繞住。

6568

storage ['stɔrɪdʒ] ['stor-]

n. 貯藏(量),貯藏庫,儲存

I put some foods in cold storage.
我放一些食物在冷凍庫。

6569

commentary ['kɑmən'tɛrɪ]

n. 註釋,解說詞,評論

The reporters will give a sport commentary.
記者們將會做體育評論。

6570

prune [prun] [prɪun]

v. 剪除,裁剪

The tree needs pruning.
這棵樹需要修剪。

6571

theatrical [θɪr'ætrɪkl]

adj. 戲劇性的,戲劇的

He is a theatrical agent.
他是戲劇經紀人。

6572

sermon ['sɝmən]

n. 訓誡,說教,布道

We had to listen to a long sermon in the church.
我們必須在教堂聽冗長的布道。

6573

crust [krʌst]

n. 外殼,硬殼,麵包皮 vt. 蓋以硬皮

I like to eat sandwiches with the crusts.
我喜歡吃有麵包皮的三明治。

6574

braid [bred]

v. 編織 n. 編織物

May always wears her hair in braids to school.
玫常常綁辮子去學校。

6575

dissident ['dɪsədənt]

n. 持不同政見者 v. 有異議,不同意

Political dissidents criticize the government on TV everyday. 持不同政見者每天在電視上批評政府。

6576

antonym ['æntə,nɪm]

n. 反義詞

That is a dictionary of synonyms and antonyms.
那是同義詞跟反義詞的字典。

6577

nurture ['nɝtʃɚ] n. 養育,教育,教養,營養品

vt. 養育,給與營養物,教養,培育

Children were nurtured by their parents.
小孩被他們父母親所教養。

6578

wholly ['holɪ]

adv. 整個,統統,全部,專門地,整體地

This is a wholly perfect solution.
這是一個整體上完美的解決方式。

6579

shrewd [ʃrud]

adj. 精明

Peter is a shrewd businessman.

彼得是很精明的生意人。

6580

unsuccessful [ˌʌnsək'sɛsfəl]

adj. 不成功的,失敗的

They had an unsuccessful attempt to do the experiment.

他們想做這個實驗的企圖失敗了。

6581

arena [ə'rinə]

n. 競技場,舞臺

We watched a game in a sport arena.

我們在體育競技場上觀賞比賽。

6582

bass [bes]

n. 低音部,男低音,低音樂器　adj. 低音的

He is good at bass and drums.

他很擅長低音樂器和鼓。

6583

milestone ['maɪlston]

n. 里程碑,里程標,重要事件,轉捩點

The Great Wall of China is an important milestone in Chinese history. 萬里長城是中國歷史上的重要事件。

6584

prophet ['prɑfɪt]

n. 先知,預言者,提倡者

He counted himself a prophet.

他自許自己為先知。

6585

stoop [stup]

n. 彎腰,屈背,屈服　vt. 俯曲,辱沒

Dave stooped down to pick up the thing.

大衛彎腰撿東西。

6586

nominee [ˌnɑmə'ni]

n. 被提名的人,被任命者

He is a nominee for the post of vice president.

他被提名為副總統。

6587

norm [nɔrm]

n. 標準,規範

Don't violate the norms of civilized society.

不要違反文明社會的標準。

6588

spectrum ['spɛktrəm]

n. 光,光譜,型譜,頻譜,範圍,各層次,系列,幅度

He has a broad spectrum of interests.

他有廣泛的興趣。

6589

contaminate [kən'tæməˌnet]

v. 汙染

The drinking water has become contaminated.

飲用水被汙染。

6590

streak [strik]

v. 飛跑,加上條紋,使成條紋(狀)　n. 條紋,痕跡

There was a streak of blood on her cheek.

她臉上有一條血的痕跡。

6591
liberation [ˌlɪbəˈreʃən]
n. 釋放,解放,解放運動
That book talked about liberation.
這本書談到有關於解放運動。

6592
trek [trɛk]
vi. (徒步)短途旅行,旅行
n. 艱難的旅程,牛拉車旅行,艱苦跋涉
We spent the summer trekking in the foothills of the Himalayas.
我們夏天徒步旅行在喜馬拉雅山山麓。

6593
reproduction [ˌriprəˈdʌkʃən]
n. 繁殖,再現,複製品
This is a reproduction of the painting.
這是這幅畫的複製品。

6594
scenario [sɪˈnɛrɪˌo] [-ˈnær-] [-ˈnɑr-]
n. 想定,遊戲的關,或是某一特定情節,設想
The worst-case scenario is that the shop will be closed.
最糟糕的情況是這家店將會被關。

6595
ridge [rɪdʒ] n. 背脊,山脊,屋脊,山脈,犁壟
v. 起皺,成脊狀延伸,翻土作壟
We walked along the ridge all day.
我們沿著山脊走了一整天。

6596
trauma [ˈtrɔmə] [ˈtraʊmə]
n. [醫]外傷,損傷,挫折,痛苦經歷
People have traumas such as death or divorce.
人有挫折例如死亡或離婚。

6597
martial [ˈmɑrʃəl]
adj. 戰爭的,軍事的,尚武的,威武的
He is listening to martial music.
他正在聽軍樂。

6598
yearn [jɜn]
vi. 渴望,想念,懷念,向往
Hannah yearned for a baby.
漢娜渴望一個小孩。

6599
orient [ˈorɪˌɛnt] [ˈɔrɪˌɛnt]
vt. 朝東,確認方向,轉至(特定方向),以…為方向
n. 東方,東方諸國(指地中海以東各國)
There is a course that is oriented towards management.
有一堂課以管理為主。

6600
rhythmic [ˈrɪðmɪk]
adj. 節奏的,合拍的
I like music with a rhythmic beat.
我喜歡有節奏的音樂。

6601

janitor ['dʒænətɚ]

n. (大樓、學校、辦公室的)清潔工,工友,門房,看門人

The janitor looks after a school.

工友看守學校。

6602

hound [haʊnd]

n. 獵犬 vt. 帶獵犬狩獵,卑鄙的人,追捕,激勵,使追逐

The hound picked up bones.

這隻獵犬將骨頭撿起來。

6603

ponder ['pandɚ]

v. 沉思,考慮

She pondered over his words for a while.

她沉思了他的話一下。

6604

layout ['le,aʊt]

n. 布局,安排,設計

The layout of the street is clear.

這條街的布局很清楚。

6605

dispensable [dɪ'spɛnsəbl]

adj. 不是必要的,可有可無的

They regard money as dispensable.

他們認為錢可有可無。

6606

nuisance ['njusn̩s]

n. 討厭的人或東西,麻煩事,損害

I don't want to be a nuisance here.

我不想要成為討厭的人。

6607

generator ['dʒɛnəretɚ]

n. 發電機,產生器

The factory's generators were used during the power shortage. 工廠發電機因應電力缺乏時被使用。

6608

exaggeration [ɪg,zædʒə'reʃən]

n. 誇張,誇大之詞

It would be an exaggeration to say that he likes me.

說他喜歡我有些誇張。

6609

astronomer [ə'strɑnəmɚ]

n. 天文學家

He is an astronomer.

他是一位天文學家。

6610

autograph ['ɔtə,græf]

n. 親筆簽名,手稿 v. 署名

Can you sign your autograph here?

你可以在此簽名嗎?

6611

toad [tod]

n. [動]蟾蜍,癩蛤蟆,討厭的傢伙

A toad looks like a frog.

蟾蜍看似像青蛙。

6612

carol ['kærəl]

n. 歡樂的歌,頌歌,(尤指)耶誕節頌歌 v. 歌頌,歡唱

She sang a Christmas carol.

她唱聖誕歌。

6613 discrimination [dɪˌskrɪməˈneʃən]

n. 辨別,區別,識別力,辨別力,歧視

We shouldn't have sexual discrimination.

我們不該有性別歧視。

6614 poke [pok]

n. 刺,戳,懶漢,袋子 vi. 戳,刺,捅,伸出,刺探,閒蕩

She poked him in the ribs.

她戳他肋骨。

6615 truant [ˈtruənt]

n. 逃避者 adj. 逃避的,怠惰的 v. 逃學,偷休息

A number of pupils have been truanting.

很多學生逃學。

6616 diplomacy [dɪˈploməsɪ]

n. 外交

He is interested in international diplomacy.

他對國際外交有興趣。

6617 footstep [ˈfʊtˌstɛp]

n. 腳步,腳步聲,一步跨出去的距離

I saw footsteps in the snow.

我在雪地上看到足印。

6618 weld [wɛld]

vt. 焊接 n. 焊接,焊縫

The car has a new part welded on.

這部車有焊接上新的部分。

6619 graph [græf]

n. 圖表,曲線圖

The graph shows house prices have raised gradually.

這張圖表顯示房價逐漸攀升。

6620 asylum [əˈsaɪləm]

n. 庇護,收容所,救濟院,精神病院

He lives in an asylum.

他住在收容所。

6621 consolation [ˌkɑnsəˈleʃne]

n. (被)安慰,起安慰作用的人或事物

The children were a great consolation to him when his wife left him.

自從他太太離開他後,小孩是他最大的慰藉。

6622 conceive [kənˈsiv]

vt. 構思,以為,持有 vi. 懷孕,考慮,設想

He conceived the idea of transforming water into electricity. 他有構思將水轉為電。

6623 solo [ˈsolo]

n. 獨奏曲 adj. 單獨的

That was his first solo flight.

這是他第一次獨自飛行。

6624

perception [pə'sɛpʃən]

n. 理解,感知,感覺,洞察力

Children's perceptions of the world are very limited.

小孩對這個世界的理解很有限。

6625

supplement ['sʌplə,mɛnt]

n. 補遺,補充,附錄,增刊 v. 補充

Their sponsorship is a supplement to our funding.

他們的贊助將對我們基金會有所供給。

6626

hermit ['hɜmɪt]

n. 隱士,隱居者

A hermit does not meet or talk to other people.

隱士不跟人見面或談天。

6627

nucleus ['njuklɪəs] ['nɪu-] ['nu-]

n. 核子,核心

He is the nucleus of an effective team.

他是這個團隊的核心。

6628

molecule ['mɑlə,kjul] ['mɑlə,kɪul]

n. [化]分子,些微

Water is a very important molecule.

水是重要的分子。

6629

whine [hwaɪn]

n. 抱怨,牢騷,哀鳴 vi. 報怨聲,哭訴,發牢騷,發嗚嗚聲

Please stop whining.

請停止抱怨。

6630

primarily ['praɪ,mɛrəlɪ] [-ɪlɪ] ['praɪmər-]

adv. 主要地,根本上

The advertisement is aimed primarily at young people.

這個廣告主要是針對年輕人。

6631

salmon ['sæmən]

n. [魚]鮭魚,大麻哈魚,鮮肉色

I like to eat salmon.

我喜歡吃鮭魚。

6632

notify ['notə,faɪ]

v. 通報

We were notified that our article had been adopted.

我們被通知說我們的文章已經被採用。

6633

kin [kɪn] n. 家屬(集合稱),親戚,同族,血緣關係, 家族 adj. 有親屬關係的,性質類似的,同類的

We'll notify his next of kin of his accident.

我們會通知他的近親家屬他的意外。

6634

injustice [ɪn'dʒʌstɪs]

n. 不公平,不講道義

We should focus on the injustice of slavery.

我們應該關注不公平的奴隸對待。

6635

glitter ['glɪtə]

vi. 閃閃發光,閃爍,閃光 n. 閃光

The diamond glittered in the party.

鑽石在舞會上閃閃發光。

6636

exotic [ɪgˈzɑtɪk]

adj. 異國情調的,外來的,奇異的

There are exotic birds standing on the ground.

有珍稀鳥類站在地上。

6637

span [spæn]

n. 跨度,跨距,範圍 v. 橫越

Over a span of ten years, he became a strong man.

這十年來他變成很強壯。

6638

corporate [ˈkɔrpərət]

adj. 社團的,法人的,共同的,全體的

Paul is a manager of corporate communications.

保羅是公共傳播的經理。

6639

credible [ˈkrɛdəbl]

adj. 可信的,可靠的

Her excuse was credible.

她的理由很可信。

6640

viable [ˈvaɪəbl]

adj. 能養活的,能生育的,可行的

Can you come up with one viable solution?

你可以想出一個可行的方法嗎?

6641

postulate [ˈpɑstʃəlɪt] [-ˌlet]

n. 假定,基本條件,基本原理 vi. 要求,假設

It has been postulated that the earth is round.

曾有人假設地球是圓的。

6642

herb [hɝb]

n. 藥草,香草

There is a herb garden in front of his house.

他房子前面有一個香草花園。

6643

concise [kənˈsaɪs]

adj. 簡明的,簡練的

This is a concise dictionary.

這是一本簡明字典。

6644

nibble [ˈnɪbl]

n. 半位元組,細咬,輕咬,啃,點心

v. 一點一點地咬,細咬,吹毛求疵,對～略感興趣

He nibbled on the cookies carefully. 他輕啃著餅乾。

6645

linguist [ˈlɪŋgwɪst]

n. 語言學家

He is a linguist.

他是語言學家。

6646

vulnerable [ˈvʌlnərəbl]

adj. 易受攻擊的,易受…的攻擊,脆弱的

Children are most vulnerable to get hurt within their own home. 小孩最容易在家裡受傷。

6647

ethical [ˈɛθɪkl]

adj. 與倫理有關

He has the highest ethical standards.

他有最高的道德標準。

6648

variation [ˌvɛrɪˈeʃən] [ˌver-] [ˌvær-]

n. 變更,變化,變異,變種,[音]變奏,變調

The cookie is really just a variation of the bread.

餅乾其實只是麵包的變化。

6649

pyramid [ˈpɪrəmɪd]

n. 金字塔,錐體,金字塔形的物體,金字塔式的架構

At the top of the pyramid are the rich.

在金字塔頂端是有錢人。

6650

flick [flɪk]

v. 快速的輕打,輕彈,輕輕拂去,(翅)拍動,(旗)飄揚

n. 輕打,瀏覽

The dog's tail flicked from side to side.

狗的尾巴左右擺動。

6651

apprentice [əˈprɛntɪs]

n. 學徒 v. 當學徒

She works at the chef's as an apprentice.

她在廚師那裡當學徒。

6652

constitutional [ˌkɑnstəˈtjuʃənl] [-ˈtɪu-] [-ˈtu-]

adj. 構成的,增強體質的,憲法的,擁護憲法的

Everyone has a constitutional right to privacy.

每個人都有憲法隱私權利。

6653

unnecessary [ʌnˈnɛsəˌsɛrɪ]

adj. 不必要的,多餘的

You should reduce an unnecessary expense.

你應該減少不必要的花費。

6654

raft [ræft]

n. 筏,救生艇,橡皮船,大量 vt. 筏運,製成筏

People fell out of the raft.

人從救生艇掉下來。

6655

resume [rɪˈzum] [-ˈzjum] [-ˈzɪum]

v. 繼續,恢復(職位,席位等) [rɛzuˈme] n. 履歷,摘要

I will send my resume to you tomorrow.

我明天會寄給你履歷。

6656

botany [ˈbɑtn̩ɪ]

n. 植物學

He majors in botany.

他主修植物學。

6657

imperative [ɪmˈpɛrətɪv]

n. 命令,誡命,需要,規則,祈使語氣

adj. 命令的,強制的,緊急的,必要的,勢在必行的

It is imperative that you should go to bed on time.

你需要準時睡覺。

6658

pulse [pʌls]

n. 脈搏,脈衝,震動 v. 搏動,震動

The doctor checked his pulse.

醫生檢查他的脈搏。

6659

wholesale ['hol‚sel]

n. 批發,躉售 adj. 批發的,[喻]大規模的

We bought the dress with a wholesale price.

我們用批發價買這個洋裝。

6660

unwilling [ʌn'wɪlɪŋ]

adj. 不願意的,勉強的

He was unwilling to go to the party.

他不願意去舞會。

6661

insistence [ɪn'sɪstəns]

n. 堅持,堅決主張

At her father's insistence, she became a lawyer.

由於她爸爸堅持,她成為律師。

6662

subsequent ['ʌbsɪ‚kwɛnt]

adj. 後來的,並發的

I haven't read the subsequent pages of the book.

我還沒讀後來的頁數。

6663

vocal ['vokl]

adj. 發嗓音的,聲音的,有聲的,歌唱的 n. 母音,聲樂作品

I like to listen to vocal music.

我喜歡聽聲樂。

6664

installment [ɪn'stɔlmənt]

n. 分期付款,就職,安置

A loan will be paid by monthly installments.

每月要分期付款繳貸款。

6665

hiss [hɪs]

v. 嘶嘶作聲,用噓聲表示

The wind blows with a loud hissing noise.

風嘶嘶作聲。

6666

flutter ['flʌtɚ] n. 擺動,鼓翼,煩擾

vt. 飛舞,拍(翅),使焦急,使飄動,使揮動

A small bird fluttered past the house.

有一隻小鳥拍翅飛過房子。

6667

fret [frɛt]

v. (使)煩惱,(使)焦急,(使)腐蝕,(使)磨損

She's always fretting about the future.

她總是擔心未來。

6668

thrift [θrɪft]

n. 節儉,節約,[植]海石竹

Thrift is the habit of saving money.

節約是省錢的習慣。

6669

quantum ['kwɑntəm]

n. 量,額,[物]量子,量子論

He won a Nobel Prize in quantum mechanics.

他以量子機械獲得諾貝爾獎。

6670

ordeal [ɔr'dil] [ɔr'diəl] ['ɔrd-]

n. 嚴酷的考驗,痛苦的經驗,折磨

She went through the ordeal of the task.

她經歷了任務的考驗。

6671

shiver ['ʃɪvɚ]

v. 顫抖,打碎,碎裂 n. 發抖,(無法控制的)顫抖,碎片

Jenny stood shivering.

珍妮站著發抖。

6672

descriptive [dɪ'skrɪptɪv]

adj. 描述的,敘述的

The subject adopted a simpler and more descriptive title.

該主題採取更簡單且更能描述的標題。

6673

infinite ['ɪnfənɪt]

n. 無限的東西(如空間,時間),[數]無窮大

adj. 無窮的,無限的,無數的,極大的

We have an infinite universe. 我們有無窮的宇宙。

6674

crude [krud] [krɪud]

adj. 粗糙的,天然的

The picture is a crude drawing of a face.

這張圖是臉的大致畫法。

6675

disbelief [ˌdɪsbə'lif]

n. 懷疑,不信

I hold disbelief on him.

我懷疑他。

6676

heave [hiv]

n. 舉起 v. 舉起,起伏

Allen heaved his suitcase onto the closet.

艾倫舉起他的行李放到衣櫃上。

6677

eruption [ɪ'rʌpʃən]

n. 爆發,火山灰,[醫]出疹

The volcanic eruption of Mt. Vesuvius began on 18th March 1944.

維蘇威火山在 1944 年 3 月 18 日爆發。

6678

escort ['ɛskɔrt]

n. 護衛(隊),護送,陪同(人員),護衛隊 v. 護衛,護送,陪同

He goes outside under police escort.

他在警方護送下走出去。

6679

orchard ['ɔrtʃɚd]

n. 果園,果園裡的全部果樹,(美俚)棒球場

He has a cherry orchard.

他有櫻桃果園。

6680

unprecedented [ʌn'prɛsəˌdɛntɪd]

adj. 空前的,前所未有的

It is an unprecedented idea.

這是個前所未有的構想。

6681

insure [ɪnˈʃʊr]

v. 投保,保證

The vase is insured for 1 million.

這個花瓶投保一百萬。

6682

clench [klɛntʃ]

n. 牢牢抓住,釘緊,敲彎的釘頭

v. 緊握,(拳頭)牢牢地抓住,確定,敲彎

He clenched his fists. 他緊握著拳頭。

6683

cavity [ˈkævətɪ]

n. 洞,空穴,[解剖]腔

Put herbs inside the body cavity of the chicken.

請將香草塞入雞的胸腔內。

6684

trample [ˈtræmp!]

n. 踩踏,蹂躪 v. 踐踏,踩壞,輕視

There was a small fence to stop people trampling on the grass. 有一個圍籬阻止人們踐踏草地。

6685

mustard [ˈmʌstɚd]

n. 芥菜,芥末,芥末色

This is a jar of mustard.

這是一瓶芥末。

6686

legislation [ˌlɛdʒɪsˈleʃən]

n. 立法,法律的制定(或通過)

They support the legislation on abortion.

他們支持墮胎的立法。

6687

thrive [θraɪv]

v. 興旺,繁榮,旺盛,茂盛生長

There are plants that thrive in tropical rainforests.

有些植物在熱帶雨林中茂盛生長。

6688

profile [ˈprofaɪl]

n. 剖面,側面,外形,輪廓,簡述,印象 v. 概述,簡介

I saw her face in profile.

我看到她臉的輪廓。

6689

penetrate [ˈpɛnəˌtret]

vt. 穿透,滲透,看穿,洞察 vi. 刺入,看穿,滲透,彌漫

Sunlight penetrated the windows in the morning.

早晨的陽光穿透窗戶。

6690

rip [rɪp]

v. 撕,剝,劈,鋸,裂開,撕裂 n. 裂口,裂縫

Sue ripped the letter open.

蘇將信撕開。

6691

jingle [ˈdʒɪŋg!]

n. 叮噹聲 v. (使)作叮噹聲,(使)押韻

I could hear the jingle of coins in his pocket.

我可以聽到他口袋中硬幣的叮噹聲。

6692

ostrich [ˈɔstrɪtʃ] [ˈɑstrɪtʃ]

n. 鴕鳥,鴕鳥般的人

They like to eat ostrich eggs.

他們喜歡吃鴕鳥蛋。

6693

warrior ['wɔrɪə] ['wɑr-] [-rjɚ]

n. 戰士,勇士,武士,戰鬥,尚武,鼓吹戰爭的人
adj. 戰鬥的,尚武的

He is a noble warrior. 他是高貴的勇士。

6694

awe [ɔ]

n. 畏懼,敬畏,畏怯,驚嘆 vt. 使敬畏,使驚嘆

The observers were in awe of the destructive power of
the new weapon.

觀察員對新武器的破壞力感到畏懼。

6695

tackle ['tækl]

n. 工具,滑車,用具,裝備

vt. 固定,應付(難事等),處理,解決,抓住

You need to tackle the problem.

你需要處理這個問題。

6696

humanitarian [hju͵mænə'tɛrɪən] [hɪʊ-]

adj. 人道主義的,慈善的 [-'ter-] [͵hjumænə-] [͵hɪʊ-]

They promise to provide humanitarian aid.
他們承諾給予人道支援。

6697

subjective [səb'dʒɛktɪv]

adj. 主觀的,個人的

He has a subjective point of view.
他有個人的觀點。

6698

tart [tɑrt]

adj. 酸的,辛辣的,尖酸的,刻薄的
n. 果餡餅,小烘餅 v. (指女人)濃妝豔抹

I ate an apple tart. 我吃了蘋果塔。

6699

harass [hə'ræs]

v. 煩惱,騷擾

She has complained of being harassed by him.
她抱怨被他騷擾。

6700

pane [pen]

n. 長方塊,尤指窗格,窗格玻璃,邊,面,(一片)玻璃

The ground is as clear as a pane of glass.
地板乾淨如一片玻璃。

6701

optional ['ɑpʃənl]

adj. 可選擇的,隨意的

There are three optional courses this semester.
這學期有三堂選修課。

6702

decorative ['dɛkərətɪv]

adj. 裝飾的

The mirror is decorative.
這個鏡子是裝飾用的。

6703 outlaw [ˈaʊtˌlɔ] n. 歹徒,逃犯,喪失公權者

v. 將…放逐,宣布…為不合法

They plan to outlaw the carrying of knives.

他們計劃取締攜帶刀具。

6704 administer [ədˈmɪnəstɚ]

v. 管理,給予,執行

Our office administers the affairs of social welfare.

我們的辦公室管理社會福利事務。

6705 bog [bɑg] [bɔg]

n. 沼澤 vi. 陷於泥沼,陷入,拘泥

Don't get bogged down in minor details.

不要拘泥於細節。

6706 rivalry [ˈraɪvḷrɪ]

n. 競爭,競賽,敵對,敵對狀態

There has always been intense rivalry between him and me. 在他跟我之間有強烈的競爭。

6707 prospective [prəˈspɛktɪv]

adj. 可能的,潛在的,預期的

We are looking for a prospective buyer.

我們在尋找潛在的買家。

6708 retail [ˈritel]

n. 零售 v. 零售,述說(特指他人的事)

We are looking for more retail outlets.

我們在找零售暢貨中心。

6709 squat [skwɑt]

v. 蹲坐,蹲伏 adj. 蹲著的

Children were squatting on the floor silently.

小孩安靜地蹲坐在地板上。

6710 forge [fɔrdʒ] [fordʒ]

v. 穩步前進,鑄造,偽造,鍛鍊

She forged a new career in the mechanics field.

她在機械學領域中鍛鍊新的職涯。

6711 weird [wɪrd]

adj. 怪異的,超自然的,神祕的,不可思議的,超乎事理之外的

n. (古)(蘇格蘭)命運,預言,符咒

She's a weird girl.

她是一個怪怪的女生。

6712 reflective [rɪˈflɛktɪv]

adj. 沉思的,反光的,反射的,典型的

Look at the quiet and reflective man.

看這個沉思的男人。

6713 toll [tol]

n. 通行稅(費),費,代價,鐘聲

vt. 徵收,敲鐘,鳴(鐘)(特指宣布死亡),勾引,引誘

This is a toll road. 這條路需要通行費。

6714

scroll [skrol]

n. 卷軸,卷形物,名冊 v. (使)成卷形

He scrolled up the document.

他卷起檔案。

6715

idiot ['ɪdɪət]

n. 白癡,愚人,傻瓜,笨蛋

It is impolite to call any person idiot.

叫任何人白癡是不禮貌的。

6716

elevate ['ɛlə,vet]

vt. 舉起,提拔,振奮,提升…的職位

He tried to elevate his spirits of the song.

他試著要提升歌曲的意境。

6717

whiskey ['hwɪskɪ]

n. 威士忌酒 adj. 威士忌酒的

He drinks a bottle of whisky.

他喝一瓶威士忌酒。

6718

occurrence [ə'kɜəns]

n. 發生,出現,事件,發生的事情

An earthquake in the area is a common occurrence.

地震事件在這個區域很普遍。

6719

mode [mod]

n. 方式,模式,樣式,時尚

They have a relaxed mode of life.

他們過著很休閒的生活模式。

6720

tribunal [trɪ'bjunl̩] [traɪ-]

n. 法官席,審判者席,(特等)法庭

She went to a tribunal yesterday.

她昨天去法庭。

6721

hospitable ['hɑs'pɪtəbl̩]

adj. 好客的,招待周到的,(植物生長條件)適宜的,
(環境)舒適的

The local people are very hospitable.

當地人非常好客。

6722

spur [spɝ]

n. 踢馬刺,刺激物,(鳥,蟲等的)距,刺激

v. 鞭策,刺激,疾馳,驅策

The increase in salary was a spur to their production.

工資增加推動它們的生產。

6723

hoof [hʊf] [huf]

n. 蹄 v. 踢

Hoof is the hard foot of an animal.

蹄是動物的堅硬足部。

6724
strain [stren]

n. 過度的疲勞,緊張,壓力,拉傷,性格特點,旋律

v. 拉緊,扯緊,(使)緊張,盡力,拉傷,過度使用

I've strained a muscle in my back.

我拉傷了我背上的肌肉。

6725
voltage ['voltɪdʒ]

n. [電工]電壓,伏特數

The lamp is low voltage.

這盞燈是低電壓。

6726
slam [slæm]

v. 砰地關上,砰地放下,猛力抨擊,衝擊

n. 砰,猛擊,撞擊,衝擊

I heard she slammed the door angrily.

我聽說她生氣地甩上門。

6727
popularity [ˌpɑpjə'lærətɪ]

n. 普及,流行,聲望

He wins popularity with the students.

他贏得學生的聲望。

6728
rash [ræʃ]

adj. 輕率的,匆忙的,魯莽的

n. [醫]皮疹,大量,令人不快的事物

Don't do anything rash. 不要魯莽行事。

6729
muse [mjuz]

v. 沉思,深思 n. [希神]繆斯女神,沉思,靈感來源

He mused on how he could get through the difficulties.

他沉思關於他如何度過困難。

6730
bully ['bulɪ]

vt. 威嚇,脅迫,橫行霸道 n. 欺凌弱小者

The fat boy was a bully at school.

胖男孩在學校欺凌弱小。

6731
reconstruction [ˌrikən'strʌkʃən]

n. 重建,改造

The doorway is a reconstruction of his work.

這個入口是他重建的作品。

6732
saddle ['sædl]

n. 鞍,鞍狀物 v. 承受

We sat for eight hours on the saddle.

我們坐在馬鞍上八個小時。

6733
stump [stʌmp] n. 樹樁,殘餘,菸頭

v. 掘去樹樁,砍成樹樁,絆倒,截去

There is a stump by the road.

路邊有一截樹樁。

6734

slaughter ['slɔtɚ]

n. v. 屠宰,殘殺,屠殺

Those pigs were taken for slaughter.

這些豬被帶去屠宰。

6735

pillar ['pɪlɚ]

n. [建]柱子,棟樑,重要的支持者

He is the pillar of the family.

他是家庭支柱。

6736

grumble ['grʌmbl]

v. 抱怨地表示,嘟囔地說　n. 怨言,滿腹牢騷

She's always grumbling to me.

她總是跟我抱怨。

6737

motive ['motɪv]

n. 動機,目的　adj. 發動的,運動的

Can you tell me the killer's motive?

你可以跟我說這個殺手的動機嗎？

6738

excess [ɪk'sɛs]

n. 過度,剩於,無節制,超過,超額　adj. 過度的,額外的

I can't eat any excess fat from the meat.

我不能再從肉類吃任何多餘脂肪。

6739

transcription [træn'skrɪpʃən]

n. 抄寫,抄本

There are errors in the transcription.

在抄本中有些錯誤。

6740

irrelevant [ɪ'rɛləvənt] [ɪr'rɛl-]

adj. 不相關的,不切題的

We shouldn't focus too much on irrelevant details.

我們不應該注意太多無關緊要的細節。

6741

outlook ['aʊt.lʊk]

n. 景色,風光,觀點,見解,展望,前景

He had a practical outlook on his work.

他在他的工作上有特殊的觀點。

6742

terrace ['tɛrəs]

n. 梯田的一層,梯田,房屋之平頂,露臺,陽臺,傾斜的平地　adj. (女服)疊層式的

My room has a terrace. 我的房間有陽台。

6743

slay [sle]

v. 殺死,宰殺,殺害

Two passengers were slained by the robbers.

兩個旅客被搶匪殺害。

6744

scope [skop]

n. (活動)範圍,機會,餘地

Her job offers very little scope for social relationship.

她的工作提供很少的社交機會。

6745

accumulation [ə.kjumjə'leʃən] [ə.krum-]

n. 積聚,堆積物

I seem to have an accumulation of photos.

我似乎累積很多相片。

6746

vomit ['vɑmɪt]

n. 嘔吐,嘔吐物,催吐劑 vt. 吐出,嘔吐

The bad smell made her vomit.

不好的味道讓她嘔吐。

6747

vicar ['vɪkɚ]

n. 教區牧師

The vicar lowered his voice.

教區牧師降低他的聲音。

6748

genetic [dʒə'nɛtɪk]

adj. 遺傳的,起源的,基因的

We are influenced by genetic and environmental factors.

我們被基因跟環境因素影響。

6749

undergo [ˌʌndɚ'go]

vt. 經歷,遭受

My mother underwent terrible hardships last year.

我的媽媽去年經歷了可怕的苦難。

6750

astray [ə'stre]

adv. 迷途地,入歧途地

The dogs had gone astray in the forest.

這些狗在森林迷路。

6751

authentic [ɔ'θɛntɪk]

adj. 確實的,有根據的,可靠的,逼真的,可信的

I don't know if the sculpture is authentic.

我不知道木雕品是否是真的。

6752

wail [wel]

v. 悲嘆,哀號,悲痛(某人的悲慘遭遇)

n. 慟哭,哀訴

Praying at the Wailing Wall has been a Jewish custom for centuries.

在哭牆祈禱是數百年以來的猶太習俗。

6753

massive ['mæsɪv]

adj. 厚重的,大塊的,魁偉的,結實的,大量的

I can't carry a massive rock.

我不能攜帶這巨大的石頭。

6754

scar [skɑr]

n. 傷痕,疤痕 v. 結疤,使留下傷痕,創傷

There is a scar on his cheek.

在他臉頰上有個疤痕。

6755

extracurricular [ˌɛkstrəkə'rɪkjələ]

adj. 課外的,業餘的

They always join extracurricular activities.

他們總是參加課外活動。

6756

chant [tʃænt]

n. 聖歌,叫喊聲,簡短的曲調 v. 叫喊,以歌讚頌

They sang chants.

他們唱聖歌。

6757

outlet [ˈaʊtˌlɛt]

n. 出口,出路

She needed to find an outlet for her lost.

她因迷路而需要找到出口。

6758

patriot [ˈpetrɪət] [(美)ˌ-at] [(英)ˈpætrɪət]

n. 愛國者

A patriot loves his country.

愛國者愛他的國家。

6759

marine [məˈrin] n. 艦隊,水兵,海運業

adj. 海的,海產的,航海的,船舶的,海運的

He is a marine biologist.

他是一個海洋生物學家。

6760

peck [pɛk]

v. 啄,啄食

n. 啄食,啄痕,輕吻,配克(容量單位,等於 2 加侖)

Chickens pecked around the yard.

小雞在庭院啄食。

6761

peacock [ˈpikɑk]

n. 孔雀 v. 炫耀

The zoo has kept a peacock since 1929.

動物園自 1929 年就有飼養孔雀。

6762

rumble [ˈrʌmbl̩] v. 隆隆聲,轆轆行駛,低沉地說

n. 隆隆聲,轆轆聲,吵嚷聲

We could hear trucks rumbling far away.

我們聽到卡車在遠處發出隆隆聲。

6763

indifferent [ɪnˈdɪfərənt]

adj. 冷漠的,不關心的,一般的

He is indifferent to you.

他對你不關心。

6764

corps [kɔr] [kor]

n. 軍團,兵隊,團,兵種,技術兵種,特殊兵種,學生聯合會,一群人(從事工作的)

The hospital needs a corps of trained and experienced doctor.

這家醫院需要一群訓練跟有經驗的醫生。

6765

spike [spaɪk]

n. 穗,長釘,釘鞋,女高跟鞋

v. 用大釘釘,用長而尖之物刺,穿刺

There are a row of spikes on a wall.

牆上有一排長釘。

6766

render [ˈrɛndɚ]

v. 煎熬,給予,提供,致使,報答,回報,使得

Hundreds of people were rendered homeless by the flood.
數百人在洪水後變得無家可歸。

6767

hypocrisy [hɪˈpɑkrəsɪ]

n. 偽善

It's hypocrisy for them to pretend that they really want to do it. 他們假裝他們真的想做這件事很偽善。

6768

disciple [dɪˈsaɪpl̩]

n. 信徒,弟子,門徒

He is a disciple of the writer.
他是這位作家的弟子。

6769

pedestrian [pəˈdɛstrɪən]

n. 步行者 adj. 徒步的,呆板的,通俗的

Two pedestrians were hurt when the car bumped against them. 當車子撞到他們,兩位行人受傷了。

6770

cater [ˈketɚ]

vi. 備辦食物,滿足(需要),投合

The chef will be catering the wedding.
這位主廚會為婚禮準備食物。

6771

tournament [ˈtɜnəmənt] [ˈtʊr]

n. 比賽,錦標賽,聯賽

I hope I can win this tournament.
我希望我能贏得這場錦標賽。

6772

allergy [ˈælɚdʒɪ]

n. [醫]敏感症,(口)反感

I have an allergy to dolls.
我對洋娃娃反感。

6773

animate [ˈænəmet]

v. 鼓舞,使有生氣,將～製成動畫

adj. 生氣勃勃的,栩栩如生的,生氣勃勃的,動畫片的

"Sponge Bob Square Pants" is an American animated television series.

海綿寶寶是一部美國動畫影集。

6774

sensitivity [ˌsɛnsəˈtɪvətɪ]

n. 敏感,靈敏(度),靈敏性

Teachers have sensitivity to the needs of children.
老師對學生的需求很敏感。

6775

beverage [ˈbɛvərɪdʒ]

n. 飲料

I can't drink alcoholic beverages before driving a car.
開車前我不喝含有酒精的飲料。

6776

reproduce [ˌriprəˈdjus] [-ˈdrus] [-ˈdus]

v. 繁殖,再生,複製,使…在腦海中重現,再現

The results are reproduced in page 2.
這些結果重載於第 2 頁。

6777

pluck [plʌk]

n. 勇氣 v. 拔去(雞,鴨等)毛,採集

She plucked out a white hair.

她拔出一根白頭髮。

6778

dissuade [dɪ'swed]

vt. 勸阻

I tried to dissuade him from his foolish intention.

我試圖勸阻他愚蠢的意圖。

6779

auditorium [ˌɔdə'torɪəm]

n. 聽眾席,觀眾席,(美)會堂,禮堂

The actors and actresses are rehearsing at the auditorium.

男演員跟女演員在禮堂排演。

6780

tactic ['tæktɪk]

n. 策略,戰略

They tried all kinds of tactics to succeed.

他們嘗試各種策略讓其成功。

6781

exploration ['ɛkspləˌreʃən]

n. 探險,探勘,探測,傷處等的探查,探察術

We need oil exploration facilities in the North Sea.

在北海,我們需要在石油探勘設備。

6782

tact [tækt]

n. 機智,手法,老練 vt. 操作性應答

Solving the problem required great tact.

解決這個問題需要手法。

6783

scandal ['skændl̩]

n. 醜行,醜聞,誹謗,恥辱,流言蜚語

He has been involved in a political scandal.

他牽連在政治醜聞裡。

6784

provision [prə'vɪʒən]

n. 供應,(一批)供應品,預備,防備,規定

v. 為…提供所需(尤指食物)

The government is responsible for childcare provision.

政府對小孩的飲食供應須負責。

6785

transformation [ˌtrænsfə'meʃən]

n. 變化,轉化,改適,改革,轉換

In recent years, he has undergone a gradual transformation. 在近幾年,他經歷了逐步的轉變。

6786

unload [ʌn'lod]

vi. 卸貨,退子彈 vt. 擺脫…之負擔,傾銷,卸

The driver unloaded some food from the truck.

駕駛從卡車卸下了部分食物。

6787

sodium ['sodɪəm]

n. [化]鈉

Nowadays, people consume far more sodium than they have to. 現在人們攝取鈉超過所需量。

6788

diverse [daɪˈvɜs]

adj. 不同的,變化多的

In the USA, people are from diverse cultures.

在美國,人們來自於不同文化。

6789

tuberculosis [tjuˌbɜkjəˈlosɪs] [tru-] [tu-] [tə-]

n. 肺結核

I have suffered from tuberculosis.

我得了肺結核。

6790

procession [prəˈsɛʃən] [proˈsɛʃən]

n. 行列,隊伍,遊行

Here comes a funeral procession.

喪禮隊伍來到這。

6791

imprison [ɪmˈprɪzn̩]

v. 監禁,關押,監禁,收監,監禁

The policemen imprisoned the criminals.

員警監禁罪犯。

6792

shred [ʃrɛd]

n. 碎片,破布,少量剩餘,最少量 v. 撕碎,切碎

A shred of paper is on the table.

一個切碎的紙張在桌子上。

6793

solidarity [ˌsɑləˈdærəti]

n. 團結

He made a gesture of solidarity.

他做了團結的手勢。

6794

highlight [ˈhaɪˌlaɪt]

n. 加亮區,精彩場面,最顯著(重要)部分

vt. 加亮,使顯著,以強光照射,突出,標出～

Your resume should highlight your working experiences.

你的履歷表應該突顯出你的工作經驗。

6795

refine [rɪˈfaɪn]

vt. 精煉,精製,使文雅高尚

The book shows the process of refining oil.

這本書顯示精煉油的過程。

6796

arrogant [ˈærəgənt]

adj. 傲慢的,自大的

He has an arrogant attitude.

他的態度很自大。

6797

layman [ˈlemən]

n. 外行,門外漢

Can you explain this in layman's terms?

你可以用簡單的方式解釋嗎?

6798

publicize [ˈpʌblɪˌsaɪz]

v. 宣揚,傳播

The theory was widely publicized.

這個理論廣為宣傳。

6799 segment [ˈsɛgmənt]

n. 段,節,片斷 v. 分割

She divided the painting into segments.

她將畫區分成幾部分。

6800 prescribe [prɪˈskraɪb]

v. 指示,規定,處方,開藥

Here are the drugs prescribed for his disease.

這是為他的病開的藥。

6801 haunt [hɔnt] [hɑnt]

v. 神鬼出沒,難以忘卻 n. 常去的場所

This is a haunted house.

這是一間鬼屋。

6802 uncertain [ʌnˈsɝtn̩] [-ˈsɝtɪn]

adj. 無常的,不確定的,不可預測的,靠不住的

They're both uncertain about the future.

他們對未來不確定。

6803 shrub [ʃrʌb]

n. 灌木,灌木叢

I planted evergreen shrubs in my garden.

我在花園種常綠灌木。

6804 forsake [fɚˈsek]

vt. 放棄,拋棄

The homeless children were forsaken by their parents.

這些無家可歸的小孩被父母遺棄。

6805 fragment [ˈfrægmənt] [frægˈmɛnt]

n. 碎片,斷片,片段 v. 破碎,碎裂

Glass fragments spread across the table.

玻璃碎片散布在桌上。

6806 valiant [ˈvæljənt]

adj. 勇敢的,英勇的 n. 勇敢的人

They are valiant warriors.

他們是勇士。

6807 miser [ˈmaɪzɚ]

n. 守財奴,吝嗇鬼,鑿井機

A miser hates spending money.

守財奴討厭花錢。

6808 shrine [ʃraɪn]

n. 神龕,神殿,神祠,聖地

They visit the shrine of Mecca.

他們參訪麥加神殿。

6809 divert [dəˈvɝt] [daɪ-]

v. 轉移,轉向,使高興

The woman diverted people's attention away from the speech. 該女子在演講中轉移人們的注意力。

6810 provincial [prəˈvɪnʃəl]

adj. 省的,守舊的 n. 外鄉人

There will be a provincial election coming.

有個省級選舉即將來到。

6811

taunt [tɔnt] [tɑnt]

n. 辱罵,嘲弄

The children taunted him about his height.
小孩嘲笑他的身高。

6812

yeast [jist]

n. 酵母,發酵粉

The bread is made of wheat and baked with yeast.
麵包是由麥和酵母烘烤而成。

6813

drizzle ['drɪz]

n. 細雨　v. 下毛毛雨

A drizzle was falling so let's go inside.
開始下毛毛雨了,所以我們進去裡面。

6814

umpire ['ʌmpaɪr]

n. 仲裁人,裁判員　v. 仲裁,作裁判

We need someone to umpire a game of baseball.
我們需要某人為了棒球賽做裁判。

6815

erode [ɪ'rod]

vt. 侵蝕,腐蝕,使變化　vi. 受腐蝕,逐漸消蝕掉

The rocks have gradually been eroded away by heavy seas. 這些石頭已經被海水逐漸腐蝕。

6816

rascal ['ræsk]

n. 流氓,傢伙,壞蛋,淘氣鬼,搗蛋鬼

You lucky rascal!
你這幸運的傢伙!

6817

corruption [kə'rʌpʃən]

n. 腐敗,貪汙,墮落

Newspapers made allegations of corruption in the government. 報紙指控政府貪汙。

6818

diversify [daɪ'vɜsəfaɪ]

v. 使多樣化,作多樣性的投資

The company is planning to diversify into other businesses. 公司計畫要作多樣性的投資。

6819

melancholy ['mɛləkɑlɪ]

n. adj. 憂鬱

He is the reason for your melancholy.
他是你憂鬱的原因。

6820

excel [ɪk'sɛl]

v. 優秀,勝過他人,突出

She has always excelled in cooking.
她常常有突出的廚藝。

6821

helpless ['hɛlplɪs]

adj. 無助的,無能的,沒用的

He began to feel helpless.
他開始感覺很無助。

6822

diminish [də'mɪnɪʃ]

v. (使)減少,(使)變小

The country's power is rapidly diminishing.
這個國家的權力正在迅速減少。

6823

victor ['vɪktɚ] n. 勝利者

Our team had two defeats and three victories, finally we became a victor.

我們隊兩敗三勝，最終我們成了勝利者。

6824

reinforce [ˌriɪn'fors] [-'fɔrs]

vt. 增強,加強,加固

The film reinforces the idea that women should be strong nowadays.

這部電影加強一個想法，女人現在應該要堅強。

6825

exceed [ɪk'sid]

vt. 超過,勝過

The price will exceed $100.

價格超過 100 元。

6826

complexion [kəm'plɛkʃən]

n. 面色,膚色,情況,局面

She has fair complexion.

她膚色均勻。

6827

undergraduate [ˌʌndɚ'gædʒʊɪt] [-ˌet]

n. 大學肄業生(尚未取得學位的),大學生

They are second-year undergraduates.

他們是大學二年級。

6828

abbreviate [ə'brɪvɪˌet]

v. 縮寫,省略,縮短,簡化

'Dormitory' is usually abbreviated to 'dorm'.

宿舍可以被縮寫成 dorm。

6829

maintenance ['mentənəns] ['mentɪnəns]

n. 維護,保持,生活費用,扶養

The cost of maintenance is really high.

維護的成本非常高。

6830

vow [vaʊ]

n. 誓約　v. 宣誓,立誓,發誓

Robert made a vow that he will love his wife forever.

羅伯特發誓要永遠愛他的太太。

6831

presumably [prɪ'zuməblɪ] [-'zɪum-] [-zjum-]

adv. 推測起來,大概

It's raining, which presumably means that you can't go out. 現在下雨你大概不能出去。

6832

precedent ['prɛsədənt]

n. 先例,實例

The party set a precedent for future case.

該政黨為了未來案例樹立了先例。

6833

dual ['djuəl] ['dɪuəl] ['duəl]

adj. 雙的,二重的,雙重

She has dual nationality.

她有雙重國籍。

6834

stance [stæns]

n. 姿態,立場

I don't like the newspaper's stance on the war.
我不喜歡這報紙對戰爭的立場。

6835

modernize ['mɑdən,aɪz]

v. 使現代化

The country is investing 1 million to modernize its capital city. 這個國家投資一百萬使首都現代化。

6836

ecstasy ['ɛkstəsɪ]

n. 入迷,恍惚,昏迷,迷幻藥

He freaks out on ecstasy.
他染上了迷幻藥的毒癮。

6837

vacancy ['vekənsɪ]

n. 空白,空缺,空閒,空虛

A bulletin board has information about job vacancies.
公告欄有工作空缺的資訊。

6838

foil [fɔɪl]

n. 箔,金屬薄片,[建]葉形片,烘托,襯托

vt. 襯托,阻止,擋開,挫敗,貼箔於

Cover the fish with silver foil and bake for a while.

把魚包在銀箔內並烤一會兒。

6839

caress [kəˈrɛs]

v. 奉承,,哄騙,愛撫,接吻,撫愛 n. 愛撫如親吻,擁抱

His hands gently caressed her face.
他的手溫柔的撫摸她的臉。

6840

spectacular [spɛkˈtækjələ]

adj. 引人入勝的,壯觀的 n. 壯觀的景色

The country has spectacular scenery.
這個國家有壯觀的景色。

6841

familiarity

[fə,mɪlɪˈærətɪ] [fə,mɪljɪˈærətɪ] [fə,mɪlˈjærətɪ]

n. 熟悉,通曉,親密,熟悉,精通

I miss the familiarity of my hometown.

我想念我家鄉的熟悉感。

6842

jade [dʒed]

n. 碧玉,翡翠,老馬 v. (使)疲倦

This is a jade necklace.
這是一個翡翠項鍊。

6843

crumb [krʌm]

n. 碎屑,麵包屑,少許 vt. 搓碎,弄碎

I like to eat bread crumbs.
我喜歡吃麵包屑。

6844

worsen ['wɜsn̩]

v. (使)變得更壞,惡化,損害

The situation is steadily worsening.

這個狀況逐漸惡化。

6845

poach [potʃ]

vt. vi. 水煮(荷包蛋),把…踏成泥漿,侵入,偷獵,竊取

I like to put poached eggs on toast.

我喜歡放水煮蛋在土司上。

6846

compassionate [kəm'pæʃənɪt]

adj. 富於同情心的

He is a compassionate man.

他是富於同情心的人。

6847

lest [lɛst]

conj. 唯恐,免得

She turned away from the window lest everyone can catch her. 她從窗邊轉身過去,免得大家注意到她。

6848

alligator ['ælə,getə]

n. 產於美洲的鱷魚

Alligator shoes can be very expensive.

鱷魚皮製鞋很貴。

6849

mattress ['mætrəs] ['mætrɪs]

n. 床墊,空氣墊

We sleep on a soft mattress.

我們睡在軟床墊上。

6850

rotate ['rotet]

v. 使旋轉,轉動

The chef rotated the fish through baking for several times.

廚師在烤魚時翻轉幾次。

6851

prosecute ['prɑsɪ,kjut] [-kɪut]

vt. vi. 實行,從事,告發,起訴

The company was prosecuted for bribery.

這個公司因為行賄而起訴。

6852

outright ['aʊt,raɪt]

adj. 直率的,徹底的,完全的

adv. 直率地,痛快地,立刻地,全部地

His request was met with an outright refusal.

他的請求遭到了徹底的拒絕。

6853

repress [rɪ'prɛs]

vt. (美)再壓,補充加壓 vi. 壓制

Repressing our feelings doesn't mean they would go away. 壓抑我們的感情並不意味著感受會自動離開。

6854

lottery ['lɑtərɪ]

n. 彩券

He won a lottery.

他贏得樂透。

6855

personnel [pɝsn'ɛl]

n. 人員,職員

All personnel have insurance.

全部的員工都有保險。

6856

referee [ˌrɛfəˈri]

n. 仲裁人,調解人,裁判 v. 仲裁,裁判

The teacher often acts as a referee for his students.

老師通常當他的學生的仲裁人。

6857

sanctuary ['sæŋktʃʊˌɛrɪ]

n. 避難所

The park is a sanctuary for birds.

這個公園是鳥的避難所。

6858

insufficient [ˌɪnsəˈfɪʃənt]

adj. 不足的,不夠的 n. 不足

His salary was insufficient for his family.

他的薪水對他家人而言不夠。

6859

staple ['stepl̩]

n. 釘書釘,釘,產品(或商品),主要成分,來源
adj. 主要的,常用的,大宗生產的

I need some staples. 我需要一些釘書釘。

6860

stabilize ['steblˌaɪz]

v. 穩定

The government tried to stabilize prices.

政府試著要穩定物價。

6861

truly ['trulɪ] ['trɪulɪ]

adv. 真實地,真正地,確實地

I'm truly sorry about this.

我真的對這件事很抱歉。

6862

psychiatric [ˌsaɪkɪˈætrɪk]

adj. 精神病學的,精神病治療的

He was sent to a psychiatric hospital.

他被送到精神病院。

6863

tempt [tɛmpt]

vt. 誘惑,引誘,吸引,使感興趣,考驗,試探

The ad tempts me to buy the product.

這個廣告吸引我買這個產品。

6864

lyric ['lɪrɪk]

n. 抒情詩,歌詞 adj. 吟唱的,抒情的

I like the music and lyrics by Rodgers.

我喜歡羅傑斯的音樂跟歌詞。

6865

vibration [vaɪˈbreʃən]

n. 震動,顫動,搖動,擺動

We could feel the vibrations from the earthquake.

我們能夠感覺地震的震動。

6866

oblong ['ablɔŋ]

n. 長方形,橢圓形 adj. 長方形的,橢圓形的

This is an oblong table.

這是一張橢圓形的桌子。

6867

literate ['lɪtərɪt]

n. 學者,有學識的人

adj. 有文化的,有閱讀和寫作能力的

He is a literate. 他是學者。

6868

oblige [ə'blaɪdʒ]

vt. 迫使,施恩於…,使感激

I was obliged to do it.
我被迫要做這件事。

6869

shoplift ['ʃɑp,lɪft]

v. 從商店中偷商品

Shoplifting is illegal.
從商店中偷商品是非法。

6870

gust [gʌst] n. 陣風,一陣狂風,(雨,冰雹,煙,火,

聲音等的),(感情的)迸發,洶湧

A sudden gust of wind blew his coat off.
突來的狂風將他的外套吹掉。

6871

ingenuity

[,ɪndʒə'nuətɪ] [,ɪndʒə'nruətɪ] [,ɪndʒə'njuətɪ]

n. 機靈,獨創性,精巧,靈活性,創造力

The problem tested the ingenuity of students.

這個問題測試學生的創造力。

6872

speculate ['spɛkjə,let]

vi. 推測,思索,做投機買賣

A fortune teller speculated about what might happen.
算命師推測將會發生什麼事。

6873

adaptation [,ədæp'teʃən] [,ædæp-]

n. 適應,改編,改寫本

This is an adaptation of the bestselling book.
這是暢銷書的改編版。

6874

reverse [rɪ'vɝs]

v. 顛倒,倒轉 n. 倒檔位置,背面,反面

He wanted to reverse the procedure.
他想要顛倒步驟。

6875

superstition [,supɚ'stɪʃən] [,sɪu-] [,sju-]

n. 迷信

According to superstition, black cats bring bad luck.
根據迷信，黑貓帶來惡運。

6876

compassion [kəm'pæʃən]

n. 同情,憐憫

The nurse shows compassion for the sick.
這位護士對病人表現同情。

6877

rouse [rɑʊz] [rɑʊs]

v. 喚醒,激起,使振奮,驚起 n. 覺醒,奮起

The noise roused the neighbors.
噪音吵醒鄰居。

6878

glisten ['glɪsn̩]

v. 閃光

Her hair glistens under the sunlight.
她的頭髮在陽光下閃耀。

6879

gorgeous [gɔrdʒəs]

adj. 華麗的,燦爛的,美麗的

You look gorgeous.
你看起來很漂亮。

6880

outrage ['aʊt.redʒ]

n. 暴行,侮辱,憤怒,不法的行為

vt. 凌辱,引起…義憤,對~施暴

There were bomb outrages in London.
倫敦有炸彈暴行。

6881

emigration [.ɛmə'greʃən]

n. 移民出境,僑居,移民

I am not an emigration.
我不是移民。

6882

smash [smæʃ]

v. 打碎,粉碎,打破,破碎,猛烈碰撞,用力撞開,擊穿,闖過,搗毀,打敗,使結束 n. 打碎,破碎聲

The glass bowl smashed into pieces.
玻璃碗粉碎。

6883

serene [sə'rin]

adj. 平靜的,寧靜的,安詳的

The child's face was serene.
這個小孩的臉很平靜。

6884

peddle ['pɛdl̩]

vi. 挑賣,沿街叫賣 vt. 叫賣,散播

He worked as a salesman peddling clothes and brushes.
他是沿街叫賣衣服和牙刷的小販。

6885

currency ['kɜənsɪ]

n. 流通,通貨,貨幣,通用,流行,流傳

The theory has received wide currency.
這個理論廣為流通。

6886

perseverance [.pɜsə'vɪrəns]

n. 堅定不移,毅力,韌性,不屈不撓的精神

It took perseverance to overcome his difficulties.
克服他的困難需要毅力。

6887

sandal ['sændl̩]

n. 涼鞋,檀香,便鞋 v. 穿上便鞋

I bought a pair of sandals.
我買一雙涼鞋。

6888
mingle ['mɪŋg!]

v. (使)混合,相交,混雜其中

Her perfume mingled with the smell of her hair.

她的香水味混雜著頭髮氣味。

6889
intensity [ɪn'tɛnsətɪ]

n. 強烈,劇烈,強度

The intensity of the earthquake was frightening.

地震的強度很嚇人。

6890
thermometer [θəˈmɑmətə]

n. 溫度計,體溫計

I bought a digital thermometer.

我買了電子體溫計。

6891
retaliate [rɪˈtælɪˌet]

v. 報復,反擊,復仇

He retaliates against the attack.

他對這攻擊反擊。

6892
viewer ['vjuə]

n. 電視觀眾,閱讀器

The ad attracted millions of viewers.

這個廣告吸引很多觀眾。

6893
ebb [ɛb]

n. 退,弱,退潮,衰落 vi. 潮退,衰退

He is watching the ebb tide.

他正在看潮退。

6894
yarn [jɑrn]

n. 紗,紗線,故事,奇談

The old man would often spin us a yarn about life.

老人通常說有關生命的故事。

6895
besiege [bɪˈsidʒ]

vt. 圍困,圍攻,包圍,使某人應接不暇,團團圍住

Paris was besieged and forced to surrender.

巴黎被圍困,被迫投降。

6896
ulcer ['ʌlsə]

n. 潰瘍,腐爛物

He has a stomach ulcer.

他有胃潰瘍。

6897
exile ['ɛgzaɪl] ['ɛksaɪl] [ɪg'zaɪl]

n. 放逐,充軍,流放,流犯

vt. 放逐,使背井離鄉

He was sent into exile. 他被流放。

6898
hygiene ['haɪdʒin]

n. 衛生,衛生學

Washing your hands is personal hygiene.

洗手是個人衛生。

6899
stink [stɪŋk]

v. 發出臭味

It stinks of socks in here.

這裡有襪子的臭味。

6900

eccentric [ɪk'sɛntrɪk] [ɛk-]

adj. 古怪 n. 行為古怪的人

He has an eccentric aunt.

他有個古怪的阿姨。

6901

legislature ['lɛdʒɪsˌletʃɚ]

n. 立法機關,立法機構

This is the state legislature of California.

這是加州的立法機關。

6902

vein [ven]

n. 血管,靜脈,葉脈,礦脈,礦脈床,礦層,岩脈

vt. 使成脈絡,分布於

The nurse was trying to find a vein in his arm.

護士試著找他手臂的血管。

6903

revival [rɪ'vaɪvl̩]

n. 甦醒,復興,復活,再生

People have expectations of economic revival.

人對經濟復甦抱有期望。

6904

maple ['mepl̩]

n. [植]楓,楓木,淡棕色

There are maple trees in Canada.

加拿大有楓葉樹。

6905

motto ['mɑto]

n. 座右銘,格言,題詞,箴言

No pain, no gain. That's my motto.

我的座右銘,一分耕耘,一分收穫。

6906

unfair [ʌn'fɛr] [-'fær]

adj. 不公平的,不公正的

It would be unfair to let you go.

讓你走並不公平。

6907

juvenile ['dʒuvənl̩] [-ˌnaɪl]

adj. 青少年的,幼稚的 n. 青少年,少年讀物

He has a very juvenile behavior.

他的行為很幼稚。

6908

prior ['praɪɚ]

adj. 優先的,在前的

Please give us prior notice if you want us to move.

如果你要我們搬走的話,請事先通知我們。

6909

petroleum [pə'trolɪəm]

n. 石油

They are petroleum-based products.

這是石油製品。

6910

texture ['tɛkstʃɚ]

n. (織品的)質地,(木材,岩石等的)紋理,(皮膚)肌理,

(文藝作品)結構

Her skirt is made of the smooth texture of silk.

她的裙子是由質地光滑的絲綢製作成的。

6915

blonde [blɑnd]

adj. 金黃色的 n. 金髮碧眼的女人

She has blonde hair.

她有金髮。

6911

celebrity [sə'lɛbrətɪ]

n. 名聲,名人

He is a famous sporting celebrity.

他是有名的運動名人。

6916

aborigine [ˌæbə'rɪdʒəˌni]

n. 土著,原居民,土生動物(或植物)群

He is an aborigine.

他是原住民。

6912

credibility [ˌkrɛdə'bɪlətɪ]

n. 可信性

The rumor has damaged his credibility as a leader.

謠言損害他身為一個領導者的信譽。

6917

stray [stre]

v. 迷路,偏離,漂泊,漂泊遊蕩

adj. 迷路的,離群的,偶遇的

n. 無主的寵物,離群的人

There are stray dogs and cats on the street.

街上有流浪狗和貓。

6913

curb [kɜb]

v. 控制,抑制,限定,約束(不好的事物),控制,限制

n. 路邊

Pedestrians walked on the curb outside her house.

行人在她家房子外的路上行走。

6918

sustain [sə'sten]

vt. 支撐,撐住,維持,持續

She decided to sustain the children's interest.

她決定要維持小孩的興趣。

6914

noticeable ['notɪsəbl̩]

adj. 顯而易見的,值得注意的

His English has had a noticeable improvement.

他的英文有顯而易見的進步。

6919

reservoir ['rɛzɚˌvɔr] [-ˌvwɑr]

n. 水庫,蓄水池,貯備,貯藏

This is an oil reservoir.

這是油槽。

6920

hypocrite [ˈhɪpəˌkrɪt]

n. 偽君子,偽善者

Charles was a liar and a hypocrite.

查爾斯是騙子和偽君子。

6921

marshal [ˈmɑrʃəl]

n. (英國)陸軍元帥,空軍元帥,元帥,(美國)執法官,
　治安官,(一些美國城市的)警察局長,消防局長,
　典禮官,執行官,司儀官,司儀

vi. 排列,集合

He is the Marshal of the Royal Army.

他是皇家陸軍的元帥。

6922

graze [grez]

v. 放牧,吃草,擦傷,擦過　n. 擦破處

Sheep were grazing on the grass.

羊在草地上吃草。

6923

sway [swe]

v. 搖擺,搖動

The flowers were swaying in the wind.

花在風中搖擺。

6924

cuisine [kwɪˈzin]

n. 廚房烹調法,烹飪,烹調,風味,通常指昂貴的飯店
　中的飯菜,菜餚

I like French cuisine. 我喜歡法式料理。

6925

posture [ˈpɑstʃɚ]

n. (身體的)姿勢,體態,狀態,情況,心境,態度

v. 擺姿勢

Poor posture can lead to back pains.

姿勢不良導致背痛。

6926

gorilla [gəˈrɪlə]

n. 彪形大漢,暴徒,打手,大猩猩,壯而殘暴的男人,
　(俚)歹徒

The guy is a gorilla. 這個人是彪形大漢。

6927

fume [fjum] [fɪum]

n. (濃烈或難聞的)煙,氣體,一陣憤怒
v. 用煙燻,冒煙,發怒

She is fuming at him. 她對他生氣。

6928

rib [rɪb]

n. 肋骨

He likes to eat ribs of beef.

他喜歡吃牛肋骨。

6929

shun [ʃʌn]

vt. 避開,避免,迴避,(英)立正之口令,立正

An actor shuns publicity.

演員避免宣傳。

6930

hereafter [hɪrˈæftə]

adv. 今後,從此以後,死後的生命,來世

He believes in God and a life hereafter.

他相信上帝和死後的生活。

6931

addict [əˈdɪkt] [ˈædɪkt]

vt. 使沉溺,使上癮 n. 入迷的人,有癮的人

He is a video game addict.

他沉迷於電玩。

6932

ethnic [ˈɛθnɪk]

adj. 人種的,種族的,異教徒的

People are from different ethnic groups in USA.

美國有不同種族的族群。

6933

trophy [ˈtrofɪ]

n. 戰利品,獎品 vt. 用戰利品裝飾,授予⋯獎品

They won a trophy.

他們贏得一個戰利品。

6934

brace [bres]

n. 支柱,帶子,振作精神 adj. 曲柄的

He wears a brace.

他戴支架。

6935

pessimism [ˈpɛsəmɪzəm]

n. 悲觀,悲觀主義

I'm not sure I believe that pessimism really exists.

我不確定我相信悲觀主義的存在。

6936

hurdle [ˈhɜdl]

n. 籬笆,欄,障礙,跨欄,活動籬笆

v. 用籬笆圍住,跳過(欄柵),克服(障礙)

The weather will be the biggest hurdle.

天氣將是最大的障礙。

6937

aisle [aɪl]

n. 走廊,過道

Do you want an aisle seat or a window seat?

你要靠走廊的位置還是要靠窗的位置?

6938

oyster [ˈɔɪstə]

n. [動]牡蠣,蠔,貝類,[俚]沉默寡言的人

v. (牡蠣)採集,養殖

I like to eat oysters. 我喜歡吃牡蠣。

6939

gender [ˈdʒɛndə] n. 性別,性,種類

Women are sometimes denied working opportunities solely because of their gender.

女性有時只是因為性別而被拒絕工作的機會。

6940

pharmacist [ˈfɑrməsɪst]

n. 配藥者,藥劑師

She works as a pharmacist.

她是一位藥劑師。

6941
optimism [ˈɑptəmɪzəm]
n. 樂觀,樂觀主義
He believes in optimism.
他相信樂觀主意。

6942
chef [ʃɛf]
n. 廚師,主廚
He is a chef.
他是主廚。

6943
stylish [ˈstaɪlɪʃ]
adj. 時髦的,漂亮的,流行的
She wears a stylish skirt.
她穿時髦的裙子。

6944
oasis [oˈesɪs]
n. (沙漠中)綠洲,(不毛之地中的)沃洲,舒適的地方
There is no oasis in the desert.
沙漠沒有綠洲。

6945
lizard [ˈlɪzɚd]
n. [動]蜥蜴
You can see lizards in the zoo.
你可以在動物園看到蜥蜴。

6946
vacuum [ˈvækjʊəm]
n. 真空,空間,真空吸塵器
adj. 真空的,產生真空的,利用真空的
I bought a vacuum machine. 我買了真空吸塵器。

6947
separately [ˈsɛpərətlɪ] [ˈsɛprətlɪ]
adv. 個別地,分離地
They left separately.
他們個別地離開。

6948
unification [ˌjunəfəˈkeʃən]
n. 統一,合一,一致
The unification of Germany is an issue.
德國統一是一個議題。

S3 高中三年級 編號 6949～6984

6949
environmentalist [ɪnˌvaɪərənˈmɛntlɪst]
n. 環境保護論者,環境論者,環境論信奉者
He is an environmentalist.
他是個環保主義者。

6950
terribly [ˈtɛrəblɪ]
adv. 非常,極度地
I'm terribly sorry to have kept you waiting.
我十分抱歉讓你久等。

6951
happiness [ˈhæpɪnɪs]
n. 幸福,快樂
Happiness lies in hard work.
幸福在於努力工作。

6952

porridge ['pɔrɪdʒ] ['pɑrɪdʒ]

n. 粥,麥片粥

I am eating porridge.

我在吃麥片粥。

6953

jewelry ['dʒuəlrɪ]

n. 珠寶,珠寶類

He has lots of jewelry.

他有很多珠寶。

6954

Soviet ['sovɪɪt] [-ət] [-vɪˌɛt] [ˌsovɪ'ɛt]

n. 代表會議,勞工代表會議,蘇聯,蘇維埃

adj. 蘇聯的,蘇維埃的

Soviet Union is a communist country.

蘇維埃(蘇聯)聯盟是共產主義國家。

6955

Africa ['æfrɪkə]

n. 非洲

Have you been to Africa?

你有到過非洲嗎？

6956

physically ['fɪzɪkl̩ɪ]

adv. 身體上地,物理上,根據自然法則地

I felt physically sick.

我覺得身體不適。

6957

gently ['dʒɛntlɪ]

adv. 溫和地,溫柔地,輕輕地

He touched her shoulder gently.

他輕輕地碰觸她的肩膀。

6958

wasteful ['westfəl]

adj. 浪費的,不經濟的

The software is very wasteful of memory.

這個軟體很浪費記憶體。

6959

unkind [ʌn'kaɪnd]

adj. 不仁慈的,刻薄的,無情的,不體諒的,不厚道的,
    不親切的

Her husband is very unkind to her.

她的丈夫對她很不好。

6960

spaceship ['spesˌʃɪp]

n. 太空船

I saw a spaceship in the sky.

我在天空看到太空船。

6961

lab [læb]

n. 實驗室,研究室

He is in the school science lab.

他在學校實驗室裡。

6962

untie [ʌn'taɪ]

vt. 解開,解放,解決 vi. 鬆開,解開

Peter untied his shoelaces.

彼得解開他的鞋帶。

6963

unhealthy [ʌn'hɛlθɪ]

adj. 不健康的,有病的,對身體有害的,不良的

Eating chips is unhealthy.

吃洋芋片很不健康。

6964

fictional ['fɪkʃənl]

adj. 虛構的,小說式的,編造的

This is a fictional story.

這是一個虛構的故事。

6965

oxen ['ɑksn]

n. 牛,公牛(複數)

Oxen are plural forms.

oxen 是公牛的複數形式。

6966

pessimist ['pɛsəmɪst]

n. 悲觀論者,悲觀主義者

I am a pessimist.

我是悲觀主義者。

6967

southwards ['saʊθwədz]

adv. 往南地

A bird flies southwards.

鳥往南飛。

6968

regularly ['rɛgjələlɪ]

adv. 有規律地,有規則地,整齊地,勻稱地

I take a health exam regularly.

我定期做健檢。

6969

differently ['dɪfərəntlɪ]

adv. 不同地

Things could have turned out quite differently.

事情也可以變成完全不同。

6970

clearly ['klɪrlɪ]

adv. 明朗地,明顯地,無疑地,清楚地

I know the details clearly.

我清楚地知道細節。

6971

uneven [ʌn'ivən]

adj. 不平坦的,不平均的,不均勻的,奇數的

The road is uneven.

這條路不平。

6972

optimist ['ɑptəmɪst]

n. 樂天派,樂觀者

He is an optimist.

他是樂天派。

6973

factual ['fæktʃʊəl]

adj. 事實的,實際的,根據事實的

Can you show me factual evidence?

你可以給我看事實的證據嗎？

6974 teeth [tiθ]

n. 牙齒

He gritted his teeth.

他磨牙。

6975 peas [piz]

n. 豌豆

I ate peas.

我吃豌豆。

6976 hoe [ho]

n. 鋤頭 v. 用鋤耕地,鋤

I have a hoe.

我有一個鋤頭。

6977 pollinate ['pɑləˌnet]

vt. 對…授粉

Flowers were pollinated by bees.

花經蜜蜂授粉。

6978 abracadabra [ˌæbrəkəˈdæbrə]

n. 咒語,胡言亂語,驅病符咒文寫成上尖下寬的三角形那一種

He is saying abracadabra. 他在說咒語。

6979 correctly [kəˈrɛtlɪ]

adv. 恰當地,正確地

He answers the question correctly.

他正確地回答問題。

6980 inconsiderate [ˌɪnkənˈsɪdərɪt] [-ˈsɪdrɪt]

adj. 不顧及別人的,輕率的

It was very inconsiderate of you to keep us waiting.

你真不體貼讓我們等那麼久。

6981 teammate ['timˌmet]

n. 隊友

He is my teammate.

他是我的隊友。

6982 pollen ['pɑlən]

n. 花粉 vt. 傳授花粉給

Flowers have pollen.

花有花粉。

6983 animation [ˌænəˈmeʃən]

n. 活潑,有生氣,動畫

I watch animation everyday.

我每天看卡通片。

6984 younger ['jʌŋgɚ]

n. 年紀較小者 adj. 較年輕的

He is my younger brother.

他是我的弟弟。

VQC
單字力　附　錄

附錄一 國立華僑高中單字能力管理辦法(一)

國立華僑實驗高級中學「英文單字能力檢測」實施要點

980915 訂定

主旨：為發展學校特色，提升學生英文能力，強化學校競爭力，訂定本要點。

說明：希望藉檢測及獎勵，提升學生英文單字量，建立學校特色；為學生英語學習奠定基礎，增加升學競爭力，因此訂定「英文單字能力檢測實施要點」。

辦法：

一、藉由「零憶連英文單字檢定」，於每學期期初及期末進行英文單字檢測，以拼寫成績為基準，掌握學生英文單字能力情況。

二、主辦單位：教務處、圖書館

三、協辦單位：英文科

四、實施對象：高中部同學

五、測驗標準：

1. 檢測採練習版，分五級，以拼寫成績須達 70 分以上為合格。

級數	字數	級數	字數	級數	字數	級數	字數	級數	字數
一級	3000 字	二級	4000 字	三級	4500 字	四級	5000 字	五級	6000 字

2. 挑戰為比賽版，分二級，以拼寫成績須達 70 分以上為合格。

級數	字　　數	級數	字　　數
乙級	4471～6788 字	甲級	3162～8029 字

六、各級單字表公布在本校網站上。

學生需經英文教師評定等級後，始可參加檢定。每學期需通過一級，畢業需達到五級（6000 字）以上的水準。

七、測驗方式，可全班至設備組進行檢測，或個人至圖書館進行檢測。

八、獎勵標準如下：

1. 合格之學生者依憑證記嘉獎壹次及英文平時總成績酌予加 1～2 分。

2. 合格人數過半之班級，導師及英文教師建請嘉獎乙次；全班皆通過者，導師及英文教師建請嘉獎兩次。或另予獎勵。

3. 主辦、協辦及監事之同仁，著有績效者酌予獎勵。或另予獎勵。

4. 凡通過挑戰組各級者，均頒獎狀乙張（如附）及嘉獎二次獎勵之。

九、本要點自 98 學年度入學之新生開始實施。高二以上同學自由參加。

十、本要點經主管會議通過後，由教務處指導、圖書館推動執行，修訂亦同。

附件一

受　獎　者：高三○班　○○○

受獎事由：通過本校英文單字能力檢測
　　　　　乙級（4471～6788字）

拼寫	看英選中	聽英選中	總分
71	75	80	226

成績優良殊堪嘉許
特頒獎狀以資鼓勵

中華民國　九十八　年　九　月　　日

附件二

受 獎 者：高三○班　○○○

受獎事由：通過本校英文單字能力檢測

　　　　　甲級（3162～8029 字）

拼寫	看英選中	聽英選中	總分
71	75	80	226

成效卓著殊堪嘉許

特頒獎狀以資鼓勵

中華民國　九十八　年　九　月　　日

附錄二　國立華僑高中單字能力管理辦法(二)

國立華僑實驗高級中學「英文單字能力檢測」活動辦法

2009.9.22 訂定

壹、活動目的

藉由活動的舉辦，增進本校學生英文單字基礎能力，提升學生英文能力。

貳、活動依據

本校「英文單字能力檢測」實施要點。

參、辦理單位

一、主辦單位：教務處、圖書館

二、協辦單位：英文科

肆、參加對象

本校高中部學生。

伍、檢測方式

一、英文檢定單字參考表，設在本校網站右邊（英文單字大賽參考單字表）。

二、程度檢定：

(一) 通過級別：凡參與檢定之同學，均採用練習版，分五級

　　高一上需通過第一級 3000 字（高中一年級）

　　高一下需通過第二級 4000 字（高職三年級）

　　高二上需通過第三級 4500 字（高中二年級）

　　高二下需通過第四級 5000 字（技院一年級）

　　高三上需通過第五級 6000 字（高中三年級）

(二) 檢定三項：測驗一（拼字）、測驗三（聽英選中），成績均須達 70 分以上為合格。

(三) 使用時間：測驗一 20 分鐘、測驗三 10 分鐘，計 30 分鐘。

(四) 初測於 10 月底前完成，檢定安排在 12 月。

三、能力挑戰：

(一) 採用比賽版，分二級。凡經檢定通過第五級之同學，或英文教師及導師評定不需檢定之同學，始可參加。

　　乙級須通過 4471～6788 字；

　　甲級須通過 3162～8029 字。

(二) 檢定三項：測驗一（拼字）、測驗三（聽英選中）、測驗五（看中選音），成績均須達 70 分以上為合格。

(三) 使用時間：測驗一 20 分鐘、測驗三 10 分鐘、測驗五 10 分鐘，計 40 分鐘。

(四) 檢測一律在圖書館進行，需先向櫃台報名。

陸、參加方式：分兩類（如附件一、二）

　　一、班級施測：安排自習課或班會課，全班至設備組進行檢定。

　　二、自由報名：每週一至圖書館登記，每週限 20 名，額滿為止；午休時間施測。

柒、獎勵標準：

　　一、合格之學生者依憑證記嘉獎壹次及英文平時總成績酌予加 1～3 分。

　　二、合格人數過半之班級，導師及英文教師建請嘉獎乙次；全班皆通過者，導師及
　　　　英文教師建請嘉獎兩次。或另予獎勵。

　　三、凡通過挑戰組各級者，均頒獎狀乙張及嘉獎二次獎勵之。

　　四、主辦、協辦及監事之同仁，著有績效者酌予獎勵。或另予獎勵。

　　增附：

　　　　1. 第一名班級，同學、導師及任課教師均嘉獎 2 次，班級獎金 3000 元；
　　　　　 第二名班級，同學、導師及任課教師均嘉獎 1 次，班級獎金 2000 元；
　　　　　 第三名班級，同學、導師及任課教師均嘉獎 1 次，班級獎金 1000 元。

　　　　2. 成績進步最多的班級，同學、導師及任課教師均嘉獎 1 次，班級獎金 1000 元。

　　　　3. 上述所有獎勵擇優辦理。

　　　　4. 沒有進入前三名之班級，同學達到獎勵標準者亦嘉獎乙次。

　　　　5. 凡拼字平均成績達 55 分以上之班級，每班另獎勵 1000 元；
　　　　　 凡拼字平均成績達 60 分以上之班級，每班另獎勵 2000 元。
　　　　　 如高二各班同學參加檢定達上述標準者，分別獎勵 2000 元及 3000 元。

　　　　6. 各班成績進步最多的前三名同學，特別嘉獎乙次（不受獎勵辦法所限）。

捌、其它規定

　　一、監考人員由教務處及圖書館安排同仁擔任，導師或英文教師從旁協助。

　　二、檢定日程及時間，由各班班長統一抽籤決定。

　　三、不得攜帶電子字典、手機、字表（小抄）入場。

　　四、作弊者一律取消資格，並通知學務處依校規處理。

　　五、現場學生若發生急症，中斷檢測，學生另行至圖書館補測。

　　六、如遇停電導致檢測中斷，則另訂日期重測。

　　七、若電腦當機，必須舉手請監考人員處理；可攜帶個人常用之耳機。

　　八、本要點自 98 學年度入學之新生開始實施。高二以上同學自由參加。

　　九、本辦法未盡事宜，得另行公告之。

附件一

國立華僑實驗高級中 98 學年度第一學期「英文單字能力檢測」

班級		導師			日期	年月日	地點			
座號	姓　名	拼寫	聽英選中	備註	座號	姓　　名	拼寫	聽英選中	備註	

監考人員簽名：

附件二

國立華僑高中學生英文單字能力檢測

成績登記表

班　級	學 生 姓 名	級　　別	字　數	登 記 師 長	
		級	字		
拼寫成績	聽英選中成績	看中選音成績	總成績	合　格	不合格

測驗日期：　　年　　月　　日

圖書館留存

國立華僑高中學生英文單字能力檢測

成績登記表

班　級	學 生 姓 名	級　　別	字　數	登 記 師 長	
		級	字		
拼寫成績	聽英選中成績	看中選音成績	總成績	合　格	不合格

測驗日期：　　年　　月　　日

英文教師留存

國立華僑高中學生英文單字能力檢測

成績登記表

班　級	學 生 姓 名	級　　別	字　數	參 賽 學 生 簽 名	
		級	字		
拼寫成績	聽英選中成績	看中選音成績	總成績	合　格	不合格

測驗日期：　　年　　月　　日

學生留存

附錄三 台北縣南山中學單字力管理辦法

英文單字能力管制辦法

980820 處務會議修正

主旨：為發展學校特色，提升學生英文能力，強化學校競爭力，訂定本辦法。

說明：教務處「成績五標管制辦法」為針對學生個人之措施，而英文教學成效除由英文科任課教師負起教學成效責任外，希望藉由導師班級經營，共同提升學生英文單字量，建立學校特色，為學校未來發展雙語教學奠定基礎，共同提升學生英文能力，增加升學競爭力，因此訂定「英文單字能力管制辦法」為導師班級經營之一部分。

辦法：

一、藉由「零憶連英文單字記憶法」，並配合五標觀念，於每學期期初及期末進行英文單字檢測，以拼寫成績為基準，掌握學生英文單字能力情況。

二、參與對象為國中部各班及高中職部各班。

三、目標訂定如下：分成十四級以拼寫成績須達 70 分以上為合格

級數	字數	級數	字數	級數	字數	級數	字數
一級	500字	五級	1700字	九級	3300字	十三級	6000字
二級	750字	六級	2000字	十級	4000字	十四級	7000字
三級	1000字	七級	2600字	十一級	4500字		
四級	1350字	八級	3000字	十二級	5000字		

班級 每學期全班達成率70%、全班進階率80%					
國中普通班	級數字數		國中特殊班	級數字數	
國一上	三級	1000字	國一上	五級	1700字
國一下	四級	1350字	國一下	六級	2000字
國二上	五級	1700字	國二上	七級	2600字
國二下	六級	2000字	國二下	八級	3000字

班級 每學期全班達成率 70%、全班進階率 80%		
資訊、資處	級數字數	
職一上	四級　1350 字	
職一下	六級　2000 字	
職二上	七級　2600 字	
職二下	九級　3300 字	
職三上	十級　4000 字	

班級 每學期全班達成率 70%、全班進階率 80%			
普科一般班	級數字數	普科特殊班	級數字數
普一上	七級　2600 字	普一上	八級　3000 字
普一下	九級　3300 字	普一下	十級　4000 字
普二上	十級　4000 字	普二上	十二級　5000 字
普二下	十二級　5000 字	普二下	十三級　6000 字
普三	十三級　6000 字	普三	十四級　7000 字

四、達成目標酌予獎勵如下：

　　國中部個人進階者，憑證記嘉獎（每學期最多記到小功乙次），全班達標者，記嘉獎兩次，各班進步最多前三名頒發獎狀。

　　職科個人達標者，憑證記嘉獎壹次，英文平時總成績憑證進階加分，最多加到滿分為止（職科最低門檻三級）。

　　普科個人達標者，憑證記嘉獎壹次，英文平時總成績憑證進階加分，最多加到滿分為止（普科最低門檻五級）。

五、每學期初測判定學生單字能力位階，期末後測判定學生進退狀況。個人須達成進階目標，未達進階及低成就同學：週三夜輔或週六由教學組規劃參加補救教學。

六、週三夜輔或週六全天開放電腦 301 教室給同學上網申請到校練習。

七、「英文單字能力管制辦法」列為導師責任制重要措施之一，教務處得依據班級表現適時給予導師獎勵。

八、各階段單字能力目標得依學生學習狀況適時修正調整。

九、本辦法經教務處會議討論通過後由教務處推動執行，修訂亦同。

備註：

　　1. 本辦法適用於 98 學年度入學之新生。

　　2. 每班每週至少安排一節課由導師協助監督學生練習。

　　3. 除練習光碟外，英文單字口袋書，由教務處印製後提供學生使用。

筆記欄

筆記欄

感謝您購買本書，為了提供更好的品質與服務，填妥以下欄位資料後，傳真或對折寄回本公司，我們將隨時提供最新出版、升學或活動等資訊。

· 姓名：　　　　　　　　　　　性別：□男　　□女

· 出生年月日：　　　年　　　月　　　日

· 身分：□老師　　□學生 (請填類科：　　　　　　　　　)　　□其他

· 任職或就讀學校：　　　　　　　　　 /　　　年　　　　班

· 地址：□□□□□ (請寫郵遞區號)

　　　　市 (縣)　　　　區 (市 / 鄉 / 鎮)　　　里 (村)

　　　　路 (街)　　　段　　　巷　　　弄　　　號

· 聯絡電話：

· **email**：

1. **購買地點**
   □學校　□補習班　□團體　□郵購　□書店　□ PChome　□其他

2. **您從哪裡得知本書？**
   □學校老師介紹　□補習班老師　□同學　□ DM 廣告傳單　□書店　□ PChome　□其他

3. **請填寫是哪位老師推薦您這本書？**
   老師姓名：＿＿＿＿＿＿＿＿，任教學校 / 補習班：＿＿＿＿＿＿＿，聯絡方式：＿＿＿＿＿＿

4. **您對本書的整體印象如何？**
   □非常滿意　□滿意　□普通　□不滿意　□非常不滿意

5. **您對本書內容深度是否滿意？**
   □非常滿意　□滿意　□普通　□不滿意　□非常不滿意 (因為：□太難　□太簡單)

6. **您覺得本書每一章的篇幅長短是否適合研讀？**
   □適合　□普通　□不適合　　(因為：□太長　□太短)

7. **您最□喜歡 / □不喜歡本書的哪些章節？**
   ＿＿＿＿＿＿＿＿＿＿＿＿＿＿＿＿＿＿＿＿＿原因：＿＿＿＿＿＿＿＿＿＿＿＿＿＿＿＿

8. **您喜歡本書的版面編輯方式嗎？**
   □非常喜歡　□喜歡　□普通　□不喜歡　□非常不喜歡

   理由是：＿＿＿＿＿＿＿＿＿＿＿＿＿＿＿＿＿＿＿＿＿＿＿＿＿＿＿＿＿＿＿＿

9. **您認為本書有哪些值得肯定之處？**
   ＿＿＿＿＿＿＿＿＿＿＿＿＿＿＿＿＿＿＿＿＿＿＿＿＿＿＿＿＿＿＿＿＿＿＿＿＿

10. **您認為本書有哪些需要再改進之處？**
   ＿＿＿＿＿＿＿＿＿＿＿＿＿＿＿＿＿＿＿＿＿＿＿＿＿＿＿＿＿＿＿＿＿＿＿＿＿

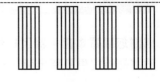

24257　新北市新莊區中正路 649 號 7 樓

台科大圖書股份有限公司 收

姓名：

年齡：　　　　　　　　性別：☐男　☐女

地址：　　　縣　　　鄉鎮
　　　　　　市　　　市區
　　　　　路(街)　段　巷　弄　　號

※為便於處理，請填寫郵遞區號

請沿此線對折裝訂寄回

勘誤表　　　　　　　　　　　　　　　　　　　PF002

頁碼	行數	可疑或不當之處	建議字句

謝謝您熱心的指正！

地址：新北市新莊區中正路 649 號 7 樓　　電話：(02)2908-5945　　傳真：(02)2908-6347

如果您對本公司圖書內容有任何
寶貴意見，請撥～ **Bube專線**
0800-000-599
將有專人竭誠為您服務!!

Bube

全民英文單字力檢定VQC 7000字級

書 號：PF002　　　　　附VQC線上英文單字能力檢測系統 2011年 12月初版

編 著 者▌劉振華
責任編輯▌陳怡秀
美術製作▌陳美齡
法律顧問▌吳志勇　律師
登記字號▌局版北市業字第1227號

發 行 所▌台科大圖書股份有限公司
地　　址▌新北市新莊區中正路649號7樓
電　　話▌(02) 2908-5945
傳　　真▌(02) 2908-6347
網　　址▌www.tiked.com.tw
E－mail▌service@tiked.com.tw

營業處各服務中心專線：
　　　　總 公 司：(02)2908-5945　　桃園服務中心：(03)463-5285
　　　　台北服務中心：(02)2908-5945　　嘉義服務中心：(05)284-4779
　　　　台中服務中心：(04)2263-5882　　高雄服務中心：(07)555-7947

郵購帳號▌19133960
戶　 名▌台科大圖書股份有限公司
　　　　※郵撥訂購未滿＄1500元者，請付郵資，本島地區＄100元／外島地區＄200元
客服專線▌0800-000-599
網路購書▌www.tiked.com.tw